I0762951

HEADLIGHTS

ALSO BY CJ LEEDE

Maeve Fly

American Rapture

HEADLIGHTS

CJ LEEDE

TOR PUBLISHING GROUP
NEW YORK

This is a work of fiction. All of the names, characters, organizations, places, and events portrayed in this work are either products of the author's imagination or used fictitiously.

HEADLIGHTS

Interior art from Shutterstock

A Nightfire Book
Published by Tom Doherty Associates / Tor Publishing Group
120 Broadway
New York, NY 10271

www.torpublishinggroup.com

EU Representative: Macmillan Publishers Ireland Ltd., 1st Floor, The Liffey Trust Centre, 117–126 Sheriff Street Upper, Dublin 1, D01 YC43

The Library of Congress Cataloging-in-Publication Data is available upon request.

ISBN 978-1-250-85795-8 (hardcover)
ISBN 978-1-250-85796-5 (ebook)

First Edition: 2026

Printed in the United States of America

10 9 8 7 6 5 4 3 2 1

For Nick and Bug,
Our lights are on for you, always

Over this odd world, this half the world that's dark now, I have to hunt a thing that lives on tears.

—Thomas Harris, *The Silence of the Lambs*

You shine on, boy.

—Stephen King, *The Shining*

HEADLIGHTS

COLORADO

Somewhere far off there is a motel and a gas station. Farther still, restaurants and houses.

At intervals, headlights cut through the night. Emphasize how black and looming, how impenetrable the road, and the dark.

An occasional car with the occasional passenger, two headlight beams stretching before them. The night swallowing the light.

And beneath it all, silent and waiting,

For a traveler to know when it is too late, when the last breath escapes his body, and his blood slows to a crawl and then stop,

There are heartbeats in the dark.

I

ROCKY MOUNTAIN HIGH

1

Then

"Is it the Bad Decision?"

I hear Mom's question, but it takes me a second to tear my eyes away from the screen.

She stands in the dressing area. The too-bright mirror bulb lighting her from the back. She's brushing her hair. The mirror behind her is clean the way she likes it, and the door to the bathroom is open with the light on and the shower curtain pulled back. It's the only part of our room that isn't orange and yellow—white shower, white curtain, white toilet and floor. Mom says the curtain is off-white. I can't tell the difference.

I don't want to leave, but she says it's almost time. I nod my head to answer her question.

"Are we going now?" I ask. We haven't packed yet, but she has her makeup on.

"Don't you worry, we'll have dinner first, then I'll get us ready."

I'm cross-legged on the orange and yellow carpet, two feet from the television screen, wearing my socks and long johns. My favorite movie is on, *Take Me Home*, the John Denver story. My mom loves it too. Right now, John Denver—not real John Denver but the actor named Chad Lowe who plays him—goes off with the girl at the party on tour. That's the Bad Decision.

"Why is it bad again?" I ask, even though I know why.

She smiles, says for the hundredth time, "A Bad Decision is one that you regret making, and one that takes you away from what really makes you happy. A Bad Decision is when you betray yourself for what you *think* will make you happy even if you know deep down it won't."

Happy.

We've lived at the Happy Inn for the last six months. We had to try a couple rooms before we found one that didn't give me a Bad

Feeling, that didn't have shadows in it. She said that was okay, that my Bad Feelings are important to listen to. She says some people have special antennas that pick up special signals, and she knew since I was little that I'm one of them.

At first the clowns on the sign and in the office scared me, and I didn't like the bright yellow and orange carpet and blankets in our room, but I like the sunrise paintings, and I like the VHS player my mom bought us so I can watch my favorite movies. I like the way she hums and sings along to all the songs in *Take Me Home* while I watch, and the way she ruffles my hair when she walks by to show me she loves me more than anything.

I like that *he* hasn't come.

"What kind of pizza are we getting?" I ask.

"Whatever you want, my Danny boy."

Danny isn't my real name. My mom wanted to name me that, but my dad said my name was going to be Calvin, just like his. When he comes around, we have to call me Calvin, but he hasn't come in a long time. Here in the motel, I'm Danny. It's our secret. *A shining name for my shining boy*, Mom says. It's from that book she's always carrying around, that dirty crinkled old paperback she's had as long as I can remember, that comes to every new place we live. But she says I'm not allowed to read it, not until I'm older.

I check the clock. It's Friday, which is pizza day, but we can't order until five. That's the rule. It's only 4:56, but it's been dark outside for a while already. The news says it'll be a cold winter. Mom keeps talking about it too. She turns back to the mirror and fixes her lipstick. She touches one of the glass root beer bottles on the counter, the ones we always have on special occasions. Mom seems nervous. My heart beats faster. Bad Feeling in my stomach.

I want her to talk. Tell me it's okay.

"Mom, what kind of pizza are you—"

"Shh," she says, smoothing down her hair. "You'll miss your favorite part."

I turn back to the TV. John goes back to Annie and says sorry by playing "Annie's Song," which he just wrote for her. My mom and Annie don't look alike, Annie has brown hair and pale skin, and my mom's hair is *bleached like Dolly's*, and her skin is tan. But they remind me of each other just the same. Safe and warm and smiling. My hair is darker than my mom's, but it's not as dark as Dad's, and I hope it stays that way.

I watch the clock. I'm *not* afraid. I'm not. Wherever we go next, we'll be together. But . . .

"Mom, I have a Bad Feeling."

She turns, looks at me, and for a second listens to me. Then a funny look comes over her face, and I don't know what it means.

She comes and stands in front of me, bends down and puts her hands on my shoulders. "I . . . made a Bad Decision. Trying to keep your dad in our lives. I . . . I'm so sorry, Danny. But you and me, we're gonna go somewhere he can't find us, okay? Somewhere safe and happy where he'll never get us again. It's all gonna be just fine."

I want to cry, but I nod instead. It's 4:59. One minute until I can pick up the phone and put in the number for the pizza place. Maybe the Feeling will go away, maybe I'm just being a baby. John sings "Annie's Song" to Annie, and Mom hums along in the bathroom, swaying back and forth, putting her makeup and jewelry in cases. She moves the root beer bottles over to the side. Outside the closed blinds, the dark.

Mom says "Annie's Song" makes you feel like the whole world will be okay. Normally I agree, I think it sounds like there's nothing to be scared of and no whispers in the night or Bad Feelings or shadows, and there's only Rocky Mountains and clean air and flying and cowboy dancing and horses. That's how the movie makes me feel, and every John Denver song. Pine trees and airplanes and John's leather hat. We live in the part of Colorado with packed dirt and buildings, the mountains far off. But John and Annie in *Take Me Home* are all the way *in* the mountains, in the trees, beside big rushing water.

"Are we really gonna go to Aspen?" I ask. "Like John and Annie?"

She turns and smiles, nods her head, and I almost think I see a tear on her face.

The musty mold smell comes up from the carpet like it does every night, there's the brown spots on the *popcorn ceiling* and the smoke detector we always take off the wall because it never stops beeping. I love it here. Mom and me, Danny. The Happy Inn. My mom in blue jeans and a jean jacket and a white *halter top*. Her turquoise jewelry and big belt buckle. I'm sad to leave, even if it is to go to Aspen. I still have the Bad Feeling.

Five o'clock. I pause the movie, and I pick up and dial the phone.

Someone pounds on the door.

The phone slips in my hand.

Hello? the person says through the receiver.

The pounding comes again. My heart thumps, and I turn to my mom.

Mom is frozen, in the dressing area, holding her brush tight in her hand.

I know where the Bad Feeling came from now. We both do.

She looks at the door, then me, then around the room. There are no other doors here, only the one that goes out front. And we both know who's standing out there.

She takes a step. I shake my head, beg her not to open it. He keeps pounding. It doesn't stop. She takes another step. I shake my head, please, please, no. She stops beside me.

"I love you, my shining boy. I'd sing and write and play all the songs for you, you know that, right? You know that you're my everything?" She's scared. Mom is scared. I shake my head again, my whole body is shaking.

"Don't open it," I say. "Please."

But she just whispers, "You're my Danny boy." She kisses me on the head.

The voice on the phone says *Hello?* one more time, and then a dial tone comes through.

The pounding on the door gets louder, Dad yelling.

Mom goes to it, reaches for the chain.

John Denver is frozen on the screen, looking into Annie's eyes, playing his guitar.

Mom slides the chain from the lock.

2

Now

Today is the first day of the rest of my life.

I open my eyes, sit up. Utah sun rising outside the window. Pink, orange through the blinds, glowing lines of light across the sheets, over my legs. My neck is stiff. Pain in my right leg, same as always. Shrapnel from an IED, my first tour. Pain in my chest . . .

Which happens any time I think of *her.*

Today is—

John Denver's voice lingers in my ears, floats around me in the room. Why did I dream of her? I haven't, in so long. I haven't thought of that song, *any* of his songs, in . . . I don't know. I've pretty fucking stridently avoided John Denver for the whole of my adult life.

But . . . today *is* the day, so I guess . . . or . . . I don't know. *Fuck.*

I breathe, close my eyes. At least there are no shadows.

I get out of bed, turn on the fan for new noise, drown out the music that isn't there. In the bathroom, I take a piss, splash cold water on my face. Step back into the bedroom, drop down, and do what I always do. But today it's different, new almost. Today, my last day.

Push-ups. Sit-ups. Diamond push-ups, box jumps on the crate. My body knows. Feet on the floor, back on the floor, forearms on the floor. Feet on the floor, then the crate. Pain in my leg. In my back. Pain in my left Achilles. Box jumps, jump lunges, jump squats. The heat before the sweat breaks through. The split second of relief when it comes. The drip of it down the skin, to the floor. My muscles push and flex. Contract, extend. I catch the pull-up bar, start my count.

I look around, breathe through my nose. White walls, white carpet. Mattress on a box spring. White sheets, workout equipment, bookshelf. Four years here, in Salt Lake City. A feeling grabs my chest. But it's not a *Bad Feeling,* and it's not a buried memory.

I think . . . It's gratitude. To this place, for giving me a fresh start.

Any kind of reason to live. This apartment complex, brand new. No shadows, no past of mine or anyone else's.

I get my twenty, swing, and land on the carpet. See myself, moving through the space, since day one. See myself change. I was thirty when I got here. I'd just lost everything.

Those first two years were spent just trying to get past the failure. And by get past, I guess I mean become properly acquainted with it, learn to accept its enduring presence in my life. The unsolvable case, the divorce. Everything that led to both. My adoptive—but real in every way that counts—parents, gone, taken from me in an instant. That's of course without touching any of the deep past stuff. Which I don't think about anymore. Which I never think about.

Today is the first—

I push harder.

I can't believe I didn't kill myself. It would've solved so much, at least for me. Mostly didn't do it because of Josie. I knew she'd picture me drinking over the divorce papers, fantasizing about blowing my brains out—which I did . . . drink and fantasize—and then finally going through with it. She'd carry that weight forever. And I've put her through enough already.

But maybe the real reason, the one that got all the way through to me, was because *he* hasn't done it yet. Rotting in his cell in Sterling and pushing through, day after day. And if he hasn't, then I sure as shit won't either.

Still, the music. There, just at the edges. Hovering, between atoms, between breaths, slipping through the walls and into my skin. It's not the worst song. The one I won't even let myself think the name of, the one that played *that night*. But still, today . . .

Could *she* be—

I slam my hand against the pull-up bar. *The fuck is wrong with me.*

I run the shower. I'm here. In this bathroom, in this apartment. Bright lights. Mostly clean toilet. White cabinets. The giant empty spot above the sink where the mirror was before I ripped it out on day one. I buzz my hair and use an electric shaver on my face so I don't have to look at myself. I've got a system. And like my reserve status, it keeps me feeling sharp. Ready. I step under the spray, let the bathroom fill with steam. Feet on porcelain. Water on my face. John Denver—

The third year here, I chased a sense of purpose. An idea. *Be of service again.* Find a way to help the world when I was so fucking useless for so long. I've been a reservist for years, ever since I got back from my second tour. One weekend a month going out to Aurora from Denver, then Riverton from Salt Lake, to put on my cammies and stay in the fight. A big circle jerk of dudes who want to punish themselves and play Rambo, who just can't let it all go. One boot out the door. Josie always hated it, that I wouldn't just quit. But how do you explain how hard it is to come back to normal life after being there? You can't. Come back, or explain it. Still, she used to keep my Bronze Star with a V on the wall where everyone could see it. I don't know where it is now. Doesn't matter.

The big plan. Decided to reactivate. Fly out to Camp Pendleton and train and do one last tour to prove that I can be something useful to this world. To be back in the line of fire, to feel alive in a way I just can't in myself anymore. Helping, *trying.*

Today is—

I squeeze my eyes shut and scrub the shampoo in harder, turn the water temperature up.

This last year, the fourth year. Pursuing the goal. Putting one foot in front of the other. Each day, pressing farther forward and farther away from the past. The Bureau holds no joy anymore, could never hold anything but pain and shame and fucking helplessness. But I've worked, every day. I've shown up. I breathe and I eat and I say hi or nod to anyone who passes. I exercise. I go to bed and wake up and drink coffee and get dressed, and I do it knowing there is an end in sight. Another tour. Another shot at making a difference.

And even . . . I don't let myself think it all the time. Hardly ever. It seems too good to be true, and if there's one thing life has taught me, it's that if something seems that way it probably is. But . . . the secret hope, the real dream.

When my next tour is done, when I've done my part and proved that I can be of even minor use to someone somewhere in this world—assuming I walk out alive—I'll finally do it. Head into the mountains. Build myself a cabin. Just me, four walls, and no mirrors. No Bureau, no shadows. A small town nearby, maybe a couple buddies at the local dive. Fires in the woodstove. Even a dog. I've always wanted to rescue one, and I don't care what it looks like, just a four-legged creature to walk with me and share my dinner. Hell, I'll take three legs, whatever. If I make it that far, maybe then I can just . . . *live*. Whatever that means.

I think, briefly, of Whileago Manor. Then I don't let myself think of it anymore.

Because after today, I'm officially retired from the FBI and headed off once again to report for active duty. Feel the sand in my teeth and the wind on my face.

I inspect my body when I step out of the shower. Thirty-four isn't twenty-four, but I've kept it in check. Meat and veggies, only drinking when I really need it. Which . . . you know. But I've done my best. All the tattoos, probably the most money I've spent on anything, besides Josie's ring. Scenes of a life, this story of mine. Mostly concealed when I'm dressed. Half the time I'm not even sure why I want them on me. This life, these memories. Maybe just want to convince myself that the good stuff actually happened. That I didn't just dream it up in the darkest moments.

That music, still there, still just—

"Hey," I say, out loud, to the empty bathroom. I close my eyes. "*Please.*" I mean please stop, please leave me alone, please not now. I mean, *None of you have popped up here in four years, and I can't have you start today. I can't have you follow me to—*

I mean, desperately, terribly,

Please, maybe, if you're her. Or them. If you're any of them—

It stops.

Fan blade whirring in my bedroom. Nothing else.

I dress, don't let myself feel anything. Tape up some more boxes, let the Salt Lake City morning news play on the living room TV. I drink my coffee, stare out the window that looks out over the apartment complex's parking lot, then beyond to an open and dying field. A handful of black birds swoops and caws, fighting over a half-eaten piece of what looks like meat. Ripping small pieces from it in the grass.

A feeling, in the gut.

It's hard, sometimes, to differentiate them. Guilt. Fear, disappointment, anger, grief, dread. They all start to blur together, eventually amount to the generic pit in the stomach and occasional moment of confusion as to what's causing it. The acceptance that you may never find out. Unless it's dread. You find out pretty quick if it's dread, because then something bad comes to follow.

What it's not is a *Bad Feeling.* And what it's not is a—I can't even think of the word. It's so stupid. To think that a grown man could have gotten this far in life believing that he could see . . .

What it's not is *her.* Them.

I don't know what's gotten into me. I check the time, flip off the TV.

It's my last day as an investigator in the whole of my mortal life, and I'm gonna walk in there with my head held high. Even if I don't deserve to. I've got a flight after work, I'll get to San Diego early, give myself a few days before training starts up. I paid a buddy to come and drive the boxes and my car, drop it all off in Denver at Whileago Manor, and leave it for me to grab when—if—I get back. I would've happily left Denver out of it entirely, would even more happily never go back at all. But I know I'll have to, eventually. Deal with the house. Deal with . . . Well, we'll see. Maybe I'll come back in a flag-covered coffin and won't have to do it after all. I lift my coffee cup to the birds.

"Cheers, motherfuckers," I say.

I grab my jacket from the back of my chair for the last time, swing it over my shoulders.

There's a knock at the door.

I pause. Jacket half on in the living room.

Again, the knock. No one's ever knocked on my door. Not once, since I moved here. I hear someone swear on the other side.

I slowly step over and open it.

I am assaulted by a brisk bright morning. The kind that nearly blinds you with the brilliance of other people's lives. Utah sun, Mormon God light.

And standing here in it . . .

Jack Murphy.

I blink.

"Dan," Jack says.

Jack Murphy, on my doorstep. His car parked in the loading zone behind him.

"Jack," I say. It comes out like a question, which . . . is how I mean it.

"I'd like to come in. If you don't mind."

Jack squints at me, shifts his weight from one foot to the other, his thinning hair catching the light, his signature old scratched aviators hanging from the breast pocket of his shirt. He needs a shave. He looks fuckin' terrible. I wonder if I should say that, if he'd still find it funny, or if too much time has passed. God, I really haven't seen him since . . .

"What are you doing here?" I ask.

"Dan, I'd like to come in."

"Yeah. Uh, sure." I step aside, and he brushes past me, and he smells like he's been smoking. I've never seen him smoke.

I offer him the single La-Z-Boy chair in the living room. I sit on a packed and sealed box of books, putting myself considerably below Jack's line of sight, which is fitting in more ways than one. Jack looks down at me, starts to say something, then stops.

Has he turned fifty already? Fifty shouldn't look like this. Fifty's young these days. It's eight hours from Denver to Salt Lake, so he hasn't slept all night, but it's more than that. I watch my old friend take off his hat and rub his face with his hands. The pit in my stomach. The *Feeling*. Shit. No. It's just a shock, to see him older. That's all.

I worked for Jack most of my career, up until I transferred to Utah four years ago. I haven't seen him in all this time, and the way the years have worn on him . . .

"Do you have any coffee?" Jack says.

"Yeah. Right." I stand, head to the kitchen. I'm relieved to get away from him.

Jack takes in the apartment, and I glance around too. White walls, no art. One chair, the one he's sitting on, TV tray with a lamp on it. It's embarrassing. Him seeing this place. This place I was just feeling so grateful for and proud of. His eyes snag on one of the boxes.

"You just move in here?"

I start a new pot of coffee, glad for something to do with my hands.

"Um, no. I'm movin' out, actually. Today."

"Today?"

I nod. Don't look at him. "Yeah. Uh, put in my resignation a few weeks ago. Time to move on." I say it like Hank or Willie would, facing the coffeepot, my body angled now to keep Jack out of my line of sight. I sound stupid saying it. But still . . . it feels good. To remind myself.

The last tour. The cabin.

Today is the first—

Shit. Hot coffee on my hand. I shake it, bring it to my mouth.

I pour a new mug, holding my hands steady, and take it to my former boss and friend. The one who sits here, unexplained, a state over from where he should be. Not at work. Not at home. Not with his kids, who should be—*are*, I guess—maybe ten or eleven now.

"Jack," I say, and I know there's no answer I could want. "Why did you come here?"

He takes a long moment to drink the coffee. He stares at the empty bottom of it and then brings his eyes up to mine. New wrinkles, dark circles. Eyes a little bloodshot.

"I'm sorry, Dan."

"Sorry for what?"

He stares at me, that Bad Feeling in my stomach growing, making itself known, and—

"He's back," Jack says.

The birds outside fall silent.

Suspension, the second after a blown frag.

A cosmos and a planet and an aching, devastating pulse. I hear my own heart, feel it pounding through me, pushing against the apartment walls. Throbbing through the earth.

Today is—

"He's back, Dan," Jack Murphy says.

I am here and not here. I am a thousand places at once.

"No," I say. I might say it more than once.

Jack exhales long and slow, stares out the window over the parking lot and the field, and eventually, carefully, sets the mug down on the floor. He shakes his head. Doesn't stop shaking his head, rubs his face. "Could be a copycat. Could be multiple copycats. But . . ."

"Multiple?" I ask. It's a plea. This apartment, too tight with the both of us here.

I've never had anyone in this room before. My brain brings this thought to the forefront, pushes everything else aside. The few women who've come go straight to the bedroom, slip out before morning. That I should share this space with another human one time before leaving, that Jack should show up today of all days.

Today is—

"Two," Jack says. "Two, about a week apart. We've kept it out of the news so far, but—"

Two.

Tears burn the backs of my eyes. I don't have it in me now to be embarrassed. There's no need. Jack knows. We all know. Jack drove eight hours through the night to tell me.

No, he had to tell me, yeah. But *Jack* needed it, for *him*. He needed to remember that there is a world outside of Colorado, that there is a world untouched by these . . . What? *Crimes* has never done it justice. Atrocities, abominations? I felt the impulse myself, a hundred times during the investigation. So many aimless drives, so many nights spent drunk at the bar or on the floor of the house or in Jack's garage chasing the moment of a blackout. Anything to drown out the details of the case, even for a second. Anything to solve any fucking part of it.

Jack drove eight hours to my packed-up apartment on the first day of the rest of my life because that's what this case is. All of us, infected, poisoned, trying forever to get out from under this impossible weight. In our line of work, we're supposed to be at least a little immune to the effects of violence. We've seen our share by now, have had to inflict it ourselves in our worst moments. How fucking stupid I was to think it could ever be over.

He's back.

There's no apartment. No La-Z-Boy.

It's me and a highway. Me and a motel.

Me and a bathtub full of blood.

Jack is watching me.

"You're sure?" I say. My voice, again, a plea. Again, if it were anyone else in front of me, I would be ashamed.

"DNA's a match, the hair. If they're copycats, they might be in league with him. Or at least know something we don't. It's happening again, Dan. It's real."

I look out over the parking lot and the field, the birds who've resumed their struggle, the packed book box sturdy beneath me. All I can do is breathe. All I can do is exist.

"You get a U-Haul already?" Jack asks.

"I'm, uh . . ." My eyes on the field.

Blood.

I clear my throat. Look back to Jack Murphy, can barely hear myself talking. "I'm leaving the furniture. Putting boxes in my car. But . . . I reactivated. I'm going to Pendleton."

"What?"

"Yeah," I say. "Going back on active duty. Do another tour."

Jack stares at me. "Are you fucking kidding?" he asks.

He looks around. I come back to the room, try to. I feel him seeing it, a thirty-four-year-old failure desperate to get back to the front lines. To feel that my life is not being wasted. To feel I am worth anything at all.

"This is your case, Dan."

Blood. Bathtub. Motel parking lot.

"We want you on it. You know it's yours."

Bodies, limbs, skins flayed off corpses.

This case conflating my memories, dragging the moments up out of order. Crowding my vision with so much red.

"I couldn't solve it," I say. "You could get anyone. After all the press, I mean . . ."

But I know. Others have tried, of course they have. It wasn't their fault. Wasn't their failure. It was *my* case. And now, because of me, because *I* couldn't . . .

It's here. Happening again. People are dying. People are being . . .

"Don't run away from this," Jack says. "Help us. Please. There's a reason it was yours."

Because of that *thing*, what he thinks I can do. That thing that is a complete fantasy.

My shining boy.

Jack Murphy in my apartment. Birds cawing louder through the window.

Sand in my eyelids, the brush of starched new fatigues. The weight of an M4, ushering civilians to safety.

A cabin in the mountains or forest. New friends. A dog to share my dinner. The birds ripping meat from the carcass.

Blood in my eyes. My eyes in the mirror. Blood on the tiles, my skin and my hands, and—

John Denver's voice tearing through the air.

Today is the first day of the rest of my life.

I close the trunk of my car on the boxes, my remaining life packed inside.

I follow Jack all the way back to Colorado.

3

We stare through the one-way glass into the interrogation room.

The fastest route between Salt Lake and Denver is the one that cuts up through Wyoming, avoids the Rockies altogether. We stopped for a meal halfway through the driving day, small-talked to catch up. Neither of us there, not really. A shadow moved in the corner of the diner, the first I'd seen in so long. Stress response, coming back here. I pressed my hands to my eyes.

We hit traffic, a protest clogging the streets. Colorado Subarus—the back of them caked in mud, like always—stalled in front of the protestors. One of them holding a sign that said PROTECT OUR ECOSYSTEMS. Another with a photo of a wolf that said STOP THE SLAUGHTER.

Every mile heading back, an ounce of hope undone.

Now, standing here again, it's like none of the last four years happened at all. How many times have Jack and I stood side by side in this very spot? How did I ever think I could escape any of it? Shadows I pushed past on the way inside the building.

Not real. My brain just . . .

Before us on the other side of the glass, another bewildered killer, another victim. A kid. He's terrified. Not small, by any means, he's gotta be six five, but the personality, the *himness*, more sensitive than the linebacker physique would suggest. It doesn't help that he's crying.

"I told you," he says to the agents sitting across from him. Tillman, if I have to go off the back of his head, and Garcia, the prosecutor on the case, who's letting Tillman do the talking. "I don't remember *anything*," the kid says. "I can't . . . There's no way I did it. I couldn't have."

Jack turns the volume down on the speaker between rooms, slides a file over to me.

"Name's Pete Noland. Pretty beloved kid. Last thing he remembers is climbing out his girlfriend's window in Greeley to walk to his car he'd parked in a field. No record, lives with and takes care of his grandmother. Waived rights to a lawyer, called the police right when he came to. Did the polygraph on him, not that we needed to. Same as the others."

"Let me hear him," I say. Jack turns the volume back up.

Pete Noland studies his hands on the table, shuffles his feet on the floor. His eyes travel up slowly from his hands and meet Tillman's. "So this is it, right? I'm one of *them* now. Somehow, I'm . . ."

He trails off, but his gaze doesn't falter. I feel it. He's a strong kid, an important kid, as much as any kid can be. The kind of kid who grows into the kind of man who can make a difference in the world.

"One of who, Pete?" Definitely Tillman. He's always been the worst.

"I don't want to say it. They say it's bad luck to say it." Pete leans back in his seat and shuffles his feet again. "Though I guess I can't imagine my luck getting any worse." He tries for a smile, but falters when he sees Tillman's face.

"Let's hear the order of events, Pete. One more time, if you don't mind."

"Um, yeah, okay. I can . . ." He sits up. "So I said goodnight to Lucy, and I climbed out the window, and then . . ." He shifts in his seat again. "And then I'm walking on the side of the highway like fifteen miles from her house, and I'm naked and barefoot, and there's this . . . thing on my shoulders."

"What was the thing on your shoulders, Pete?"

Pete clears his throat, and his eyes fill up again. He uses the back of one cuffed hand to brush a tear away. After a moment, he says, "My uncle hunts." He takes a breath. "I've never had the stomach for it, but . . . you know, I know a hide. I mean, who doesn't?" His voice cracks on the last word. "But human skin, it doesn't . . ." His skin goes pale. "It feels different."

"Did you realize immediately that you were wearing Ramona Lopez's skin?"

"Please," Pete says, leaning back and choking on a sob. "Please don't say her name."

"When did you first meet Ramona Lopez, Pete?"

"I told you, I never met her in my life! I have no clue who she is or why—"

He doubles over onto the table.

Pete's sobs echo through the interrogation room and through to us, bounce off the walls and the floor and ceiling and my brain. The kind of unselfconscious anguish that humans only experience a handful of times in a life after the toddler years, if they're lucky. When they are reduced to nothing but a singular pain, when they would do anything, truly anything, to get away from themselves. All the sobs of all the killers. Every one of them.

There is a word he doesn't want to say. The one the internet has so lovingly bestowed on the killers who walk the highways, wearing or dragging human skins. The one the public decided is bad luck. The word spreading on whispers, as if having a name could possibly make these murders worse. *Drifters*, they call them.

"Turn it off," I say.

Jack reaches forward. The sound cuts. We don't need to hear it.

Pete Noland, like all the rest, blacked out in the dark of the Colorado night. He came back to consciousness hours later on the side of a highway miles from where he started, naked and wearing the skin of a person he'd ostensibly never met before like a cloak. With a single brown hair tied around his tongue in a knot, a hair that did not belong to him, or his girlfriend, or the victim, or anyone else he knew, and which was an exact DNA match to every one of the hairs pulled out of every mouth of every one of the killers.

The victims' blood under the Drifters' fingernails, in every case. Eight killers and eight victims over the course of a year, six years ago. Eight strands of one person's hair tied around their tongues, staying in place through the Drifters' eating of the bodies, or tied there after eating. Or the Drifters *aren't* the ones eating the bodies. We just don't know. And the phones—both the victims' and the Drifters'. We get a warrant with the cell phone companies. And every time, the data stops right around the time and location the Drifter would have intercepted the victim. Just glitches and goes black. Sometimes we find the phones with the victims' bodies, sometimes with the Drifters' and the victims' clothes. But they never yield any information. All of it a shitstorm of *we don't know.*

And everything coming to an abrupt stop five years ago, a year after the murders started.

Pete's victim, the skin he carried, a forty-one-year-old single mother of two nurse practitioner who was walking home from work to relieve her ex-mother-in-law of babysitting when she was intercepted. Ramona Lopez, like the others, was skinned alive with an unrecovered knife—the striation marks on the skin matching those of a dull blade, like all the others—and tossed in a drainage pipe beneath the road about ten miles back from where Pete regained consciousness.

"You said there were two," I hear myself say. Everything happening in a way that doesn't quite add up with the natural progression of time, a delay between words and thoughts. A strange sort of pressure in the air. The déjà vu of being back in a place I never thought I'd ever step foot in again. Somehow suddenly being a person I never thought I'd be again.

Jack tosses me another file. Same story, more or less. Thirty-two-year-old highway patrolwoman came to consciousness wearing the skin of a fifty-eight-year-old male gas station attendant. Hair in her mouth tied around her tongue. Like all the others, like Pete, she was barefoot and naked, walking on the side of the highway, covered in blood. Her victim found just the same as Pete's, skinned alive in a different drainage pipe on a different stretch of road. Both the killers' and the victims' clothing left piled near the body, just like all the ones before. Her dashcam and bodycam glitched out at the time of the murder, static and black screen, like seemingly every security camera and cell phone and electronic device within one hundred feet of the crimes.

Both cases look identical to the old ones, except—

"They didn't eat the victims after they skinned them," I say. Again, that strange delay.

"No." Jack looks thoughtfully at the teenager through the glass. "This time they didn't."

He doesn't have to say they don't know why. Why these people would do this, why they wouldn't remember any of it. Why it started, why it stopped, why it's back again. *We don't know why* is the whole of this fucking nightmare and has been from the beginning. The cannibalism of the corpses is public knowledge. Why would someone change it now, copycat or otherwise?

The one piece that is *not* public knowledge, the piece of evidence we've managed to keep under wraps even now, are the hairs tied around the killers' tongues. I check the files even though Jack already told me. These two new hair strands are a match to all the ones from before.

Eight murders, all taking place in and just outside Denver. And eight dead bodies, seemingly random. No gender, age, ethnic, racial, or socioeconomic patterns. This thing, seemingly indiscriminate, both among the killers and the victims.

And then one day the murders just stopped. We knew nothing. And we had the families of sixteen victims as far as I was concerned, to deal with, not just eight. And there was the press. We couldn't squash it, one true crime podcast picked it up and then suddenly the whole of the internet was taking it upon themselves to solve the case for us, muddling any information we may have found. Oliver Wright, the father of the first victim and a prominent real estate developer in town, put all his resources into making sure each case was taken to court and the Drifters were convicted and kept in jail.

And us, scouring the whole of the state to try and solve even some small piece of this puzzle. *Nothing.* This case that's destroyed so many lives. Small pittance compared to what the others suffered, but it destroyed my marriage, any sense of self I'd cobbled together over the years. And then.

Just over a year after the last murder, and about a month after Josie left me for good, my parents and I were on our way to a show at Red Rocks, and a drunk driver in a semitruck smashed the left side of the car. The left side of the car where they both were sitting. By the time I woke up in the hospital, they were already gone.

I called it quits and applied for the transfer.

Case, marriage, family. I don't know what I could possibly be doing here now. Maybe I'm still sleeping back in Salt Lake and this is a nightmare. Maybe none of it is happening at all.

Pete Noland in the chair, sobbing to Tillman and Garcia. Five years since the last murder, and almost four years since my parents died. And this thing somehow back twice in a week. The perpetrator escalating. Before, the closest together were a month apart.

Again, the infuriating question. The interminable and repeating, nauseating question.

Why?

"We scoured their computers and phones, these new ones, absolutely nothing, all the phones cut out, so no location data on movements. No shared page visits, no clubs or forums. Cyber's monitoring Reddit and the chat rooms. They've noted it's been quiet so far, aside from this one user. Posted something a few months back saying they knew the Dri—the *killers* were gonna come back. Has this stupid username, '*Wizdumteller*.' We're looking into it. Not sure if anyone told you, but not too long after you left we got word of a docuseries in the works and squashed it pretty quickly, but for a year or two there the internet was blowing up so much, we had to put a full team on handling it all."

I was recognized in the first year in Utah and stopped going out other than for work for a long time after. "Has anyone been to the girlfriend's house yet?" I ask. "The one Pete snuck out of?"

"No. Car's still there though, far as I know."

Pete isn't crying anymore. He has leaned back in his chair and turned his face partway up to the ceiling. Shock. Brain shut down to static. Tillman still talking to him, moving his hands in an overstated *I'm on your side* kind of way. What a prick. Pete just staring up at the ceiling. Maybe beyond it.

"He's lookin' to God," Jack says.

Last I checked, all the previous killers are sitting in jail cells still bewildered by the fact that this is now their life. Still unable to recover a single memory from the time in which they committed atrocities upon people they maintain even now are total strangers to them.

I don't say anything. We both know what's gonna happen to Pete Noland. We both know this kid's life is over before it's even begun. It'd be kinder to stick a gun in his hand and put him in front of enemy fire.

Jack closes the file.

We both know there's no place for God in any of this.

4

It almost never rains in Colorado. Everyone here will tell you that. *Over three hundred days of sun a year.* They say it like a TV slogan they're paid to repeat, as if the whole state were an insistent advertisement of itself. I sit in my car, in the night, rain falling hard. Jack's gone home to his family. Home for dinner where people are waiting for him. He invited me, but I can't do it.

I don't remember walking from the office to the car, don't remember half of today. I peel off my work jacket and reach behind me until I find the brown leather one I wear off duty. I shrug it on. Watch the raindrops fall in my headlights.

It's getting dark early, mid-November somehow already. It was late in the day when Jack and I pulled up to the office, I don't know how many hours ago. There are always at least a couple agents working, and sometimes, inside, it's hard to tell what time it is. This case, being back, distorting the world, stretching it. It was like this before too. Hard, sometimes, for any of us to stay tied to reality.

Jack showing me sites on the map. All of it, too slow and too fast. Out of time and completely inevitable. The two new cases in blue, the eight old ones in red. Still, no discernible patterns. Ramona Lopez's murder out by Adams City, the gas station attendant down by Littleton. All the others scattered. I don't have to look at them. I've recited the places and names of the victims so many times I can do it in my sleep, often do hear them in my sleep. Though less and less in the last couple years.

My old desk upstairs, empty. Cleared off for me. The nameplate I'd thrown in the trash on my last day just sitting right there. Like they always knew I'd return.

Special Agent Daniel Stansfield.

Shadows drifting in the corners, watching me.

Everyone desperate for someone else to take this on. And of course it would be me. I've already borne the brunt of the backlash, I can take it. I *should* be the one to deal with it. The guy who'd been unstoppable for years, had once been the recipient of awards and special commendations and cracked nearly every case put in front of him. The guy who couldn't solve this one, was responsible for all the lives lost.

The guy who is back.

I drop my forehead to the steering wheel.

I'm not working at that fucking desk. I'm not staying. I can't believe I'm here at all.

The night, the dark.

My shining boy.

Pounding on the door.

I jump, reach for my pistol.

Not pounding. Knocking, tapping, on my window. On the car window in the rain.

I breathe, slow my heart, take in the figure blurred through the raindrops on the glass, knocking. The car is fogged up. It takes me a second to move.

I roll down the window. I know who it is before she bends down, droplets dripping from her hair, catching in her eyelashes, on her lips. It hits like a punch to the chest. Even now, I can barely breathe looking at her.

"Wanted to make me wait, did you?" She looks no different than she did when I left. Still way too pretty for this job. Still way too certain of herself for anyone to really feel comfortable around her. I thought I'd dodged this bullet, at least for today, Jack said she was out on a call.

But here she is. Here we are.

"Hey, Josie," I say. And her name on my tongue rips me open again. In just this second, all the work of the past four years undone.

"Hey yourself." She stares at me through the open window, bites the inside of her cheek the same way she has a thousand times before, squints through the rain. "Murphy filled me in."

I don't know what to say.

"Guess I shouldn't be surprised you'd come," she says.

"Yeah. I didn't, uh . . ." An emotion threatening, I don't know what. I clear my throat. "I didn't mean to. It's been a long day."

"Yeah," she says. Same way she always says it, like she's laughing a little bit at me with whatever internal monologue she's got running. Even now. Even with this. I can't believe I was ever married to her. Even more can't believe I'm not married to her now.

"Where you headed?"

"I—" I have no idea. I missed my flight to California. Book another flight? Find a hotel for the night? I sure as shit am not heading to my parents' house. "I might go for a run," I say.

She squints at me again, looks out into the night, the rain. "Hop out," she says.

"What?"

"Hop out, Stansfield. I'm driving."

"Josie, I'm really not in the—"

She reaches through the window and unlocks the door, opens it. She grabs my arm and pulls me out of the car. I let her because it's the way it's always been with us.

The car ride is quick and silent to the edge of town, save for the rain on the windshield and the roof. The tight space filled with the crisp citrus soap scent of her. We don't speak. My whole body is tensed, and I try not to breathe in too deeply. Finally, she parks, and I nearly throw myself out the door and into the rain to escape it.

It's cold.

If the rain came in another week or so, it'd be sleet, maybe even snow. But tonight, just a bitter cold rain in a bitter cold town. This whole place telling me to turn around.

Still, I look to the neon roadhouse in front of me. Lit up like a red, green, orange beacon in the night. We step inside.

Just like the Bureau office, Mama Tried hasn't changed at all in my time away. The same roadside dive, same flickering neon signs and pool tables and tin beer logos. Antlers, skulls, and taxidermy hanging in the spaces between everything else. Same jukebox in the corner, Skee-Ball machine, and pool table. Same Leslie behind the bar top. She smiles as we shake the water off us, hair piled on her head the way it always is, shirt lifted and tied above her belly button like always, providing half her tips. A Colorado flag behind her and all the liquor bottles.

"No shit." Leslie throws her rag down on the bar and plants her hands on her hips. "Daniel and Josie Stansfield in my bar again. Never thought I'd see the day."

"Hey, Les," I say.

"Maynor," Josie says.

"What's that?" Leslie says.

Josie clears her throat. "It's Maynor. Now."

My feet stop for half a second, and Josie brushes past me.

"Well, that makes more sense, I guess, Josie Maynor. Suits you." Leslie pours two glasses of Wild Turkey, neat, pushes them toward Josie, who's reached the bar. "How you been?" Leslie's asking me. It's very warm, suddenly. Having trouble breathing. I take off my jacket.

"Oh, yeah. Been okay," I say.

She nods the nod of someone who's kept bar for a very long time. "I'll keep 'em comin'."

We sit at the same corner booth we've always sat in, neither of us hesitating. Elk and caribou antlers hanging on the wall above us, and a taxidermy fox holding a bottle of Odell IPA. Fat Tire and 90 Shilling metal signs, an old framed Avalanche jersey, the original Broncos D logo in a frame. Photographs of Leslie around Colorado, on mountains, at Nuggets games. It's the only place we would sit. We are both, Josie and me, if nothing else, creatures of habit. I take a deep breath and brace myself against the music playing through the bar. Tell myself it's fine, clench my jaw. I can be normal and sit in a bar with music playing just like everyone fucking else.

"So," I say, once we've both settled and she's leaning back against the leather of the booth, her chin jutting out a little, exposing the perfect smooth dark skin of a throat I haven't run my fingers over in years above the neckline of her gray hoodie. Her jacket and mine strewn over the side of the booth, both wet. Her hair wet, and curlier, because of it.

Josie's always been one to slouch when off the job. College athlete. She wears her title like a trench coat, and the second it's off, you see she's only ever a sweats-on-the-couch kind of girl beneath it. The sweatshirts hiding a single butterfly tattoo over her heart for the mom she lost ten years ago, the same spot she presses her palm to now, always does when she's uneasy.

Her hand squeezing mine when she got that tattoo, tears streaming down her face, shop lights overhead flickering.

"So?" she says.

"You haven't been back here," I say.

"Yeah. I dunno, it always kind of felt like our place." She says this, again with that smile, and I know better than to let it affect me. I *know.*

"No new ink," she says, eyes running over my arms. I look down at what she can see in my T-shirt. I shake my head, but it's a lie. Just nothing new on my arms. She doesn't need to know that. Maynor.

"You changed your name." I can't hold her eye, saying it. I sweep the room. A couple dancing on the open floor in front of the bar, the guy in a faded Rockies hat, the woman in cowboy boots and a skirt. We used to come here like that. Pearl snaps and dress boots, Josie in a short dress, out for a night on the town. Live band twice a week. Her soft laugh as she'd tuck her head into my shoulder on a slow song.

When I turn back, she's watching me. She drinks from her glass, presses it to her lips. The surreality of this entire day pressing in. Sitting across from someone who was there for such a significant portion of my life, was not only there but was instrumental in the making of me. Someone who knows everything about me, who I know everything about. And yet . . . There's a gap. I know nothing of the last four years of her life. How is that even possible?

"Of course I changed my name," she says. "Wouldn't you?"

I shrug, look away again, search for something to take me away from this conversation and this day and those fucking images in the files and Pete Noland staring up at the ceiling. I squeeze my eyes shut. When I open them, her expression has shifted. She's angry.

"What the fuck are you thinking, Daniel?"

"What?"

"Murphy said you're going back on active duty. You're seriously gonna go back there?"

"Josie, come on. I don't need—"

"I don't care what you need. Clearly you don't either, because getting back in fatigues isn't it."

"You always liked me in my cammies." I shouldn't flirt with her. What am I—

"You're running."

"I'm not running."

"Bullshit. You *hated* it over there. It fucked you up, and I cannot fathom why you could possibly want to go back unless it's just to d—"

"Josie," I say.

"So that's it," her voice quit. "You're trying to end it. You're trying to—"

"Josie," I say again. My heart racing.

The dancing couple step closer in to each other. Leslie flips on the pink and red twinkly lights that run across the ceiling throughout the bar. I think maybe I just need to stand up and leave.

"Sorry," Josie says. And then, "You know what, though, I'm really not. Is this . . . Are you trying to punish me? Punish us all by going over there and letting someone kill you? That's what this is, right?"

"Believe it or not, this isn't about you."

"Daniel—"

Pete Noland sitting in the chair. Jack in my apartment.

I press my palms to my eyes. "This is . . . not the day I thought it was going to be," I say. To my ex-wife. To my ex-wife with her maiden name, in our old seat at our bar. So much for flirting. I down the whiskey.

We sit for a while in silence. Leslie brings us another round. I don't touch mine. The couple sways to Willie Nelson. *You were always on my mind.*

When Josie speaks again, her voice is gentler, but she's not letting it go. Like always. "Getting yourself killed won't fix anything."

"Says the fed."

"I'll have you know I haven't been shot at in about"—she checks her watch—"five hours."

I give her an imitation of a smile. Her eyes catch on it, then she looks away.

And I see it there. For half a second. She looks young, and I can see her back at the beginning. Us meeting when we were just kids at Quantico and I was fresh off my last tour. I *was* fucked up, and she got me through a lot of it, the night terrors, the flashbacks. We joked and told everyone our getting together and FBI training was pretty much just like *Starship Troopers*—her favorite movie—chaos and long steamy group showers among taut and toned cadets (sadly very untrue), and camaraderie over a shared enemy. But the enemy was theoretical, some mob boss. Or they were real, but we hadn't met them, just online work, remote. I hated *Starship Troopers* (aside from the shower scene), but I never told Josie that. The way they all cheer when the enemy bugs feel fear. These kids, who inflicted that pain. Who created that fear. Which I guess is the point of the whole thing.

The divorce rate for the average American couple is 50 to 60 percent. For FBI agents, it's 70 to 80. It's rare for us to get married, rarer to stay married. But when we both got assigned to Denver, of all the offices in the whole country, it seemed like fate. Especially because being assigned to a field office in your hometown is pretty much unheard of, and we were both from Colorado. So it felt like we were the kids to break the odds. Like the world somehow wanted it for us.

Like John and Annie in *Take Me Ho—*

"So," she says, "all it took was one conversation with Jack Murphy to bring you back?"

"Haven't changed my mind," I say. I reach for the new glass, down it. "I'm still going."

She nods slowly, bites the inside of her cheek again, finishes the glass in front of her, her eyes never leaving my face. I don't want to feel it, don't want to sit inside the gravity of her.

I'm in it though. I'm here. And fuck it all if being near her doesn't just feel like home.

Is she looking at me that way because she feels the same?

"You think it's the same guy?" she asks.

I should tell her she shouldn't have faith in my ability to answer that question. That I'm as clueless as anyone, maybe more than everyone. I shake my head, not in answer but in a lack of one. I don't know anything. Not who the person coercing the killers is, or whether it's drugs—though nothing ever pops up in toxicology—a cult, or a conspiracy. Who the hairs belong to—the calling card of the actual killer most likely, but never enough as evidence to let the blacked-out murderers off the hook. Not with the juries and judges moved by their outrage, and guys like Oliver Wright pushing their might into it.

And maybe it *is* the individuals doing it. Maybe they're all copycats of an original and are just the best fucking actors I've ever seen. We just know nothing. And the top of the pile of the nothing I know is how and why I'm sitting here again, letting myself pretend for a minute that I didn't lose the woman in front of me a long time ago.

"What's up with Whileago? You goin' there tonight?" she asks.

"Fuck no," I say, flinching at the name.

"Seriously? You're just . . . *not* gonna go? Is it like . . . holding up okay?"

I shrug.

"No one's been over there?" She says it in the disappointed, certain, accusatory tone of a woman who's been let down a hundred times.

"I mean . . . not as far as I know."

"Well, you'd be the only one to know, it's your hou—"

"I don't want to talk about it," I say. And I mean it. I really fucking don't want to talk about it. Or think about it. *How* am I here?

Josie clears her throat. "So," she says, her voice taking on a slight hint of uncertainty. Nervousness even. "You're back now, which, you know, I thought you probably wouldn't be. Like ever. But, um, there's something I should maybe tell you." She fidgets with her empty glass. "You know," she says, "since you are back."

I wait for her to speak.

"Nat," she says, "Tillman. I mean, obviously you know who Nat is. Um, so he and I have been . . . seeing each other. For a while now. He . . . he moved into the house, with me. I just thought, you know . . . that you should know."

I stare at her.

"What?" I say.

"Well, I mean, it's been four years. And after everything that went down, you know, Nat was there. He's been there for me. I know you never really liked him, but he's a good guy. And . . . we're happy."

Lucinda Williams comes on over the speakers. Out of the corner of my eye, I see Leslie pouring again. As if sensing that I need to get absolutely obliterated. A shadow lingers near her behind the bar. Leslie pouring one for me and one for the woman shacking up with . . .

Nat fucking *Tillman*?

No. No to all of this.

I stand, stumble almost, over to the bathroom. I shove myself into a stall and unzip my jeans to piss. I'm shaking again. With what? Rage? Exhaustion? Déjà vu? I put my hand on the wall for stability, for something that isn't going to be pulled out from under me.

The first day of the rest of my life is a seriously fucked-up time travel back through the rabbit hole, and now this. *Tillman* living in my old house with Josie. Tillman sleeping in my bed, plopping down at the end of the day on my couch that Josie and I picked out together, watching my TV and eating off our plates that we were given at our wedding.

Jesus Christ. Josie still uses my streaming logins. I thought it was sweet. The one way we've been tied together, the one thread holding us from afar, even if we never spoke again in the whole rest of our lives. I don't watch movies anyway, not since I was a kid, and then again when I was married to her. But every now and then I look, see what she's watching, try to picture what she's doing. Sure, I did it more two years ago than now, but every so often . . .

But *Tillman* is the one watching those movies. *With* her. All her sci-fi movies. I remember now, the guy believes in UFOs. He drinks out of an *X-Files* mug at the office that says I WANT TO BELIEVE. Tillman probably in a fucking *Starship Troopers* T-shirt or something, making her popcorn and making her laugh because Josie would never be with anyone who didn't make her laugh. It was maybe the biggest way I failed her in the end—any humor in me, the case did away with completely.

But those images. The look on every single one of those people who killed and didn't remember doing it.

I *believe* them. Maybe I shouldn't. I probably shouldn't. But I can't help it. They're all so horrified. How do you make jokes after that? How do you do anything? Sixteen lives ruined. Now twenty. Twenty lives. And that's not even the whole of it. There's all the lives theirs touched. Countless victims unspoken for. Parents, siblings, children, friends. How does anyone come back from that? From the stigma and the lifetime of their names being googled to find only brutalities that had nothing to do with them. This poisonous thing spreading like rot, further and further, until it destroys all of us.

My parents and I had been discussing the case, on the way out to Red Rocks, when the truck lights swept through the night and blinded us.

I close my eyes, hold the wall for support.

The answer is, you don't come back from any of it. You pack up your life and head off to war. You leave your shithole past behind you and don't let yourself get sucked back in.

I button my pants and step over to the sink, run my hands under the water, my eyes on the flow of it over my skin. I check my watch. It's almost nine. This day has gone on forever, and I need it to end. I let my eyes raise to the spot in front of me that's always been graffitied wall.

It isn't this time.

Blood.

Fuck.

Blood.

I jump back and swear.

Blood in a bathtub.

I hold my arm up over my eyes.

Blood overflowing the bathtub and crawling out over the tiles and—

I swear again, turn around. This bathroom has never had a mirror in it. Never. It was one of the best things about this place. Who needs a fucking mirror in the men's room? And who decided one day to spend the dumb fuckin' money to add it? I think I'm gonna be sick.

Finally, turned away, I open my eyes and stare at the stalls. After a few minutes, the blood recedes from my vision. Someone's scribbled on the wall DEFEND THE WILD, CO NEEDS WOLVES. Someone else has scribbled over it DEFEND YOURSELF. KILL 'EM ALL. A flyer is stuck to the wall that says FEELING LOST? FIND YOURSELF IN YAMPA, over a photograph of a white dome in a field.

Things have changed. This bar has changed. I've changed, even if it doesn't feel like it coming back here. I've grown past all this, have made peace with the fact that I will not solve this case. That there is nothing I can do to get my life back.

I have a choice in this. I have a plan and people counting on me. I don't have to sit here and watch Josie and Tillman have their happy love affair, and the faces of all my former colleagues and friends looking at me with such pity, my life so full of shame and guilt and every feeling that will eat a person alive, has eaten me alive forever.

I do not have to walk back into Whileago Manor, or deal with this motherfucking mirror in this bar bathroom.

My stuff is still packed. I can just get on the road tonight and drive to San Diego. Call Murphy from the highway and tell him I'm not the guy. I haven't had too much to drink yet. I can do this. I can get on with my life and get the fuck out of this place.

I grab a paper towel, keeping my eyes down this time, again that relief creeping back into me, that sense that things might start to look up. Today is the day I'm going to leave it all behind, for good. Maybe this is a test from the universe or whatever fucked-up gods there are, and the only way to pass is to turn my back on it. To walk all the way away and never look back.

I dry my hands and toss the paper towel into the trash can a few feet away.

It goes right in.

And then I do smile. Just once, just for a moment.

That is, until the screaming starts.

5

Josie.

I run. I'm unarmed. I'm not thinking about anything, just her.

I find her in the bar in shooting stance, pistol trained on the chest of a man standing near the door.

She's talking to him. The scream wasn't hers. My brain takes in the information out of order. The person screaming is the man Josie is pointing her gun at. The person screaming is dripping rainwater and blood.

Thirties, tall, male. Hysterical.

The person screaming is naked and wearing someone's skin.

Here.

Almost at once, he seems to realize there's something on his shoulders. He reaches around with shaking hands to remove it, holding it out in front of his face. An entire human pelt hangs there, before the whole of Mama Tried. Deflated face, black hair shaved tight to the scalp, no feet or hands. The screaming man's volume surges as he takes it in, eyes frantic, searching around the bar, blood and rainwater dripping down to the floor.

He drops the skin to the ground. Turns, doubles over, vomits beside it. He stumbles on bloody, bare feet. Unsure where to go, vomit dribbling over his lip and tears and rainwater streaming down his face through the blood smeared all over.

Leslie hangs up the bar phone. She's called it in to the local cops.

This can't be happening. Here. Now. In person. I reach slowly for my own cell and shoot Jack a text with one hand. Josie takes a step forward toward the man. The Drifter. He flinches back from her. She slowly sets the gun down, still talking, still trying to calm him.

I back myself through the exit, into the wet night, sprint around to the front. I don't know which direction he came from. The rain, still pelting the ground, the parked cars, me. I don't have my jacket, but I don't feel the cold. I don't feel anything.

I run to the car for a flashlight, move the beam over the slick pavement. Make a full sweep of the parking lot. I head down the road to the east, and then to the west. My limbs electric, every heartbeat, every moment. He's here. One of them is here. *Now.* Third in a week.

We've never had access to an actual crime scene, never even knew where the skinnings had taken place. And now, here I am, witness to this man fresh off his kill. And I'm sweeping the road again and again, back and forth. The rain pelting incessantly, taunting me. Back and forth, I run and slow. There have to be tracks, there has to be *something.* Feet pounding on wet asphalt, my feet, asphalt I've trod a thousand times. The red, orange, green from the Mama Tried sign reflected on the blacktop, the surface slick like a mirror. *Find something. Anything.*

Three in one week. This one in the bar we're in.

I stop. Stare out into the night through the rain. Open road stretching in both directions from the parking lot, nothing but black beyond.

This one bringing the crime *to us.*

There's nothing out here.

I grab my pistol from the car and head back to the front door that the Drifter just walked through, minutes before me. Through the front window, I see him. See Josie too. I slow. He doesn't even know she's there. In the light of the bar, pink-red lights twinkling above them, surrounded by the cold wet night.

The man's fallen to his knees, no longer screaming. He's sobbing. Like Pete. I'd bet like the highway patrolwoman too. Josie kneels beside him, speaking low and soft. The man who had an identity of his own before tonight, who was a person with people who loved him and dreams and wants and needs.

Just as the sirens reach my ears, the man's anguished cries become words.

How did I get here?

6

Red and blue flash over Josie's face, in the Mama Tried parking lot, talking to Jack. Both of them dealing with DPD. The rain has paused. Left the ground slick and the air thick, but allowing us all a moment to convene. The screaming man is no longer screaming. Wrapped in a space blanket and shut in the back of a cop car. He's a university professor. His name is Everett Brown, and the last thing he remembers was over forty-eight hours ago, thirty miles outside of Boulder.

All the rest of the killers blacked out for twelve hours or less and walked less than thirty miles during the night. Everett's feet are raw and bloodied, torn open from what very well could have been thirty miles of walking, but part of me wonders if it might have been even more. I don't know how he could have walked during the day without being seen. In the vomit pile, we found a long hair tied in a knot. Someone from forensics took it in for testing, along with the skin.

"Stansfield, with me," Jack says, and I follow him into a car, two others with us. "Say hello to your team." It takes me a moment to realize he's said this to me. *My* team. Jack tells me their names. I don't hear him. I'm not staying. Still, I know Garcia, and I give her a silent nod. Not typical for her to come, but this case . . . She looks just the same as she always does—black hair slicked back, clothing pressed and perfect, efficient no-nonsense look on her face. Another agent I don't know. Josie in the parking lot. Who I was just sitting across from, and the killer, and—

We're moving. Driving.

The rain ruined any chance of us chasing footprints, but the couple in the bar said they saw Everett coming from the west so that's where we're headed.

Red and blue lights in the dark of night, the sweep of our headlight beams. All of this, some kind of dream, a great black avalanche.

We hit a three-way intersection and plug Everett's last known location into the map. If he fits the pattern at all aside from the differences we've already identified, the body should be back closer to where he started. But which road did he arrive here on? He could've come from the one straight ahead or the one veering north. We're assuming he only walked the roadways, assuming that, like the other murders, we'll find the body beside the road in a drainpipe. We're assuming a whole fucking lot.

We head north, stop at intervals. Every drain, ditch, dip in the ground. The night is balmy, unusually humid. The rain's still holding off, but we feel it there, hovering. Letting us know it'll be back and we won't know when. My clothes are still wet, the night clinging to my skin.

People from here aren't suited to moisture. You can see it, in the cracks and joints of elbows, hands, crow's feet. Us who belong to the mountains, the high plains. Hearty and craggy as red rock. But in the moisture, we soften and sweat. In the moisture we break.

Jack is quiet. I am quiet. The others are quiet. Everything feels wrong.

Bad Feeling.

"Clear. Nothing over here," someone says. "Let's move."

The wind pushes through the grasses on either side of the road. Outside the car, I pause. Another empty ditch below us. But . . .

I glance over to Jack, to the members of the team—*my* team. They walk through the night with their flashlights. The new one shivers. She must not be local. So many people moving in all the time. New suburbs built every day, the city expanding faster than anyone can keep up with.

They don't feel it, the others. The thing pressing in on my skull, scratching at the back of my brain. Not that it's real. I don't have some special power, and I certainly—

I turn. I can't help it.

The black of the fields. The road stretching behind us, darker than usual. It's not normally this dark. The moon and stars blotted out by this strange humidity, hanging around us, dampening the world. Sealing us in.

Someone's here, in the field. I can feel it.

I grasp my gun and the cold barrel of the flashlight, take a careful step forward.

I sweep the beam slowly through the grass. Blade after blade, miles of it sprawling ahead. I hear Jack's faint voice ten or fifteen yards behind me. I take another step, away from them. Another. Deeper into the night.

More pressure. An ache.

A throbbing, disordered pulse.

VOOM.

A sound like hawk wings in a metal barn. Like a vacuum purge in space.

VOOM.

I take another step. My eyes unable to see anything outside the range of the flashlight beam.

The grass moves.

On the left.

I turn, whip the beam through the field.

No. Shit. My right.

I swing the light—

VOOM.

Darkness.

A crack. Behind me.

I smell something now, though I can't say exactly what it is. Old, forgotten. Like . . . a memory just out of grasp. Bitter, maybe a little chemical.

VOOM.

Everett Brown's screams, echoed on the wind. Surging, growing, stampeding.

I turn again.

"Shit, Stansfield!"

I turn back, heart thundering.

I'm far . . . so far from them. From the road. That can't be right, can it? A hundred meters, more. It was just a few steps. I shine the light again, and . . .

That . . . *pressure.*

That sound.

Jack calls again.

I wait. Watch, and listen.

But there's no sound, no rustling.

Just a gentle sway in the wind, throughout the field. Grass bowing under its sweeping weight.

Still . . . I take another step, away from Jack.

Something pulling. *Wanting.*

The night. Or something in it. It's almost . . .

Alive.

"Stansfield! They found him!"

A drainpipe off the side of the highway ten miles northeast. DPD and FBI swarming the grass on both sides of the highway, blocking the whole thing off.

Jack stops on the road past the barricade to talk to the other detectives, assesses the scene.

I move to follow him, and someone's hand is on my chest. I look down at it, then up at a young guy in a DPD jacket. "This is an active crime scene," he says. "You need valid identification."

The female agent next to him, older than me, shakes her head at the kid. She stares openly, lifts the corner of her mouth in a smile. I just step past them when she says to him, "You don't know who that is?"

Low grass gives way beneath my boots, heading down into the muddy ditch beside the road, the ground slipping, shifting. Nothing visible beyond our floodlights. Whatever I felt in the field before didn't follow us here. Or what I imagined in the field.

Here, now, beneath the crime scene tent, a small hunched figure crouches at the edge of the floodlight on the grass, maybe fifteen feet from the asphalt, a series of items laid in front of and beside her on two tarps on the ground. The crime scene photographer moves around, documenting the items, camera flashing at the tarp next to her, the yellow evidence markers. I'd looked for her, at the bar, but she wasn't there. My chest tightens, seeing her now.

"Daphne," I say. "Anything good?"

The woman's head turns slowly until nearly black eyes land on my face. She's changed her hair a little, has new glasses. But otherwise the same. She maintains her crouch and neutral expression and says, "Daniel is back, is he?" Doing her Gollum impression, one she does because it makes me uncomfortable. And because it also sometimes makes me laugh.

"For tonight, my precious," I say.

The photographer steps over to talk to someone. I bend down beside Daphne, the familiar feel of her eyes on my skin, taking me in as though I were one of the thousands of insect specimens she keeps pinned to the walls inside her home. Always smelling faintly of chemicals and carrying in her purse at all times a cyanide killing jar in case she should happen upon something "wonderful."

"Just pieces," she says. Shreds of fabric and skin that she's assembled on the cloth in front of her. She's already bagged up a hand. The photographer steps in and snaps a few more photos. The shadows move. I feel her watching me again.

"We were told they'd found the body," I say.

She shakes her head. "Just the hands and feet, a couple slivers of skin. And the killer's clothes, I would guess. They said he was quite tall, at the bar. And these," she says, indicating the body parts in front of her, "make me think the victim is smaller."

"Only one set of clothing?"

She nods, eyes unblinking. She's thinking.

Chaos, all around. Jack swearing, shouting at the cops. Saying they shouldn't have said they found a body if they didn't find a *fucking body*. Radio chatter, rerouted traffic.

We're closer in now, nearer to houses and stores. Some kind of new residential development a handful of miles away. Their light bleeds through to us, at the edges of the night. Hanging even more otherworldly in this unusual fog.

Crickets in the grass. Too many voices.

A pile of items on a tarp, a couple feet from us. A Styrofoam gas station cup, food wrappers, a cigarette pack, small pieces of plastic. Tons of them. Shit that crowds the earth, multiplies faster than we do. Daphne's made the pile, cleared every item of mud in her floodlight. Put the yellow markers beside them.

"This all come from the drainpipe?" I ask, bending down beside her.

She nods. "Just past it in the grass. They're all looking for more now."

Mud all over her gloved hands. "Where'd you dig?" I ask.

She glances to me. "Knew you'd be back. The others didn't think so, but I knew."

"I don't know where I am," I say.

"You used to be good at this."

Anyone else, and I'd bristle. But it's Daphne. "Maybe. Not now."

She narrows her eyes and looks up at the sky. "Wanna know what I think?"

"Guessin' I'm gonna hear it either way."

"No," she says, turning her attention back to the items in front of her. "It doesn't matter what I think."

I lean to the side, just enough so our shoulders touch. Just enough to say I missed her. And I realize I really did. Not once in four years did I reach out to her. When I left, I said I needed a clean break. And I did, I think, in the beginning. But then, I just . . . didn't call. Time kept moving, and I sort of just . . . I guess I disappeared on her. My friend.

"You okay?" I ask. "These days, I mean." God, what kind of dickhead has to ask that? What kind of dickhead asks that in a moment like this?

Her dimples show, just for a second. Then she nods toward the drainpipe, the trail she cleared in the mud leading out from it. Officers spread out through the field, on the other side of the highway, redoubling efforts. "Go be useful, Stansfield," she says.

I hesitate, want to say more, but she's right. We have to keep moving.

I step away from Daphne. Crouch down, to where the ground's already been tilled, closer to the road. I touch the mud, the cold dankness of it. Inhale. It rained hard. Water would have pushed things out pretty far. I ask Daphne what each of the yellow tents and their numbers represent. Try to imagine that hard heavy rain washing it all from the pipe. Hands, feet, T-shirt, jeans, all the trash. Unfocus my eyes and try to follow. Not the path the others dug, but the one that's intuitive, the one that feels . . . right. Out into the grass.

A few paces out, I bend down, stretch my hands in the earth, the mud. Move forward a few more steps, drop to my hands and knees. Grope in the mud.

Again. Forward, deeper into the night.

Again. Forward, dig. Crawl, search. Away from the road, away from the light. Dig, crawl, search.

Until I sit back on my heels. There's nothing here. At least not in this spot.

And why would there be? Why would *I* of all people find it?

My shining boy.

Of course there's nothing. Some washed-up asshole digging in the dirt, playing make-believe that he can somehow *sense* things, know things that other people can't. The truth is, I was a scared kid who always thought there were things going bump in the night. And in my twenties, I was just . . . lucky. That's what it all came down to, just shit-all luck. Luck that put Josie and me in the same town after training. Luck that got my whole squadron out when we were surrounded by enemy fire, holed up in a lookout tower. Luck that led me to solving a few big cases young. And part of that was just knowing how to read people. Just . . . watching. Survival mechanism, probably. But the problem is when people start to put too much faith in you. The problem is when your luck runs out and you're no longer the guy everyone thinks you are. The guy they were all counting on you to be.

I stand, knees wet, hands and clothes filthy. Head swimming with lights and voices and the day that will never end. Daphne stands now at the edge of the road. I'm not gonna find anything. I'm tired. I finally have my life in my own hands, and today I just . . . I don't know. I lost control, and it's time to get it back. Boots squelching in Colorado mud.

Daphne, by the road in her new glasses, studying something. I fucked up. She doesn't have anything to do with Josie, or Jack, or any of it. I was so desperate to get away from this, away from everything. And now I've missed out on four years of a friend's life. And I'm shipping out, may not even get a chance. Maybe this proves I'm making the right move. I don't make anyone's life better, haven't in a long time. My notice is already in. I don't work here, and I can walk away right now, just step out into the night and call a fuckin' car to come and pick me up and—

Snap.

I stop. A feeling, beneath my boot.

Something breaking.

I step back, put my foot down again.

Another snap. Plastic.

More trash? But Daphne wouldn't have missed it. Maybe something I dropped . . . Or maybe she just hasn't come this far out yet.

I step back, bend down. Reach my hand out for the item in the grass—red, maybe pink. Hard to tell with mud on it, here in the strange foggy dark. I can tell I broke it though. Two, no, three items. Or one item, but now in three pieces. Two matching halves, and one of them broken in two. I pick them up, the three pieces, hold them before my face in the floodlights. Start to wipe the mud from them. And—

Sweat. The humidity.

No.

I'm cracking.

Voom.

That pressure, that strange . . .

The lights are too bright. The air too close, everything.

"Daniel?" Daphne's voice. But the whole of the world is turning, and I feel it. I feel the motion in this vast empty darkness that only gets darker every day.

I look up at her walking toward me, the floodlights behind her nearly blinding. I ask, "Am I dreaming?"

She picks up her pace. "Hey, are you—"

John Denver's voice floats to me on the wind. The other song, the worst song.

No.

A dream. All of this has to be . . .

This plastic in my hand, twenty-nine years ago.

This plastic in my hand now. It's not red. Not pink.

Voom.

It's orange. Orange, with a yellow smiling clown on one side.

Running through the parking lot, throwing it up in the air and catching it. Mom calling from inside.

"Danny!"

Voom.

The pieces fall from my hands. The wind blows in the grass, and the Colorado soil softens the landing. I don't need to see what it says on the back.

Daphne stops a foot away. Her eyes find it on the ground.

Three pieces of an orange and yellow plastic motel room key tag. With words in white cursive on the side. Words that form when Daphne bends down and fits the pieces together.

FREE SMILE WITH EVERY STAY AT THE HAPPY INN!

7

A motel by the side of the road, south of Denver on I-25, a flickering neon blue WANDER INN sign. We, and a SWAT team, pull up to the front parking lot. The motel lights shine in my eyes.

I could have driven this way a hundred times and not known it was the same road, the same motel. When I was a kid, it was wide open stretches, nothing around but open road in black night. Now, houses. New developments everywhere, a sea of brown roofs, strip malls, subdivisions. All their lights so bright. Nearly suffocating.

I was told the Happy Inn was torn to the ground.

You know you're my shining boy.

The Wander Inn now, it's been painted blue and white, given a cosmetic overhaul. But it didn't fall. It's the same structure. I'd know it anywhere. This place hasn't died. It hasn't even been reconfigured. Just soft colors added, mountain flowers on the front office sign. Befitting a motel near these new neighborhoods. The road itself a main artery now, no longer a back road. No more carnival-saturated orange and yellow. No more clowns.

But the Happy Inn is still here.

Officers jump out of vehicles, feet on pavement. The main office is over on the right with the Innkeepers' Suite, a little apartment and garage where Sherie used to live, same as it used to be. The rooms on the left. The towering sign in the middle.

Mom stands and walks to the door of our room, Dad's fist pounding from outside.

"ROSE, OPEN THIS DOOR RIGHT NOW!"

Mom, please don't—

Shh, Danny.

"DON'T YOU FUCKING TALK TO MY SON! LET ME IN!"

I'm out of the car, somehow. Standing on the asphalt. Pavement? I don't—

Mom looks scared. She turns to me. "Put your boots on, Danny, okay? Get your boots on and go for a little walk while Daddy and I talk."

She opens the door, and he stumbles in.

Wander Inn. Happy Inn.

Glitches in time. Static. Pressure.

Wearing too-big cowboy boots, the ones my mom found for me at a thrift shop. The ones she said I'd grow into. That we both thought John Denver would wear.

A tired couple is dragged out from the apartment attached to the office, the innkeepers. Jack asks for a manifest log. The plastic key tag pieces shoved in front of them, the innkeepers' eyes wide.

"I . . . I haven't seen one of those in years. Not since the renovation. Not since we took over. I don't . . . Where did you say you found it?"

SWAT starts at the nearest room. I drift behind them. As they knock on doors, push into empty rooms. Ask if they can look around inside the occupied ones. Probable cause, warrants. I don't know how Jack's handling it.

Dad trips on his way inside, stumbles. His head swings around, looking for me. He pushes past my mom.

"Danny, get outside," my mom says.

"You think you can take him from me?" Dad yells.

"Mom!" Hiding between the beds.

"Shh, Danny, it's okay. Calvin, let's just talk, okay? Let's just—I wasn't—"

Outdoor walkway, lights flickering. Static, in the air.

"That's not his name, Rose!"

Bad Feeling. *Bad Feeling.*

A black Cadillac, in the final parking spot out front. Thirty paces from the room. My room. Mine and Mom's.

Glitch. Static.

I blink. No Cadillac.

Glitch, again.

Yes, there is. It's there, and I'm staring at it.

"Calvin, let's get Danny outside, and then we'll talk, okay?"

He's crying. Dad is crying, stumbling, running his hands over his head. "I can't even look at you. I can't believe you would do this. How could you do this?"

He leans on the wall, his head resting on a sunset painting, knocking it crooked. He breathes, heavy, through his nose. It's loud. So loud. "Haven't I given you everything? You wanted space, you wanted—I can't—"

I don't mean to, but a sound comes from my throat. I'm scared, and I'm shaking.

Mom's eyes cut to me, and she shakes her head, to say be quiet. *She takes a step.*

I'm here. On the mat. In front of the room, just outside.

Blood on my cowboy boots.

Someone on the SWAT team steps in front of me, knocks, and puts his ear to the door.

I blink. The motel is the Happy Inn again. Orange, yellow, I—

Blink again.

Mom crying too. Both of them crying.

"Go wait outside, honey, okay? Go take a little walk, and Mommy will—"

Two officers, knocking on the door. One of them young, new. A third and fourth holding formation. I'm just standing, just—

"How could you do this?! How could you!" Dad yells.

"Police!"

It's cold outside. I didn't get a jacket before they made me leave.

"Calvin, please—"

A slap, a loud one. Mom screaming now.

I turn the knob, but they've locked me out. I pound on the door. Yell for my mom.

The officers knock, pound on the door again.

Footsteps come. The owner, Sherie, runs through the parking lot, asks what's the matter. Mom yelling inside, Mom screaming, and I can't get to her, and—

Orange, then blue. Two motels, two times. Glitching, flashing.

The young officer abruptly stops knocking. Leans in to the door. Listens.

He signals to the others. Crouches down, cocks his gun. He knocks one more time. No answer. But this time I hear it too.

A whisper. A muffled cry, from inside the room.

The whimper I'd made that night. It sounds just like me.

Sherie unlocks the door.

They kick the door in. The forward two officers step into the room, the other two flanking, turned, holding position.

Already a stench wafts out from the room. One of them says, *Jesus Christ.* The other stops, frozen.

"Danny!"

"Dan, what the fuck are you doing?" Jack says. He pushes past me to get inside.

Dad, in the dressing area. Holding Mom by her hair.

"That's not our son's name, Rose! How dare you do this, how could you—"

Jack turns to me, eyes frantic. "Paramedics. Now."

Mom whimpers, cries.

Dad's face contorts with rage. He slams her head into the sink.

I scream.

"Clear out! Get her out, and get forensics in here!"

MOM!

My legs are warm, wet.

"Stansfield! What the fuck is wrong with you!"

I blink. I lift my hand, speak words. Radio the paramedics. Force my legs to move.

Orange. Blue. Orange. Static. Glitch.

He picks her back up, yells into the side of her face. Crying. Howling. "Why?"

Mom's eyes lock on me. She looks dazed. Blood on her head. Her eyes half-closed, still crying. She opens her mouth and says to me, "I'm sorry."

Dad reaches up and twists something sharp and shiny against her neck.

I run for her, trip over the TV remote. I fall to the carpet.

The movie starts again, John Denver singing "Annie's Song." It's loud, louder than before.

Mom reaches up, grabs her throat above the turquoise necklace.

She's bleeding.

Dad pushes her, hard, into the bathroom. She slams against the shower wall and slides down into the tub. She doesn't fight him. John Denver sings, Mom in the bathtub. Blood, and—

I shove off the carpet.

MOM!

Not screaming, not moving, she's just—

MOM!

Dad stands. He's crying. Crying, so hard. The mirror, splattered with red. He raises his eyes to the mirror. Where they land on me.

Sirens. Dad's eyes on me. "Annie's Song."

Sirens.

Mom!

I—

I'm here. Standing in our room, looking at the mirror.

No blood in this bathroom. White, still clean.

Dad is here, in the mirror, though. Hard jaw, hard brown-green eyes.

Dad's eyes on me.

Dad in every mirror. In all the years since.

Blood—

I turn, force myself to take in the room. No one's looking at the bathroom. There's no blood there, no body. Everyone in the motel room is focused on the bed.

The bed is covered in blood. It has seeped through the sheets and spilled off the sides to the blue floral carpet.

On it is a man with no skin. Missing hands and feet, like all the other skinned victims. His raw exposed body is duct-taped in a side-lying position to the bed, tape looped down under the mattress. It holds him there.

Him, and the woman in the bed, who is taped in beside him. The two of them, facing in toward each other, as if they are lovers.

"Annie's Song" in my ears. Mom screaming.

The woman in the bed is alive.

SWAT cuts the tape, officers rushing to try to help her up. She has trouble moving. She wears a blood-soaked tank top, hiking pants, socks but no shoes. There's a tattoo on her arm, obscured by the blood. With the help of the others, she's off the bed, touches down on the carpet. It takes a minute. Even then, she can't hold her weight, collapses against one of them. A large double piece of duct tape covers her mouth. She whimpers, but it's weak. She opens exhausted eyelids as Jack yells to the officers. Garcia is there, talking to the woman, saying she's going to remove the tape.

The song keeps playing. I still hear it. Everyone must hear it, it's so loud.

The glitch. An orange room. The past pushing itself up and—

Garcia swears. The woman from the bed lifts her eyes.

Jack is telling me to do something. Everyone talking, saying different things. Sirens. Sound and movement, and my father in the mirror.

Pressure. Static. Pulse. That sound.

VOOM.

You fill up my senses, come fill me again.

The woman from the bed stares up at me.

They rip the duct tape from her mouth. She chokes a sob, spits something on the floor.

Dad's eyes on mine, and the song playing. Dad, through his tears.

Her eyes lift to mine again.

The thing on the floor, what was in her mouth.

It's a human tongue.

8

Dark room. Familiar sheets. Familiar side table. I found it at an antique store off the side of the highway on the way to meet up with Josie's family for Christmas, a couple hours south.

Roadside pit stops, friendly people. So many lives on a planet all the time, so many in a single town. Everyone intimately familiar with a different patch of dust and earth, with a different slice of sky, claiming it for themselves.

I reach over, grab my phone to check the time. But when my fingers wrap around it and tug it free of the charging cord, it . . . feels different. I blink. Rub my eyes.

It's not my phone. It's Josie's.

My eyes are unfocused, the room unsteady. Did I drink last night? My stomach and muscles start to dissent in a way that makes me think I did. The light infiltrating my eyes through the slit in the curtains and the phone screen in front of me.

An image, blurry behind the password prompt. Josie's passcode is our anniversary. I type it in, but the phone buzzes in protest. I try again, still no luck. I need to know what time it is, and it's too small in the corner. *Jesus, what did I drink?* For the hell of it, I type in 1234.

The phone unlocks.

The image on my wife's home screen is one of her. And a man. The man is not me. I blink through dry eyes.

Josie and Nat Tillman at Red Rocks, Dead & Co playing behind them, and they're . . .

Kissing.

I drop the phone, push myself up and out of the bed. I run to the bathroom, the bathroom that used to be mine.

How the fuck am I here?

I vomit, just barely make it to the toilet. Stand, sway on my feet. This bathroom with another man's toothbrush. With another man's . . . hair products? Fingerprints and toothpaste, spit in the sink, and I'm gonna be sick again.

I stand, and—

Blood, bathtub—

Fuck. Where's the curtain we installed over the mirror? Why isn't the fucking mirror covered?

Because Josie took it down. Because I don't live here, and I haven't for a long time. And because Nat Tillman does and he's normal and doesn't have to cover mirrors, and—

The bathroom mirror. My dad.

The Happy Inn.

Everything, all of it rushes in. A torrent of memory, a day that lasted lifetimes.

The woman with the tongue taped in her mouth.

The woman in my old room. Staring at me.

I stumble back through the bedroom, out into the hall and to the living room. Voices sound from the front porch through the open door.

The world spinning, I lean around the corner to find Tillman and Josie sitting there on the other side of the open front door in the Adirondack chairs. Admiring a crisp fall sunrise and talking to each other so casually and comfortably I have to hold the wall to steady myself. Breathe until the framed hall photos come into focus. People I don't recognize, with Josie and Tillman at the holidays. The happy couple stand with a cardboard sign on top of a 14er.

The woman in the motel room. That look in her eyes.

"Yeah, but is he sick? I mean, going down like that . . . You remember I had that uncle who had the tumor and didn't know it. Maybe he's got cancer." Tillman's voice.

"He doesn't have cancer," my wife, ex-wife, says. "There's . . . It's just complicated."

"You don't have to protect him. I mean, if it's gonna impede his work . . ."

I fainted last night. That's what happened. I passed out, on the scene. Who brought me here? Did *Tillman* carry me? And if it all did . . . happen . . . it's a mercy, a not insignificant one, Josie keeping my secret even now.

I shove off the wall. Walk as carefully as I can down the hall with my balance off and push the door open. The desk, twin bed that could accommodate guests but really is always just covered with files and romance novels, maybe a half-clean sweatshirt or two. I try not to inhale the smell of her in this room, try not to see her hunched over those files and biting the inside of her lip in concentration, an audiobook of one of those romances playing from her cell phone in the corner, a seasonal over-scented candle lit beside it, flickering.

I step over to the window and undo the latch. My muscles still don't work the way they should, and it's hard to push the window open. I'm just able to lift it. I raise one leg and shove it through the opening, have to hop a couple times to do it. None of my limbs going where I think they will. I stick an arm through and pull my torso into the window frame with leverage from my hand on the outside of the house. I duck my head under, still facing the room. Pull my body out, and when I'm just there, just almost free save for one foot, I pause.

I push myself back halfway under, straddling the windowsill.

Under one of the sweatshirts, beside a stack of files. Just sticking out . . . An old photograph of the two of us. Josie and me, at city hall. Her, smiling in her white dress, my brown leather jacket shrugged over it in the cold, our family and friends. Me in a pearl snap shirt and embroidered suit and cowboy hat, smiling at her. Looking so happy. So blissfully, momentarily weightless.

I am frozen, half in and half out of the house. Staring at the photograph, the one she has out on the bed. The one she must have been looking at.

I hear the porch door open and close. Josie's and Tillman's voices carry in from the living room. I swear. Push myself further out the window. My foot, the one still inside, catches on one such over-scented candle, and it falls to the floor with a crash.

"Daniel?" Josie calls from the hall.

I swear again. Outside, the dizziness hits me even harder, and my bare feet crunch through the grass, dry and full of burrs because we've never landscaped back here.

"Daniel!" Josie calls from her office. "What the fuck are you doing?"

I run, trip, the too-bright rising sun in my eyes. Around the side of the house and through the front yard to the street. The front door creaks open, and Josie says, "Daniel, come back."

I keep walking, can't run anymore, am too dizzy. But I walk until my feet hit the asphalt.

"Daniel, you've got ketamine in your system, they gave you a shot. Jack said you freaked out," she says. "I have your stuff!"

I ignore her. Though the confirmation that there's a drug in my system is a bit of comfort.

"Daniel, your shoes!"

I'm not looking back. Not going to see Josie in my house with another guy.

Orange-yellow-red leaves litter everything, pile up in front lawns and sail through the air. I don't recognize half the houses. Every neighborhood in all the world getting gentrified or expanded or upgraded, one at a time.

Then there is the hand on my shoulder, and I turn to her. Josie drops my boots on the ground, holds out a plastic grocery bag. "Phone, wallet, keys." She looks me over. "I can't believe you had to go back there. I'm so sorry. If there's . . ." She trails off, concern in her eyes.

"I didn't know it was still there," I say.

"I didn't either. But . . . Dan. Mama Tried, and then that motel. I mean, is someone trying to . . . ?" *Trying to get to you* is what she doesn't say. *Trying to involve you.* Of course I'm thinking the same thing. Of course I fucking am. Of course if anyone at the office does even a little digging into the motel's history, I'll be off the case in a second. I'm beyond compromised.

Not that I'm on this case. Not that I'm staying.

They don't print kids' names in the press for murder cases. And I was adopted so fast after it happened, my name changed almost immediately. As far as I've found in all my years, there's nothing official besides the foster care and adoption agency's records tying me anywhere to Rose and Calvin Keller of the Happy Inn murder. And the adoption agency's since gone out of business, and things slip through the cracks in foster care all the time. But if someone were to start digging, someone with all our resources looking specifically into that murder in that motel room, what would they find?

I'm not staying. This isn't my life anymore, and it hasn't been for a long time.

The motel. The Happy Inn.

The woman. The look in her eyes. Who was she? And how is she a part of this?

And why did she . . . Why did I feel, looking at her . . .

Josie reaches out, her hands on my shoulders. She wraps her arms around me, pulls me into a hug. That citrus scent of her. I need to try to resist, need to resist falling back into this life. Josie understands, as much as anyone can. She knows. This love and respect between us, support. What made us great, when we were great. Even if it wasn't enough in the end. Even if it, like everything else, slipped through the cracks made by the case. The cracks I made. I open my eyes, hadn't realized I closed them. See my old street, my old house, my old life. I see, from Josie's arms.

Nat Tillman standing on my front porch holding a mug I bought.

I close my eyes again, take a breath. I push away from Josie.

Down the road, I pull on my boots, shake my phone out of the plastic bag, and call Jack.

"They're keeping her at the hospital another day, said no visitors yet," Jack says before I say anything. "They're worried about her kidney levels, may have been without water more than two days. We've got Everett Brown in custody. No ID on the girl yet. Take a beat. Get yourself together."

"Jack. I passed out at a crime scene."

"You passed out, then tried to slug the paramedics lookin' at you."

I swear. "That explains the drugs I guess."

"Look, you haven't been out in the field in a while. Salt Lake said you've been requesting desk duty, which I can understand. You're just getting your sea legs again."

"I think . . . I think I have to go, Jack. I think I can't be on this one."

"When they go big, we're one step away from catching them, you know that."

"I think . . ." The killers are getting personal, personal with *me*, and it seems very likely that whoever is orchestrating all this is trying to get to me. Only Josie knows.

I have to tell him.

One of Jack's kids yells something in the background. Jack puts his hand over the phone, says something back.

People are dead. Lives ruined. Because someone wants to get to me? Because the killer wants me rattled? Who have I ever pissed off so much? Unless . . . Unless it's because I couldn't solve it before. Unless someone is taunting me now, or trying to get even. Because I couldn't do it? One of the former victims' friends or family? Or . . .

"Trying to get everyone out the door," Jack says. "Always something with kids." In the background, doors slamming, voices overlapping. "Okay. Stansfield, what were you saying?"

I'm gonna say it, am about to. Somehow, I actually say, "Anyone look into that motel yet?"

Those are the words from my mouth. Those words, and nothing else. I stare at the cell phone, as if it somehow betrayed me. As if I don't betray myself every fuckin' day.

"Not sure. Why, you got something?"

"Yeah. I'll . . . send you and the team all of it. I stayed there, one time. As a kid. That's how I knew about the key. There was a murder, almost thirty years ago. You remember, the guy killing his wife?" My voice is steady, doesn't break once. I'm doing this. Fuck, I'm doing this.

"Oh shit," Jack says. "That was there? What were their names? Kacey?"

"Keller," I say.

"Right. I remember, kind of. Same room?"

I say, "You know what, let me do the legwork. I'll send everyone what I find."

"So. You'll stay then," he says. Doing nothing to hide the eager hope in his voice.

Someone making me return to the Happy Inn. Someone using this to taunt me.

The look in that woman's eyes.

Al-Anbar sand. Final tour. Forest cabin.

I don't want to stay. Of course I don't. But . . .

You fill up my senses,

Maybe I need to. Maybe just long enough, once and for all.

Come fill me again.

To take this fucker down.

"Okay," I say into an indifferent Denver morning. "Yeah . . . I'll stay."

II

HERE YOU COME AGAIN

1

I drive to the gated far section of Cherry Hills, where the land extends alongside the High Line Canal, sixty or seventy miles of trail that began as an irrigation project and then became a staple urban recreation path for the city. It moves through grasslands, wetlands, woodlands, host to all kinds of wildlife.

Whileago Manor is accessed by a private drive near Foxhill Road, surrounded by a seemingly spontaneous copse of trees so thick you can't see past it. If a person didn't know to look for the house, they would never even know it was here.

I take the turn for the drive, after very nearly missing it. The branches and leaves of the tree tunnel scratch at the edges of the car, so dense now that no sunlight permeates. My parents never let it get overgrown. At least, not like this.

I don't want to be here. I'm sweating. Maybe it's the drugs. I took a cab to Mama Tried to pick the car up, then drove here to shower, pull myself together. What a freakin' joke.

I hit a downed branch, and the car jolts. I turn on my brights, shine the lights through the tree tunnel, can't even see the end of it.

A figure runs across the tunnel through the headlights.

I squeeze my eyes. Breathe.

Just a shadow. Just a figment. I open my eyes again, and it's like I've been swallowed by the earth itself. By the past. By every mistake I've ever made. The tunnel, stretching, pulling me.

I can feel more of them, the shadows. Sense them waiting just ahead beyond the trees. Waking at my approach. I'm six years old again. Driving through this tunnel for the first time, and the branches are reaching, reaching for me, and—

My phone rings. I grab it. My breaths steady. I force them to.

"What's your office ETA?" Jack says.

"Uh . . . five minutes," I say, closing my eyes against something else moving through the trees.

"You're not stopping by the house?"

"I—" I thought I was. But now, being here—

BOOM!

I swear, loudly.

"Jesus, Daniel, what?"

I breathe. *Oh nothing, Jack, a shadow just slammed my goddamned window. No big deal. It doesn't exist, but it scared the shit out of me.*

I clear my throat. "Thought a bird hit my window." I refuse to look to the left where the thing is. I put the car in reverse. This was a terrible idea.

"Right. Okay. Well, so . . . I gotta tell you something," Jack says.

"Okay," I say. I back out through the trees, keep my eyes on the light behind me through the rearview.

"As you know, uh, case is cold. *Was* cold, before this. And we kept it open, 'course. But uh, you know time passed, and . . ."

"Yeah."

I'm almost out, almost back in the sun. Keep it steady, slow your heart.

"So I'm gonna have you workin' with cold cases on it. Since they've been covering things."

"Okay," I say. Breathe. Just a little more, then I'm there. "I like Kowalski. That's fine."

"Kowalski quit. Retired, actually."

Finally I break free of the trees, pull out away from Whileago Manor into the sun. I stop the car. Collect myself, hear what Jack said.

I try to run through that department, think of who might be next in line to take over. "So who am I working with?" I ask.

Jack doesn't say anything for a moment.

"Hello?"

"Yeah . . . I'm here," he says.

And then a terrible sinking feeling that has nothing to do with the giant haunted house that I couldn't face today.

"Who's in charge of cold cases now, Jack?"

* * *

Nat fucking Tillman stands outside the front door to the building, staring up at the sky.

Wiry climber build, black hair, a tan from time outdoors. Supremely punchable face.

I forgot that he does this, just stands around and cranes his neck up at the clouds like a stoner, which I actually don't think he is, which somehow makes it worse. He startles as we approach, as if he were not waiting here for us to arrive. He reluctantly draws his eyes down.

"It's a clear one," he says with a smile.

"Tillman," Jack says, nodding. He catches my eye to say, *Be nice*, holds the door for us to the building.

"Excited to work with ya, buddy," Tillman says. "We've done a lot since you've been gone, and—"

I step past him.

Daphne stands in front of my desk when we arrive. It's rare to see her outside of the DPD forensics lab or Mama Tried, but I'm happy to. Sometimes in the past she would come over to deliver information to us in person, just to get out for a bit. It's a strange space to occupy, not knowing what her life has been like. Like Josie. Jack. Everyone. All my fault.

"Doctors still won't let us in, but we have her medical report," she says in her gravelly discordant voice. She often liaises with the hospitals, as she grew up in a family of prominent doctors and knows or can pull strings with most everyone, at least in the Denver area.

"Let's hear it," Jack says.

"Scattered contusions. No sign of sexual assault. Blunt force trauma to the back of the skull. Could be handle of a knife. Her skin is in bad shape from the tape. She's lost some of it on her arms and face. Should heal."

"Okay," I say. "Anything else?"

"The body of the John Doe was skinned alive, same as the others, but his tongue was also removed."

"We know," I say, feeling a little sick again.

"And it was taped inside Hannah Lawrence's mouth."

Hannah Lawrence.

My mind catches on her name. Almost like . . .

I say it out loud, I think. Maybe? I don't mean to. A chill runs over my arms, my heart racing.

Hannah.

An intense sense of inevitability, déjà vu, maybe. I don't know.

A shadow moves at the corner of the room.

"Right. Yes. We got an ID. Frazier, your new officer, she just put this here before you walked in. Hannah Lawrence woke up in the hospital, freaked out about being there, nurses had to up her meds."

Daphne slides another file to me. I open it.

"She's still conscious?" I ask.

"No. She was. But now . . . they'll update us when she's ready."

Hannah Lawrence. Twenty-eight, ranger, US Forest Service. She left a psychology PhD program at Colorado State for a yearlong stint in California, then returned and joined the USFS. Born and raised in Durango, parents both dead, last living in Arizona. No siblings, spouse, or children. No criminal record. Frazier stuck a Post-it on top of everything else that says NO SOCIAL MEDIA. She's stationed at a cabin in the Pike National Forest near the Colorado Trail / Indian Creek Trail junction. There's a photo of her, in a ranger uniform, serious expression. Athletic, strong. Her eyes slightly upturned at the edges, the color of them a light, almost translucent green. Freckles across her nose, that tattoo of something, just below her sleeve. Dark not-quite-blond hair down her shoulders.

She's beautiful. Painfully, almost. Not a useful thought. Wildly inappropriate. My chest tightens up, looking at her photo, and I shake my head. Have to stop whatever that is. My heart pounding.

"We send a team to the cabin yet?" I ask Jack and Daphne.

Jack says, "There's one on their way. Thought you'd need a minute. But you and Tillman can do a double check when you're ready."

I nod, look to Daphne.

"From her dehydration level and the motel manifest," she says, "we think she was in that room for forty-eight to fifty-two hours. No water, no food. She held his tongue in there for two or three days and didn't bite down and didn't lose her lunch, so to speak. I think she's my hero. If it's appropriate to say."

"It's not," Jack says.

Daphne shrugs.

Hannah. Her name a whisper in the back of my skull. In that same room as my mother. They don't look alike. But if someone was trying to get to me, trying to make a point . . . If they didn't know Rose—she was taller, a couple inches maybe, her skin less freckled, hair bleached, eyes brown—but had seen just a photo maybe, they might think Hannah could be a stand-in.

Hannah Lawrence.

I hand the file to Jack, who hands it to Tillman. I feel relieved, somehow, not seeing her photo anymore. But also a little sick, dizzy. I shake it off, try to catch Daphne's eye.

"Okay, well, that's all for now," Daphne says, not quite meeting mine. "Back to all my dead friends. I'll get you an ID on the John Doe soon as I can."

Daphne leaves, and I'm alone with Jack and Tillman.

"Well, then," Jack says. If he had a thought he doesn't finish it.

We go over all they've compiled while I've been gone. Hannah Lawrence there, in the background of everything. I'm anxious to get to the cabin, but I need the rundown on everything else. Tillman's already interviewed Kimberly Chen, the first Drifter since the hiatus, and the family of her victim, gas station attendant Ross Thompson. Then of course I was there for Pete Noland. "Pete's victim?" I ask.

"Ramona Lopez," Tillman says.

"Have we gotten anything from her family or friends?"

"Her mom, Angela, she can come in tomorrow. Then with the chat rooms . . . This *Wizdumteller* definitely seems to have a lot of support. We've been lookin' into it, but we can't find 'em, and that seems significant to me. But for today, I think we should go to the cabin," Tillman says, snapping the file closed. Then he looks around and furrows his brow. "I mean, uh, of course, if that's what you think."

I exhale a long breath, wish for a fucking lobotomy. Jack stands behind me, puts a hand on my shoulder, and says, "Let me know if you find anything."

I say to Tillman, "Be downstairs in five."

I walk to Frazier's desk before Tillman can respond.

"Hey," I say when I get within a few feet of her. She has bright red hair and a birthmark on the side of her face I didn't notice before. She's knocking back a coffee and reading something on her computer. "Great work this morning. Thanks for getting that together."

She looks up, surprised, and smiles. "Thanks," she says, a bit of an accent I can't place.

"You up for a hike by any chance?" I ask. *Be my buffer with Tillman, please.*

Her eyebrows shoot up. "Going up to her cabin?"

I nod. She pushes back her chair and bends to lift up her pant leg. There's a prosthesis there. She's young, under thirty. She smiles apologetically. "I'm fine in the field, but once it comes to the mountains, long climbs"—she shrugs—"I'll be more useful to you down here."

"Military?"

"Cop. Boston."

Ah, there's the accent. "When did you get here?" I ask instead.

"Finished up training a few months ago, got assigned here first thing."

"Well," I say, "good work so far. Where're they holding Everett Brown?"

"County, for the moment."

"Tillman already interviewed him? When I was out?"

She nods slowly.

"Call 'em and tell them I'm coming this evening, just me. Ask for Ray."

"You got it."

I write down my cell and hand it to her. "Text me with whatever you have, doesn't matter time of day, night, the second you get something I want to hear about it. This case is . . . I'm glad to have a good team on it. We need it."

She nods. Then I exhale, brace myself for the hike.

She clears her throat. I realize it's been a moment, and I still haven't moved. She says, "Uh, whatever it's worth, sir, and off the record, of course. But . . . he's really shit at Ping-Pong."

"What?"

"Special Agent Tillman. We play sometimes, all of us. They put a table downstairs to, like, boost morale or something. He's the worst I've ever seen."

2

The Indian Creek trailhead route is closed indefinitely for maintenance, so we have to access it from the South Platte River Trailhead for the Colorado Trail off County Road 97. Which means a longer hike.

Boots crunching on gravel. I haven't been out in nature in a long time, or at Colorado altitude. Salt Lake isn't far behind, but it's different here. I forgot how much I love it, the burn of the thin air in my lungs. Muscles flexing and stretching as we climb.

Tillman stomps behind me. "Can you imagine livin' out here? How'd ya get your groceries?" He hasn't brought up the whole me-sleeping-in-his-bed thing, but I can feel how badly he wants to, the conversation practically a third party with us on our hiking date. "What a frickin' glorious life," he says, up to the sky.

I keep walking. We still have four miles to go. I try to watch the trail, the trees, for signs, clues. Try to listen in. But there's nothing. Just birds and woods and mountains and views. Just nature. It's beautiful.

After a while, Tillman's throat clears.

"So, uh, about . . ." he says.

I close my eyes. *There it is.*

"You know it's no big thing, you crashin' at our place. You're welcome to stay longer too, long as you want really. Though Josie did say you've got some big place out in Cherry Hills. I know someone who was at your parents' wake, said it was a great place, *real* big—"

"Hey," I say, turned back to him. "Could we just . . . walk in silence?"

"Yeah. Okay."

I pick up my pace.

"All I'm sayin' is if you don't wanna stay in your big ol' fancy mansion that was left to you in the nicest part of town, you're welcome to crash at our place. Just maybe next time you take the guest room. Main bedroom was the easiest to drag you to, but the guest bed gives me a real crick in my—"

It's only eight miles from the trailhead, but it feels so remote up here. Green grass on either side of a well-maintained thin dirt trail. Pines, flowers. We pass a moose at one point. Start to gain elevation, the trail taking an upward turn.

Hannah Lawrence.

Solitary life, at least mostly, I'd imagine. To Tillman's point, I want to look into how she gets supplies up here, how often she goes down and where she goes when she does. Obviously the location of the crime was significant, significant to *me*, anyway. Which is what I think it was meant to be. But what about Hannah? Why this girl? Why bring a third person into this at all?

This matters. *She* matters. I can feel it in the air up here as we near her cabin, a sort of thick crackling rightness. Or wrongness, I don't know, I just . . . *want* it. Want to be near it. Want to know how and why I am a part of it. Want . . . to be near *her*. No. I clear my throat. That's not—

Tillman trips and stumbles behind me. I don't turn around. I remind myself that he's working for me on this case. Technically. It should make it better. It doesn't. The dude is, at the end of the day—maybe even at the end of *today*—fucking my wife. Ex-wife. Whatever.

The sun filters in through the trees, and the unexpected heat releases a pine smell familiar to anyone who's grown up in these parts. Ponderosa. Smells almost like butterscotch. I breathe it in. It's peaceful up here. Quiet. I can see how someone would be drawn to this life. It isn't all that different, maybe, from the one I've been planning . . . dreaming of, at least, after my tour. After I've proved that I deserve it.

What did Josie say? *Getting yourself killed won't—*

I look up, suddenly, and there it is.

The cabin. Two hundred square feet, less. Tucked back away

from the trail in the trees. A bell on a hook hangs above the door, and a brittle mat sits in front of it on the ground. One word printed on the door: RANGER, in black letters. Crime scene tape across a perimeter, attached to trees. The two crime scene investigators step out and come over to us. We introduce ourselves, and they say they were told we were coming.

"We've done our sweep. Got everything we need. No sign of struggle. Up to you, but I think we can turn it back over to her for whenever she comes back, don't have to leave it active."

Tillman's staring up past the trees to the sky. I nod and thank them.

"Here," one says, handing a key over. "We locked it up. Ranger came by and gave us this. Said he'd get it when we're done, be down at the trailhead in a bit for questions."

We thank them, and they head back down. Tillman and I approach the cabin, slipping on our gloves and booties, ducking under the crime scene tape.

They were right. There's no sign of a struggle here, at least not from outside. The mat squared just so, door locked. No scratches against any of the window casings or the doorframe.

Inside the cabin, a plain twin-sized bed is built into the wall with just one sheet, one blanket, and one pillow on it. Tight-fitted. A single wooden chair and a small one-person table sits on one side of the room. An electric heater and generator-powered kitchen comprised of a self-contained sink, toaster oven, griddle, and electric kettle on the other. A small cubbyhole of a room with a composting toilet in it, entered through a wood pocket door by the kitchen. Three windows in total, none large enough for a human body to get through, just enough to let in a little light. Simple white blinds pulled down over them. The wood of the furniture is all one color, some kind of light pine. The whole place is spartan. Except the one wall.

I take a step closer, hold my breath.

All of it, the entire wall, is covered in playing cards. Each card with a sketch of an animal, a view, plant life. At least three full decks' worth, maybe more. Covering nearly every square inch of it. When I step up close, I see how meticulous and detailed each sketch is. How beautiful. They're . . . amazing, actually. All of them, labeled and dated next to the rank and suit. Bobcats, insects, bears, chipmunks, coyotes, foxes, birds.

These moments in time, quiet encounters. I reach up and trail my gloved fingers over the edge of an ace of clubs with a mountain lion on it. The girl who was in the motel room, the room from my childhood. *She* drew these. I can't imagine how much time it must have taken, the thought and devotion that went into each one. It feels intimate, seeing them. Like we shouldn't be here. Something of her soul exposed in these drawings. In a cooler, we find film canisters. No camera. In a drawer, film rolls full of the shots she must draw from, the photos she must take. I hold them up to the light while Tillman gets cell phone shots of the space. On the film, close-ups of animals, of flying wings. I try to picture the stillness required to capture these images, the patience and quiet.

I open another drawer. Clothing. Simple, utilitarian. Lavender sachets in the corners, to ward off certain bugs. The clothes smell of it. I softly close the drawer.

"Wow. She really digs nature," Tillman says. He changed before the hike into a Phish *Farmhouse* shirt and a Smokey Bear beanie. My blood pressure goes up looking at him.

The cabin is clean. That's already clear. No blood, no scratches or scuffs, no sign of struggle. Assuming no one came in and cleaned the place, it probably hasn't been abandoned for that long—three, maybe four or five days, tops. I glance up at the wall of drawings again.

We document the orientation and state of the room, but I think it's probably a waste. She wasn't taken from here. My gut tells me, and the evidence does. Still, somehow, I think . . . we learned something. We learned something about Hannah Lawrence, even if I'm not quite sure exactly what it is. And something tells me it's going to matter.

Something tells me *she* matters.

Tillman steps back outside first.

My heart races for some reason I can't identify, looking around the space. A dizzy feeling jolting through me.

And in a split second of insanity, just me alone in Hannah Lawrence's cabin, I unpin one card from the wall.

I slide it into my pocket.

"Can we play some music?" Tillman asks in the car.

"No music," I say. "Podcast, or talk radio, or whatever. Or silence. No music."

"You don't like music?"

"No."

"Who doesn't like music?"

"Do you want to listen to something, or not?"

"Yeah. Okay. I got just the thing."

He puts on a paranormal podcast about an abandoned mining town.

We pulled down the crime scene tape at the cabin. The ranger met us at the trailhead and gave us his info, but he didn't know anything. Just recently took over in the office where they keep all the spare keys. But I might call and follow up later.

"You ever have any paranormal experiences?" Tillman asks.

As he says it, a shadow appears, then disappears, on the side of the highway.

"Why would you ask me that?" I say.

"Why wouldn't I?" he says. Then after a moment, "I ask everyone."

"No," I say, gripping the wheel harder.

"Lot of ghost stories, 'round here," Tillman says. "Cults, hauntings, cryptids. All kinds of wild stuff. Colorado's a hotspot. I feel like it maybe has to do with the geothermal activity."

"Hm," I say.

"Lot of UFOs too, all kinds of stuff in the skies. All it takes is just keep lookin' up."

"Right," I say, willing myself to breathe.

"You seem like someone who maybe doesn't believe."

"I—"

"You know it surprised me that Josie's a believer, but—"

"Dude, respectfully, can you please shut the fuck up."

He throws his hands up and sticks a toothpick in his mouth. "Jeez, man, she said you were weird about mirrors. Nothin' about music or the paranormal. Anything else I should avoid?"

I drop Tillman off at the office as the sun slides behind the mountains. He steps out of the car and looks up immediately to the sky. Then he turns and starts to bend back down to say something else. Before he can, I pull out of the lot.

3

Dark blue-gray bleeds in to dampen the world, sweeping in a cold wind. Fall descends so quickly on us here. Winter, even faster. Then it sits, for months. Snow a thick numbing blanket that seeps into tendons and ligaments, fingers, toes, brains. Colorado winter unlike any other on earth, somehow simultaneously harsh and friendly. People from here will fight anyone who seems to imply that any other place might make them happier—California, say—that Colorado is not the happiest place on earth, that *WE, COLORADANS, are not SO SO HAPPY.*

A strange darkness, a snow-shifting haze. Eight of the top ten states of highest suicide rates are in the Mountain West. Tourists flock from all over to see the Rockies, to hike or scramble them, ski, snowboard, sled, horseback ride, take a gondola and drink a hot chocolate, in a hot tub at some resort. And those of us who live here, so insistent of our happiness, as we scrape ice from our windshields and pour salt on the ground, chain our tires. As we check for the locations of exits in our movie theaters and put in metal detectors at schools, as we glance up to the mountains for the weather, for the time of day. As we shore up our houses against disproportionately high levels of radon poisoning in the soil, try and keep it from seeping through the cracks into our lives to poison us.

Denver. Low red and brown brick buildings and houses. Always, that strange heaviness of the sky here, even on all our sunny days. A dirt-packed cow town at the western edge of the Great Plains, masquerading as a city, shadowed on the west by distant mountains that dictate everything about our lives. Our sports teams named for them, seasons determined by them. Always at the outskirts, those mountains always forty-five minutes away by car, at least. We the town of settlers who crossed all those plains just to give up before the good part.

Hannah Lawrence who lives in them.

Her drawing in my pocket. The way my palms sweat thinking about it.

Her face behind my eyes. Pulling at me.

My phone pings with another text from Frazier. I glance at it.

Everett Brown, environmental sciences professor at CU and the man who walked into Mama Tried wearing the skin of the John Doe we found taped in next to Hannah Lawrence. He is also, it turns out, a member of an online chat forum called DRIFTERS: SEEKING THE TRUTH and has been for the last five years. One of the chat rooms this *Wizdumteller* that Tillman flagged is a part of. *Wizdumteller* who kept saying the murders were going to start up again. I pull over and read through what Frazier sent. Before all this, I didn't even know chat rooms were still a thing, but this one's pretty active.

He lives with his wife in Erie in some new development called Rock Creek, and she teaches at a nearby public elementary school. He's got one arrest for assaulting a cop at a climate demonstration in Boulder, otherwise clean record.

I call Jack, go over it all with him. I hear Emily in the background talking to the kids. I watch the black steel traffic lights change.

Everett Brown could have kidnapped Hannah Lawrence sometime forty-eight or more hours before he brought her to the Wander Inn—kidnapping location unknown, though we can probably rule out the cabin—and duct-taped her to the man he skinned. Cell records show Hannah's phone has been off or dead for five days, but that could be normal for someone living her lifestyle. Everett's phone was left at his house four days ago when he was last seen by his wife. The next time he was reported seen was at Mama Tried. After the motel room, Everett walked farther and longer than any of the others before him had walked, in order to get to the bar where Josie and I were sitting. He knew I was here, or someone did. Days are left unaccounted for. How can someone walk naked wearing a skin in the daytime without being seen?

The three recent murders deviated from those before the hiatus in that the killers did not eat the skinned victims before walking down the side of the road. And then there comes Hannah with a dead man's tongue in her mouth. Hannah, alive, the first in all this.

I've visited every family of every victim and killer from before, their places of work, interviewed their colleagues, friends, exes, bosses, neighbors. Stepped inside their homes, seen their cars and pets and children and lives. Lives that are over now, every one of them put away forever, or put in the ground.

Geese honk as they waddle down the street outside the detention center. The city is overrun with them. I read that recently the goose populations have gotten so out of control that the city is now feeding the birds to the ever-growing unhoused human population. This city somehow sprawling with new homes, and more and more people who don't have one.

I pull into the jail parking facility. Josie is calling. I hesitate, consider not answering, but then . . . I clear my throat. "Josie. Hi."

"Wow," she says.

"What?" I say.

"You sound like before."

I sigh. "What do you want?"

"I think we should talk."

"About?"

"You know what about."

Her voice still makes my heart do something stupid in my chest. And maybe, as a goose waddles out into the street in front of my car, as the evening grows colder in a town I'd rather do fucking anything than be in, maybe *I* feel resentment in this moment too.

I put the car in park.

"I gotta go, Jo," I say. And I force myself to hang up.

Everett Brown sits in the chair across from me, large ears, slightly unkempt hair. Dark circles. He looks as haunted as the others before him did, but there's an air of acceptance about him, surrender. He's thin, thirty-six years old, just two years older than me. We probably grew up on the same shows, same ads, same prom playlists. But while I've been training, strategizing, running and lifting and investigating, he's been in libraries, in classrooms, theorizing, learning. I wonder if that's more the life my parents envisioned for me. Doesn't matter now.

"You doin' okay in here?" I ask.

Everett nods. His hands are shaking, just a little. Of course he's not okay.

"Good," I say and lean back in my chair, think about the terror on his face in the bar. This guy who taped Hannah Lawrence and the John Doe to the bed. This man who's been in those chat rooms. "I know my colleague already came in and interviewed you," I say. "But do you mind if we just start over, from the beginning?"

"I dunno, got a lot of important places to be," he says. Then, after a second, "Sure."

"Could we start with what you remember from that night?"

His eyes go distant. He rubs his ear.

"Um, I was on an evening walk," he says. "After getting back from work, before dinner."

"Four days ago," I say.

"I . . . I guess so. I don't know."

"Says here it's what your wife said."

"When can I see her again?"

"I'll see what I can do," I say. "You went for a walk straight out your front door."

He nods, defeated. "I was just a few streets over, on Sagebrush. It was just at the beginning. I do it every night."

"How long do you normally walk for?"

"Thirty minutes, sometimes an hour."

"And you stay in your development normally?"

"Yeah."

I nod. "Okay. You're walking on Sagebrush. Then what?"

"It was like . . . Have you ever read any of that stuff about time and space being a fabric and theoretically it could be folded and changed the way we perceive it? Or move us somewhere else entirely? Not linear and not fixed points, you know, but it can be . . . adjusted. It's not my area of expertise. I don't know if it makes sense, but that's the best I can do, I guess. To explain it. That's what it felt like."

I turn his answer over for a moment, let it hang.

"What is your area of expertise?" I ask.

"Organismal ecology. Basically the way living organisms relate to each other."

"And you've always wanted to do that?"

"I was in cellular biology, before. It was the wolf reintroductions that got me interested."

"That what made you hit a cop? That stuff gets pretty heated."

He blinks. "No, that was . . . No."

"So . . . the wolves. It's been controversial?"

He lets out a bitter laugh. "Yeah, you could say that."

I watch him.

"When settlers got here," he says, "they immediately killed off all the bison and elk, shipped 'em back east. That was the wolves' food source. Those same men brought in livestock, stuck penned-in cows on the plains. Wolves had to eat, and now they had nothing else. And the trappers needed a frontier enemy, besides Native folks—and we all know how the Europeans treated them. The wolves became that. The emblematic epitome of the wild. If the frontiersmen could dominate the wolves, then they'd have proven to the world that they'd beaten the West into submission. The land was officially theirs. They strung up the wolves' carcasses by the hundreds. Next thing we know, gray wolves—the most widely distributed predatory mammal in the world, this keystone animal—we shrank their territory to nothing, and they became the villains in our storybooks and the trophies on our mantels. Otherwise, just a distant memory."

"But they've been gone so long, right? Bringing them back now—"

"When you kill an apex predator, it sets off a chain effect that can obliterate entire ecosystems. *Now* it's a coyote problem, all of 'em sneaking into yards, eating dogs and cats, attacking kids. They're everywhere. And it's because we took out their predator and competition. Foxes are endangered because now coyotes outcompete them. Deer populations have skyrocketed. Too many deer leads to too little vegetation and an increase in illness—*human* illness. No wolves, more moose and elk, they eat all the saplings. No more aspen trees, whole forests taken out. Can you guess how much life a forest holds? Every time we tweak anything, *everything* is affected. We just do this everywhere all the time. Eradicate entire species, send shock waves through the earth. It's hurting *us*, ultimately. But we can't see it. We've just decided that of all the almost nine million estimated species on the earth, only one matters."

I watch him a minute. I consider him. This.

I nod. After another moment, I say, "You were on your walk. On Sagebrush."

He nods. When I don't say any more, he says, "Sometimes I just want to see. You know? Like what is it all for? What matters *so much more* about us and the breaths we take and our wants and fears than those of any other living breathing creature? That hour before the curtains are shut in people's houses, but the lights are on. Walking by, glancing in—not to be weird, or . . . to just . . . *witness* something. People sitting or playing on lawns, kids running, grandparents with a glass of wine or a cigarette or an iced tea. Human life, bonds, family units. It can be beautiful, this thing we're destroying the world for. Sometimes I feel like I need to see that. Sometimes seeing it from the outside makes me realize."

"What's the exact last moment you remember before you were at the bar?"

"It was evening. I passed a house, saw a family cooking dinner. And then . . . There was no break in the walking. I picked my foot up in Rock Creek, and when I set it down again, I was still walking and it was full night. I wasn't in my development or anywhere near my house. I was cold, my body felt, I dunno, sore, and exhausted. Terrible. Like I hadn't slept in days, or maybe ever. My feet hurt. I looked around, and there was this one glowing building in the dark.

"It felt like the strangest dream. Me, in this dark cold endless night, and that bright warm building in front of me. Neon and Christmas lights. I could hear music, even. And the sort of dream logic just told me I had to get inside to the light, had to get out of the cold dark. I had a cloak around my shoulders, and I pulled it tight. I walked toward the neon sign and the lit-up building, out of the dark."

"And then?"

Everett takes a breath. "Well, when I stepped inside, into the light of this bar, it felt . . . *real*. Suddenly not like a dream. Like stepping inside the building brought me back to this world, somehow. Woke me up. And there was a woman in front of me, the first person I saw. That agent. And she looked at me like I was a monster, which . . . made me look at myself. When I looked down, I saw blood. It—I guess I just started screaming. I can't believe she didn't shoot me.

I would've shot me. Got lucky. Or probably *unlucky* . . . anyway. That's . . . what happened."

"Do you know now what happened in the time between walking near your house and ending up at the bar? Has anyone told you?"

Everett swallows. His voice breaks a bit when he says, "They said that skin I was wearing, that I killed that person. They said I . . . kidnapped a girl?"

"Do you know where you took them? What you did with them?"

"Can you imagine someone telling you not only that there are multiple nights of your life you don't remember at all, but also that you somehow did things that are *so unfathomably horrific*, things that you *know* you are completely incapable of, that it all feels like some elaborate joke? And then they tell you they have proof that you did it? Proof that something you have no memory of happening at all, that honestly makes you sick to even hear about, *actually* took place, and now, suddenly, your life is just . . . over."

"No," I say, after a moment. "I can't imagine." But I know that we're capable of so much worse than we think we are. War will show you that. Life, sometimes.

"There was a hair, tied into a knot, in your vomit at the bar. Do you remember there being a hair in your mouth?"

He stares at me. "What?"

"There was—"

"Is she okay? The girl?"

"How did you know her?" I ask.

"I'm telling you, I don't even know her name, or what she looks like."

"Your fingerprints are on the duct tape that was sealing her mouth shut," I say.

He runs his hands over his face. "I don't even know what the fuck hotel it was. Please," he says. "Just tell me, is she okay?"

"Do you know who I am?" I ask.

"Daniel Stansfield. Tell me."

"How did you know I was back in Denver?"

He shakes his head, distraught.

"She's okay," I say. "How do you know who I am?"

"Everyone knows who you are."

"How did you know I was back?"

"I didn't know you left."

"The chat rooms didn't talk about me leaving?"

"I don't do that stuff anymore."

"You don't go in the chat rooms?"

"Look, it was . . . My wife got into all that stuff a while ago, and she got me into it, and it was a stressful time, and it was just this thing to let off steam. As soon as I realized it was affecting investigations and lives, as soon as I realized, I guess, how *real* this whole thing is . . ."

"By 'all that stuff,' you mean like true crime?"

A pause, a slight shift in the air. "Yeah," he says.

"You used to log on after your evening walks?"

"Yeah, I guess, sometimes before. Look, like I said, it was stupid, and a long time ago. It's easy to get caught up in stuff like that—religion, whatever, stuff you think you need."

"Did you know that one of the chat rooms you belong to has an entry and exit log?"

"Yeah, that sounds right, I dunno."

"And your username is *CanisLoopus*?"

"Was," he says. "Look, I really . . . I told you, that was not a great moment of my life. Could we—"

"Because of your arrest."

"That and just family stuff, life."

"The assault. Was that around that time?"

"Man, it wasn't . . . My students organized a climate protest, and one of the cops who came to break it up put a hand on this girl from my freshman seminar. She was so small, and he was so big with that gun on his belt. It just . . . You don't put your hands on an eighteen-year-old. You don't bring guns on a college campus. It was a protest. Just students with signs. Something in me snapped, seeing it, his hands on one of those kids. But I didn't hit him, just pulled his hand off her. Guess that's what they call assault."

"I have a report here, for the chat room. It shows that you've logged in a lot over the last year or so. About three times a week on average."

Everett looks puzzled. "But . . . I haven't."

"Here, you can take a look."

"I . . . don't know what to say. Maybe I got hacked." But a look crosses his face, some kind of understanding maybe.

"Do you know who might have hacked you?" I ask.

"No." It's a lie. I can feel it.

"Is there anyone you can think of in your time on the internet who might be pulling some strings on all this? Anyone who could be in charge?"

A flash of panic, there and then gone, but clear as day. "Not that I can think of," he says. His jaw is tight.

"What about this—*Wizdumteller*? They seem to be the organizer of a lot of these online conversations. They said they knew that the murders were going to start back up again."

Everett's face goes blank, his knuckles white where his hands grip each other in his lap. "I really don't want to talk about the chat rooms anymore. It's bad enough that everything I've ever done with my life is going to be forgotten for this *murder* I don't remember committing and have no connection to at all. I don't need to be remembered as one of those freaks too."

"Okay," I say. "I just have one more question for now."

He's tense, now. But he nods.

"Back in your early chat room days, you said you thought every one of these killers was guilty, you suspected that they had found each other, online, like you and your chat room friends did, and came up with this whole elaborate plan. What do you think now, if you could guess?"

"I don't have to guess."

"Really?"

"None of this is the work of people. People can't do this."

"What do you mean?"

"I've never liked religion. But . . . I don't know if it's God or spaghetti monster or something else. I just know it's bigger than us. A hell of a lot bigger. I had no idea what this was like, before. I hadn't felt it."

"You don't seem afraid of what's going to happen, if you're found guilty," I say.

"I *will* be found guilty, because you're not gonna solve anything. And I'm not even accusing you, that's just how it's going. I can't stop thinking every second about my career and my students and my wife and every day of my life that I took for granted that I'm never getting back. I'm so terrified I can hardly breathe. I had no idea fear could be so paralyzing and all-consuming and lonely. I just sit here, and— But . . . I'm a lot of shameful things, but stupid isn't one of them. Least . . . not anymore."

Everett looks up at me and holds my gaze straight on, leans forward. "If it's something bigger than us, and it *is*, then we won't be able to stop it. Avalanche is coming, and we're in the path whether we like it or not. I've been there, deep inside it. I'm there now. Fuck, I'm *all* the way down. And it is so dark.

"And I feel sorry for you," he says. "'Cause somehow, something tells me before this is all over, you're gonna join me down here too."

4

The looming homes, larger than anyone needs. The trees. The quiet. I grip the wheel as hard as I can and force myself to take the turns.

Everett Brown's words ringing in my ears. Hannah Lawrence's drawing in my pocket.

I remind myself I am choosing this. Driving into the night. Headed back to a place I swore I'd never return to in the whole of my life. A place I couldn't make myself go before. I remind myself I am choosing all of this.

At least I know there'll be whiskey.

Once again, the private drive. The overgrown trees. The outskirts of Cherry Hills. Remembering that first time, driving down the tree tunnel with the social worker. This time I just go, don't let myself hesitate again. I shove my foot to the pedal, and I surge forward, hitting the downed branch, pushing through all the leaves and vines until I am out the other side. I don't realize I've been holding my breath until I reach the clearing.

A hundred meters of lawn in front of me, the long winding gravel drive, illuminated only by my headlights. The house is dark. The gardens dead and rotted, the vines barely clinging to life, still climbing up the grand over-the-top walls of Whileago Manor. I haven't seen the great stone structure in four years. Music pushes its way in, moves along the edges of the house, the sides of my skull. Dolly, Waylon, Hank. As if in the space between molecules, pushed into me by the night wind. All the songs. All the life and memories.

I shut off the engine. My hands are shaking. I get out, step foot on the grounds.

I feel something waking. I feel all of them. I will my heart to steady.

Gravel crunches beneath my boots. I input the garage code, realize it won't work while the power is out. There's a manual latch hidden around the side. An owl calls from one of the trees at the edge of the lawn. After a couple tries, the door finally creaks and lifts. I take a shaky breath, keep my eyes on the task in front of me. Catch movement out of the corner of my eye, ignore it.

In the garage, I use my cell phone light to see my way past the cobweb-covered paintings on the walls, ice scrapers, snowshoes, cross-country skis on their hooks. The sculpture in the middle of the six-car garage, some kind of deity or goddess, I can't remember from where. It was my mother's doing—Marianne Stansfield—she always loved for there to be something beautiful, in every room. Even one you might only just pass through. Her tastes always a little eclectic.

I try the switch even though I know there will be no light.

The door to the mudroom is unlocked. The music pushes in again, threads, short clips of voices. My heart pounds.

Something clatters to the ground somewhere in the dark.

"Stop it," I say, out loud.

The music stops. I open the door.

The hall between the mudroom and the kitchen is still full of family photographs, images of my parents on their many adventures, others with their arms around me. My graduation, Josie and me at our wedding. All of it an assault in the cell phone flashlight beam, the reflection glaring back at me from the glass. My boots creak on the floorboards.

In front of the gallery wall, on the bench with boots beneath it, sits a stack of handouts from my parents' funeral, CELEBRATING THE LIVES OF NOEL AND MARIANNE STANSFIELD.

In books and movies, characters always have one big life event, that singular *thing* that defines them from the past. The one bad thing that happened that made them *who they are*. But in reality, with real people, it's five big things, ten. A hundred. You go to war and see and do things you can never take back. You see death in so many forms through your job that you're constantly shocked at the capacity humans have for cruelty. You build a marriage and watch yourself destroy it. You even learn you can lose parents twice, it turns out.

You can lose a whole hell of a lot.

The smell in here is horrendous.

Past the hall, in the kitchen, I cover my nose and mouth with my arm. On the enormous center island sit vases overflowing with long-since rotted flowers. Maybe fifteen of them. A casserole dish full of fungus and mold. The stench nearly unbearable. I walk to the fridge and open it. All the dishes, the sympathy foods at room temperature. I close it immediately and gag, run to throw up in the sink. The tap at least still works, after a few sputtering tries.

Off the kitchen to my left is the informal dining room, then the formal one down a hall beyond it. I turn the other way, step through the opening to the right instead, to the house's grand formal entry. A large round table in the middle with more rotting flowers. My mother loved giant arrangements, in three- or four-foot vases, changed them out weekly, themed around holidays or events in our lives. Everything sort of mountain lodge meets eccentric collector.

Behind the table, matching large staircases sweep from either side of the room up to the second floor. Beneath and behind them lies the sprawling living room and the thirty-foot-high floor-to-ceiling windows looking out over the lawn and the trees that surround it.

And of course, the mountains beyond.

My phone light sweeping over everything, the darkness swallowing the rest.

Before the entry table and opposite the living room, is the front door, massive frame carved in oak. The one I first passed through, that first day here. Clinging to the social worker's hand as we stepped through the enormous entryway. As I approached the table—taller than me—and walked around it, into the living room. I was six years old, and I'd never seen an indoor space so large, a ceiling so high. I didn't know indoors could be this big. It made me feel as though I'd done something wrong, a feeling I wouldn't come to understand for a long time.

The social worker and I sat down across from Noel and Marianne Stansfield. The couple was in their fifties, so much older than my actual parents, more than double their age. Marianne wore scarves and layers and colors and jewelry, and Noel wore a green sweater. They offered me every kind of snack I'd seen, and some I hadn't, all laid out on plates made of wood and woven baskets and hammered metal that I would later learn were only a small sampling of the treasures they had brought back with them from all around the world. Hobby travelers, bohemians, philanthropists. Not that I knew what any of that was. Not yet.

I couldn't stop looking at the ceiling, couldn't stop wondering how tall it was. The windows overlooking the outdoors. Noel was talking about how they'd always wanted a son, had always wanted to adopt, once they had accomplished everything else they wanted in life.

I was staring out the window. The social worker touched my arm.

Blood.

My mom and my dad and—

I pulled my arm back, my heart racing.

"I'm sorry," she said. "I didn't know if you could hear me." She had already talked to me about my name, about how I could change it and go by something new if I wanted. They gave me a list of ideas to help but said it was my choice. I picked Daniel because it was close to Danny like Rose had called me, and I didn't want my dad's name. But I still didn't always remember to respond to it.

Marianne Stansfield cleared her throat across from us. "We can't imagine what you've been through, what any of it's been like . . . We know that we *can't* know. But we have space, we're both retired so we have all the time, and we promise to work every single day to give you the best, most wonderful life possible. If you want it, that is. Or . . . if you want us."

I grab my chest here, now, in this dark empty house. The pain of their absence, a terrible living thing.

I go to the wall, try the living room switches, which of course don't work. I head for the giant hearth. Sit down, pile on some wood that still rests beside it, reach for the matches and start the fire, just as Noel showed me.

I stand up again. I can't. Can't be still in here, can't sit with this *pain*. I stand beside the fireplace, nearly as tall as I am, and I watch the room darken in contrast to the glow of the flame, rub my chest with my palm. Breathe through it. Will I ever not be drowning in this?

Noel, my father, in this same room, even older, sitting across from me and letting out a long sigh. "You don't have to do this, Daniel. There's nothing to prove."

Me, opposite him, just as I was on that first day. But now, eighteen, holding enlistment papers in my hand. "I don't want to disappoint you. It's not . . ." But I broke off. Because I didn't know what it was. Or I did, but I didn't know how to explain it to him. How I couldn't live this life, couldn't accept that it was mine or that I would ever deserve it. How in the moments in which I'd start to forget myself, start to enjoy any of it, *her* face would return to me. The motel room that could almost feel like a nightmare or dream. How my whole life I'd been outrunning this one person, and also so desperately, pathetically, hoping she'd return.

"Hey." Noel leaned forward. He had aged, was nearly seventy, and it showed. He reached over the coffee table and took hold of my hand. "You could never, ever disappoint me, kid."

I knew they were getting up there, but I wasn't ready. I was so far from ready.

We'd gotten tickets a while before for the four of us to see Willie Nelson play at Red Rocks—Mom, Dad, Josie, and me. My parents closer to eighty than seventy now. The divorce initiated, Josie wasn't coming. My dad insisted on driving, like he always had, and I didn't fight him. I sat in the passenger seat, and my mom sat in the back, and we were talking about the case. A grown man riding to a concert with his parents, talking about his failures.

A grown man who'd let his aging father drive.

When the truck came at us from the side, I saw the split second in which I might have reacted if I had been in the driver's seat. Saw what my dad didn't. Both my parents on the left side of the car, their bodies silhouetted in the truck's headlight beams.

Bright, brighter, so blindingly white that I thought I'd never see again. All the sound in the world, the crash so painfully loud, and then,

Silence.

My parents, the people who'd given me everything. The truck driver hit his head in the crash, also died on impact. I was the only one who survived.

I stuck it out for a couple months, moved back in here, planned a funeral, worked day and night to make any sort of headway on the case. Walked into the snow and onto the road and asked, *Please take me instead. Please, let them have a little more time. Please, give them back.*

And when it was clear that my marriage was lost, my parents weren't coming back, and the investigation was going cold, I said fuck all of this and left Colorado.

The one thing my parents asked for, the one request in their lengthy will that continues to give generously to charities now and will for many decades, was this:

Don't sell the house. Don't let anyone else live there unless they live with you. It's *yours.*

As if it heard me, a door creaks open upstairs.

I run my hands over my face.

Yeah. And then there's the other thing.

At the end of my first visit, I got a tour of the house.

There were six bedrooms in addition to Noel and Marianne's, and they said I could choose which one I wanted. They thought I would choose the big one downstairs, just down the hall from theirs, or one of the other big ones upstairs. But I knew immediately there was only one room I could take, and it was the smallest, in the corner of the upper floor. It wasn't set up as a bedroom, but instead some kind of study with a wooden desk in the middle of it.

"Could I have this one?" I asked.

The Stansfields and the social worker shared a look. They'd later tell me they thought I'd picked the smallest room in the house because I was used to small spaces, because all of this was too overwhelming. And of course it was. It would be forever. But what I didn't tell them until years later, until the terror only partially kept me up at night and I'd learned how to get by on the few hours of rest the house would give me, was that I couldn't take the other rooms because:

I got a *Bad Feeling* in them, too bad to ignore. And—perhaps the more important thing—

The other rooms were already taken.

Footsteps creak above me as I sit in the living room in the dark. Music starts to play.

I press my palms to my eyes. I've never wanted this, to be terrified of every place, Bad Feelings everywhere. As a kid, to find shadows standing at the foot of my bed, watching me with a detached neutral curiosity that I instinctively knew was dangerous. I'd always seen shadows, but here, in this house, they were so much stronger, more vivid. So much more powerful.

Nightmares. Overactive imagination. I only partly told the Stansfields about it. They'd put me in therapy to process what had happened at the Happy Inn, and I told my therapist once, about the Bad Feelings, told him how my birth mother thought I had a special gift—"*my shining boy.*"

But my birth parents were young, tortured people, and my therapist suggested that maybe I was holding on to the idea of having some kind of *shine* as a way to hold on to my birth mom, the same way I picked Daniel for my name from the list. It was all in my head, something put there by a woman I barely ever knew and some old book she carried around.

And if it was *real*, what a shit thing, what an unforgivably fucked-up thing, that I would be visited by all these ghosts, and never the woman who was supposed to have been my mother.

Never her, and never Marianne or Noel.

Another creak upstairs. This old house the worst place for a kid with Bad Feelings and night terrors and traumatic memories. But my parents were so loving and warm that the house became more about that than anything else. They filled this place with love, chased out the shadows—or at least shined bright enough to keep them at bay.

But they're gone, and now I stand in a haunted old house with no electricity and a lifetime of nightmares to share it with. And the loss that is so profound, it's nearly blinding.

I don't mean to, but—

I say, "Mom, Dad, if either of you is here . . ."

The music stops. I exhale.

"Because none of this is real," I say in the quiet of the house. Because I'm just a sentimental asshole with PTS who would grasp for anything at all.

Another creak upstairs.

I go back to the garage, holding my breath through the kitchen, and grab the Drifter case files from where I left them four years ago. Copies of the files I am definitely not supposed to have made.

They're all stored digitally, but I try to avoid the computer when I can. Too easy to catch a reflection in the black of the screen. I clear the books, baskets, decorative items off the enormous living room coffee table, wipe away some of the accumulated dust. Lay out the files, one by one. Eight of them on the coffee table, the rest on the rug on the floor, all around the living room. I add the new ones.

I use my cell phone light to head through the side passage in the foyer to the lower stairwell. I pass a cold spot in the dark, a shadow drifting. I don't let myself acknowledge the Feeling in my stomach. I tell myself I don't hear the whisper, feel the touch on my skin.

My parents were the third owners of Whileago Manor, though they were the first to call it that. When Noel got on the phone with his parents after purchasing it and they asked if he and Marianne had named the home (a tradition in their family), Noel said, "Yeah we named it a while ago." He was going to save the unveiling until they'd properly settled in. But Noel's dad was hard of hearing, and "Whileago" just stuck.

Cobwebs catch on my face, and I cough and spit, try to clear them from my mouth and eyes. I walk through the lower living room, past the wine cellar and the gym. I open the storage room door, go to the far corner where the candles, flashlights, and matches are, and grab as much as I can carry. Something moves past the doorway behind me, the same shadow from the stairwell. I take a breath.

The house was built in the late 1800s, one of the only houses here at that time, and long before this was a neighborhood. Since its original construction, it's been expanded and renovated by each of its subsequent owners. In one of the rooms on the top floor, there's a huge vintage trunk containing the history of all the inhabitants. The first owners died here, and their photo albums, journals, various deeds and documents remained with the house in the trunk. The second owners must have had some kind of sentimental streak because they put it in their will that they wanted their lives similarly documented and left with the house. And then it became tradition, and my parents wanted the same. In the corner of this storage room, a cardboard box of Marianne's and Noel's lives sits on the floor, one I haven't opened, haven't done anything with. All the things I'm meant to go through and put into the trunk upstairs with all the other former owners'.

All the things I can't face.

Once I was past the initial *post-trauma period* as a kid (this is what my therapist called it), my dad wanted to show me the trunk, tell me of the history of the people who were here before us. But the Bad Feeling hung around it like a shroud, and I didn't want to go near it.

Three sets of owners of this house, all contributing to its history and legacy. And the fourth one, now letting it all rot.

Back upstairs in the living room, I light six candles among the files, put two flashlights on either side of it all facing in. I've got a third one to use as I read. I add another log to the fire. My stomach rumbles. I fish out my phone again, put in a delivery order from the local Chinese place. Every now and then Josie and I would pick it up on our way over here to see my parents. I only realize after I've hung up that I placed the order for the four of us, our usual. I call them back and change it. I turn to the corner of the great room, swing open the French doors to the bar. The alcove is dark and dusty like everything else, wallpapered in an Egyptian pattern Marianne loved. I grab one of the six bottles of whiskey and step back over to the files.

I reach into my pocket slowly and pull Hannah Lawrence's drawing from it. My heart pounds again. I turn it back and forth.

A fox, sketched on the six of spades. Did I mean to grab that one, or was it just there in front of my hand? I think of her. Picture her. Hannah, alone, in that cabin. Creating this. My senses on full alert suddenly, adrenaline coursing.

Why? Just because she was in my old room at the motel?

I'm not sure if it's more than that. Not sure why thinking of her makes me need to run, or do something. Anything. Why I took this card from her cabin.

The candlelight flickers over the card. I drop it, watch it slowly fall and land on top of one of the files.

Another creak upstairs, and the music drifts back in. A shadow darts past the stairs.

This card. Hannah Lawrence.

The whole of a city holding its breath.

Something feels different this time. Strained, inevitable.

Like it was always all coming to this.

It's six AM when the phone rings. I fell asleep on the floor, slumped against the mantel, a file splayed open on my lap. Photos of bite marks on the former bodies. The images capturing my midnight attention, an itch in the back of my brain.

The bite marks on the last two bodies before the hiatus seemed to indicate a smaller or missing canine in the person cannibalizing them. Meaning it very well could have been the same person eating the last two bodies before the haitus, and either it was a different person than the one who ate the previous bodies, or they lost or chipped a canine between the sixth and seventh killings. Forensics deemed it inconclusive. It probably is a dead end. So many pieces, crooked useless paths. And me, going over it all still. Following it straight off a cliff.

The candles have all burned down, the fire gone out.

Whileago Manor is dark and silent.

Jack's voice on the phone. "Dan," he says. "She's awake."

5

Denver sunrise, clouds over mountains, geese and dry branches and a waking city. Front lawns covered in leaves, brown roofs, brick and wood and steel.

My mom—Rose—in a pink dress, sitting on a big rock in a river. Me sitting beside her.

Her crinkled old paperback sticking out of the picnic basket, with our sodas and snacks.

She reaches for my hand, bruises on her face. A tear in her eye.

"She requested a nose plug," Jack says, putting his cell phone back in his pocket.

I'm at the office, boots on office carpet. That memory—what is wrong with me?

I don't know that river, have no other memory of ever being there. Wherever *there* is.

I shake my head.

Jack, Tillman, and I stand on the other side of the one-way glass of the interrogation room. Jack checks the time. Ten more minutes until she arrives from the hospital.

Hannah Lawrence. Hannah, who is coming here. Garcia and Frazier have gone to get her, at one of their suggestions that maybe she should only be in close proximity to women after what happened.

"Nose plug?" Tillman asks.

Jack shrugs. "They said after the motel, she doesn't want to smell anyone."

We take this in, all of us. She was taped into that bed with a dead man for days with his tongue in her mouth.

Hannah Lawrence coming here.

A shadow moves at the edge of the room. When I started here, there were only a couple, but the number grew, especially when the case gained momentum. Crowding, waiting until I was alone in an elevator, staircase, bathroom, until it was late, my nerves on a hair trigger. Appearing before me suddenly, shoving something to the floor.

Externalizations of stress. Hallucinations. It's a trauma response.

I drop the files I'm carrying on the table. Tillman for once is silent. All three of us tense, waiting. The question of Hannah, the potential implications of her part in this. Tillman is sitting across the observation room, closer to the door. Jack's loosened his tie. I sit, stand back up again.

I startle when the door to the interrogation room opens. I glance down at my watch. Ten minutes have passed, I'm not sure how. Time stretching, warping.

She walks in.

I can't breathe.

I don't know what comes over me. But seeing her, Hannah Lawrence, I feel as though I've lived this moment before. Or I knew it was coming, or— Of course I knew. It's more . . . Why is my heart racing like this?

Her hair's pulled back into a ponytail, that dark almost-not-blond. Bruising discolors her temple and left eye, and the lower half of her face is red and slightly raw from the duct tape. Wearing a dark green hoodie and sweatpants, clearly too large for her. The hospital partners with a charity that gives clothes to discharged patients whose clothing is soiled when they're admitted, and the sweats are probably from there. She's limping, keeping as far away from Garcia as possible, flinching back any time Garcia steps too close. She's got that nose plug in.

"You okay?" Garcia says, her blazer wrinkle-free as always. She's a good calming presence to put with witnesses and suspects, radiating the calm composure of someone who has her life together, who understands what you're going through but also has no tolerance for funny business.

Hannah nods, and the movement is jerky. There's a bandage on the top of her right hand, probably from the IV. Garcia goes to stand behind the chair facing away from us, leaving the other chair for Hannah. Hannah slowly moves over to it, lowers herself to sit, wincing.

She looks down, brow furrowed in pain, catches her breath. Then she glances behind Garcia to the mirror. Her eyes—that pale almost translucent green—widen, and I think that maybe she can see us, that maybe she has somehow penetrated the one-way glass. My pulse goes haywire. But then I realize she's seeing herself like this, maybe for the first time, bruised, changed. By what happened.

Frazier steps into the observation room with us, stands right by the shadow in the corner. She looks shaken. The shadow moves toward her. I swallow, remind myself it isn't real.

"Thank you so much for being here," Garcia says to Hannah in the other room.

"Did I have a choice?" Hannah's voice is raw, hoarse. Low and melodic, even rough as it is now.

"Um, yes," Garcia says. "We could have spoken anywhere."

"They didn't tell me," Hannah says.

"Oh. I'm sorry. Are you okay to continue?"

She glances around the room, sinks lower in the chair, covers her nose with her hand. "Hard to be indoors." She closes her eyes, clears her throat. "Does that window open?"

Garcia glances over, then back to Hannah, shakes her head. "No, I'm sorry."

"Okay. Um, if we can do this fast—" Clears her throat again, shifts in her seat.

"Do you need anything else? Water?"

Hannah hesitates, then nods. Frazier leaves the observation room again and steps into the interrogation room with a water bottle. When she sets it down in front of Hannah, Hannah leans back as far from her as possible, face a little pale.

"All right," Garcia says after Frazier leaves. "If you're okay with it, I'd like to walk through the last couple days that you remember and work our way up to the motel. If at any point it's too much or you need to take a break, that's completely fine. We can get you anything you need. And we'll try to get you out of here as fast as possible."

Frazier steps back into our room. Still, that shadow is there.

"Whenever you're ready," Garcia says.

Hannah takes a sip of the water. "Right. Um . . . the last couple days," she says, "before. Pretty normal. I was clearing brush from some trails, checking backpacker permits, though there were only one or two, um, backpackers. That's normal for this time of year. Don't need a permit for a day hike, so it's just . . ." She takes another breath. She takes another sip.

"I was down in the prairie grass. I heard something behind me, a twig snap. I turned, and then . . . I don't remember anything. I heard it snap, I turned. And then I was . . ." She trails off. "Sorry," she says, and it comes out more like a whisper.

"It's okay. You're doing great."

"I was in the grass, then I was in the motel. That's it. I can't remember anything else."

"What were you doing down there?"

"What?"

"You said you were—"

"Oh. I uh . . . I was trying to photograph something, a fox. Did you, or did someone, find my camera? Did I have it in the motel?"

"I'll ask around. You were photographing a fox?"

"Desert kit fox. They're endangered, it's really rare to see one."

"Would you be able to point it out to us on a map? Where you were in the prairie grass, with the twig snap?"

"Yeah. I mean . . . of course."

Garcia motions with her hand, and Frazier leaves the observation room again. "You know the mountains pretty well?" Garcia asks.

"Yes?" She says it like it should be the most obvious thing in the world.

"How long have you been a ranger?"

"Five years, give or take."

"Pretty long time. How often do you come down to town?"

"Every two, three weeks, I come down for a resupply."

"You see a lot of people up there? A lot of foot traffic near your cabin?"

"Not really, except during peak season."

"You ever get lonely up there?"

Hannah stares at her for a minute, and . . . that look again. Like Garcia's asked the dumbest question in the world. I almost want to laugh.

"No," Hannah eventually says. And I see it there, behind the anxiety and pain. She's got fight in her.

Frazier walks in, sets a map on the table in front of Hannah. Hannah leans away again, her breath coming faster at the proximity. She points immediately to a spot on the map.

"Wow. Pretty far from your cabin," Garcia says.

Hannah shrugs, relaxes when Frazier moves away again.

"How many miles?"

"Twelve or so, probably."

"That's a lot."

"Oh, um. Not really?"

"You hike a lot? That part of the job?"

"Not for everyone, but for me."

"You ever worry about your safety out there? Have anything to protect yourself?"

"I wasn't taken from my cabin," she says. "I was down closer to people."

Garcia pauses, seems to consider. "But you don't remember being taken."

Hannah looks agitated, glances around the room again.

"You have a background in psychology," Garcia says. "What made you switch to—"

"I was awake when he put the tongue in my mouth," Hannah says.

Garcia stills.

"That's what you want to know," Hannah says. "I'll tell you." She braces herself. "I know those plains. I know how to stalk and what it is to be stalked, and I heard and sensed *nothing*. Until that twig snapped. And then in the next second I was in a motel room with my arms duct-taped behind my back and my legs taped together, and I couldn't move. I was paralyzed, I guess. I figured he must have given me something. And I, um . . ."

She closes her eyes. A strand of her hair falls loose over her face. She tucks it back.

"The guy on the ground," she says, "most of his skin was off already. I couldn't see his face. It was hidden, from where I was. But he was still alive, for a while."

"How did you know he was still alive?"

"He was screaming. Trying to. There was something in his mouth or it was muffled. But the screaming . . . I couldn't hear at first, at all, like I was deaf or something, for a while, just this static, and like pressure. But then when my hearing came back I heard it, and the man with the knife, he bent down and did something to the screaming man. I figured out not too long after that he had cut out his tongue. But the man on the floor, he kept making sounds after that, kept crying for help, then moaning. I knew he was dead eventually when he stopped."

Garcia pauses, silent. "And what happened next?" she says after a moment.

"The guy with the knife turned to me. It smelled like a slaughterhouse. I can't . . ." Her eyes start to tear up, but she blinks, doesn't let them. "I can't get the smell out of my nose."

"Did you recognize this man? Either of them?"

Hannah shakes her head. "No. I'd never seen him. I'd know. I don't see, you know, so many people. Um. The knife was strange. The blade was maybe off-white? Kind of homemade looking. And . . . He came toward me. I couldn't move, at all. I tried. I couldn't fight him. He turned me on my side and taped me down to the bed, facing in. Then he took the man from the floor and put him in with me, taped us together, so we'd be looking into each other's faces. The last thing he did was put the tongue in my mouth. I don't remember him leaving. I was in and out the rest of the time. Some light came in through the shades, but it was hard to tell how much time was passing or how long it was in between each time I was awake."

"We think that you were in there for almost three days."

Hannah takes this in.

"Did the man with the knife say anything? When he was doing all this, did he speak?"

Hannah shakes her head. "Not that I can remember."

"And would you be able to identify him if we showed you a photograph lineup?"

Hannah nods.

"Can you think of anyone, anyone at all, who would want to harm you?"

"No."

Something in my senses prickles at this. I think she's lying.

Maybe. It's the first lie I've felt from her. It grates on me, more than normal.

Frazier goes in one last time, sets some photographs on the table in front of Hannah, who flinches back more than before. The shadow slips into the room with Frazier. Stays after she leaves.

I watch the shadow move slowly around the interrogation room behind Hannah.

Hannah leans forward to look at the photographs, Garcia putting them all side by side.

The shadow slides against the wall, coming around to the window side of the room. Moving as though it wants something.

Hannah stills.

She lifts her head. Her eyes go wide again as she tenses.

Hannah staring at the shadow that doesn't exist.

"Is everything okay?" Garcia says.

Hannah watches it for another moment.

And . . . I'd almost think . . .

She can *see* it.

Then she blinks, looks down at the photos, and nods her chin toward one of them. I can see from here it's Everett Brown.

"You're sure?" Garcia asks. "You can look closer."

Hannah looks to the shadow again, on edge. After a long minute, she turns back to the table and takes hold of the photographs.

She throws herself back from the chair. Stumbles away from Garcia and the shadow. The photos scatter over the floor with a whoosh, the chair clattering as she backs up against the wall.

"Whoa, are you okay?" Garcia says.

"Who gave you this?" Hannah says.

"What?" Garcia says.

"This photograph. These photos. Who printed these out?"

"Frazier, you met her—"

"No. It wasn't." Hey eyes dart behind Garcia to the glass. "Who's back there?" she says.

"No one. Maybe an agent or two, but I assure you, everyone is—"

"Do you hear that music?" Hannah closes her eyes, breathes, holds herself back against the wall. "*No*," she says. "I can't hear it again."

Garcia says, "Are you sure you're all right, we can—"

"This song. I heard it in the motel."

"What song?"

"John Denver. You don't hear it? What the fuck is happening?" Her words are frantic now, looking from Garcia to the shadow to us on the other side of the mirror. She squints at the glass. I know she can't see through, of course she can't. But if I didn't know better, I'd swear . . .

That dizziness washes over me again, and I can't breathe.

Garcia turns to see what Hannah is looking at, seems not to see us or anything else out of the ordinary, turns back to Hannah. "He was playing music in the motel?" Garcia asks.

"It . . . yeah," Hannah says, keeping herself against the wall. "After he left," she says. "When we were alone. The dead man, and me."

"What was the music, did you know the song?"

"That John Denver song. *You fill up my senses.* That one. It played over and over again. I forgot, until now. Why are you playing it?"

Garcia says, "Hannah, can we get you—"

She looks to the shadow, then back to the glass. "I want to go," she says.

"Um, yes. Just— Could you ever take us? To where you heard the twig snap. We could drive you to the trail, or if you want a place to stay down here while you recover, we can get you one."

Hannah seems to take a long moment to comprehend what Garcia is asking.

"I'm going back to my cabin," she says, with finality. "But you can drive me to the trailhead. Just you two." She looks back to the glass again. As though she can see right to me.

Garcia says, "No problem. We can—"

"You really don't hear that music?" Hannah says, and this time she's imploring, begging.

"No," Garcia says quietly, "It's a lot of stress, and we've got resources, things we can—"

Hannah looks to Garcia, to the shadow, to the mirror glass again.

She closes her eyes, body seized up, her brow furrowed in pain.

One tear falls.

6

Do you hear that music?

I stand behind the one-way glass. *Annie's Song.* The motel. Hannah, seeing the shadow. Hannah, hearing that song. Hannah Lawrence, touching the photos *I* held before Frazier took them in. Hannah Lawrence staring through the glass right at me. Someone played that song, in the motel. Someone fucking with me. Her?

Why?

I blink. I'm the last one in the room. They've all walked out after her. I shove myself up from my chair, throw myself out the door. She's across the floor being escorted through the desks, headed toward the elevators.

Frazier hangs back, waiting for me. She eyes me, but doesn't say anything.

I clear my throat, try to remember where I am. Hannah with Garcia, her location my only focus. "Can you do the hike?" I say to Frazier as we walk.

"Looks like it's pretty close to one of the trailheads. Should be fine," Frazier says.

"Okay. You're sure."

"Yeah. Feels worth it, anyway. With this."

"What do you think?" I ask her, barely.

"I think this is all pretty fucking crazy."

Hannah and Garcia step into an elevator. We cross the floor, wait for the next one. Step in, breathe, descend. Before we pass through the doors downstairs, I say to Frazier, "Take her to eat, if she'll let you. Get her whatever she needs. We'll need to talk to her again."

And then . . . we're outside.

And there she is. Her back to us. Slowly getting in the car.

Frazier and I walk toward them. I feel like I'm walking into a firefight. We've got Everett Brown detained, but without answers, we don't know if anyone else will try to get to Hannah. She's the only person brought into this who wasn't one of the killers and who walked away. We need to protect her. And yet . . .

Do you hear that music?

Frazier steps to the passenger side. The windows roll down. Hannah's head pushes out the window behind Frazier for fresh air. Claustrophobic before the motel, or just since? I stand at Garcia's side. I don't know where Jack and Tillman went. I don't know anything.

"Make sure she gets to the cabin," I say to Garcia, somehow. She looks me up and down. We've worked together for years, know each other well. "Please," I say.

She nods, debates whether to say more, a question on her face. Probably about the papers, Hannah asking who touched them.

"I'll call you," she says. I nod. She gets in.

As the car pulls away, I get one glimpse of her. One glimpse of Hannah Lawrence sitting in the back seat, leaning out the window.

And as they turn out of the lot, she looks back with an expression I can't even begin to read and that I know I will turn over in my head again and again for a very long time.

Anger, confusion, hurt, fear.

Recognition on her face.

As she looks right at me.

Back upstairs, I step into the interrogation room, stand where Hannah stood. Try to feel something, somehow. To understand. This space she occupied just minutes ago, molecules, breath. I force my eyes up and to the mirror wall.

Blood, bathtub,

Dad—

I close my eyes and take a step back, exhale.

She couldn't have seen me through it, it's just a mirror. There's no way.

I breathe through the moment, and I open my eyes to look down, check my watch. Ramona Lopez's mother is coming. I run my hands over my face and look at the chair Hannah was sitting in.

I look up to find more shadows moving in the room.

They all rush toward me.

7

The house that Pete Noland snuck out of the night he killed Ramona Lopez sits on twenty acres just outside of Greeley. Tillman and I pass through the city on the way up. Elitch Gardens, Meow Wolf, Mile High, warehouses, downtown skyscrapers, factories, the Adventure Forest on our right, bright letters painted on a giant wooden pod that kids run in and out of: WE ARE ALIVE IN A LIVING WORLD.

The city giving way to hay bales and pump jacks, junkyards and open fields as we head north. We take the exit for Greeley. Drive through the old-timey, charming downtown, a strong putrid smell permeating the car, the air outside notably warm. Tillman's podcast talks about a haunted themed restaurant.

My mind is occupied by Hannah Lawrence. Her eyes on mine, leaving the lot. My heart pounding.

Before we got in the car, Ramona Lopez's mother came in for her interview. She was crying too hard to give us anything other than that no one had any reason to hurt Ramona, and that Ramona Lopez was walking home from work at St. Mary's Hospital near Eagle's Nest when she would have been intercepted. The reports say her phone was found on the side of 76. I hadn't heard of Eagle's Nest. I put it in the search bar of my phone, try to focus, try not to think about Hannah Lawrence.

Eagle's Nest. New development, out by Aurora.

"Jeez, what a smell," Tillman says. "What is that?"

Right. Tillman who probably only goes into the mountains, hiking, climbing on weekends. Who wouldn't have come out this way. It does smell terrible to be fair. Meat, methane, blood. I say, "Greeley. It's the town. The smell is worse before a snow."

"Why?"

"Gets warm before a snow, and humid, it—"

"No, I know that. But why the town?"

I nod to the stockyards and meatpacking plants we're passing, and Tillman sees them too. "The farms and all the cow methane don't help either. It's a whole thing," I say. "How long have you been here again?" There might be a little shade in my tone.

"Six years."

"Hm," I say.

Tillman is silent for a moment. Then he takes a deep loud breath, stretches, and says, "Man, I just feel like I need to *move* today. Shake all this shit off."

I was able to squeeze in a morning workout between Jack's call and Hannah arriving for the interview. The basement gym at Whileago is dusty, and I still haven't got the power back on, but sweating out that much whiskey feels shitty in the dark or the light of day, so who cares. After what happened in the office though, I could use more too.

Tillman groans and stretches loudly, again.

"Maybe hit the gym," I say, as the podcast prattles on. *"I swear, bacon and eggs just flyin' across the kitchen! Would sometimes hit you right in the face!"*

"Not really a gym guy, I'm about the fresh air, ya know? We live in a freakin' wonderland. Real waste not to explore it."

As if suddenly remembering that he hasn't done it in ten minutes, he leans forward and looks up to the sky through the windshield.

It's brown, wide open, windy. Despite the college nearby, the town feels quiet. Aside from the construction. A lot of nearly identical apartment buildings going up off the main roads, farms surrounding. So many new developments all the time.

We pull up to the Wheely property. Pete Noland's girlfriend, Lucy Wheely, and her dad, Frank, the residents. A sign sits out front that says IF YOU VOTED FOR WOLF REINTRODUCTION, YOU'RE NOT WELCOME HERE.

We walk up the front porch steps. The first thing he says when he opens the door is, "If I had known that boy was sneakin' into my little girl's room, he probably wouldn't have been the one going to jail, if you know what I'm sayin'." Frank Wheely is stout, but strong. Has eyes that look hard but carry sadness, wears a flannel button-down and a vintage Broncos hat.

"Sure, yeah," Tillman says, adjusting his beanie.

"Mr. Wheely," I say. "We just have a few questions for Lucy if that's okay, and if possible we'd like to take a look around the property, see where Pete's car was parked."

"Lucy's out. But I'll show you the car."

Someone steps into the hall behind him. He closes the door before we can see, says, "Gonna show you somethin' else too."

It's an old farmhouse with a solid, new fence around the perimeter of the property. The land well maintained but brown because of the time of year. I bet it's beautiful in the summer. We walk out behind the house and Frank leads us over to a barn, cattle grazing beyond it in a large enclosure. Inside, the smell of manure, hay, and old wood fills the space. Frank steps over to a small office, then comes back with photographs. He hands one to each of us. Close-ups of bloody wounds on a cow's neck. Another of a calf with its entrails ripped from its belly, spilled out in the grass and half-eaten by something.

"What is this?" I ask, flipping the photos over.

"That is what happens when wolves are put back on our land. Three of 'em attacked one of our cows and a calf. I scared 'em off, but not before they did this. Neither of my cows made it," he says. "That in your hands is as clear evidence of wolf depredation as you're gonna get. And if that isn't enough"—he holds up his hand, shows us the half tooth in his palm—"I dug this out of her throat."

The tooth . . . a sense. Something prickling.

I say, "This isn't our—"

"Cops aren't doin' shit. Government's allowing it. I get one paycheck a year, and I need to send my kid to college. We didn't ask for it. Nobody asked for this, and someone's gotta do something. I killed one of the wolves I saw, and it was in my rights to do it, seein' it happen. But if you don't see it, if you're just a little late, law isn't on your side."

"We're here investigating a murder case," I say.

"This *is* murder. Each of these cows is a life."

"Till you send 'em for processing," Tillman says. He's wandered to the side of the barn, is leaning down over a stack of hay bales, inspecting one closely. "I thought we've got a pretty good depredation compensation policy in place these days. Hopefully you got your money. This looks like good hay."

"It is," Frank says. And the quiet danger in his tone is clear.

"I'll make a note," I say, smoothing it over. Tillman's a goddamn liability. "See if I can send someone out, find the right department."

We leave the barn. Frank and I walk ahead, Tillman traipsing behind us like a child. I apologize for him. Frank says, "We're helpless here. We look after this land, we tend it, my family for four generations. And the state's just sent in a bunch of predators we're not allowed to shoot if they come after our livestock. Airlifted 'em from freaking Canada. For what? Someone's gotta do something. No one makin' these laws gives a shit about us. Predators sneak in, in the fuckin' night, and we can't . . ."

I glance over and try to pretend I don't catch the emotion in his voice, the way he swipes beneath his eye as he takes a deep breath. After a long minute, he says, "She's my kid, ya know? And this boy was here, and I didn't even know it. And what he did to that lady . . . I just keep askin' myself, what if he'd done it to Lucy? If he was capable of that, what if he . . ."

I nod. Because what else is there to say.

He collects himself. "We hear a howl," he says, "and all it means is death."

We walk around a large paddock to reach a lower field where we find Pete's car.

"They told me not to touch it," he says. "You takin' it today?"

"I can send someone," I say. Tillman and I slip on our gloves. "You find the keys?"

He shakes his head no, tells us he's gotta make a call from the house. We tell him we'll be gone soon, and he starts to walk back the way we came, around the paddock.

"The lengths we used to go to to get a little action," Tillman says, when Frank's gone. "Guess nothin' changes." He taps the top of Pete's car, then looks up to the sky again. He's talking about a kid who's never gonna see daylight again outside of a prison yard if things keep going this way. For one second I very seriously consider doing the world a favor and punching him in the face.

I step around the car and bend down, get Tillman out of my line of sight and try to view Pete's path from all angles. Was he intercepted, coerced? No traces of any kind of substance in his system. No contusions, nothing to suggest he could have been physically assaulted. But I just can't believe he planned to do this. Unless . . . Tillman's right about one thing. Teen boys might do a lot for a little action. We should talk to the girlfriend.

I watch the grass, the sky, the roads. Feel the wind, listen to the quiet. This last land Pete Noland walked on before his life was ripped from him forever. Or because he chose to throw it away. I rub my neck, my eyes on the cows. That photo Frank showed us, the teeth marks in the throat.

Teeth marks.

That strange pressure in the air.

The field the other night, Everett Brown abducting Hannah out in the middle of nowhere, in the plains grass. The grass in the wind, something moving in the dark, something I couldn't see. And Pete's car, here in this hayfield. We're dealing with someone who knows land, who can move freely through the outdoors. Who keeps using cover of night.

Movement, to our left. I turn, in shooting stance. There's a girl there, a teenager. She throws her arms up, stumbles back from us. "Oh my god, sorry. I didn't mean . . ."

I lower my weapon. "Lucy Wheely?" Tillman says. The girl steps over wearing a Lord Huron T-shirt over a long-sleeve, and jeans. She looks terrified. She's clearly been crying.

"Hi," she says.

I say, "Hi. We're—"

"My dad doesn't want me talkin' to you, but . . ." She shifts on her feet, tucks her hair behind her ear. "But I just wanted to say. You don't know us, and I know what it looks like. I get how . . ." She takes a shaky inhale. "A lot of people have two sides to them. People say that they never knew someone had a dark side until they snap. Until they do something terrible one day . . . But if there is one person in this world who's not like that, who's good and only good and not even in an annoying way, just like really genuine and . . ." She turns pleading eyes on us. "Pete would never hurt anyone, I'm telling you. Please help—"

BEEP BEEP BEEP BEEP BEEP!

Lucy and I both jump at the same time.

Pete's car alarm blasts through the day, sends a flock of nearby geese sailing into the sky. Tillman stands beside it, his hand on the door handle, a sheepish look on his face. "Whoops," he says. "Sorry, didn't know it was locked!"

Frank Wheely runs out of the house and jogs toward us through the field.

8

We spent twenty minutes trying to figure out how to get the fuckin' car alarm off without a key, then I had to apologize to the Wheelys again for Tillman's absolute stupidity. Not to mention, we didn't get to properly ask Lucy anything while we had the chance. We drove around for a bit after, took all the roads around the property, but didn't find anything.

"What the fuck was that?" I ask Tillman as we head back to Denver. When I am calm enough to speak.

"Just clumsy," he says.

"*Clumsy?* Are you serious?"

"That girl didn't know anything."

"Why do you say that?"

He shrugs.

"Well, we can't know because we didn't get a chance to ask her."

We drive with the podcast playing. And as we pull back into town Tillman checks his watch for what must be the eighteenth time since we got back in the car.

"Got somewhere better to be?" I say, taking a turn for South Broadway.

"We just try and get home for dinner, no matter what's . . ." He trails off as we both remember that he's talking about my ex-wife. He's anxious to go home and eat dinner with Josie. It's only four thirty, so I guess they do it early. Five-thirty dinner, then back to work, or if they don't have to, then time for a movie, time for a fuckin' nature walk.

He starts to say, "Sorry, if—"

"I'll drop you off after this," I say. I turn up the volume on his stupid podcast.

Lady Justice Brewing Company sits in a nondescript parking lot off Broadway, a stretch people call the Green Mile for all the dispensaries. On the way we pass the Mayan Theater, Wizard's Chest, Mutiny Information Cafe. My parents used to bring me to these places. I like this part of Denver, where the punk scene lived—maybe still does, I don't know—where there's more than sports and strip malls.

The brewery, welcoming, colorful, is decorated for Christmas already, a small fake wood-paneled living room set up with a fake fireplace, stockings, Christmas lights. Skis rest against the walls, tinsel hangs from the ceiling. By one door stands a cardboard cutout of Dolly Parton in a Santa hat and cowboy boots, hanging an ornament on a fake aspen tree. In the corner living room setup, a family plays a card game. One of the kids colors on a sheet of paper.

My mind drifts back to the playing card in my pocket. My heart pounds. I shouldn't be carrying it. Don't know why I can't let it go. Why I am acting completely insane.

Kimberly Chen, the highway patrolwoman and first killer back after the five-year hiatus, has out-of-state parents and a local brother. We're told that David Chen is here but that we'll have to wait until the end of his shift to speak to him—another thirty minutes. Which means I am spending thirty stationary minutes with Nat Tillman after that absolute shitshow in Greeley. Which means I most definitely need a beer.

We go to the counter and get the hazy they recommend on draft. A shadow drifts in and out from the employee room. Nat explains, unsolicited, the difference between a hazy, milkshake, session, sour, West Coast. He's still talking when we sit down at a table and I text Daphne.

Dinner soon?

I take a sip, and I get a text back almost immediately. But it's not from Daphne, it's Josie.

We really need to talk. I don't feel good about this. Kinda think you shouldn't either.

I knock back the beer. Tillman's still talking when I stand and get us each another.

"Oh no, I can't. Thanks though, man." I've just set two glasses down on the table.

"What?"

"I'm really just a one beer kind of guy. Two, I mean, woof, you don't want to see me."

"You—"

"I get wild."

"You drink two beers, and get . . . wild."

He nods his head solemnly. "One night I was with some buddies o' mine, back up in Oregon. That's where I'm from. Don't know if you know that. We were slingin' some brewskies, and I had like three of 'em. And one of my buddies dared me to a race to the top of Ruckel Ridge, which, if you don't know, is a real dangerous hike. Can be, if you're not careful. Just a real scramble, slick mossy rocks, and there's this part called the Catwalk that's just like a foot wide, straight cliff down, and I'm tellin' ya, we were running! So yeah. Gotta limit myself to one, 'cause when I drink I just throw caution to the wind!"

He happily bobs his head to the Phish song playing on the speakers. An Avalanche game plays on the TV behind the bar. I sit back down and pull both glasses toward me. My phone buzzes, Josie again.

I'm serious, call me.

I pull out my notebook and start writing things down, everything Frank and Lucy Wheely said, everything I noticed in the field. Try to lower my blood pressure.

"Pete didn't go the way we thought he did," Tillman says. "Gotta redraw the map."

It takes me a second to register that Tillman is actually talking about the case. "What?"

"I don't think he walked on the road we thought he did. I think he took the other one around the side of the property."

"What are you talking about?"

"When I set off the car alarm. Frank Wheely didn't take the same route coming to us as we all walked before—from the house, around the paddock. He took a cut-through path."

I set my pen down, look at him.

"Pete Noland's clothes," he says. "When we found them, there was a piece of grass stuck to the bottom of his boot, wedged in between the grooves. Timothy grass isn't common here. You need it to be wetter for it to grow. But it's real in demand, people think it makes premium hay, so it's like a point of pride if anyone's got it—it's a thing. Except it's common up in the northwest, since . . .

wetter. Anyway, Frank Wheely's got a patch of it, down on the other side of the house, the one we didn't walk on. Pete didn't go the way we thought he did. And I wanted to see if Frank was gonna show us some route I hadn't thought of when he came to us from the house. Also see if he was lying about finding the car keys. Seems like he wasn't." He shrugs. "So, may not matter, but Pete didn't go back to his car. Someone intercepted him and made him go the other way from the house. Or he planned to go that other way all along."

At the front, a delivery is made, kegs brought in through the door and set just inside. Something about a truck blocking the back entrance. Two employees start carrying them, one by one, through the taproom. Tillman watches and says, "It's like the skies. Flight paths can tell you a lot. And we're in the Central Flyway here." He winks.

"You don't have working theories," I say. "Nothing listed in any of the files." It's a question. Nat Tillman, who set off that car alarm on purpose.

"Do you meditate?" Tillman asks. "I do," he says when I don't answer. "Every day, for the last ten years. You don't need to write things down. I got it all logged right up here." He touches his head. "Caffeine's the other thing that'll screw ya, I don't touch the stuff."

I take a breath. "Tillman. Do you have a working theory?"

"Don't think we're there yet, compadre. Just gotta keep takin' it all in. Eyes to the skies."

He's up then, off his stool, and walking over to the employee struggling with one of the kegs. He asks if he can help her with it and lifts it off the ground with strength I'm surprised he possesses, and which makes my mood significantly worse.

I get a text from Daphne, but not about catching up. It's an ID on the John Doe from the motel room, the one taped into the bed with Hannah Lawrence. She sends it to Jack, Frazier, Tillman, Garcia, and me. Frazier sends a follow-up PDF report through the FBI server a few minutes later.

Tony Howell. Twenty-six years old. Geological survey analyst for a major oil and gas company. Lived with his brother, socials showing him out with friends, volunteering at shelters. From his outward persona, a very well-loved guy.

I read through the preliminary report, and something catches my eye. His company office, in another area I haven't heard of.

Granite Ridge. All these names of these new developments, all these stupid meaningless nature references. Eagle's Nest, where Ramona Lopez's hospital is; Rock Creek, where Everett Brown lives with his wife. And something occurs to me. Something so glaringly obvious that I cannot believe it didn't before. I search for the owner of each of these developments. Different LLCs.

But all one developer.

WrightStar. I exhale a long slow breath.

The very first victim in all this, six years ago, was a fourteen-year-old girl. Claire Wright. None of us will ever forget it.

Claire's father, Oliver Wright, is the developer on Rock Creek, Eagle's Nest, Granite Ridge.

I don't want to get ahead of myself. Years ago we found a connection with a guy named Ryder Smith who went to the same high school as two of the victims and one of the killers. While at that school, years before—and unrelated to this case, we ultimately determined—Ryder took a fake gun to school and threatened to kill everyone. Jack interviewed him in jail, but he was a dead end. It was a straw grasp anyway.

But Oliver Wright . . .

I look up who owns the high school that Ryder Smith, those victims, and that Drifter all went to. It takes a minute and a number of searches, but I find an article. WRIGHTSTAR ACQUIRES FORTY ACRES OF PROPERTY IN WEST DENVER, INCLUDING HIGH SCHOOL AND LOCAL BUSINESSES.

My glass suddenly knocks over onto the table with a clang. Beer spilling over my notebook, down into my lap. I stand, look around to see a shadow darting away, then quickly try and mop up the beer with some napkins.

What the hell? This shadow came and knocked my beer over? Motherfucker. The father of the family in the corner eyes me, wary. I reach for more napkins. Did *I* knock it over?

Tillman says, coming up behind me, "You okay, brother?" I turn to find him and a young guy, maybe twenty-three, twenty-four, standing there. Lean, sharp, grief and shock written on every inch of him.

"Stansfield, this is David Chen, Kimberly's brother. He's got about two minutes to speak to us, then he's gonna be about his day. Thank you again for your time," he says to David.

"Look," David says. "I'm exhausted and I'm just trying to keep it together, okay? I'm just . . ." He wipes a tear and adjusts his hat, turns to Tillman. "If you hadn't helped with the kegs, I wouldn't be talking to you at all. This whole thing . . . My sister is the best person I know, and she is my rock. She would never ever do this."

"We understand," Tillman says. "What happened that night? You said you talked?"

"Yeah. I was on the phone with her. She was making her rounds on Eighty-Five. And she suddenly just stopped talking and said, 'What is *that*?' And I said, 'What?' but she didn't answer me. It was quiet for a long minute, and then I asked, 'What?' again, and she said, 'Hold on a second. There's something in the road.' She sounded worried, freaked, even.

"Then she put the phone down on the seat, but I could still hear. She does that, and I can always hear her talking in the background, whoever she's pulled over responding to her. But this time I couldn't hear any talking. This time I heard grasshoppers, I heard her boots. And then . . . I don't know how to explain it better than . . . it was like this sort of wind turbine, almost. The sound. Or a giant vacuum. Like . . . *VOOM*. It happened a few times, three or four. And then, I didn't hear her boots anymore, and the sound stopped. Even the grasshoppers. It was just silent. And the phone cut out. She didn't call back and didn't answer when I called her. So I called nine-one-one and told them where she was. When they got there, there was no sign of anything. Just her abandoned patrol car."

That sound. What I heard in the field. I start to say, "And did you—"

"Look," David says, "I already answered the cops when I called them. I know who you are, and I know what this whole thing is, and I just cannot get my head around the fact that this is our lives now, or that we are in any way a part of it. Okay? Like my sister I've known my entire life just decided on a whim to put down the phone and kill and *skin* someone she pulled over on the side of the highway? And now she's in jail? She has a cat, a life, a family. She would never do any of this.

"So please don't sit here questioning me when I've already told the cops everything. Get out there and do your job, because if there's any chance of my sister, or me, or anyone else getting out of any of this, it's you just finally figuring this the fuck out. *Please*."

On our way out, we pass the family in the corner.

My eye catches on the marker drawing the kid has been making, sitting between his parents.

A long spindly creature with antlers or horns. I stare at it for a second.

I dodge another shadow as we step out the door.

9

"We need to talk to Oliver Wright again," I say to Tillman back in the lot. He leans against the side of the car, looks up at the sky. Clouds have rolled in, and in the gray light the city looks like the purgatory it is. I tell him about the new connection with these last three murders, the WrightStar developments. He's already read over what Frazier and Daphne sent.

He furrows his brow. "Josie and Jack are investigating him," he says. "Oliver Wright."

"What?"

"White-collar stuff. Fraud, I think." He shrugs. "Wouldn't hurt for us to talk with him."

We wrap up this super fun day by lingering in the parking lot near each other, making calls. Leaves fall from the oak trees, squirrels zipping at the edges of the parking lot. A magpie pecks at an overturned take-out container that's fallen from a trash can.

"Got good news and bad news," Tillman says when we get back in the car.

I start the engine, the podcast turning back on automatically.

"So Mona Brown, Everett Brown's wife, she's down to talk to us," he says.

"Great," I say. "When?"

"Tomorrow morning, first thing. But she had a stipulation."

"Okay."

"Yeah, so she doesn't actually want to talk to us . . . she wants to talk to . . . me."

"To you."

"Yeah, or like, more specifically, to anyone. Just not . . . you."

"Not *me*?"

David Chen's voice. *Get out there and do your job because—*

"Right," I say.

We get on the road, the sun starting to lower behind the mountains. "Wright's assistant's getting back to us tomorrow," I tell him. "But I say we just stop by if we don't hear—"

"Holy shit!" Tillman exclaims.

I swerve, heart pounding.

Enemy fire, Dad in the mirror,

Scan the road for danger, the car.

"Oh, hey now—"

Blood, bullets, glass raining down, land mine blowing, sand, screams and blood and—

"Hey, hey," Tillman says. "Sorry, brother, didn't mean to—"

Truck coming from the side, Marianne's head slamming into the window

"Whoa. Do you wanna pull over?"

"You can't," I say. I breathe, do the breathing. I make myself say, "You can't fuckin' do that. Not in my car."

"Okay, okay, I'm sorry. Can I drive, or—"

"I'm fine, just gimme a sec."

I calm, make myself. The podcast talks about the haunting of Cheesman Park and the bodies buried there.

"Why did you yell?" I say after a minute, gripping the wheel. "Did you see something?"

"In the sky," Tillman says. "Saw a light, didn't look like a plane . . . thought it might be a . . . Sorry, dude. I didn't realize . . ."

I feel him watching me, getting a whole picture. How fucked up I am, how much I can't get past anything in my life. How Josie dodged a big fuckin' bullet by getting away from me. He'll want to talk about it in bed tonight with her, my episode in the car, what it must have been like for her to be with me for so many years. She'll volunteer some anecdote, more than one, moments when the past hit me in the face while I was with her and I couldn't deal with it.

"What is your deal with the UFOs?" I say. "Seriously, what the fuck is it about them that you need to see? There's all kinds of shit in the skies, all the time. Who fucking cares."

He doesn't answer. For once he shuts his mouth. We listen to the podcast, and the sun disappears, leaving us with another cold blue fade into night.

I drop him off in front of the house I bought back when my life was still mine.

I turn off the podcast and drive.

10

I drive, up and down 85, where Kimberly Chen would have been when she got off the phone with her brother, his words echoing in my ears. I drive past the victims' houses, the killers', from the last three murders. All of them. I think of the sound David Chen talked about. I think of the one piece of all this that most seems to stick out, the one total break in the pattern.

I pull her card out of my pocket while driving. The fox she drew. I try to picture her in the cabin now. A lamp on, sketching. In the quiet? With that radio playing? Living alone for so long, away from people, does something to you. Changes you. Shifts how you relate to other humans. The way I felt looking at her. The way I still feel. My heart still fucking pounding. I have to stop with whatever this is. I gotta get myself together.

Daphne still won't reply to my texts. I wonder if I'll find her at Mama Tried. Maybe I shouldn't if she doesn't want to see me. I don't know. I call Murphy. "You home or out?" I say.

"Home, but come over."

"Okay," I say.

"Daniel," he says. "Come to the front door, they want to see you."

I pull into the driveway ten minutes later. Jack's wife, Emily, stands in the doorway with a hand on her hip and the other in front of her face to block the shine from my headlights. I cut the engine. Grab the flowers I picked up on the way and go to greet her. Her red hair is tied back, a little more gray in it than before, and she's wearing a turtleneck and jeans.

"Only been waitin' here for four years," she says, the light from their house shining behind her.

Jack, like Daphne. I haven't seen his family in so long. I spent all this time so relieved that I wasn't here, all this time grateful to stay away. If I'm being honest I just didn't let myself think about everything I was leaving behind, the people I wasn't showing up for. Convinced myself somehow that they'd be happier with me gone—maybe they were. Shit agent, shit husband, shit friend, shit person. I run my hand through my hair, look down at the flowers, clear my throat. "I'm sorry," I say, meeting her eye. "I just . . . couldn't face it," I say. "No excuse."

She looks me up and down. "You look healthy."

I shrug.

"Happy?"

"Not really."

She barks out a laugh and pulls me into a hug. I put my arms around her too.

"He's missed you," she says in my ear. "We all have." Then she releases me and takes the flowers. "C'mon," she says. "Kids are excited to see you. It'll only take a second."

She closes the door on the night.

Their house smells like home-cooked dinner and pine needles. Soft glowing lights. A carpeted, wood-paneled living room with framed family photographs, trophies, awards, art projects. One half of the room is a mess of half-opened boxes, ornaments. Christmas lights and tinsel spilling out onto the floor, a tree already sitting in the corner by the front window.

"We're gettin' a head start on Christmas this year," Emily says.

A boy sits on the couch, homework in front of him, one hand tapping a pencil, the other twisting a fidget spinner. On the floor by the tree, a girl tries to untangle string lights. I hardly recognize either of them. Seven to eleven is a huge jump. I can't really believe it.

"Kids, you remember Uncle Danny?"

They both stare at me a long second, then jump up, homework and toys and lights flying, run at me, tackle me in a simultaneous hug. Their voices climb over each other,

"Uncle Danny, where have you been? You missed my birthdays!"

"Were you fighting in the war again?"

"Casa Bonita reopened! Will you go with us?"

"My friend says war is just a bunch of—"

"Dad said you don't live with Aunt Josie anymore."

"That's enough," Emily says. "Give Uncle Danny a second."

I take a step back and breathe. Fight through the tightness in my chest. I clear my throat and bend down on one knee. My voice isn't quite level when I say, "I really missed you guys."

In the garage, Jack's pouring drinks for us. All his tools organized on one wall, lamplight. I've always loved this space, how they've set it up with an old rug and a couple chairs and couch, next to the Charger he's been fixing up forever. Someone's put a bunch of rainbow Christmas string lights crisscrossing over the top of it plugged in and lit up. There's a fake-fireplace heater going in the corner of the sitting area setup, and a sign hung up on the wall above the couch that says SANTA'S WORKSHOP. Two coolers between the chairs and couch as side tables, and a beer fridge in the corner. Jack's pouring us bourbon for tonight though. He's got a Santa hat on. His aviators still hanging from his shirt. Always on him somewhere.

"Cheers, asswipe," he says, handing a glass to me.

"Watch it, I'll call HR."

"We're off the clock."

"Good one."

He sits down on the couch. "Kids attack you?"

"I didn't mind," I say, taking one of the chairs. "Nice hat."

"They said I have to wear it at home every day November first until January first."

"That's a big job."

"Someone's gotta do it." He adjusts the hat, settles in. After a long minute, he says, "It's weird, you know. Having you back. Four years is nothin', but—"

"The kids grow really fast," I say.

"Yeah. Not to kick you while you're down, but Brianna cried when we first told her you'd left. Two nights in a row."

I take a sip. A big one.

A posterboard rests against the wall, a school project. It says across the top:

OUR FRIENDS THE WOLVES. Then a bunch of facts in circles around the posterboard, images of wolves pasted around them:

WOLVES WILL ADOPT ORPHANED OR ABANDONED YOUNG

WOLVES MOURN WHEN ANOTHER WOLF DIES

WOLVES HAVE COMPLEX FAMILY DYNAMICS AND ARE VERY PLAYFUL

ONLY 1% OF LIVESTOCK DEATHS ARE FROM WOLVES

GRAY WOLVES MATE FOR LIFE

"You didn't have to do it, you know," Jack says.

"What?" I say.

"Big fat medical center donation *anonymously* comes in, suddenly the doctor calling to check in all the time, *how's she feeling, can we do anything, let us know what you need.*"

"I don't know what you're talking about," I say. Brianna's epileptic. It's been a struggle for years, but she has great parents, and they're on top of it. "Has she been okay?" I ask. "She looks good, happy."

"Couple bad ones, but yeah. She's good. She's strong. Wish she didn't have to be, but . . ."

"I'm glad. I'm sorry," I say. "That I haven't checked in. It's . . . I'm sorry."

He watches me, takes a sip. Says, "I get it. You had a shit hand. Thank you for donating. But you *are* like the worst rich guy."

"I'm not—"

"You would be, if you didn't just hemorrhage it out to charities—not that I'm complaining, mind you. But to not even get like a beautiful car out of it. Something!"

"The only thing I want is some answers, and for people to stop dying."

"Yeah, well, don't we all."

"Tillman said you and Josie are looking into Oliver Wright. He developed a few of the properties some of the victims live and work on. Obviously, in addition to Claire being our first victim. I think it's worth looking into on our end."

"Well, he developed half this town. Least in the last decade. But we're gonna get him soon on financials. He's like any rich asshole. Sorry . . . you know what I mean. But he's been gaming the system for years."

"You don't think he could be involved in this?"

"I don't know. I mean, have you ever talked to him?"

"Not in a while," I say.

"Look, I get theoretically that there are sick fucks out there who could hurt their own kids. And he's a pain in the ass. But . . . he's really fucked up from what happened to his daughter. Like *really.* So, could he be tied to the murders? Sure, maybe, but . . . I dunno. Being a parent is like . . . you would do literally anything for your kid. *Anything.* You think you know yourself, and then you have these little people, and suddenly you're like, I don't know who I am at all. But I know I would die before letting anything happen to them. And his kid is gone. Fourteen years old. And the way it happened . . . I just can't imagine what that does to someone. I feel sorry for him."

"It could make a person into a monster."

"Yeah. I mean, he could be responsible for the murders after. I don't have a fuckin' clue, but I'll look on our end and see if there's anything that could possibly tie him in to it, and you guys do it too. Might be able to get some of the Drifters retried without him breathing down everyone's necks too." He takes a sip. "Any other leads?"

Hannah Lawrence, my brain says. *Hannah Lawrence, the outlier, who might somehow be the key to everything.* My hand twitches, wants to reach in my pocket, for the card.

My eyes find Brianna's posterboard project again. Something . . .

I pause. Glance up to the little window in the corner that looks out over the front yard, think I catch movement.

I wait, tense. But there's nothing there. Of course there isn't.

"I'll send you everything," I say. "Everett Brown's lying about logging in to the chat rooms. I gotta look at those transcripts tonight. So far, those two feel the most promising."

"Thank you," Jack says after another long minute. "Thank you for what you did for Brianna, and thank you for coming back. I . . . we needed you on this."

"I don't know," I say.

"Dan, I've seen you solve shit no one could, and in record time. This case is fucked up, and there's no one who could've figured it out. I mean, we've been trying. We haven't stopped. But you . . . you just know how to see things, things that people wouldn't think to look at. And I think this Drifter thing just got your confidence, put up some kind of block for you. But you *are* the best we have. And I know grief does a lot of weird shit to people, but you can do this. If someone's gonna figure this thing out, I know it's you."

The fake fire crackles in the heater, wind blows against the house. And I remember what I should have this whole time. The man across from me, he's not just a boss or friend. He's family. He and Emily never had to invite me in to be a part of their lives, even now. I don't want to lie to him. Not about something as big as this. It might help the case even. Maybe . . . I just. I think I have to tell him. The Happy Inn. My birth parents. My connection to all this.

I take a deep breath. I don't know what's right and what's not and if me telling him jeopardizes us even having a chance of solving this. But I say, "Jack—"

"I'm sorry," he says. "About Nat and Josie. I shoulda told you. And I mean it sucks. She just really went for it, I guess."

I exhale. "Can we not?" I say, running my hands over my face.

"You know . . . he's a good agent. He's annoying—like Emily and I have *not* invited them over, just so you know. Team D forever. Obviously. And truth be told, I just don't really wanna hang out with him. But." He shrugs. "Take a look at his notes, he saw stuff I couldn't, before. Not that it, you know, led to anything. But it's never the same urgency with cold cases, you know that. I think we might actually have a shot at this. Maybe, with the two of you . . ."

He lets it hang there. The possibility of a future in which we aren't buried under the weight of this all the time. I down the drink. I can't do it. I'm not doing it, telling him, I guess.

I keep my voice even as I say, "That was a real dick move you pulled."

"Well, how was I supposed to know you wouldn't want to partner with the climberbro Deadhead who's taken your job and your house and your wife?"

It's late when Jack and I step out of the garage. The lights are on the tree. Bret's gone to bed. "Mom said I could stay up to see you put the star on," Brianna says.

I look to Jack and then back to her. "Me?"

Emily laughs. "Okay, to be fair, this is sweet, but it's also because last year Jack did it, and the whole tree fell down. We lost like eight ornaments."

"Santa works in mysterious ways," Jack says, tucking her under his arm, kissing her head.

I hang the star, and I promise them I'll come for Thanksgiving, as if I'm doing them some kind of favor. As if they're not rescuing *me* in every way. As I fix it in its place, movement catches my eye again, outside. I turn to the window.

Blood, bathtub—

I close my eyes against my reflection in the glass. I force a breath and open them again, look above and past my reflection, out into the night.

Pressure, a strange . . . pull.

Bad Feeling.

"I gotta go," I say. "Thank you, guys, so much."

I hug them and step out the door. It closes behind me, sealing in the warmth of the house.

I scan the night for any movement, any life. Quiet suburb, waning moon through the trees.

I have a Bad Feeling.

I walk to my car, boots crunching on November grass and fallen leaves, the air chilled enough that I see my breath. Yellow-white streetlamps illuminated up and down the cul-de-sac.

I pull my keys out of my jacket, and there's movement out of the corner of my eye.

I turn just as a black shape rushes forward, throws me back against the car.

I can't see, am blind suddenly. Something shoves its fist down my throat, blocks my airway. All I see is black. Panic, as I try to breathe. I drop to my knees in the grass beside the driveway, choke, hold my hands to my throat. I can't breathe.

Rose and me on a rock, in a river. Someone singing Blaze Foley.

If I could only fly.

The thing releases me. I drop forward to my hands, forehead to the grass. I wheeze in a breath. That image. The same place. Same memory—not memory—that hit me in the office. When were Rose and I ever at a river?

When I've recovered enough to sit up, the shadow is gone. The lights are turned off in Jack and Emily's house. I know I'm crazy, that this isn't real. Grief does this, PTS does, rips the air from your lungs, makes you think you've—but . . . Still, just . . .

Just in case, I say, out loud and into the night.

"Not them."

The words barely rasp out after what it just did to my throat. This is what happens, when they start to come for me. Or when the grief does. Or PTS. Or I don't know, but—

"Not this family," I say. "You stay the fuck away from them."

I shake my head to clear the half-memory—not memory—of my birth mom, get myself in the car.

I pull away from the Murphys' house, the streetlights flickering, one by one, as I pass.

11

I hired a cleaning service for Whileago Manor. When I get back now, it's less dusty, and the smell is gone. In some ways it's worse, cleaner like this. Looks more the way it did when my parents were here. But dark, empty.

As if to contradict me, footsteps pound upstairs. A door slams in the basement. The lights of the entry and living room glow at my approach. The power's still off. I go to the wall switch to double-check. I walk to the living room and sit by the hearth, start piling on the logs.

A glass bottle smashes to the floor of the bar. A shadow moves along the wall.

"Jesus. I am not doing this," I say. "*We're not fucking doing this.*"

Stillness, silence. Save for the crackle of the fire, the pop of it catching.

My heart going wild like always. Kid in the motel, kid with the murdered mom, kid in the haunted house, kid at war. Therapist once showed me a report on what constant fight-or-flight can do to a body, over time. No matter which way I play it, I'm fucked. Heart attack's comin', any day now, and that's gonna be that. You can only push it so far for so long.

I go to the bar and pour myself a whiskey, knock it back. Ignore the mess on the floor.

"You're not real, and you're not fucking helpful, and I swear to god, if you—"

The lights flash brighter, then stop glowing. Dim down to darkness. I take another drink.

"Thank you," I say.

Back by the fireplace, I spread out the files again, on the coffee table and floor, walk in and around them, the fire glowing at my back.

I pull the fox drawing from my pocket, Hannah's card. Set it down with all the photographs and reports, everything compiled on this case over the past six years. All these names, faces and stories and relations and connections or lack of connections. Twenty-three now with the three recent murders—Kimberly Chen, Ross Thompson, Pete Noland, Ramona Lopez, Everett Brown, Tony Howell, and Hannah Lawrence. Seven new names here.

So why can I only think of Hannah?

I open my laptop, close my eyes against the black, then search for her again. I use a hotspot for service from my phone, remotely log in to my work desktop, and read over Frazier and Garcia's memo. They got her safely back to the cabin, noted how she was able to hike even injured, that they found her camera and asked if they could develop the film. She'd been protective of it, had insisted she get it back after they got it developed, said she wanted to see the photo she'd taken of the fox.

Hannah Lawrence. Her name, even. Like a part of me knew she would always be involved in this, like I've somehow heard it before.

Have I?

I search through the files, try and find any way she could have been even tangentially associated with anyone else here. Any way I could have ever come across her.

One thing about PTS is that sometimes there are gaps. These memories of Rose surfacing now could be that. You get blank spaces in your life, periods of time your brain shuts you out from, and sometimes it'll spit them back at you out of nowhere. Could I have met Hannah before and just not remember? Is that why seeing her makes me feel . . .

I touch the edges of the sketch. Drop it and run my hands over my head.

My heart, that lightheaded nausea.

The murder that ended the hiatus—Kimberly Chen as the "Drifter"—was November 2. The second—Pete Noland and Ramona Lopez—November 10. The third—with Everett Brown, Tony Howell, and Hannah Lawrence—was November 16, three days before I arrived here. Eight days between the first two, six between the second and the third. And November 16 was the six-year anniversary of the very first murder, of Claire Wright. Could it be Oliver Wright acting in revenge?

I check the clock on the computer. It's the 21st now, two days since I was at the motel.

That third murder in the motel the only one seemingly targeting me specifically, on the anniversary of Claire Wright's death, the beginning of all of this. Is it possible there won't be any more? That whoever's doing this just wanted me to have to go back there? There's nothing worse for me. If it's about torture, that was it. What else could they do? They've already made me go back to the worst moment of my life.

Could Wright have found out about my past?

Is it just wishful thinking to hope that was the grand finale? Is another murder coming any day now, and because I'm so goddamned slow, because none of us can make any kind of headway on this thing, more lives will be stolen? *For what?*

I turn to the digital forensic and HTML reports, narrowing the search to lines to *Wizdumteller*, the seeming mystery leader of this chatroom thing, and *CanisLoopus*, Everett Brown's handle. I start with the most recent posts from these last couple months.

Wizdumteller, 10/15: Do you think our friends in blue have gotten a little complacent? Do you think they have any idea what we can do? (Shall we show them?)

10/28: Little birdie told me our gumshoe might be flying the coop. What will WW have to say about that?

11/1: Wake up, my friends. The boogeyman is back. Think we'll get a show?

There are so many of these. Dating all the way back to the early murders. For years this shit has been going on, and . . . the "gumshoe." Is that me? My actual name is mentioned so many times I can't quite get my head around it. *Daniel Stansfield*. Just there, typed up by all these true crime enthusiasts positing their theories, trying to solve the case. Or alerting the others when new information is available.

But *Wizdumteller* doesn't use my name, just "the gumshoe" a number of times. Ten, or more. A lot of folks chiming in, some saying they personally knew one of the Drifters or victims. Everett Brown's contributions, back when he made them, were mostly trying to piece together evidence from what was available on the internet—much of said "evidence" being wildly incorrect.

But this *Wizdumteller* is something different. I think.

Talking about "the WW"—whatever that is—and "the boogeyman" repeatedly. Almost longingly. Making cryptic claims and promises for years. And while they never have many direct replies on their posts, there are always hundreds of likes on them. The rare comment they do get, a *salute* emoji or an "amen." This person has a following of some kind, people who know who they are. Who put a "like" on everything they ever say, almost immediately. But this last post was the first time Wizdumteller said they knew another murder was coming. If we can interpret it that way. I don't know, could just be a crazy person who loves attention and trolling. But we need to find them, see if there's anything there. The fact that we *haven't* found them yet seems like something.

A door slams upstairs. Music starts to play, soft, low. I turn. The record arm has dropped, the vinyl starting to turn. Dolly Parton's voice carries through the room. *Here you come again.*

"Stop," I say, to the house. To the shadows. I can't lose focus, need to figure out—

"You don't have to face it alone," Marianne says. "I'm here with you, for all of it."

"Hey," I say. "I'm serious."

Marianne kneeling on the floor before me in the living room. The nightmares so bad I hardly slept. Remembering what happened in the motel, seeing it again, nightmares where my dad came and found me here, did to Marianne and Noel and me what he did to my mom. Nightmares where the shadow people came into my room and stood over me and grabbed me and suffocated me, and—

I blink, hard. Try to pull back to the present. "I said stop it," I say. But I am here and not here, the house bending time, pulling me—

Every night, the music. No matter what I did. John Denver's voice in my room. Marianne read me this story about a very brave cowboy who faces his fears. So one night, when the shadows were everywhere and the music was so loud I could hardly breathe, I went downstairs where she was reading by the fire, and I said, "I don't want to be scared of the music anymore."

"Please—" I say. "I can't—"

But I'm there. I remember it.

She sat with me, and we went through record after record. All the country music records in the house, playing them in the living room, me crying and shaking and Marianne holding me so tight. All except John Denver. Not him. More than once she said it was enough, thought we should stop. But I said we had to keep going. We stayed up all night, did it again the next night, and Noel joined us, sat on the floor, and brought hot chocolate over.

Again and again, we sat in this room, listened to the songs that Rose and I used to play, until the crying got a little better, I shook a little less. Until I could eat a snack while we were listening, until I could play with my toy horses and sometimes read and sometimes even fall asleep leaning on one of my parents. Until it didn't terrify me. After a while, Marianne decided we'd learn to "cowboy dance." Rose and I had danced a couple times at the Happy Inn. But it was nice, to really learn. We took lessons, Marianne and me, and we learned to two-step and cowboy waltz, and we'd sometimes do it here in the living room while Noel laughed and cheered us on, told stories from when he was my age. I even took rodeo swing classes and taught Josie a few of those moves when we got together years later.

The lights glow, the music getting louder. I can't pull myself back to the present.

I was a teenager, and Marianne looked at me and said, "You scared us, you know. We had no idea if we were helping or making things so much worse. But then, we started to look forward to the evenings with you, the sun setting over the mountains, the record spinning, eating dinner on the floor. Willie, Waylon, Dolly, Hank, Lee Hazlewood, John Prine, all of them. I loved getting to experience it all with you. You are such a great adventure, Daniel."

Marianne and Noel bringing me back to life, Josie the final eventual piece.

I fell in love with music again, with dancing, with life.

And then.

Sitting in the mudroom with a box of funeral handouts. The closets, the pantry, refrigerator, washing machine full. Everything full and ready to move forward as always.

But they were gone. And I haven't put on a record since.

They're gone.

The files on the floor in front of me, blurred in my vision.

I can't understand how any of us are supposed to find the will to carry on when carrying on just means surviving, and surviving just means somehow keeping your lungs breathing and your heart beating through every loss, through every heartbreak. Surviving means just staying here longer to feel it more. Again and again, losing everyone you love. Until you're the one someone else is mourning.

"Here You Come Again" playing, a song Marianne and I danced to a hundred times before, that Rose loved before that.

I'm on my feet. I don't want this music, I don't want these memories. This stupid fucking machine spinning this thing round and round, and this house that has never cared what I want, that has tortured me from the moment I first stepped through its doors, if in nothing else that it brought me more happiness than I ever deserved and then ripped it all away.

I remove the record from the turntable, slip it back in its sleeve, and shove it on the shelf.

Upstairs, another thump, footsteps, running now. A crash.

I swear, take the stairs up two at a time, my heart racing again, racing as always, and I follow the steps to the end of the hall. The lights glowing up here. Pulsing, on and off.

A slow creak as the door at the end of the hall opens.

The room with the trunk in it. Three doors down and across the hall from my childhood room. Always the one with the most of this stuff going on. Sounds of feet going in and out all night, whispers. Marianne and Noel of course never heard it.

I go to my room, the one I still haven't slept in since I've been back, and grab a key from the desk drawer. I cross the hall, the lights glowing, dim. I get to the room with the trunk. The trunk with all the lives of all the former owners of the house until my parents. The one I still haven't opened and haven't transferred their things into.

The lights glow in here too, over the antique four-poster bed, side tables, armoire. The trunk, large enough for me to lie down in if I wanted to. The whole place buzzing.

There's something on the bed.

I take a step forward, and another. Someone's left a book here, or actually two. My mom's old paperback copy and the plastic-wrapped first edition Noel later got me.

Both of them *The Shining*.

I've never opened either, never read it. I watched the movie once, but it was hard for me to get through, given . . . everything. I forgot I put them here, after the funeral. Not sure what I thought, maybe that even if I couldn't bring myself to open the trunk, maybe I could make some kind of offering. Or maybe I just couldn't look at them anymore.

"We are not doing this," I say again.

I leave the room and lock the door behind me.

Downstairs, the record is somehow back on the turntable, spinning. Dolly's voice carries through the house. The fire pops in the hearth. Another murder could be coming any day now. We're probably running on borrowed time. All these names. These relationships, histories, connections . . . I just have to make the right one. All these files before me, and I know there's something I'm missing. Something right in front of me.

There's got to be something.

Files, bite marks, maps, notes, photos. All of us caught up in this thing, spinning round and round like the record under the needle.

I open the files and get back to work.

12

I'm standing on a mountain pass, wearing cowboy boots, my nice jeans, a pearl snap, my cowboy hat. All black. A red bolo. The sun glints off the snow on the granite ridgeline, the Rockies surrounding me on all sides. The wind blows, harsh, and cold. Lee Hazlewood plays, from somewhere. Everywhere. Echoing up from the sheer canyons to the mountaintops. "Your Sweet Love."

The sky an impossible blue, the craggy granite ridgeline rising and falling around me. The clouds hovering below. It's just the peaks and ridges up here. Just the sky and me.

I look out over the great windy cold expanse, and I feel . . .

Something warm, solid, in front of me. I turn back.

Hannah Lawrence is here, a foot away.

The wind whips her hair over her face. She's wearing a red dress with little orange and yellow flowers on it. There are no bruises on her.

She's so beautiful, eyes bright, cheeks and nose a little red from the cold. It hurts, looking at her. Too much feeling. Makes no sense. She's—

"You gonna ask me to dance?" she says.

She doesn't wait for me to answer, takes a step forward.

She steps in close, and I don't think. I just reach out. I take her in my arms. The only heat up here, her and me.

She smells like ponderosa pine. She smells like something I've dreamt of before. Dreamt her before. Is that possible?

And we're turning, turning, together.

I've never seen anything so beautiful as this view, these mountains.

I've never felt anything like . . . *Her.* In my arms.

She feels . . .

Hannah Lawrence.

She tilts her face up to me, those light green eyes on mine. "Do you get it yet? Can you see?"

I shake my head. Her eyes, her mouth, the tilt up at the corner of her lips. The feel of her in my arms. The wind ruffling our clothes, chilling our skin. I can't think, looking at her. Feeling her.

Her body pressed to mine. We stop turning.

Hannah Lawrence and me on a mountaintop.

She leans forward, stretches up on her toes. Her cheek brushing against mine.

Her lips so close to my ear I can nearly feel them, her breath on my skin.

"It's so simple," she whispers. Her hand presses to my chest, slides up my neck, to the side of my face. She leans in closer, her lips brushing my ear. "It's right in front of your—"

I don't hear her. As I notice the fabric of her dress.

The wind whips hard against us, threatening my balance. My stomach turns over.

It's not flowers on her dress.

It's tiny clown faces.

Free Smile with Every Stay at the Happy Inn.

Hannah, whispering in my ear.

Dizzy, nausea, confusion, cold, want—

Hannah, holding me tighter. Hannah, who won't let me go.

A wolf howls in the distance.

Do you get it yet?

Do you get it?

Three forty-five AM. I'm in the car, headed out toward Morrison. It's dark. Headlights, in front of me on the road, nothing else.

Mom, Dad, motel, Whileago Manor, Bagram, motel, blood, shadows, motel,

Hannah Lawrence.

Her body in my arms. Her breath against my ear.

Do you get it yet?

Waking up in a sweat. Dizzy. The dream, all the files.

Hypnagogia—hypnagogic and hypnopompic hallucinations.

Images, movements, sounds, shapes, upon waking, falling asleep. They come with sleep disorders, which come with PTS. Shadows might stalk you, do anything they want because they move freely and you are a mortal human, and you're paralyzed in your sleep.

But if the shadows come when you're fully awake, the hallucinations, then they don't call it hypnagogia. They call it psychosis because you've lost your fucking mind.

You've lost your mind, and *you're just like him,*

just like him, up in his jail cell, your mom's blood on his hands, his eyes in the mirror, his eyes, your eyes, you're

just like—

The old paperback on the bed. My mom annotating as she read.

"All work and no play makes—"

A figure stands in the middle of the road, in my headlights.

I slam on the brakes and swerve.

The sun rises, orange-red fingers crawling over the grass, the concrete and road, the wooden stands of Red Rocks. I run the stadium. The giant rocks on either side of it and down below, the stadium built right into them so that you feel simultaneously high up and sunken into somewhere safe.

Broad steps, legs pushing, arms pumping, thinking about Everett Brown and *Wizdumteller* and Hannah Lawrence and every victim. My breath puffing out in front of my face, as freezing day comes to claim Colorado. The temperature plummeted in the night, but no snow yet. My lungs burn, muscles ache, and I push because I am losing it here, and I need to hold it together. I push because I have to do something.

Making myself drive the road my parents died on.

That shadow in the headlights.

I trip over my feet, just catch myself before my face hits the wood and concrete in front of me. I turn, take a seat and catch my breath, look out over the amphitheater, the early morning sun, rising over the rocks.

"Hey."

I jump, reach for my gun that isn't there.

"Whoa there, soldier, didn't mean to scare you."

The sun is here now, and Josie stands before me in the light. "Thought I might find you here," she says. "Been lookin' for ya."

I lean back on my elbows, then lie all the way down, look up into the indifferent blue, catching my breath.

"Daniel, it's okay. It's okay, you're here."

Cold air, wood under my thighs, behind my knees, sweat on the side of my face, Josie's hand on my arm. She breathes with me, sits and stays and breathes. I don't know for how long, but my heart slows. I get it to slow. Josie exhales and says, "Shit, Stansfield."

I sit up and clear my throat, run my hands over my face.

"How bad is it?" she asks.

"Me missing you?" I say, trying to bring some lightness in. Trying to joke.

"You don't miss me."

She's wearing my old sweatshirt, a green USMC hoodie, beneath her outer jacket. "Tillman like you wearing that?" I ask.

She looks down at it and then back up at me. "Tillman's very open-minded," she says. A deer feeds in the grass to the side of the risers. A hawk soars overhead. "But . . . you know, I might have told him I thrifted it."

"I do," I say. "Miss you. And you haven't been lookin'. I've been at Whileago."

"I went there, last night. You weren't there."

"Oh. Jack's house," I say.

She nods. "They hate me?"

"'Course not."

She looks at me sidelong.

"I mean . . . they like me more."

She stares at me a moment, and I don't know what to read there. Then she softens, a little. "Remember Austin?"

Of course I do. On a whim after our wedding, we took a drive down to Texas and alternated dancing at the White Horse and playing pool at Casino. Always my hand in her back pocket or her head on my shoulder, always the two of us leaning on each other. We'd stayed up all night, talking about cases from the past. We never stopped, never turned it off, even on our honeymoon, this job of ours. This job that is everything we are.

"Do you . . . you think it's all gone?" I ask.

She stares at the ground again. "Maybe there were times when I didn't want it to be. I thought you'd call. When you left. In those early days, I thought maybe I'd hear from you."

"I thought you didn't want to. We were divorced."

She pulls the sleeves of the sweatshirt down over her hands, trying to figure out how to say what she wants to, bites the inside of her cheek. I don't know what I'm hoping for.

"Nat and I don't talk about work, at home," she says. "We . . . To him, the job matters, and it's important. But it's not his whole life, it's not who he is." The words hang around us in the morning air. What she's not saying, what she means, is *he's not like us*.

I nod. Because what else is there? Neither of us can turn it off, neither of us want to. But she gets a reprieve now, with him. Josie and me leaning and leaning on each other for so many years. Maybe she just wanted someone who didn't need to lean back.

"How's your case?" I ask, swallowing the lump in my throat.

She shrugs, takes a sip from her thermos. "Drawn out, stressful," she says.

"Why do we do this job again?"

I think it'll make her smile, but it doesn't. She furrows her brow. I know the look, and I know by now that it's about me.

I say, "I'm fine. Just had a bad night. It's just . . . Whileago."

She looks me up and down, then faces back out. The amphitheater before us, the stage at the bottom, and the giant rocks and hills beyond. "It's not though. Daniel, you gotta tell Jack. You shouldn't be working this case. These are major offenses you're committing, not to mention that it's fucking you up, and you're too close to it all. You're not gonna get anywhere when you're so deep in it, and frankly, it's gonna look real fuckin' suspicious when—"

I put my hand on her knee, and she stops talking. She turns to me, and I can see it all there. All the belief she ever had in me washed away. But it brings me back too. I'm here again, solid. Here on the bleachers sitting next to a woman I used to trust. Who used to trust me. A woman who I know in this moment it's completely over with, who I will never lean on again.

I know it now, here, in this bright cold morning. I have a lot of faults and a lot of messed-up tendencies and enough baggage for a hundred people.

But she's forgotten what I'm capable of.

"I'm solving this case, Josie," I say. Because there's no other choice. "And you're not gonna interfere."

And I do something I've become very good at.

I stand up and walk away.

As I drive back to Denver, I think about the figure in the headlights. The one I saw on the way here. The shadow that turned and became a person, in the same spot the truck hit us. Marianne, Noel, and me.

The shadow that became Calvin Keller.

My dad.

Or maybe it was me.

13

Everett and Mona Brown's house sits in the middle of the Rock Creek development up in Erie, in various shades of brown and beige, like all the other homes surrounding it. An elaborate security gate bars our entry until we're cleared by three different guards on the way in.

"A little intense," Tillman says.

Security cameras watch us, turn as we drive. Every house looks completely identical. We pass each one, and it feels like we're driving further into an endless state of déjà vu.

"When did this place crop up?" I ask.

Tillman shrugs. "So many of 'em, I can't keep up."

I wouldn't say that Denver was ever a pretty place to me. The mountains around it are beautiful, the towns in them and the trails there some of the most impressive in the world. But these plains that just happen to butt up against the mountains, live directly in their shadow, are just . . . that. Dust. Settlements. Strip malls and soccer fields and a big REI. Plains trying to claim something of the mountains beside them.

"Do you know the population these days?" It seems like a thing Tillman would know. Today's podcast topic is *tommy-knockers* purportedly haunting Colorado mines.

"Seven hundred thousand, give or take," he says immediately.

I remember when I was a kid. Teachers telling us Denver's population was under five hundred thousand. Who are all these people? Where did they all come from? And why are they settling here? House after house, yard after yard. Matching. All of it slipping, sliding, blurring at the edges.

We pull up out front, and I turn the car off. I say, "Anything on Everett's involvement in the chat room and relationship with *Wizdumteller*. And the motel too, ask her if she's stayed there before or if that location has any significance to her. And if she knows Hannah Lawrence or Tony Howell or ever heard Everett talking about them."

Tillman takes a slow breath and shrugs his shoulders up and down, shaking his arms out. He then turns to me and says, "My dude. I respect you, and I know this has gotta be real unfun for ya. In a lot of ways probably. Like a lot of ways. I mean, I can really see how it really sucks. But I'll tell ya one thing, and I hope you hear it because we're gonna be doin' this until we figure this whole thing out, and I think it could just be a whole lot more pleasant for us if maybe you get this through your head now."

He pulls down the mirror and checks his teeth, runs his hands over his hair, puts the mirror back up. He slaps his palms down on his thighs and turns back to me again. "I didn't get promoted for nothin'," he says, and steps out of the car.

In the doorway of the house, Mona Brown, a small woman wearing a white linen dress, her hair pulled into a messy bun, greets Tillman, and then I hear him say, "You cooking something? Smells amazing!"

She eyes me over his shoulder, stares at me a long minute, then seems to hear what Tillman said. She gives him a small smile and shuts the door behind them.

I text Tillman: See if Mona knows any of the former victims or killers too.

Tillman replies almost right away.

My dude.

Out the car window, this strange bland development that Oliver Wright built, with all its beefed-up security. I open the map on my phone and find which direction to go for Sagebrush.

I step out of the car and walk. It's cold. That strange Denver November light that's simultaneously too bright and somehow also dark feeling. House after house, Everett Brown's words repeating through my ears. No wonder he gets philosophical here. All these developments, growing, spreading, slowly taking over the prairie grasslands and even extending out toward the mountains. Being in this development, it almost feels as though it will keep going forever. As though in one blink, all of America will be brown and beige houses, brown and beige developments, brown and beige security gates and Starbucks and Jiffy Lubes and HomeGoods, and all of it will go on and on through the Great Plains and past them, until there's no wild lands anymore. Until it feels like there never were any to begin with.

An airplane flies overhead, slowly lowers toward the airport in the far distance. Guarded by Blucifer. I haven't thought of him in a while. Luis Jiménez was the artist who created the bucking blue bronco at the entrance to our city with the orange—really red—glowing eyes, to be the first welcome when someone touches down. The airport has a million secrets, people say. Secret tunnels, doomsday mosaics, two billion dollars unaccounted for publicly. Gargoyle sculptures, hidden corridors, lizard people. The internet's gone so wild with it all, the airport marketing team has started to lean in and now decorates and advertises it with all sorts of paranormal and conspiracy things.

Marianne used to read biographies on artists of all kinds—writers, sculptors, painters, dancers, filmmakers—and she used to say, *All great art has a cost.* Blucifer fell on Jiménez as he finished it. The crown jewel of Denver, claiming its maker's life. What about a place like this? What is the *cost* of erecting hundreds or even thousands of nearly identical homes? Of spreading this city deeper and wider and out in all directions? And who pays it?

Human dwellings, places to sleep, places to pay bills and watch television and exercise and cook and eat and fuck and bathe and read and dream and want and fear and scroll on our phones and hold loved ones and sit alone in the blue glow of a screen and clean and dirty and clean and dirty until we don't anymore. Until we die, like everyone else. Like we always knew we would.

Everett Brown, walking these identical streets, looking into these identical houses, ruminating on the same shit I am now, and more. Everett Brown taking steps and breaths outside that he had no idea would be some of his last as a free man. I stop walking, my gut telling me to. I look around, see if I can sense anything. I don't—

But then I glance down.

A chalk drawing on the sidewalk, right in front of my feet, of . . . what? Some kind of creature. Maybe an elk's head on a human body, but longer, spindly almost. Long pronged horns. Maybe. It's been smudged, blurred a little. Where have I seen this?

At the brewery. A kid was drawing this. Or something like it. Strange.

Above the creature, a zigzag that kind of looks like . . .

That pressure in the air.

Wizdumteller in the chat room. That thing they kept repeating.

What will the WW think of this? What will the WW do next?

Above the smudged creature are eight lines that almost seem to say "WW."

I straighten, look around. A woman sits on the front porch of the house I stand in front of, scrolling on her phone. Her front door is open. I walk up her front walk, and she realizes I'm heading her way, and stands.

"Can I help you?" she asks. She looks to be about my age, in workout clothes, a puffer, gloves, and baseball hat. A bag sits beside her on the porch, and a kid's bicycle is out front on the lawn. Waiting for a child to come out, go to school or sports practice or something.

"Hey," I say. "Sorry if this is weird, but . . . there's a chalk drawing here on the sidewalk. Do you know who did it?"

Her brow furrows, and she holds her hand above her eyes to see me better in the late fall sun. "Yeah." She glances inside, closes her front door, then crosses the front walk to meet me. I introduce myself, tell her I'm just visiting.

After a minute, she says, "I keep telling her not to—my daughter, she's into scary stuff. Watches horror movies with her dad. I keep telling her it's gonna scare the neighbors, drawing this stuff. But these neighborhood kids like to make up stories, scare each other."

"The kids here made this creature up?"

"I think so. Or maybe the ones at school. Hard to tell where these things come from, they always spread so fast."

"What is it?" I ask.

"Oh. Um, it's just a silly thing."

"Does it have a name?"

She looks uncomfortable, like she doesn't want to answer. "It's not real," she says. "Obviously."

I wait.

And finally, she sighs, a little girl stepping out the front door behind her.

"They call it a Witchwalker."

14

We pull out of Rock Creek listening to another paranormal podcast. Tillman's eyes fixed on the skies.

I say, "Have you heard of something called a Witchwalker?"

He blinks. "No, what is that?"

"Oh, um . . . maybe like. What do you know about, uh, creatures. Like paranormal—"

"Cryptids?" he says.

"Yeah, maybe. What do you know about those?"

Tillman turns to me, incredulous. "Are you telling me that Daniel Stansfield is asking about a paranormal phenomenon? On day three? I was thinkin' it was gonna take at least—"

"Tillman."

"Sheesh, buddy, okay. All jokes aside, it's a big topic. Lots of different kinds, you know?"

"Well, what *are* they?"

"What are cryptids? I think the overarching definition would probably be creatures whose existence isn't totally substantiated. You know, like, Bigfoot, Mothman. There are different schools of thought, but what I personally believe is that cryptids are creatures who are trapped between worlds. Or who accidentally stumbled into ours from theirs. And that's why we can't see 'em all the time."

"Otherworld creatures."

"Yeah. And we're just so fixed and linear in our thought processes we really can't get our brains around it, but I think there's more here than just *here*. And if there are multiple universes or realities kind of occupying the same space or sitting on top of each other, maybe sometimes a hole gets torn, or a piece gets worn down, and then . . . things are just open and start to move freely between worlds that otherwise wouldn't."

I take a long breath, blow it out as we pass fast food chains, grocery chains, fitness chains. Red, brown, beige. This was a stupid train of thought, stupid question.

"Is it possible they're just . . . not real?"

"'Course. But why are you asking?"

"What did Mona Brown say?" I ask. I see Tillman debate pressing the topic.

Instead, he leans against the passenger door to get a better upward view of the sky. "You went and interviewed Everett after I did," he says.

No use denying what he already knows. "Yeah," I say.

He nods. "I don't wanna jump to conclusions, we should check the chat room transcripts again. But . . . I think I know why he's lying about logging in."

"Why? What did she say?"

"I should rephrase. I suspect that Everett doesn't know he is lying. *CanisLoopus* has been logging in to those chat rooms and putting a like on every post by *Wizdumteller* for years. But I think it's her. Mona logging on for a long time in Everett's place. And I don't think she knows who *Wizdumteller* is, but I think she's kind of . . . in love with them. Something like that."

"In love with them."

"Yeah, I mean. You'll hear it. Worshipful, maybe."

"Hm."

"You know, the sort of *can't stop thinkin' about you, keeps me up all night* kind of tone. You know? Like . . . reverent. Obsessed."

I keep myself from tensing at that word. Obsessed. Don't know why I want to.

Hannah Lawrence's card in my pocket.

Hannah Lawrence in my dream.

I clear my throat, shift in my seat.

"She's gonna leave Everett, I think," Tillman says.

"How'd you get that?"

"She said she's been wanting a fresh start for a while. This was the final straw I guess."

"Did she admit to logging on in Everett's place in the chat room?" I ask.

He tilts his head from side to side in a way that means *kind of.*

"You can listen to the recording," he says. "But I think figuring out who *Wizdumteller* is is where we put our attention. Maybe Oliver Wright too. They're both influential. Might have the means to get people to do things for them. I mean, shit, they could be the same person."

"But she didn't give any sort of indication that she knows who it is? No direction for where to start?"

He looks up again, then back to the road. "My brother's an actor," he says. "Lives out in New York, does plays, the whole thing. And he told me there's this school of thought that instead of being *focused* on something—say, your scene partner—you should have your *attention open*. Because when you're focused on something, you're limiting what you can see. But if you have your attention open, you pick up on all these other things you wouldn't catch otherwise. And I don't really understand acting, but when he said it, it made me think of UFOs. You let yourself be open, have your *attention* on the sky, rather than *focusing* on wanting to see something. You just sort of tune in to this open field, this specific frequency, and just observe. That's when you see things you can't see otherwise."

"You're saying we shouldn't concentrate on solving this case, we should just let it . . . *appear* to us?"

He smiles at me, shrugs. "Maybe I'm just sayin' a lot of words that don't mean anything. You know, I know you don't wanna talk about it, but given that we both fell in love with the same woman, it stands to reason that we might have some other things in common. Maybe—"

My phone rings, and I mumble a *thank fucking god.*

"This is Oliver Wright's office returning your call," a voice says on the other end. "He can squeeze you in, but you'll have to come now."

Six years ago, Oliver Wright was driving with his teenage daughter, Claire, when he got a flat tire. They pulled over at a gas station. It was dark, and there was a field behind the building. Claire wandered behind the car, and she just disappeared. CCTV cut out for exactly one second, showing her there and then gone when it came back online. There was no sign of Claire Wright anywhere until the first Drifter appeared on the side of the highway twelve hours later carrying her skin.

Oliver sued the gas station company for negligence on the security camera and gave us hell trying to speed up prosecution of the Drifter who took his daughter's life. His name was Jake Evers, a fifty-two-year-old EMT, husband, father of two, and he killed himself in jail about a month after he was detained. Wright has been doggedly pressuring juries, media, and every decision-maker to keep the Drifters in jail ever since. On the one year anniversary of Claire's murder, Amber Wright, Oliver's wife and Claire's mother, overdosed.

We pull into the WrightStar complex and are greeted by a fastidious young man with a clipboard and in-ear Bluetooth after driving through the gate into the lot. "Mr. Wright has twenty minutes between appointments. Continue straight, park beyond Building C, and walk to the left."

"Thanks. Um, we didn't catch your name."

"Twenty minutes," he says, and walks away.

We find Oliver Wright sitting at a lone picnic table at the edge of a field. Slumped over a sandwich in a suit, not touching it, just staring down at it as if he doesn't know what to do with the thing. When he hears our footsteps, he straightens, turns to face us, but doesn't stand.

"Been a while," he says. "Come back to be *useful* again?"

"I'm not sure if you remember me. I'm Daniel Stansfield," I say. "This is Nat Tillman."

He runs a hand through his hair. "I'm not a fucking idiot, Stansfield. I remember you."

"Well, it's been a while, so . . . nice to see you again," I say.

"Yeah, you're right, the time my daughter was skinned alive and left in a ditch wasn't super memorable for me," Oliver says. "Thanks for jogging my memory."

"Do you mind if we sit?" I ask.

"Why are you here? Do you think I could possibly have any answers for you?"

"Do you by any chance know a man by the name of Everett Brown?" I ask.

No recognition. Just that anger, that deep furious grief.

"What about Mona Brown, Tony Howell?"

"I meet hundreds of people every month. But I don't remember them if I did."

I read the whole list, Pete Noland, Ramona Lopez, Kimberly Chen, and her victim, Ross Thompson. Hannah Lawrence. The last name gets caught momentarily in my throat.

Again, his stare. I don't think he's registered my words at all.

"Do you remember where you were the night of November tenth?"

"That was my gala."

"Your gala?"

"To raise more funds for construction."

"Oh?"

He waves his hand. "I just started again. Felt like there was no point, for a long time. Then . . . it occurred to me—maybe I could prevent this from happening to other families. Change up some of my site plans, ramp up security and safety in the existing developments, build even higher security systems in the new ones. Just a safe walk to school. Safe houses. Make sure these families won't have to go through what I did."

He works his jaw for a moment, and then takes a breath. I watch as he forces himself to pick up his sandwich and take a bite. A picture of him forms. Doing this every day. Sitting and staring out over the field alone, forcing himself to chew.

"You just started up construction again?" I ask.

Oliver nods, swallows. "Few weeks ago." A shadow moves in the field. "Been outfitting existing housing and school developments with the higher security for the last six months or so. But few weeks ago broke ground on new projects. Or more accurately projects that I stalled for years after Claire and Amber."

"Interesting you don't have security here. With all these materials," Tillman says. "Especially with all the guards and gates you have out in your housing developments."

"That's for *people*. Kids. What do I care about a bunch of fuckin' lumber and stone?"

"Pretty valuable, with how much you have. Lumber prices what they are."

Oliver looks at Tillman while he chews as though he is the biggest idiot to have ever walked the planet. I can't really blame him.

"Insurance would cover it I'm sure," he says. "Someone wants to try and take it, let 'em. It's just material. Anyway, I got so many people workin' overtime now trying to get these new projects off the ground, place is hardly ever left empty."

"We're here because a property you own, off I-25 South, was the site of a recent murder," I say.

"Oh. The motel."

"Yes. You know what happened there?"

"Yeah, they told me."

"Interesting your legal teams haven't shored up your affairs in response to it. Seems like there could be some liability issues, this happening on your property."

He laughs, takes another disgusted bite of his sandwich. "Believe me, they were on it, but I pulled them from it. Waste of time."

"What's a better use?"

"Pressuring politicians to do their fuckin' jobs so people's fuckin' kids don't get killed."

"Your lawyers were fine reallocating their efforts?"

"I pay them, they do what I tell them to. And I own the property, but it's on a forty-year lease to that couple who run it. I've never even set foot out there. You can talk to my account manager."

Tillman says, "Where were you the night of November sixteenth?"

"Fuck you."

Oliver Wright looks at Tillman now with such rage I think he might try to kill him. Tillman knew the dates. I know he did. He's trying to get a reaction out of Wright. It's a little reckless. I set my hand on my gun.

Wright's eyes catch the movement, and he glares at me. He turns back to Tillman and says, "Do your fuckin' homework if you're gonna come here. You people are a goddamned joke."

After a moment, Tillman says, "That wasn't an answer."

I start to say something when Wright drops his sandwich and levels Tillman with a cold cruel look that is probably the reason he's gotten as far as he has in life. His eyes cut to me, and he says, "You should fire this asshole, save everyone a lotta trouble." To Tillman he says, "That's the night my daughter was murdered. And the same fuckin' day, a year later, that my wife died. All her pills from all the doctors. I was in the same place I am every year. And you people being so fucking terrible at your jobs is the reason this town needs gates and guards and cameras that fucking work. 'Cause the cops and the feds don't do shit." He picks up the sandwich, throws it back down. Turns and looks out at the field.

After a minute, Oliver says, "That's where it happened." I follow the line of his eyes, see Tillman do the same. At the end of the field is a closed-down gas station. "That's the last place I saw my girl. The last time I ever heard her voice. She wanted to go shopping for some dress for a school dance, I wasn't even really listening. Wasn't really listening, and it ended up being the last conversation I ever got to have with her.

"Every day I sit here for my lunch, and I stare out at this field, and I think that if I want it bad enough, if I wish fuckin' hard enough, she'll appear back here, just as she was when she left. If I sit here long enough, I'll have my little girl back. And my wife. And on that one day each year, I go and sit on that side of the field, and I wait."

A bird calls somewhere above. Machinery whirs in the background, men yelling to each other, all the sounds of work and day.

When I speak, I keep my voice even. I say, "Why did you buy that plot of land? The one with the motel?"

Oliver Wright looks back at me, and I can't read his expression at all. I wonder if he's even really here. A shadow moves through the field, closer and closer to us.

"I built and own a third of this town. You ask me why each and every piece of land, answer nine times out of ten is that it was a good site for development or investment. I don't do the research, I don't draw up the proposals, I got guys who do that, and then I give a yes or no."

Tillman clears his throat, and Wright gives him an incredulous look, as though the idea of him speaking again is the most preposterous one he can think of.

"Nine times out of ten," Tillman says, and Wright stares at him. His assistant is walking toward us now, speaking in the Bluetooth, holding the clipboard tight to his body as he run-walks over the gravel. “What about the tenth time?” Tillman asks.

“What?”

“The tenth time in those scenarios. What makes you pick your specific plots then?”

Wright stands from the table, giving Tillman one last furious glance.

“Tenth time, it’s ’cause I fuckin’ want to.”

15

I drop Tillman off back at the office, and Josie's standing there waiting for us when we arrive. Tillman steps out of my car and jogs over to her, picks her up, and twirls her in a kiss. He sets her down, closes himself into the driver's seat, and leans out to look up at the sky. Josie says something to him, then turns to me. Holds up her hand telling me to wait. She pulls a duffel bag from the trunk and my old cowboy hat, carries them both over to me.

"Here," she says, handing me the bag through my window. "Some of your old stuff."

She steps in closer and says, "Daniel, please just talk to me. You need to excuse yourself from this. You know you do."

I take the bag from her, and the hat, and toss them in the back seat.

"I don't think you know what I need," I say.

She stares at me, shakes her head, and walks back to her car. Slams herself inside.

South of Denver, near the giant Cabela's and the hospital that now sit just up the highway from the Happy/Wander Inn, is a new restaurant overlooking I-25 and all the surrounding new developments. A higher-end establishment than has ever been here before. Steel beams, brick, and glass perched on the side of the hill, a glass wall in front of me looking over the highway, the land around it. All the new identical houses. The lowering sun casts its orange glow over the sea of brown rooves, the perpetual sprawl.

I think of Oliver Wright. He's got every resource, maybe he could coerce the Drifters into killing, promise them massive payouts, pull their families out of debt or ensure healthcare or who knows what.

But twice now—in Mama Tried and in the Happy Inn—this

thing has seemingly targeted me specifically. Could it be because I was assigned to the Drifter murder investigation and didn't save his daughter in time the night she was taken? But I was assigned to the case long after her body was found and after the next murder had taken place. It was a DPD issue before we deemed it serial, and FBI wasn't a part of it. And why the pageantry of Hannah and the motel?

I sit down at a brown leather and redbrick booth in the brown leather and redbrick restaurant. The place seems to say, we are cattlemen, and we talk around oil deals in our ostrich boots over dishes that probably all have meat in them even if it doesn't say it on the menu. I ask the waitress for a beer and whatever food she thinks is best here. A shadow comes to the table with her, waits close behind as she writes down my order. I look up, and my eyes catch on the round metal industrial candelabras. They almost look like giant leghold animal traps.

I search to see if Oliver Wright owns this property too, and all I can find is another LLC. All these people who have everything, finding loopholes and ways to own it all, to hold no liability and pay taxes like they own none of it. I think of Everett Brown, walking around Rock Creek. What is it to own anything when we die after eighty years and it just goes to someone else? We're renting it for the duration of our time here. Pretending that we can *own* land. As if it wasn't here millions of years before us and won't be here millions of years after. As if we're not all living on borrowed time. No matter how much concrete and brick we pour on it.

I get a message from Frazier. Pete Noland's girlfriend, Lucy Wheely, has been calling us nonstop. Says Pete was the only person taking care of his grandmother, wants someone to go make sure she's okay. Sorry. She's been really persistent.

I text back. Send me the info I'll take care of it.

The waitress sets a plate and a glass down in front of me, and I thank her. She's given me barbecue ribs and some sides. I take a sip of the beer and look out over I-25, try to remember if I can recall being on this stretch of the highway. We would have driven it so many times, Rose and me, going between the Happy Inn and the city.

Mom on the rock in the river, unpacking our picnic.

I love you, my Danny boy. You know that, right? You know how much I love you?

I blink. What is this memory? Where were we? Why is it—

I take a breath, press my palms to my eyes. Am I just hallucinating things now that never happened?

I pick up a rib and make myself take a bite. They're beef ribs, thick. It takes a big bite to get through. Everett and Mona Brown and the chat room, *Wizdumteller.* All the killers, all the victims. How could any one of them know about my life before? Why would they *care*?

The resignation on Everett's face, the pain on Pete Noland's. My stomach turns, and I set the food down. Pete Noland sitting alone in a cell shit-terrified about his grandmother, about everything. Kimberly Chen in another one no longer able to call her brother every night. To be with her cat.

Claire Wright murdered in the most brutal way possible at fourteen years old. Oliver left alone having to face every day with that understanding.

What I want is liquor. What I want is to never have come here at all. Denver, Whileago. If I remove myself, does it all stop? It started again when I was in Salt Lake, when I was about to leave for California. Was it because I was about to leave? Someone wanted to draw me back here, and now that they've got me . . . for what? What could they possibly want? And how could they have known what my plans were?

I take another deep breath. I gotta get home and listen to the recording of Tillman and Mona Brown's interview. See if there's anything salvageable from it. I text him, remind him to send it to me.

I call over the waitress for the check, that shadow following her, and she asks me if I want a box for the food. I automatically say yes, glance down at it.

And—

The meat on the rib.

The bite I've taken out of it. I stare, and gears start turning, ideas moving, memory, thought.

What's always bothered me about the photos of the bite marks. Those last two bodies before the hiatus, bite marks that showed a long string of meat to the right of the middle of the bite. As if one tooth just didn't sink in all the way. That one sliver of meat hanging on. A missing or broken canine. My bite here, clean.

I take another, look at it. Clean. Another. On another rib. Look at it.

Frank Wheely and the photos of the cows. *Wolf depredation.*

Teeth marks.

I know it doesn't mean anything, that we deemed it a dead end. And maybe I'm just grasping. Of course I am. But . . . the way the meat just hung on, just one or two bites where we could see it, on each of the last two bodies.

"Here you go, hon," the waitress says, putting the check and the box down in front of me. The shadow is now nearly wrapped around her.

16

Daphne isn't at Mama Tried, and she's not picking up her phone. I call the forensics lab, and they tell me she doesn't come in on Mondays. Then I remember, she volunteers weekly at the museum, down in the entomology lab.

I drive over to the Denver Museum of Nature and Science. Make some calls on the way to send a caretaker to Pete's grandmother's house. Call Frazier to ask the status of everything else. Text Tillman again to ask for the recording of his talk with Mona Brown.

I ask at the museum desk if I can go back to the lab, and they tell me visiting hours are limited there, but her shift ends soon, and they'll let her know I'm here. I get a museum ticket.

Too much spinning, circling, not connecting. Dancing and dancing through my fucking brain. I've always thought there might be something to the tooth, the canine, our early findings. To those bite marks. Why? Why can't I let it go?

I head through the main lobby, beneath dinosaur skeletons and whales, and take the first entrance to the first room. I used to come and visit as a kid. Noel and I would watch the IMAX movies on animals and weather and foreign landscapes. Get books after in the gift shop.

Gray carpet, dark ceilings with that particular spare but intentional museum lighting and built-in seats in the center for viewing all sides of the exhibit. And the large middle interactive map: EXPLORE COLORADO FROM PLAINS TO PEAKS. Beneath the sign, black and gold inlay in local granite, a 3D topographic map of the state. Buttons that can light up all eight Colorado ecosystems and show their distribution: RIPARIAN, ALPINE TUNDRA, MONTANE FOREST, SUBALPINE FOREST, MONTANE SHRUBLAND, SEMI-DESERT SHRUBLAND, GRASSLAND, PIÑON-JUNIPER WOODLAND. Others illuminate the Continental Divide and the highest and lowest elevation points in the state.

Surrounding the gray low-lit room on all sides are nearly daylight-illuminated dioramas of Colorado's ecosystems. The golden eagles in the grassland, the tarantula and tarantula hawk wasp locked in their eternal battle in the piñon-juniper woodland, marmots, kings of the alpine tundra, the tree line of the subalpine forest rich with willow, daisies, bistort, chipmunks, firs.

A father and son push the buttons that illuminate the different ecosystems on the center map, and I walk around the edges of the room, taking in each diorama, each ecosystem flourishing with flowers, weeds, trees, reptiles, mammals, birds, competition, symbiosis, life.

My chest hurts, my head. Colorado, here, displayed so reverently.

"If you've really been all around the world," I asked Noel once, "why'd you pick here?"

"Because," Noel said, "we've just always known this was home."

"But why?" I asked.

He said, "I think home is just a place that pulls on you harder than the rest."

Noel's hands on the buttons, illuminating the land.

"I'm more of a montane shrubland girl myself, but I see the appeal of piñon-juniper," Daphne says, nearly making me jump out of my skin.

I swear at the same time that she says, "Sorry. Forgot you startle easy."

Daphne is here. I calm down after a second. She waits. We stand together in front of the diorama, and I have no idea what to say.

I take her in. Glasses, a green button-down with a big pin on it that says FEAR NO WEEVIL, a backpack slung over her shoulder. She says, "Is there . . . something with the case?"

"Do you want to get dinner?" I ask.

She hesitates, watches me for a moment, glances over to a taxidermied pine marten in the flowers. Then she says, "Okay. But you're buying."

Linger Eatuary is Daphne's favorite restaurant. When we don't go to Mama Tried, we're always here. Formerly Olinger's Mortuary, which once held Buffalo Bill's remains, the warehouse-style brick building with the giant white neon cursive sign on top is an often-packed staple of Denver's restaurant scene, leaning in to their colorful history by serving some of their drinks in formaldehyde bottles. We carpool over in my car from the museum and park in the lot across the street. Inside, we're met with steel, iron, leather booths, and provocative large photographs. But Daphne and I walk straight to the elevator and take it up to the rooftop where we pass the enormous Olinger Mortuary–turned–Linger Eatuary sign and the old VW bus-turned-bar to the upper outdoor seating area looking over the city. The heat lamps are on in full force as we sit down at a table in front of the giant sign. It's cold, even with the heat lamps. She orders a drink I haven't heard of, and I get a whiskey.

"I looked for you at Mama Tried," I say.

"Oh. Yeah. Haven't been there in a while, actually."

"Really?" She used to go all the time, with Josie and me, with groups of us after work. Just her and me on a weekend to play darts and talk about life. We met on a case, and it was one of those instant friendships that just suddenly clicks into place like you'd always been meant for each other's lives. Sometimes we'd hang, the four of us, Josie, Daphne, Tess, and me.

She shrugs again.

I'm anxious, need to talk about the bite marks, but I need to be a decent friend for once too, something I maybe, hopefully, still know how to do.

"How's Tess?" I ask. I'd always liked her girlfriend.

Daphne's face darkens, and we're handed our drinks. "Cheers," she says.

"Cosmo?" I ask.

"Mocktail," she says. "I don't drink anymore. Three years in about a month."

"Wow," I say. "Congratulations." I think that's the appropriate response?

She snorts a laugh. "Thanks. It's been the right move for me."

"What prompted it? Or . . . if you don't want to—"

"Tess isn't—" She clears her throat. "We're not, um . . ."

"Oh," I say. "I'm sorry."

The waiter appears, and I lift the menu. I'm still not hungry, am about to say as much when Daphne says, "She died."

I lower the menu and look at her. The waiter pauses.

"It was sudden," Daphne says. "Some genetic thing we didn't know about. She died, and my life sucked. Really bad. And I drank too much, and that's why I . . . stopped. After a while."

"When?" I say. "When did she—"

"About a month after you left," she says.

"I'm gonna give you two a minute," the waiter says. I drop the menu to the table.

"Daphne, I'm so sorry. I didn't know. Why didn't you . . . ?"

She shrugs again. "You weren't here, and it was pretty clear you didn't want to be."

Fuck. "I'm sorry," I say again. How can I ever say it enough?

We talk about life. About everything I missed. About what a shit friend I am and how much I miss her, and Jack, and everything about life before it all fell apart. She gets cold, and I give her my jacket. It's not the same. I can feel that a part of her has shut me out, and may not ever let me back in. Has maybe shut the world out. But who could blame her?

"What's the latest?" she asks, and I know she means the case.

"Um, I have a thought," I say. "But I don't know if I'm crazy." I pull out my phone. "Look at this." I hand it over to her.

"I am looking at . . . meat."

"Right. Ribs, actually, just close up. I took a bite, and I saw it, and . . ."

"You're thinking of the teeth thing."

"Yeah. Why didn't we pursue that more? I always had a feeling about it. Or I mean . . . it always seemed like something to follow."

"Well, because it only definitively applied to some of the bodies, and because bite mark forensics are a pretty imprecise science at best."

"But did we ever call in to any dentists, or—"

"You mean start calling all the dentists in the greater Denver area and asking if they've got a client with one chipped or veneered canine?"

"No, I mean getting the dental records of each of the Drifters and then maybe going beyond if that doesn't yield anything."

"Yeah, if you want to pursue that, you can, but even if one of them matched, it's not enough to convict them. And they're *already* convicted, or at least detained indefinitely, the ones who haven't killed themselves. What you'd need is to see if anyone *else*'s teeth marks match, if some outside party lost or broke a canine right then—but that leads us back to how would you begin to narrow down a whole city, maybe a whole state, to someone who went in for dental work around that time. Assuming they would go to a dentist. Assuming we know that they had the tooth the whole time up to that point. Assuming it's all the same outside person who ate all the bodies, maybe the one who the hair belongs to, but it's just *assuming* so much that—"

I rub my hands over my face. "Yeah, I get it," I say. "Bad lead. Not a lead, I guess."

"Makes sense," she says. "Hoping. Sometimes life makes it hard. But it's good to do it."

I nod. "I'm so sorry, Daphne," I say.

She toys with her fork. "I look at dead people all day long, and I never really got it. Till Tess. Feels like someone turned off a light switch, and I'm just stumbling around in the dark trying to find it, to flip it back on. But it just . . . can't be flipped back. This thing, it just happens once and then it's done. Forever. It's so unimaginably cruel. And then you just think like, who could be shitty enough to flip it off in the first place? Who would ever do that? To find your person, that one person you want to spend your whole life with, who gets you and completes you, and then . . ."

The Linger Eatuary sign flickers, and everyone around us eats and laughs and talks and thinks and feels. This restaurant and this city and this state and this world. The dark of Denver night, hovering beyond the glow of this rooftop.

"Look," she says. "I don't mean to be . . . You know what, screw it, grief makes you just say stuff. If I'm being honest, I never thought Josie was your one. Like if there is a *one*, she just . . . I mean, she's great, but like. I don't know. She's always gotten the brighter parts of you, but there's a lot of you that's—"

"Dark?"

"Yeah. Kind of. It's not a bad thing. Some of us are just . . . We've just been places, is all. Or maybe we're just wired a way to begin with. But she and Tillman make sense to me. I think when you're ready you'll find someone new. Maybe someone you don't have to try and be like a *version* of yourself with. But just . . . you."

"I don't know," I say.

"I do. And when you find her—if you do—just . . . Seriously. I'm telling you." Her eyes fill with tears, but she keeps them on me. "Don't fucking let go."

I drive Daphne back to her car at the museum, and I get out and hug her goodnight. She lets me. I tell her she can give my jacket back another time. One more flimsy excuse to see each other, for me to try to make it all right. Make any of it right.

She steps back, puts her hands in the pockets, and pulls something out. "Do you need this?" she asks.

I look up. And I freeze.

Daphne is holding a six of spades playing card with a drawing of a fox on it.

A playing card that no one knows I took. From the wall Tillman and CSI photographed in Hannah Lawrence's cabin. Photos which would be in Hannah's file.

"Right," I say. "Yeah, thanks." I'm not breathing. Adrenaline rushing through me. It's not a huge deal. It shouldn't be. Right? I don't know. Tampering with a crime scene. Theft? More, probably.

Daphne watches me a very long moment and holds the card out. After another, I take it.

"It's good to see you, Daniel," she says, studying me like I'm one of her insects or cadavers. Like she's seeing so much more than I want her to.

Maybe too much has happened and we'll never get it back—this, us—maybe life just takes so much from a person sometimes, there's hardly any person left at all. Or maybe she knows me too well and can see all the ways I'm slipping.

I wait until she drives off, standing in the dark of the museum parking lot, the playing card in my hand for all the world to see. My fingers sliding over the silky edges of it.

The air feels different. Everything a little tighter.

Somewhere close by, coyotes yip and cackle. It sounds like it comes from everywhere at once, echoing, crackling. Static and pressure and cold. And I don't know how I know it, I can't explain, but I feel a shift in the air, a tension between atoms.

A rumble of something in the near distance, closing in.

Heading straight toward me.

17

I get in the car just as we receive an email with the security footage we requested from Rock Creek subdivision security. The video shows Everett Brown walking exactly where he said he was on Sagebrush. Walking, looking into people's yards. He's standing very near the spot where the little girl's chalk drawing was.

WW.

Witchwalker.

And then there's a 1.2-second glitch. Everett Brown is gone in the next frame.

I pull up the CCTV footage from six years ago. Fourteen-year-old Claire Wright at the gas station. There, and then gone. One second exactly on hers.

I watch them ten times, twenty, in the museum parking lot. I listen back to Tillman's interview with Everett, to my own. I drive, and I listen. I don't even know where I'm driving. My headlights cut through this town that makes me insane, that—

I have such a Bad Feeling.

I don't know where the thought comes from.

Another email ping. Tillman's uploaded his interview with Mona Brown to the file. I listen to it as I drive through the night. Tillman's right. I do think she's gonna leave Everett, and that she's been logging in as him in the chat rooms. And the way she talks about *Wizdumteller* . . . it *is* reverent. Obsessive even.

"Who is *Wizdumteller*?" Tillman asks. "Do you know?"

"No," she says.

Tillman moves on to the next question, either doesn't clock the lie that I just did, or is working toward finding it from another angle.

He doesn't though. The whole interview, and he doesn't ask her again about *Wizdumteller.*

I think she knows. I feel it.

The only other strange thing in the interview is a moment that shouldn't be strange at all. But it just . . . that prickling, the itch at the back of my skull. I start the recording over. At the very beginning of it, Tillman says, "That's a nice vase. I like the clouds on it."

"Thank you," Mona replies. "My father gave it to me."

"Where does he live?" Tillman asks.

"Out in Yam—" She clears her throat. "Yuma," she says.

And something about it. The way she says *father.* The way she just . . . I don't know. I don't know why it bothers me. But it does. Just a little stress on the word.

I run it back, listen to it again.

A third time. *My father—*

The radio flips on by itself, playing music over Tillman's and Mona's voices. I turn the radio off.

It turns back on again. Static, the air distorting a little.

Pressure in my ears.

I flip it off, try to listen to the interview, to see if there's—

A song. Now playing in the car. One I know. I hit the radio button again, try to turn the interview volume up. The music only gets louder, unbearably.

Blaze Foley's "If I Could Only Fly." But discordant. Almost like . . . there's a pulse underneath. A deep, wet heartbeat.

Blaze Foley. Rose, on the river. Her hand holding mine.

I flip the switch again, but nothing. The stupid radio keeps—

"This is what life is supposed to be," she says. "Happy. Beautiful. I love you, my—"

I'm so goddamned sick of these goddamned memories coming out of nowhere.

The smell.

A smell at the river. I've never smelled something like it before, it's kind of—

A horn blasts through the night, and I swerve just in time not to have a full head-on collision.

I pull over, cut the engine. My heart fucking racing.

The smell.

I smelled something, that first night between Mama Tried and the motel, out in the field. The night we found Hannah and Tony in the motel. Bitter, chemical.

This memory that keeps coming back. The smell that keeps coming with it, I don't know. I don't know what it is, but . . . I breathe into my hands again. I can't remember anything else.

Mom and me in the river, by the green grass and trees. Where was it?

I start the car. Why can't I remember? Where is any of this coming from? And why now?

The music picks up, grows to such a volume and such a staticky discordance that I want to punch something, want to fucking scream.

At Whileago Manor, I open my computer, looking away until the screen lights up from black. Turn on the hotspot, still no power. I still have some battery though. I go to the chat room, use the handle someone at the office created so we could log in.

I read a few recent posts. And—

A new one appears, from *Wizdumteller.*

I blink.

I wonder if it's not time to give our friends a little hint. Maybe we should say it's important to keep your eyes to the SKY.

I check the time. Posted eleven seconds ago.

The likes start pouring in immediately, shoot up before my eyes. This post coming right after I logged in. Comments—laughing faces, salutes, prayer hands. Posted just now. Is our username compromised? That must be it, they've figured out we've been logging in all this time. Or . . .

I look around the giant living room, the house I left vacant for four years. No surveillance. Could someone have broken in here? Left a camera at some point?

A record starts spinning, one I didn't put on the turntable. Ted Hawkins. "There Stands the Glass." I stand, reach for my gun. There's no one by the record player, just a shadow lurking.

Once, when I was a kid, there was a break-in. The burglar took things from pretty much every room on the main level before we realized he was in the house. But by the time he made it to the door to leave, he mysteriously dropped everything he'd grabbed. And by the time he got to the front lawn, he dropped dead of a heart attack. My parents never knew what to make of it. But I understood right away. I saw it happen out the window, the last part. The shadows got him. Now, as an adult who doesn't believe in shadows and fantasies, I realize the stress of a robbery probably just did it.

Still . . . I don't think anyone's been in here. I don't know how to explain it, but I just kind of *know.* I do a sweep anyway, check all the rooms upstairs and in the basement. If someone's here I can't find them. And if someone *was* here and has been surveilling me, well then that just sucks I guess. I could try and get one of those device finders, but I don't know, I just don't think I need it. But I've been wrong before.

I sit down again, turn back to the chat room, watch the likes come in. They keep coming.

Eyes to the sky. Eyes to the skies. Tillman. Who could he have said that in front of? Is our car bugged? Is *Tillman* a part of this? I search for the word "sky" anywhere in the chat room, but there's nothing. I search for "Witchwalker." Nothing, but a lot of mentions of "WW," all from *Wizdumteller.* Do we start contacting these hundreds of people liking these posts? Clearly they know something we don't, none of them are asking questions, for clarification. We just start asking every one of them who *Wizdumteller* is?

It's almost like they've been instructed not to comment. Like they're all following some code, or . . . I think of Tillman, what he said about Mona Brown. Obsession. Devotion. The way she spoke about *Wizdumteller.* People will do a lot for someone they're obsessed with, for someone they love. I pull up Tillman's interview with her and listen again as I head down to the basement for another workout in the dark. Seems like she might be our best bet, to see if she'll talk to me or maybe Frazier or Garcia, or have Tillman talk to her again.

My father gave it to me.

I text Frazier to see if we can get any info on Mona Brown's dad.

Mona Brown. Oliver Wright. *Wizdumteller.*

Bite marks. Motel.

Questions. So many questions.

Hannah Lawrence. My heart pounding every time I think of her.

Do you get it yet?

A call lights up my phone. Frazier.

"Hello?" I say.

"Hey," she says. "Um, you have to see this right now. Just uploaded. Hannah Lawrence's file." She sounds out of breath. Almost frantic.

I remote access Hannah's file.

New JPEGs in a folder titled "Hannah Lawrence Film Roll."

She says again, "You need to see this."

Digital copies of film photographs, with time stamps.

A small fox with large ears, 5:10 PM, the day Hannah Lawrence was taken to the Happy Inn, November 16. A bird in the grass the same day, earlier. A lizard two days before. Then . . . I squint, zoom in. A photo that looks like a mistake, a week before Hannah's abduction. Blurred, camera moving, a trailhead parking lot. And . . .

At the edge of the lot, a young man with a backpack on, stepping out of a car.

A young man who looks a lot like Tony Howell.

Hannah's camera. Hannah's film roll. Tony Howell who was taped into the bed with her at the Happy Inn. The two of them in the same place at the same time, a week and three days before we found them at the motel. Hannah taking a photo of him.

Proof of it on her camera roll.

"Oh shit," I say.

"Yeah," Frazier says. "Ran prints on the camera. Inconclusive, but . . ."

A roaring in my ears. That giant sweeping avalanche.

Hannah Lawrence might in fact be responsible for everything.

We get to Hannah's cabin a little after midnight. Her bed's made. She isn't there. My heart pounds. Was it her? Did she do this, orchestrate *all* of this? With help? Alone? Why? What could she possibly want with me or any part of my life?

We stay all night, sit outside in the mountain dark, walk a perimeter around her cabin. Tillman, Garcia, and me.

We couldn't ask her about Tony Howell before, if she knew him, because we hadn't gotten an ID. The two of them are surely connected, have to be. The only photo of a human in her film roll, and it was him.

I feel eyes on us. Am certain we are not alone. We hike all around, check everywhere. See nothing. Hear nothing.

We leave a trail camera with an automatic alert function. By morning, we decide to head down. We check her grocery store resupply spot on the way back to town in another new development I haven't seen before. The store clerks say they haven't seen her in weeks.

By the time I step through the doors of Whileago Manor, it's late morning. I haven't slept at all. I open my laptop and search for her again. Frazier already talked to the people who hired her. We called the ranger I saw before, to let us in. They know nothing more about her life than what we've already got in the files.

I'm restless, don't know what to do with myself. Am so fucking tired and wired and—

Wizdumteller. Could that be her?

I check the chat room again. Nothing new. We hiked sixteen miles, there and back. All of it.

Hannah Lawrence.

I read and I search, and sleep pulls at me, but I fight it. It's cold in the house, gray outside the windows. I build another fire. Sit back down, look for her again. I search and search for her, for anything at all. The shadows in the corners of the room, watching me. Hannah's card in my hand the whole time.

Hannah's drawing is the last thing I'm thinking of when sleep finally takes me.

My phone. Ringing again. Eyes open.

Awake in a dark house. Whileago Manor. Hannah Lawrence's card in my hand. My laptop half-closed before me.

It's evening. Did I sleep through the whole afternoon?

"Hey," Jack says through the phone. He sounds terrible, worse than before. And it jolts me back. Images of Brianna in a hospital flash before me. Of the worst possible thing.

"What's wrong?" I ask.

"It's the kid," Jack says.

And my brain doesn't compute at first.

"Pete Noland," he says.

It takes me a moment to catch up, to realize he's not talking about his family, that they're all okay. My heart rate slows. Then another moment to understand.

"He hung himself in jail," Jack says. "He's dead."

18

I'm running. In the dark, on the High Line Canal, beneath the cottonwoods, willows, green ash. I've been running, I don't know how far, how long. Headed back toward the house. The house where I'll stare at files and search things on my phone, on my computer, ask the same questions of the same people, beat my head against the fucking wall again and again.

Pete Noland is dead. Another person dead because of me. A kid.

You know, Blaze was never afraid, not of anything. He sang things that could've gotten him killed, but he did it anyway. He looked out for people, did right by 'em. Rose, talking to me in the motel. The sun shining in through the shades. Blaze Foley's voice playing on our little tape player.

For me it was John Denver. For her, it was Blaze. She talked about him all the time. How he was living in Texas in the Reagan era when he put that song "Oval Room" out. Everyone around him was scared he was gonna get shot for it. And he did get shot, but not for that. I always thought his songs were lonely, kind of sad. I liked the president one, but the others, the ones she played again and again like they held the answers to everything . . . as a kid, they just made me feel sad. Maybe just made me feel.

I don't shut out the memories, the pain. Us dancing and laughing. Her sitting up crying when she thought I was sleeping. Counting coins on the table and making me mac 'n' cheese or ramen in the microwave and reading me books from the library. My dad, when he was around. The two of them, fighting, screaming. Him holding a bottle and pulling his fist back, and—

I trip over a root. Hit the ground on my shoulder, roll to my back. The Colorado night sky above me. My heart pounding. And . . .

Pete Noland is dead. Because he couldn't handle the idea of having done this to someone. Because I couldn't get to an answer fast enough.

Because we had Hannah Lawrence in custody but I couldn't see past the fact that she was hurt and strong and familiar-seeming and beautiful. How fucking stupid can I be?

Trying to piece together a life I shattered, going to dinners, having drinks with people I wouldn't have to reconcile with if I hadn't abandoned them in the first place. Running. Running all the time, always running. I should have been working every second, should have seen what was right in front of me, should have—

There's a rustling in the trees.

I don't think, just move.

Jump up, tense.

That strange pressure.

VOOM.

The sound.

VOOM.

A footstep on dried leaves. My head snaps to a spot in the trees. It's too dark to see.

VOOM.

Another snap.

VOOM.

Another.

And—

Hannah Lawrence steps out into the moonlight.

19

She doesn't move, at first. Just waits at the edge of the path. She knows I see her, she's letting me. Then she takes a step forward, holding something in her arms.

She's wearing a ranger puffer, a sweater, jeans, boots. Her hair is loose over her shoulders.

She's here. Standing in front of me.

Watching.

"Hi," she says, after a moment.

That's it.

"Hi," I say back. Adrenaline. Breath.

"I . . . I think I need your help," she says.

Hannah Lawrence, here on my running path. Here, where she knew how to find me.

I don't have my gun, cuffs, anything. Not that I . . . Hannah Lawrence is here. I can't see her well, just enough to know it's her.

I watch us as if from above, as if we are two strangers I have never met, as I nod my head once. As I say, "Let's go inside and talk."

We walk in silence, and I am lasered in on her every movement. This woman who could be the one organizing all of this, who could be responsible for so many lost lives. She glances at me every minute or so. I don't know what she could be thinking.

We pass through the trees at the back of the property, and I feel her pause half a step when she sees the house. I keep walking, my attention still fixed on her in my periphery. We cross the lawn and come up on the French doors leading to the dining room.

I say, "What's in your arms?"

She drops it to the ground, kicks it over to me. Something wrapped in a sweatshirt. I think for half a second that it could be an explosive, that I'll reach forward, and that'll be it.

"What is it?" I ask again.

"It isn't mine, I don't know how it . . ."

I look at her, realize she seems almost afraid.

I bend down slowly and take hold of the sweatshirt, slowly unravel it, letting whatever's wrapped inside clatter onto the back patio. And I let out a long exhale.

There's dried blood on it. We've been looking for this for so long. Assuming it's the same one, assuming it's been used for every killing, which I feel in my gut, *know*, that it is and has. She told us it was strange, homemade-looking. Daphne noted the jagged striations.

The knife looks like it was hand-carved from bone. Amateur carving, but effective. A six-inch handle, a little uneven, and the blade about the same length, crude but sharp enough to skin a person.

Hannah Lawrence just brought the murder weapon to my house.

"If you let me explain . . . I just . . ."

She's right here, on my actual doorstep. The person I've been looking for all this time. The lights in the house faintly glowing, reflecting off her skin through the glass. Half her face in their yellow-orange glow, the other half in the little moonlight there is. She leans away from the door, like she'd rather do anything than go inside. My heart hammers looking at her.

I shake my head, open the door, gesture for her to walk before me.

The one I've been searching for for six years. It would make her twenty-two when it started. Doubt creeps in, questions. So many goddamned questions.

I reach down and pick up the bundle, careful not to touch the knife.

I walk us to the living room.

The shadows all hang back, silent and still for once. Waiting to see what will happen. I'm crazy, I know by now I'm crazy, but I see her gaze linger as we pass each one, could almost believe she's clocking them.

I shouldn't let her see all the files, shouldn't let her know how much I know, or more accurately how much I don't. But a part of me wants her to see. Wants her to realize what's going to happen. She's come here, and this is the end of it, and if she did this, she's going to jail for a very, very long time. Or maybe I want her to see how badly I have wanted this, how much I want to see the person responsible put away. Maybe I just want to see how she reacts.

Her fox drawing, the card, at least, is nowhere in sight.

"You can sit," I say, indicating the couch. She looks at me, and I try to read the expression there. Fear, for sure. But something else. Pain, almost. She holds her hand over her nose, keeps far away from me.

She steps around files and sits, takes in all the folders before her, the fireplace, the room. She looks up to the ceiling. I step over, set the sweatshirt-bundled knife down on floor by the hearth. I put a few logs on the fire, hold my back to her to get it started. I tell myself I'm doing it because I want to show her I'm not afraid. But I just need to take a breath. Just need a second to collect myself, not looking at her.

When I turn around, she hasn't moved. She's watching me. My phone's on the coffee table on top of one of the folders. She sits, with her hand still over her nose. The nose plug is in beneath her hand, I can just see it between her fingers.

Hannah Lawrence, here, in my house.

"This is your home?" she asks.

"How did you find me?"

The flames come to life behind me. Silence, in the living room, between us.

"Talk," I say, when she says nothing else.

"I went to get water from the stream, after you all left, and I walked for a while. I was gone maybe two hours in total. When I came back, that knife—I guess you'd call it that—was on my bed. I recognized it from the motel. It . . . Seeing it again . . ." She takes a shaky breath. "Someone broke into my cabin and left it. I don't know if it's a threat, or if they want to make it look like *I* did this, or both, but . . ." Her voice breaks a little. "I was scared."

"But you didn't see anyone."

She shakes her head. "I didn't know what to do. I just felt like I needed to leave. If someone was up there, if they had waited. I mean, there's no one else around for miles, no service. I ran."

"With the knife."

"I didn't want it on my bed, and . . ."

"And?"

"And I thought you might need to see it."

"Why me?"

"I . . ."

"How did you find me?" I ask. *All the times. All the pieces of my past. How?*

She looks around the room, her legs bouncing, brows knitted together in what looks like pain. Bruises still on her face. Just faint ones, but there. Her eyes catch on a shadow that's drifted over by the bar and the record player, that seems to be watching us.

"Hey," I say. "Look, if I'm going to believe anything you're—"

"Yeah, um . . ." But she can't look away. Another's come in from the kitchen, and Hannah's gone pale.

"They're fine," I say. "Just—"

Her attention snaps to me. Green eyes reflecting the flames behind me. "What did you say?" she asks.

"I need you to give me some answers. Give me something here."

"You see them?" The way she asks it, desperation, shock.

I take a breath. "How did you find me? Why did you come here?"

She watches me a long moment, then leans back, exhales long and slow, her hands over her face. She says, to the ceiling, "Oh my god, I . . . no wonder."

"Hey, I need you to talk to me, or we're going to—"

She sits up, and there's still that shine in her eyes, but this time it's not only fear there. "When I saw you at the office," she says. "When I *felt* you. It's because . . ."

Then something else crosses her face, and her whole demeanor changes. Fear. Distrust. She sits up slowly.

"Did you put me in that motel room?" she asks. "Were you there?"

The fire pops. It takes a moment for her question to register.

"Did *I*—" I say. "Everett Brown put you in that room. I—"

"Why did I hear that song when I touched the photographs?" she asks. "That was you, who'd held them before me. Why did I hear that song? Why did I . . . *feel* you?"

Why have I *been thinking about you every second?*

I shake my head. "I wasn't even in the state when he took you to the motel." Why am I defending myself to her? How could I possibly—

"Why did you come to me?" I ask. "Why not go to the FBI office? Why not try to find Frazier or Garcia? If you were really scared, if you really thought someone was trying to frame you? And what do you mean you *felt* me?"

This last question feels monumental. All of this . . . I try to feel my feet on the ground, focus in on the present. Her, here. But . . .

"You don't . . ." she says. She pauses, tilts her head, brow furrowed now in confusion and pain and . . . she's searching for something. "Oh." Deep disappointment on her face. "Um." She runs a hand through her hair. "Okay. I just . . ." She takes a breath, realizing something. Deciding something. "I ran down from my cabin," she says, "and I didn't stop running. Then walking. I came through Roxborough Park, through Chatfield to the High Line Canal. And I ended up where you were."

"That's like twenty miles. Twenty-five."

"Yeah," she says.

"You said I might want to see the knife. You meant to come to me."

She stares at me a second. "Yeah, I just . . . get like, feelings, sometimes. It doesn't matter. I just needed somewhere to go, and you . . . seemed like a safe place. When I saw you at the office, I just . . . felt like I knew you. I don't know."

My phone buzzes on the table. Lights up with a text, then another. My heart is thundering, and I can't process any of what she's saying. *Felt like I knew you.*

"Please," she says, almost a whisper. "I can't be locked up. Even here, in this room, I'm . . ." That panic look, her legs shaking. "I can't be in a tight space, with other people. And even . . . even if I don't go to jail because someone tried to . . . frame me? I guess? Someone was in my cabin. They could come back. I don't know what to do. I don't know where to go, or—"

"We developed your film," I say.

"What?"

"Your film roll, from your camera."

The phone buzzes on the table.

"Okay," she says, unsure.

"There was a photo of Tony Howell on it."

"Who?"

"The man who was duct-taped into the bed with you."

"What? I don't take pictures of people."

"The photo looks like a mistake. It's in the parking lot for the trailhead."

She stares at me. "Maybe whoever took me from the field took the photo after."

"Your camera was in the field when you all found it, not the parking lot. And the photo was taken before the one of the fox. A week before."

She takes this in, her legs bouncing faster. She barks a disbelieving laugh, tears filling her eyes. "What is happening right now?"

My phone lights up.

"Where were you last night?" I ask.

"I was at my cabin."

"No, you weren't."

"Yes, I was," she says, meeting my eye. Holding it. "I was there, in the woods, watching all of you."

My phone buzzes.

"You—"

"I heard you all coming, and I hid. I didn't know why you were there or what you could want, but I waited to see. And you never said what you wanted out loud, so I just . . . stayed. When you left this morning, like I said, I went to the stream and to do my rounds, and when I came back, the knife was there. And now . . . I'm here."

"The game camera."

"I disabled it right after you left."

"Then you walked twenty-five miles to get here?"

She nods. "Yeah, sounds right. I just . . ."

My phone, buzzing again.

I reach for it, allow myself to glance down, quickly.

Josie: I did it, Daniel.

I glance up at Hannah, who's leaned back again. Swiping tears from her eye. I look down, read the text again. What—

Josie: I told Jack. I had to tell him.

What?

Josie. Jack knows about the motel?

Another buzz. A message from Jack.

Jack: Daniel, where are you? We have to talk.

Hannah Lawrence sitting on my couch. Hannah Lawrence with a murder weapon.

"Maybe I shouldn't have come here," Hannah says. "This was a mistake."

Josie told Jack about the Happy Inn. About my connection to it. The one I've been lying about. I look back up at Hannah.

My phone, buzzing. Still. In my hand.

Buzz.

Hannah's scared. I don't trust her. I can't let her out of my sight until I figure out—

The shadows move, restless, near the bar. Hannah stills, clocking the movement. She tenses further, and I think she's about to make a move of some kind, I ready myself for anything.

"What's going on?" she asks. And there's so much fear in the question.

Buzz.

Daphne: I'm sorry.

"Um, just hold on," I say to Hannah. I try to catch up with all the messages. Try to watch the girl on my couch who very well might be—

Josie: What the fuck is happening right now? Is this real?

Hannah leans forward. "Look, I get why you don't believe me, but please you have to—"

Buzz.

A screenshot from Josie. A forensics report. There's a sender line at the top, from Daphne to Jack.

"Just," I say to Hannah. "Just, don't move. Okay, just give me a—"

I look back down at the report. It's a hair analysis. Run on a quarter-inch strand of hair from a brown leather jacket. There's a photo of it.

The brown leather jacket I gave last night to Daphne to borrow.

My brown leather jacket.

My eyes scan the analysis, the words that should make sense but don't.

Because this says that there was a DNA match.

A DNA match between the hair on my jacket and . . .

And the hair that was wrapped around the tongues of every single killer.

The hair wrapped around the tongue of every killer in this case, for six years. The one I have been searching for.

The hair, this says . . .

It's mine.

Jack: Stay where you are. I'm coming.

I drop the phone and lift my eyes to Hannah.

It was a long hair every time. I shave my head. And anyway, I never— It couldn't have—

But with what Josie told Jack, about my past . . .

They've matched the hair to me. Somehow . . .

Oh shit.

They're coming here. Here, where I have Hannah Lawrence in my living room.

And the murder weapon.

I lied about my connection to the case. And my hair . . .

"What is it?" Hannah says.

I have to think fast, have to make a plan.

"Oh my god," she says. "They're doing it to you too." She lets out a pained laugh. "Someone's doing it to both of us. Trying to . . ." But she trails off, watches me. Wondering if I did it. Wondering if she can trust me at all. Looking at me the same way I've been looking at her. And how would she know what the messages said? How could she possibly . . .

Unless she's a part of it. Unless *she's* trying to set me up? *Why?*

I can't move. I need to *think*.

"I . . ." I look around Whileago Manor.

"Hey—hey, look at me," Hannah Lawrence says. I do, even as I only half know who she is and who I am. "Are they coming here?"

I try to make my brain work. I nod, somehow.

"Look," she says after a second. "I don't trust you. You could be doing all of this to mess with me, or . . . I don't know. But I do know if they get here, I'm fucked, and I think you might be too. We need to go somewhere, get out of here."

Whileago Manor and all the ghosts. My DNA. My hair.

How?

"Hey, help me," she says. "We . . . I might have somewhere. For us to go. We'll figure it out. Okay? Maybe . . . maybe we can figure it out together."

That feeling of inevitability, of a great sweeping avalanche.

Hannah Lawrence, and me. The prime suspects.

Hannah Lawrence. And me.

Bad Feeling.

"Please," she says.

Bad—

Her eyes lock on mine.

I'm so fucking screwed.

III

HIGHWAYMAN

1

In the John Denver *Take Me Home* movie, once Annie and John have called it quits, Annie becomes a therapist in Aspen. She meets with a patient, and during the session, the young woman tells Annie that she was preparing to kill herself when a song came on the radio. "Poems, Prayers and Promises." It made her stop. Made her want to live. Made her realize that life is *worth* living. Just the one song, hearing it at the right moment.

Pete Noland killed himself. Josie told Jack about my past. The DNA on every single killer matches my own, and Daphne was the one who tested it, who told everyone. Hannah Lawrence, whose film roll makes her a suspect, is sitting beside me, and she brought the murder weapon to my house. The murder weapon that is now in the trunk of my car, the two of us speeding west on the highway. Hannah leans away, out the open window, her hand over her nose and the nose plug. Hannah Lawrence, who is the prime suspect—besides me.

"Leaving on a Jet Plane" plays on the car radio.

I-70 heading west is long and winding, twisting its way through the mountains, our headlights pushing into the dark ahead of us. Hannah leans as far from me as possible, her head out the window, gulping the frigid night air. It's freezing in the car, but I don't ask her to close it. She's shaking, and I'm sure it's not just from the cold.

I don't look at her, don't let myself look at her.

I glance over and look at her every fifteen minutes.

The orange glow of the dash, the occasional lampposts of the winding mountain road, against her nose, her cheek, her eyes, her throat. Shining through her hair.

And somehow . . . she smells like ponderosa pine. Just like she did in my dream. I don't know how that's possible. I don't know how any of this is.

We drive in silence, save for when she tells me to stay on this road, that she'll show me the exit. My heart pounding in my chest. Two heartbeats in my car. Hannah beside me.

And even though I've never been here, have never driven out this way, I realize where we're going. Realize I should have known it all along. Again, I wonder if I've made the biggest mistake of my life getting in this car with her. If she did organize all of this, of course this was the only place left.

John Denver's town. The city I thought my mom was taking me that night we were going to leave the Happy Inn. Where she might have been planning to.

Aspen.

And I don't know what it is, but as we drive, a sense of strong déjà vu comes over me. I watch the mountains and the small towns roll by, and I think . . . *I know this.* But I can't possibly. I've never been this way before.

And yet . . . it all looks so familiar.

We pull into Aspen just before sunrise.

We can't see much yet, bruisy dark mountains against a blue-black sky, a small town down at the base of them, with its overnight lights on. The air feels cleaner up here, the elevation gain from Denver apparent. The cold air keeps me alert, and this new thinness to it wakes me up even more. Not that I need it.

Hannah tells me to take the turn for Red Mountain, and I catch sight of an old-timey drugstore on the corner, a red half-cursive CARL'S PHARMACY sign on the outside, a shadow lingering in front of it, following us as we drive past the entrance.

A smell, in my nose. That strange bitter chemical smell. The drugstore . . .

Something's not right. Something . . .

Why does this all look so *familiar*?

Maybe the John Denver movie. I don't know if they actually shot it here, but I watched it so many times, that could maybe explain it. Still, something doesn't feel right. Correction: Nothing feels right. Everything is fucked. But something about *this place.*

I glance over at Hannah again. I swallow and turn my eyes back to the road.

We take a winding road up the mountain past enormous homes

on wide lots, and pull up in the driveway of one of them near the top. A modern home that only looks like one story from the driveway that swings by the front doors, but a peek through the glass front doors reveals an enormous multistoried glass-and-wood modern house extending down the mountain.

Hannah jumps out of the car and inputs a code that opens the garage door, gestures for me to pull in. I do. Park. Step out into a garage full of vintage ski posters and high-end sporting equipment. My car now sits next to three vintage collectors' cars—red Wagoneer, powder blue Bronco, yellow Aston Martin. It smells like Marianne and Noel's garage, a particular combination of new-car leather, high-end wooden cabinet, garage-floor epoxy. I realize Hannah hasn't come in.

I turn to the open garage door, to where she stands out in the cold. I let out a breath.

"We're going this way," she says, standing on the driveway that I'd bet anything is heated for the winter. Is this her house? *This* place? Her file said family wasn't alive, but . . .

"Where are we?" I ask, stepping over to her.

In the driveway, I watch her input the garage code again to close the door, taking note of the numbers. She doesn't answer me. And in the early morning stillness in a place that feels completely wrong and strangely, impossibly like I know it, I follow her. As she walks to the woods at the edge of the driveway. As she disappears through the trees.

I break through after her. Stand in a thick copse of aspen trees and towering pines. It smells earthy, damp, that slight decomposing smell of a fall forest, leaves beneath us.

"Watch for bears," she says, from ten feet ahead. "They like to come swim in the pool this time of year."

I glance behind us to see the lowest level of the house through the trees, where there is in fact a pool. Steam billows up from beneath and around the cover. It's currently heated. "Is someone else here?" I ask.

Hannah doesn't answer, just follows the pine needle and fallen aspen leaf path I now realize we walk, small glowing lights on either side of it, lining its edges. It's dark still, here in the trees. I can't quite see the colors, everything around us that faded dark gray-blue.

Something rustles to my left, and a chipmunk crossing the path nearly collides with my leg. Early morning birdsong, the soft crunch of Hannah's boots on the path, of mine. My breaths, nearly echoing in the quiet.

"Hannah," I say. "Where—"

"Shh." She turns back and looks at me. Her eyes once again obscured in the darkness of the woods. "We're almost there," she says. Then she turns away from me and continues down the path. I follow. Try to get my bearings. The path goes away from the house, and down. On the left side of the path is the upward slope to the street we entered the driveway from, which we can't see anymore, and to our right, a drop down through the trees down the side of the mountain. I turn back behind me and can't see the house anymore.

Something's off. Everything is. I shouldn't be here.

I turn back around, and I almost collide with Hannah.

Blood, bath—

She jumps back, puts distance between us, holds her hand over her nose. She closes her eyes, adjusts her nose plug. A look of pain on her face.

"What are you—" I say.

She takes another step backward. "I was just going to say," she gets out through uneven breaths, "be careful. When you step in." She turns her face away.

I realize there's a building behind her, suddenly. Tucked back in the trees, a small wooden structure that sits on a platform stretched out over the edge of the mountain. I can only see its side from here, and I watch as Hannah takes the path to it and then steps off the path heading downhill. Her feet find particular rocks among the packed dirt, leaves, and pine needles, as though she's done it a hundred times. Then she steps down to the front, and I can just see her legs through the gap between the slab the house sits on and the sloping mountainside below, as they suddenly lift off the ground and disappear inside.

I try to follow her steps down, but my foot slides once on the dirt, and I grab on to the nearest tree to keep myself from sliding down the mountain. I take hold of the platform the house sits on and go around to the front, the downhill side, like she did.

And I realize when I get there, there's no wall on this side. The structure has three walls, and then just opens up to the elements on the fourth side, facing out from the mountain. Hannah in the three-sided cabin—maybe two hundred fifty square feet in total—flipping switches on one wall. I assume she just hoisted herself up over the side, so I do the same.

Her back is to me as she collects wood from where it's bundled at the far left corner of the structure. She's tense, I can tell. Three wooden walls with a wooden ceiling slanted up at the open side. Wooden floors, other than the circular black firepit built into the center of the space, and built-in cabinets along the back wall. In the far corners and along all the edges of the ceiling are strip heat lamps, which mercifully are turning on. I'm still in my jogging clothes, but I threw on a black leather jacket on the way out the door. Still, it's cold.

Hannah sits down on the floor by the firepit and splinters off a piece of kindling from one of the logs with a pocketknife. Was that here, or has she had it with her the whole time?

"Where are we?" I ask. She smells of something spicy now, a new smell, something I can't identify. She tucks a small white tube into her pocket. Touches the back of her hand to her nose.

She piles the kindling and then pulls a lighter out. She holds the flame to the splinters like she's done it a million times. Her hands are red in the cold. "This is my place," she says as she works. "I don't own it, but it's mine."

"So you're a . . . squatter? Part-time?"

The kindling catches. She takes a long breath, leans back, sitting on her heels in the glow of the beginnings of a fire. Looks up at me. "No. This shelter is mine. Just not in deed. Although it was offered to me that way."

"Is the owner of the house here?" The one whose garage currently holds my car.

"No," she says.

"Are you sure?"

"Yes," she says. "He always leaves it like that—pool heated, lights on, everything up and running. He's in the Bahamas somewhere, I think. But," she says, her eyes catching over my shoulder, "you're gonna miss it. Show's comin'."

"You want me to turn around while you've got that knife in your hand?"

I have my gun. I prepare myself to have to reach for it, turn, deal with whatever's now behind me.

She shrugs. "Suit yourself," she says.

I step to the right side wall and put my back to it before I turn. And—

I'm looking out at a view.

There's no one here, no threat, as far as I can see. Beyond the trees, the town of Aspen, with lights still on from the night, glittering out and below us. And behind the town and its lights, the looming ski mountains.

And here in front of us, right here, the trees.

The aspen bark, white, spotted with gray-brown, the trees no larger around than maybe five or six inches each. But . . . all of them, here, tucked in tight together, their fall leaves on full display, trembling before us, just framing our view of the town and distant mountains.

It's beautiful. Ridiculously.

I feel something looking at it. Maybe what John Denver felt. Maybe why he chose this place. This, exactly as magical as I pictured it as a kid.

The glow of the rising sun orange and red coming in now from the west on our right, lighting up the mountains. The edge of the platform suspended out over the mountain we're on. It's . . . maybe the most exceptional view I've ever seen.

I glance to Hannah, the glow of the flames dancing on her face. She's more relaxed than I've seen her up to now. Outdoors, but with three walls guarding her back and sides. I'd be willing to bet a lot that that was the idea, that there's a reason there's no door to enter through, almost like a hunting blind.

That prickling, the sense that there is so much more here than I can see. So much more about *her.*

"Who built this place?" I ask.

"Me," she says. "I'll make us some coffee." She stands. "I have to walk around the back, there's a bear box behind the shelter. I'm not leaving."

She's asking me to trust her. I shouldn't. I don't. But I could use a second away from her, to see what I can find. I nod. She steps to the edge of the platform and swings down onto the soft ground. I hear her boots crunching on leaves.

When she's gone, I take a breath, run my hands over my head. The heat lamps are working, and her fire's come to real life. It's still cold in here, but it's more comfortable, not unbearable. About the same as the car on our way driving in. I step to the back wall and open cabinets, the few drawers. I see that one cabinet hides a whole sink and basin, another a large bin with pillows. Another is just full of books. Ecology and wildlife nonfiction, a bird guide, plant guide, hiking memoirs, books on the Ute tribe, Edward Abbey, Michener's *Centennial*, Hunter S. Thompson's *The Great Shark Hunt*. Another cabinet conceals three drawers, all of which are filled with art supplies. Sketchbooks, pencils, charcoal.

I reach into one and flip open the sketchbook. The first sketch is of a girl, lying down on a large rock, laughing up at the sky. At first I think it's Hannah, but then I see the face is a little sharper, the look there not quite hers. Darker hair, maybe. The next sketch is of a man in glasses and a sweater, thin but strong-jawed, drinking liquor from a rocks glass, looking out over a balcony. I think it's the balcony of the house we're parked at, from my quick glance earlier.

Both portraits feel intimate.

There are more sketches in here of each of these people, and even more of wildlife, close-ups of the aspen trees, their thin trunks, small nearly round leaves and famously white bark. I've never seen them in person before now, only photos.

I read once that what might look like a hundred individual aspen trees is actually all one organism, one big tree, and what we see aboveground, what looks like entire forests, could be considered just branches. I look back out at them, her view from in here. How many hours has she spent here? How much of her life is this?

I reach up and touch my pocket, feel her card there. The card that keeps getting back there somehow even when I don't mean for it to. I don't remember putting it in this jacket, something unconscious, instinctual.

I flip to the next drawing.

I spent the whole drive here trying to understand how that DNA could be mine on the Drifters. Daphne must have thought to test my hair when she saw I had Hannah's card.

Still, she's my friend. Was, maybe. For her to think I could have done those things, to have even considered it. And she didn't talk to me, went straight to Jack. And if it was my hair . . . why wouldn't they have made the match before? I guess they take DNA samples for the DoD database when we enlist in the Marines, mainly for body identification in war. But the DoD database is separate from CODIS, and the FBI has to request specific samples from the DoD in order to get them. We don't submit DNA samples for FBI work, and I've never been arrested or convicted for anything, so I wouldn't be in CODIS at all.

But how? Who could have gotten my hair? And why? And how could any strand be long enough to tie around a tongue in a knot? It has to be a mistake.

And Josie telling Jack about my past. I should have told him long before now, but . . . The connection to the case and repeated lies about it—the FBI ethics code is strict. Beyond strict. And then the DNA match.

It's bad. Really bad. And Josie and Daphne are distrustful enough of me to have submitted them. These two people who used to be two of my closest friends on earth.

"Find anything good?"

I jump at the voice behind me. Hannah stands at the entrance with a small plastic bin.

I clear my throat, close the drawer. I don't know how she got in without me hearing her. I need to be sharper, need to pull myself together. So much is happening so fast.

Hannah steps over to the other side of the cabinet wall and starts to prep the coffee. I watch her, try to glean any piece of information. There's an intensity about her movements, her gaze. This same girl who drew those sketches, who took the photographs back in her cabin near Denver. Who maybe orchestrated all these deaths. She moves comfortably in silence, is used to it. It's *me* she's not comfortable with, a fact reinforced when she steps over to give me my coffee in an earthenware mug and sets it on the floor feet from me instead of getting close enough to hand it over.

She sits on the other side of the firepit, on the floor. I lower myself down to do the same, opposite her. Look out over the aspen trees. A chipmunk runs up and down the nearest one to us. Hannah adjusts her nose plug. With the sun now beginning to cast light in the sky,

I can see the Aspen leaves are all orange, yellow, and red. I would think they'd have fallen by now, but maybe it's been a warm fall. All of this, so surreal. I look at her.

"You gotta give me something," I say.

Please tell me I am not making the worst mistake of my life. While I'm running from my friends, who also happen to be FBI agents. While I'm with a woman who very well might have killed all these people.

I bring the coffee to my nose, hesitate, then take a sip. I don't think she'd poison me. If she did want to kill me, she wouldn't do it in such a quiet way after all this spectacle. Anyway, I need the caffeine.

"The last time I was at the trailhead before the motel was three weeks ago," Hannah says, looking down into her cup. "And I just passed through and into town to buy food. That's it. I couldn't have taken a photo of someone."

"You'd never been to that motel before?"

She looks up at me now, indignation in her eyes. "Look. I'll answer your questions, and I get that you're skeptical, but I already told you all, I don't know *anything* about that motel, and I don't have any idea why I am a part of this. Okay? Not a clue. And I would really rather go the rest of my life never thinking about that motel again. Someone broke into my home. I've asked you, a stranger, someone I shouldn't trust at all, for help. Please. Just . . . I don't know what else to do."

That look in her eyes. So much fear, so much pain. But fight too.

Fuck, do I believe her?

"Okay," I say. I rub my forehead. "So someone broke into your cabin at some point, took your camera down the mountain, took a photo of someone else, put the camera back, then kidnapped you and the person they took a photo of a week later. Then took you both to the motel, killed him, put his tongue in your mouth, kept you alive, and then came back days after and put the knife on your bed. Right after we'd been there."

She looks at me with fury in her eyes. "I don't know what you want me to say," she says quietly. "I didn't do, or ask for, any of this. And yeah. Right after you all were there. For all I know, it could have been one of you who broke in and left the knife."

"We all went down the trail together. It wasn't us. Was there any other sign of forced entry at any point in the last month? Any other clues that someone might have been there without you knowing?"

She thinks, watches the chipmunk. "I have these . . . drawings. In my cabin in Pikes Forest," she says. "Just little sketches that I do, on playing cards. One of them is missing. It was after the motel, after I was taken. When I came back it was gone."

I keep my eyes on the coffee cup, my heart pounding again. *Yeah, because it's in my pocket* is probably not the best answer right now. I take another sip.

"If we're alone out here," I ask after a minute, "why aren't we inside the house?"

She hesitates, then says, "I can't be indoors with people. Or . . . I don't like to be. It's . . . hard."

"Since the motel?" I ask. This girl with this three-sided shelter. Again, that prickling.

She stares at me, then gives a slow nod, and I know it's a lie. She takes a sip of her coffee. My eyes catch on her mouth for half a second. I pull them away.

"If you want to go in the house, you can," she says. "There are showers and bathrooms, heat, all that."

"I'm good," I say. "So the guy who owns this property let you build this structure and offered you the land it's on?"

She says, exasperated, "Look, you and I could have gone to the backcountry anywhere today, but Parks law enforcement are always on the lookout for people on the run. And your car would be parked in a public lot, with that murder knife in the trunk of it. This seemed like the best option I could think of, but if you don't want—"

"I just want to know where I am. I just want to know what the fuck is going on."

"Well, that makes two of us! So *please*. Tell me. Where do we go from here? How do we fix this so that it isn't our lives anymore? That's your job, isn't it? That's what you're good at?"

"I . . ." Is that what this is? She wants to get me here and have me play out this agent narrative while she pretends to need my help? For what? Why me? Why any of this?

Do I just . . . play it out? Pretend I believe her?

But I do. Part of me does. Part of me believes her enough that I came here with her. Or maybe that was just to get a little time, find something to clear myself or get a little closer to understanding. I know *I* didn't orchestrate all this. Right? Of course I didn't.

I grabbed all the file copies before we left. Turned my phone off and took the burner I keep on a prepaid plan in case of emergency. I guess I was thinking more like apocalypse and less like running from the feds, but here we are. I shiver, the cold penetrating my jacket, even with the heat lamps. I think through options. Hannah clocks the movement. She stands and goes to the cabinet with the bedding and opens one of the bins. She mumbles something.

"What?" I say, trying to clear my brain enough to think.

"I hate these things. It's disgusting. I wish he would stop putting them in here." She's holding up two animal furs. "Keeps replacing my camp blankets with these."

"What are they?"

She looks through for something else but can't find it. She swears, then hands one of the furs over to me—drops it to the floor near me—and puts the rest back in the bin. "Mink, mostly. Lot of minks, stitched together. Foxes. The tails on the ends, those are all foxtails. That one in your hand, that's three wolf pelts stitched together."

I lift it up, hold it out. It's not big. They're not big animals. It surprises me. Makes me sad, and a little sick.

"There's a taxidermied mountain lion in the main house. You might see it through the window." She closes the bin and shoves it back in the cabinet. "Nothing makes a man look smaller than having to take down a threatened or endangered animal to feel a little power. When trappers came in the 1800s and killed off all the wolves, they would taxidermy them and put them back in the wild to photograph. Like they only realized after they were all dead that it would have been nice to see them in the wild. That these were wild, free beings that were a part of this place and should have been."

Wild, free beings. Looking at her, I think . . . yeah. That's it. Is that what's made me feel drawn to her? Made it so I can't stop thinking about her? Because I am tied to a haunted house and a haunted office and a haunted motel? Buildings that have trapped me my whole life, even when I'm not in them? Because what she is, what she *has* . . .

"The guy you're talking about," I say. "The owner of the house. Is he the one you sketched?"

She sits back down, sighs, then nods. "His name is James. I was in a tough time in my life, running from my past, from a bad thing that had happened. My . . . my best friend died, and it just sort of . . . I was passing through different towns. I met James in Sun Valley, and he just took me in. Didn't ask a lot. I told him I . . . preferred outside. And he let me do this." She gestures to the shelter. "Gave me a soft place to land when I needed it."

I was right, it wasn't the motel that made her like this. Then what was it? "And he left it here for you?" I ask.

"Some relationships are mutually beneficial. I hardly come here anymore, but he likes the idea that I might. And he did really help me. I owe him a lot. Can we—"

"How does this benefit him?" I ask, even though I can guess the answer.

She throws an angry look at me. "*You* never get lonely?" she asks.

The question. Hannah's eyes on me. Her hair falling over her shoulder. The sun starts to reach over the floorboards, cuts across her legs. My heart beating so stupidly fast looking at her.

"So the indoors thing, the being-around-people thing," I say.

"I don't want to talk about me anymore," she says. "What's next? How do we fix this?"

I study her for a minute. Then I say, "I need to look at it all again. Go over the evidence I've got, see if there's anything I missed before that I can somehow find now. Figure out next steps. Maybe if you want to sleep or something, I can work on this."

"No, I'll help," she says.

I'm about to say no. Of course I am. I'm about to say *just stay in my sight line at all times and don't fucking stab me please*. But . . . she was in that motel. She knows more than most people, whether she's a part of orchestrating it or not. And if she's *not*, then she's got just as much reason as I do to figure this thing out. Our time is limited, and really, we are so, so fucked.

"I can help you," she says. "I know we don't know each other, and I don't trust you either, but we're in this, both of us, whether we like it or not."

Birdsong, sun now streaming into the cabin, lighting her face. Her green eyes so light in the sun they look almost translucent.

"Okay," I say.

I go up to the car and grab the files. Stop and take a piss on the way back to the shelter. The woods are so quiet, the air crisp and clear. This mountain air that John Denver loved. The yellow-orange aspen leaves shimmering in the wind, one over the other, the sunlight streaming in to make them seem almost golden. Again, I think, it doesn't feel real. Hannah's shelter in the woods something close to the life I've been imagining for myself—maybe even better. The life I was going to have after proving my worth once more. So much for all that, I guess.

Walking back, a thought nags at me. I glance to the house while I still have it in view. It's enormous, hulking on the mountainside. The idea of Hannah feeling like she owes something to this James guy, the uneven power dynamic of it. It bothers me. This Drifter case has always been about influence. If I'm right, that is. If someone outside *is* coercing the killers or convincing them to do it. If that same outside person is eating the victims' bodies and putting his hair—because it can't be mine—on them.

Who have we investigated with strong influence? Oliver Wright for sure. But being here, seeing this house, it occurs to me that anyone with money can do so much. Money is freedom, which is power. Freedom to use your time however you want. Your resources. This guy buying up two lots, building this behemoth on one of them, and preserving the other for the girl who is his . . . what? Mistress? Girlfriend? Pet? I don't know why it bothers me so much. Why I'm judging it. I don't know these people. But . . .

Everything here, since the moment we arrived in Aspen, just feels charged. Dangerous.

Familiar.

Why?

When I get back to the shelter, Hannah's put out two blank sketchpads and pens. She means for us to take notes with them. The sun in the cabin, on her face.

"Here," I say, setting down the files. The ones that I should not be showing to her.

She takes half of them, opens them before her on the floor,

beside the fire. I sit down on the other side and start to do the same. What's one more criminal offense in all this?

I open Oliver Wright's file again, read through his interview transcripts from when Claire was first taken, back before I was even assigned to this and it was in DPD hands. It's hard to read. A man who'd just lost his fourteen-year-old daughter the week before. Hard to believe a person can survive that. But . . . I wonder if we should be pulling his dental records. See if maybe he veneered or repaired a canine around the time of the sixth killing. It could make a man insane, losing a daughter. But then who killed his? Could he have hired someone to do it, and then eaten her after? Could he be that fucked-up? And Daphne's right, what are the odds he'd go to a dentist in town if he broke his tooth on a *human* bone? Maybe we can bring him in. Or maybe it's stupid. Maybe all of this is. I don't know why I can't let it go.

I feel something after a while. I look up. Hannah, watching me. Our eyes meet, and they hold, for just a second. She looks away, a little flustered. I swallow, don't know why my heart is racing again.

We get back to it, and I try to focus on the files. Not on her. Not on Hannah, sitting right there. So close I could reach out and touch her.

After another ten minutes or so, I notice a shift in energy, some kind of feeling. I look up. Hannah looks . . .

"What's wrong?" I ask.

She swallows. Looks like she might faint. After a long second, nods. "Sorry," she says on a breath. "I just, um . . ."

I look down to what's in her hand. It's one of the bite mark photos. Close-ups of one of the victims' legs, the marks of human teeth and missing meat clear. I look back up to her face, drained of its color. Her eyes don't leave the page.

"Yeah," I say after a moment. "Probably should have mentioned. There are a lot of those."

She nods, swallows.

"Sorry," she says, closing the file and putting it away. "Um, vegetarian." She opens another file, and I watch her. After a moment, I do the same.

We read. I try to think in a new way, will myself to see things I haven't been able to see before now. It could be that an outside party has been setting this elaborate maze for me and put Hannah in as a part of it. Or she set this all up and put herself inside, as part of the game. Or she could be working with someone. *For* someone, even. That prickling feeling, that she's keeping things from me. That there's more here I can't see yet.

I think of the house again. I can't let it go.

"So . . . James," I say.

She looks up, watches me. That intensity. "What do you need to believe me that he's not a problem? Seriously, in no way is he a part of this. And it's not your business."

"Anything. That's what I need. Give me any piece of information. I don't know anything about you. You brought me here, and—"

"I am giving you information, I'm telling you everything! And I don't know anything about you either, but I'm not wasting time on shit that doesn't matter."

When I don't say anything, she says, "James doesn't matter. Not in this. He's not coming here. Now can we please try and figure out how we're not going to go to jail forever for something we didn't do?"

I search her face, look for anything I might not be seeing. *Some relationships are mutually beneficial.* Why does that bother me so much?

"Okay," I say at last.

She grabs the pen. "Do you mind if I . . ."

At this point, why not. I nod. I start reading through the chat room transcripts again.

Another half hour. Movement catches my attention. I look up. Hannah chewing on the end of the pen. My eyes catch on it, on her. Her lips on the pen. I look back down, force myself to. Tell my heartbeat to slow the fuck down.

I think of *Wizdumteller*, their last post. I pull out the burner phone and refresh the chat room, use a new account to be safe with the logs. I can't stop turning over their last line.

I wonder if it's not time to give our friends a little hint. Maybe we should say it's important to keep your eyes to the SKY.

I can't stop thinking it must be so much more obvious than I realize. If we're right to put attention here at all.

Hours pass, combing through the same notes, the same pages,

Hannah asking me periodic questions. At one point she says, "Are there any main suspects?"

"You mean besides us?"

"Yes."

"A developer, Oliver Wright, maybe. And a person in this chat room. Calls themself *Wizdumteller.* We haven't been able to track them, and they seem to know when the murders are coming. Those are really the best we've got at the moment."

She takes this in. "You think for sure that someone aside from the Drifters is involved?" she asks. "That they're not just all killing these people and eating them and then pretending they don't remember it?"

I say, "We don't know."

She nods, looks back to the file in her hand. She flips a few pages, and I watch her as her eyes catch on one of them. She tenses again.

"What are you reading?" I ask.

"It says, um, 'Tillman's Notes.'"

She slides the paper over to me behind the firepit, keeps the folder in her lap. I pick up the paper and glance at it. It's dated from yesterday, so it must be one of the new files Frazier last put on my desk, or the last batch I printed. The page says: *Witchwalker Mentions.* Then there's a list of links.

Tillman. Of course he would run with this. I only said the word the one time to him in the car, but never underestimate the cryptozoologist or whatever. I wonder if he put together *Witchwalker* and the *WW* from *Wizdumteller*'s posts. Something tells me he did.

We start checking the links. There isn't much. A couple low-view YouTube videos from internet paranormal people that are mostly incomprehensible. A couple Reddit threads that don't say much, talking about kids at school, spreading scary stories. I hold the phone up so Hannah and I both can see them. She seems off, a little more on edge than before. The last link is a TikTok video of a guy in Carhartts with a horse behind him, a teenager asking him, *Can you tell us about the Witchwalker?*

The man looks angry. He says, *Don't you say that word. Seriously, that's not funny. It's not—*

I squint at the screen, play the video again. I know him. Why do I . . .

Ryder Smith. Shit. He looks different now, has grown into a man. Our dead-end momentary suspect from years ago who went to the same school as a couple of the victims and one of the Drifters, who was busted for bringing in a fake gun to their high school and threatening to shoot up the student body. He was a teen at the time of these murders, there was no way he could coerce any of these adults into doing these things. And he didn't have the personality to seek control, power. Not the kind that someone like this would. Just didn't fit the profile. What he wanted was attention, to be understood, by his parents, the other kids at school. Still, it was terrible. To take even a fake gun into a school. He served the time for it.

I play the video a third time. I'm certain it's him. And I think I remember reading that he works at a horse ranch somewhere now, rehabilitation programs for at-risk youth.

Hannah drops the file to the floor.

"Are you okay?" I ask, turning back to her.

"Um. I'm feeling a little bit . . . I need to get outside."

"You . . ." I look around. We are basically outside.

"No, I, um . . . I need to move. Run. If that's okay. And I think I need food. I haven't eaten in a long time. Are you, do you care if I . . . ?"

I know the look on her face. I know it because I've had it on mine a million times. She's fighting off a panic attack. Something in the "Tillman's Notes" file or the video I was playing gave her this reaction. Does she know Ryder Smith? Is he more a part of this than we think he is? Being tied in with that word, *Witchwalker* . . .

Maybe Hannah is the best lead I can follow for the moment. It's risky—beyond risky—stupid, even. Leaving, going out in the open. Letting her call the shots on where we go and what we do. But maybe all I need is right here. This woman before me. Maybe she, as I have wondered this whole time, might really be the key to everything.

"I'll go with you," I say. And I don't give her a chance to argue.

I pack up the files in case we don't come back and carry them to the car. Hannah steps inside the house for clothes, and I start to follow her in, but another thought pulls at me. That look on her face with Tillman's notes in her hand. I reach for the folder.

The paper on top is another list. Lines that Tillman's pulled from different interviews—victims, family members, friends, killers—in which they used the word *it* instead of a personal pronoun. It's not long, only eight or so.

Why it would it want my daughter?

It must've gotten him when—

Can't sleep anymore. Scared it's coming for us too.

He's got each labeled and cross-referencing their interview. I reach for the corresponding interview transcripts. Each time, the way the lines sit in the conversation, no one would bat an eye. I've pored over these documents, for years, and I never caught these. Because why would I? What the fuck was *it*?

But these lines pulled from their context, written out alone with space around them . . . something doesn't feel right. And what would *it* mean? That we're talking about a "thing" and not a person? These are terrified people whose lives have been upended, who are trying to make sense of something that no one should have to make sense of.

I don't think it's so much *what are they saying,* as it is, *why did it scare Hannah?*

Or was it something else?

2

We drive down the mountain in James's Bronco and park at the edge of a public green space. Wide perfect stretches of grass, lush trees. And this park, this place I have never seen before, fills me with a kind of dread I can't understand.

Dizziness, nausea.

Rose. My mom, in a pink dress.

On the path in front of me.

Rose.

I *see* her.

Plain as day, in this memory.

Here.

No. That's not possible. We never—

"We can catch the trail through there," Hannah says.

My heart, thundering.

The drive into Aspen from Denver, feeling like I'd done it before. But I know I haven't. Right? Passing that old pharmacy and the entrance to this park. That overwhelming sense of déjà vu. Is it just being here with Hannah? Is it just the fact that I am somehow implicated in this case? That I can't seem to get my bearings at all?

I move in a daze, behind Hannah. She's now wearing running tights, an oversized faded purple PROTECT OUR PARKS hoodie, and a fleece headband, all of which I can only assume are hers, clothes left at the house. Her hair in a ponytail again. A pair of beat-up running shoes.

Hannah, walking before me.

Time, glitching, shaking.

Rose, Mom, walking before me.

I blink.

Ahead of Hannah, a sign that—

I don't know if I want to laugh or cry.

But of course I knew it was here. That there would be something here. Something to commemorate him. I should have expected it.

JOHN DENVER SANCTUARY.

Still . . .

I follow Hannah through an unthinkably beautiful garden, boulders with plants, flowers, trees. So dizzy. Ears ringing. My palms sweating.

That glitch. Seconds, half seconds. A past version.

Rose, in a pink dress, walking in front of me. Here.

Hannah. Now.

I blink, shake it off.

Grass so green and soft looking it almost seems fake. On some of the large stones, nearly as tall as I am, are lyrics. "The Eagle and the Hawk," "Perhaps Love," "Sunshine on My Shoulders." I follow Hannah through them, and when I see the last one by the water, the river,

The river I have been seeing and remembering—

"Rocky Mountain High."

Glitch. I'm—

Leave your shoes on the rock, Danny, come sit in the river with me.

Mom in her pink dress, beside the big stone with the lyrics. I can only read some of it, but she said it's "Rocky Mountain High."

I've been here before.

This is it. She—

We leave our shoes on the grass and take the small path down to the water. It's cold on my feet. I laugh. Mom is headed for the big rock in the middle, sets the picnic basket down and turns back to take my hand—

I blink, can barely breathe. A shadow in the river. Near the rock.

I try to catch my breath, to stop the nausea. I turn to where Hannah is.

Was. To where Hannah should be.

She's gone. Hannah is . . .

Fuck. I was caught in that memory, and now she's gotten away.

Panic. Have to think. I think if I go left, that's where she'll be. Right? Fuck, I don't know. I don't have time. I push my body to move. How fucking stupid can I be? The river—

I swear, go. My feet pound on the dirt path, catching the Rio

Grande Trail across a wooden bridge that goes over the river, onto the paved part. I don't see her.

I run faster. She couldn't have taken the car. I have the keys. She had to have gone this way. I think. I move, push, my lungs burning in the cold. It's a lot colder here than in Denver, higher up. Running feels different, harder. I take a turn, through the trees, through a path that in any other circumstance I would probably marvel at the beauty of, surrounded by towering pines and golden aspen trees. And there, just at the edge of my field of vision, at the farthest visible point on the path, I see her, running up ahead.

I sprint. Thank my fellow reservists for kicking my ass and keeping me in shape all these years. Hannah's fast, crazy fast. I don't know how long I was standing by the river back there, but it wasn't long. At least I don't think it was. I can't think about that. The river, the memory. That strange smell, and my mom and—

I see Hannah now, closer.

The river—wide and flowing—runs on our left now, an upward sloping rock face on our right. She'd said something on the drive down about running to get food, that there would be a place. I push my pace until I'm nearly even with her.

She looks back, and at first I think the look on her face is fear. But when she does it again . . . I think she's smiling, a little.

I lean forward and catch up to her, come around on her left.

Our shoulders nearly brush as she surges forward again, pushes ahead of me. Trees fly by. She weaves in and out of a couple hiking with their dog, bikes speeding around us, Hannah dodging all of them. I weave through them a moment later, push my legs. My muscles are burning. I ran far last night, I don't know how many miles, but with the cold and the altitude, and pushing my pace faster than I ever do, I feel it. Hannah ran or walked twentysomething miles to Whileago Manor. And now *this*. She said she hasn't eaten. I know she hasn't slept.

Who the fuck is this woman?

I surge forward again, and she turns to me.

"Thought you'd never catch up," she says, not breaking pace.

"Seems like you didn't want me to," I say.

"I don't," she says, and she surges forward again.

I let her run just ahead for five miles, maybe six, but keep close enough behind her. The landscape changes around us as we get farther from town. We gain elevation, the river dropping so far below us down a cliff's edge on the left that I wonder a few times if maybe she brought me up here just to push me off it. Though I guess she could have done that back up at her shelter on the mountain. The sun is high in the sky now. I pull out the phone and glance at it. It's almost eleven. Haven't slept. No closer to finding out what's going on. Chasing after a woman who makes my head spin. And my mom. The river, John Denver Sanctuary. That memory, somehow a memory in a place I don't remember ever—

My muscles burn, and I watch Hannah Lawrence running in front of me, and I can't fathom how Rose and I could have been here. How any of this is happening.

But for one second, I think, my legs hurt, my lungs burn. And despite everything, it feels so fucking good, to feel the pain. To move through it. To push in the altitude and cold. Physical pain can take something from the mental. Is that what she's doing? Does she need it too?

Maybe we're just wasting time. Probably. Precious time we really don't have. I lean forward, tell my legs to go. I meet her, then when she picks up speed, I push forward again, pass her. She passes me. A foot from me, that's it.

We do it again. She passes, then I do. I don't know how many times. I don't know because maybe I'm not thinking. I'm running and sweating and working and breathing.

The next time I surge ahead to pass her, I make the biggest mistake of my life. I turn to look at her straight on. Just once, just one moment. I catch sight of her face. Skin flushed and red in the cold, eyes bright and electrified and wild. A small smile there.

Something running toward me, from ahead. But my eyes are on her.

Hannah Lawrence is smiling at me. And—

I look forward. The thing running toward me, it's a shadow.

It collides with my body, shoves its arm down my throat.

3

I blink, and I'm in a restaurant. Sitting at a booth. Hannah across from me, adjusting her nose plug, her sweatshirt lifted to cover the lower half of her face. She sinks deeper into her side of the booth. John Denver's "Take Me Home, Country Roads" plays on the speakers. I close my eyes and take a breath. Will my heart to slow. Against the music, against everything.

I sort of remember coming in, the WOODY CREEK TAVERN sign outside, Hannah bracing when she learned the outside tables were closed, making herself step into the small indoor space. The onslaught of music as we walked inside. The low-ceilinged lively restaurant wallpapered with labeled photographs of patrons, eating, partying, laughing. Over the photos, framed posters of Hunter S. Thompson's campaign for sheriff, framed art and photos of him and his friends. A disco ball hangs from the ceiling in the middle of the room, and on the other end by the door, there's a bar with six stools, a TV playing the news behind it.

I scan the space for security cameras. I don't see any. On the wall to our right is a wooden shelf with a fishing trophy; another portrait of Hunter S. Thompson, who seems to be staring at us from behind his sunglasses; a frog lamp; a naked baby doll; and, because everything feels like the biggest fucking joke, a framed photo of John Denver holding his acoustic guitar.

I turn and clock the other diners. No one's paying any attention to us. Aspen socialites with those ridiculous wide-brimmed hats, a Hunter S. Thompson fanboy with a notebook and pen, a few grizzled old mountain men, and a table of three mountain bikers. A shadow lingers on one of the barstools, another by the door. The TV behind the bar says a storm's coming, blizzard, across the state. *Severe weather warning, stay safe.*

Hannah's anxious. No trace of the woman on that running

path, the wild freedom of her. Even huddled in the corner, in arguably the safest spot here, her back and side covered, seeing her indoors is like seeing someone entirely different. I think about her three-sided shelter. Cover, safety. Only one exit to defend. She thinks like a soldier. She thinks like someone who's had to fight for her life.

When the server comes to take our order, Hannah shrinks back from him. I ask for a burger. Hannah points to the salad on the menu. We both get coffee—her voice just audible through the sweatshirt to order it. If it were any other circumstance in which I'd find myself here, I would be getting a drink. Could really use one now.

Hannah excuses herself to use the restroom, and I almost protest after seeing how fast she can run, but at that same moment, an unfamiliar chime sounds on my person. Also, the bathroom door is right in my line of sight. I pat my outer layer and pull out the burner phone, shrug the jacket off in the warm restaurant. I have an alert: new post in the chat room from *Wizdumteller.*

Seems our last clue went a little OVER THE HEAD. Have they tried the wolf of no name?

I read over the post again. *Over the head* obviously calling back to Sky clue, right? For the life of me I still don't know what it could have anything to do with. Screw it. I don't know what else to do.

I close my eyes in the bar, reach out through my senses into the other-place. The one that doesn't exist. The one that my stupid brain says it feels, even knowing that. I repeat the phrase under my breath.

Have they tried the wolf of no name.

Have they tried—

"What are you doing?" Hannah says. I open my eyes, and she's standing beside the booth, watching me. Her eyes zeroed in on my face.

"I'm just . . . thinking," I say. I blink. She's not holding the sweatshirt over her nose anymore. She's not wearing it, in fact. Her arms, throat, chest bare. Her skin. I swallow. She watches me another moment, glances over to the bar, then sits.

She smells faintly of that something spicy again, in addition to the ponderosa smell she seems to carry with her. She slips what looks like a small medication tube into the hoodie's pocket in her lap. In her tank top, her tattoo is visible. A hyperrealistic mountain on her arm, tattooed over a thick jagged scar. Her skin is smooth and tan, all of it—

I clear my throat. Pull my eyes away. Make myself.

The song changes, another John Denver. "I Guess He'd Rather Be in Colorado." I take a sip of water and try not to throw up.

"What's your deal with John Denver?" Hannah asks, watching me. What is that expression on her face? Confusion, curiosity. Something more, maybe.

I clear my throat again. "What do you mean?"

"I mean"—she tucks her hair behind her ear—"it's been on the radio nonstop, your car radio that mysteriously doesn't turn off. It played in the motel. I heard it again when I touched the papers you'd held. Why?"

I take a breath, try to speak. It doesn't come. After a second, I try again. "You really heard 'Annie's Song' playing there?" I ask.

She nods, watching me.

And I don't know why I say it. Maybe because I need to see her reaction. To watch her eyes and know if this is somehow her doing. If she would put me through this.

"I used to live in that room," I say. "When I was a kid. And I used to listen to John Denver, all the time. There was a movie about him, and we had his autobiography." I swallow, make myself say it. "My mom used to read it to me. And the movie . . . it was playing when— I think that someone was trying to get to me by playing that music in the room."

"Trying to get to *you* . . . by playing the music for *me*."

I shrug. I've got nothing better for her. I've got nothing better for anyone else.

She takes it all in, and I don't get a lie from her. Or I mean I don't get a feeling. Not that the feelings are real. But I think the way she's watching me now, the way she takes me in, I think that was the first time she heard about me living there. Unless I'm a total idiot. Unless I'm falling for an act, hook, line and sinker. Which . . .

I look away, glance back. She's watching me, still. She swallows too, looks away, her chest rising and falling.

The server sets our food down. Hannah leans back further, a sick look crossing her face at my burger.

Right. Vegetarian.

She covers her nose again with the sleeve of the hoodie in her lap. "So," she says, not touching her food. "Was he your hero? John Denver?"

"No," I say after a minute. "He was a . . . complicated guy. His dad didn't support him early in life, and it seems maybe a lot of his life was trying to make something of himself despite and because of that. And John as an adult was gone a lot, cheated on his wife, Annie, for years. At one point, when he was away, Annie had to make a decision about trees on their property in Aspen that someone told her needed to be cut down, and she did it. The story's a little different each way. In the movie, he gets back from tour and sees the trees are gone, and he takes a chainsaw to their four-poster bed. It comes out of nowhere, this just total rage. He was big on humanitarian missions, helping the environment. He loved nature, loved their property. He was never remotely violent before that moment, was just this sort of dweeby but cool cowboy hippie out saving the world with his music and charity."

"What happened in the book version?"

I take a bite, chew, and swallow. "When Annie finally wanted a separation after he'd been gone for so long, and he'd moved out, she started hosting dinner parties and having their Aspen friends over without him. So he showed up at the house one day with a chainsaw. He says in the book that he could see she was afraid he was going to hurt her with it. He just . . . says that. No apologies. And then he pushes past her into the house and cleaves the dining table in half, the one she'd hosted at without him. He goes into their bedroom and cuts the posts off the four-poster bed. Then he drops the chainsaw and grabs her, puts his hands around her throat. And in that moment, in the narration, he says, 'I almost lost it.' Like everything that happened up to that moment was just . . . He *almost* lost it."

"Oh. So it makes sense you're obsessed with him."

I laugh. I can't help it. I take another bite. Something about the woman in front of me. Something about everything falling apart. I swallow, glance at her again.

I say after a second, "It's—I mean, I loved the music, when I was young. But it was the fact that he could be so . . . complicated, I guess. Nothing ever made me feel as safe as a kid as his songs did. I'm not excusing his behavior—you can't—but people I knew, as a kid, things I'd seen. Something about knowing that even people who might not be all the way good could give a lot of good to the world anyway . . . it made me feel hope. And he was funny." I point to the speakers. "Like this song. About a guy in New York who dreams of Colorado and the West, everything here so beautiful. Then at the end of the song, the most brutal savage line. *Up in his office, a quiet cough is all he has to show he lives in New York City.* John Denver loved *this* land, Colorado. He loved this place more than anyone. He made Colorado, to me, less dark, less terrifying. Like . . . a place worth being."

Hannah watches me, and I can't see her nose or mouth, but that bit of light is there in her eyes. It's only after I finish my food and the plate's taken away that she starts to eat hers. "What were you repeating when I sat down?" she asks. "When I came back from the bathroom?"

"*Wizdumteller*, that chat room person, posted again. *Have they tried the wolf of no name?*"

"What does that mean?" she asks.

"Million-dollar question."

"Well, No Name. I mean, could it be like the town?"

"What?"

"The town. No Name. We passed by it on the way here, right before Glenwood. It's small, like three hundred people or something. Just like a bunch of houses, maybe a hotel."

"Is there a wolf there?"

"Um . . . I don't think . . . Oh! OH! Oh my god. Yes! There's a . . ." She tucks her hair behind her ears, puts her hand over her mouth, closes her eyes, thinking. "Ranch. Sorry, was trying to picture it. I saw it once, when I went for a hike there. There's a trailhead right nearby. There's a wolf on the sign."

I pull out the phone and search "No Name CO wolf ranch."

The first thing that pops up is No Name Equine Therapy Ranch. But the images show a wolf on the sign. I click on the page, and it takes me to a website explaining the history of the ranch. Explaining how it used to be a wolf education place, but they moved to a much larger property. And Ryder Smith—the very same from that TikTok talking about a *Witchwalker*, the one who went to the same school as two of the victims and one of the Drifters and pulled that shit at his high school all those years ago—took it over. Brought in a couple horses, and provides rehabilitation for at-risk youth. Plans to expand to bigger, wider open land one day. Ryder Smith, the owner.

I clear my throat. "I know him. We thought he was attached to the case a while ago, but we dropped it."

She sits up, watching me. "So we have a plan?"

"A starting point, at least," I say.

She nods. "Okay." This girl I don't know, in a tank top and nose plug. Her hair sweaty and pulled back, light green eyes shining. That spicy smell mixed in with her ponderosa pine.

"Thank you," I say, a little out of breath.

Her eyes search my face, I don't know for what. But there's feeling there. Her brow furrows, trying to find something. I let her look.

I don't move, don't do anything. Seconds pass. She raises her eyes to mine, and . . .

What is this look? So heavy. Complicated. Charged.

My heart, racing. Her breaths coming a little faster.

She bites her bottom lip, for just half a second.

"I—"

She glances over my shoulder, then double takes.

Her face drains of all color at whatever she sees there. Something behind me.

I slowly turn around.

On the TV behind the bar, a banner streams across the bottom of the screen.

DRIFTER SERIAL MURDERS ARE BACK.

Reports of four murders since the five-year hiatus.

I think it's a mistake. It's three murders back, not four. And how do they . . .

A photo flashes of a woman on the side of the road naked and wearing the skin of a man, blurred out for the program. But plain as day. A woman I haven't seen. A new one. And someone got a photo. They got it, and it's . . . on live news.

I don't know who she is, don't recognize her, but . . . I pull out the phone, click through articles, one after another, as fast as I can.

Someone leaked that the murders have started again. It doesn't matter who, one of the victims' or killers' family or friends, probably in response to this one being recorded. People know. And there's been a fourth one. Already, since we left. Last night, there was another—

"Oh shit," Hannah says.

I turn again, but I already know what I'm going to see before I do. The bartender has stopped to watch the screen.

A second headline flashes.

WANTED FOR QUESTIONING, ARMED AND DANGEROUS.

And beneath it, two photographs.

One of Hannah. And one of me.

4

We duck into the gear shop next door that mercifully has no TV and get a couple fishing hats. I call a taxi back to town, and we hide our faces from the driver. We get the Bronco from the park and drive it back up the mountain, pack all our things into the red vintage Wagoneer in the garage. We take cash from James's house. Hannah says he won't care, but I'm taking her word for all of this. We were in the restaurant, with the news showing us plain and clear.

I grab the duffel Josie gave me from my car, the files. The knife. I pull a pair of blue jeans and my boots out of the duffel. A clean shirt. Change quickly in the garage. Hannah changes too, inside the house. She comes back out in a green sweater and her jeans. Her hiking boots. She leaves her USFS jacket in the mudroom, shrugs on a larger one, a black puffer probably belonging to a man. Belonging to James.

I catch sight of the stuffed mountain lion through a side window as we're leaving the house. Hannah's looking at it too.

We don't talk, the road stretching out before us. Hannah's window rolled down with her head leaning out, the heat on high.

"Take Me Home, Country Roads" plays on the radio. Even in this car that isn't mine. I slam my hand against the off button, and it does nothing.

Everything is fucked. Beyond fucked. Colossally world-shatteringly fucked.

And in an insane moment of dissonance, just one second, the sun glints off the hood of the red car, the mountains towering over us and those aspen trees that look like a million individuals but are just part of one staggering whole, and I think, Colorado really looks so beautiful.

* * *

We shouldn't have left the three-sided shelter. We were hidden, no paper trail, the car tucked away, no one to find us. Now we're out in the open, and a notice has been put out. How far will it be spread? They put it on the fuckin' news for god's sake, who else has been notified? Cops, probably. Highway patrol. If they get us on the cameras, if they see us . . . But we have to find out what's going on. We need to solve this. We need *something.*

"I don't think we need to worry about anyone at Woody Creek," Hannah says, as if reading my thoughts.

"Why's that?"

"They're all Aspen, maybe New York, LA. They're all people who look around for someone they deem important, and if they don't see that, they just want to be seen themselves. That's all they really want. To just be there and be admired. We're fine. From them anyway."

I consider her words. Some of them looked like influencers. Influencers have followings. Could go viral with a clip of two wanted, armed, and dangerous people on the run. I don't think I saw anyone taping us, but you can't be sure these days.

We take 82 up past Basalt, to Glenwood. The Wild West tourist traps and Doc Holliday signs, the sulfur smell of the hot springs coming through the window. All the historic redbrick stores selling Colorado merch and Old West costume pieces. We head east on 70, take the exit for No Name, and follow it up to No Name Creek Road. No Name seems to be almost nothing in terms of population—two small sections on either side of the highway of homes. Hannah said a hotel too, but I don't see it.

We find ourselves moments later in a wooded canyon, a winding road. A big drop on one side, slope up on the other. Houses at intervals on either side. The GPS glitches, shuts off. My phone refusing to tell us where to go. The radio flips on again, Lead Belly's "Springtime in the Rockies."

We come to a cul-de-sac with a trailhead on our left and an AUTHORIZED VEHICLES ONLY sign for the long windy road ahead.

"I thought there was a sign," Hannah says. "I remember one. But . . ."

There's no sign. Maybe we were supposed to turn right off the highway instead of left. Maybe this was a wild goose chase and we're no closer to finding what we're looking for.

"But this looks familiar otherwise? And you remember a wolf on a sign here?"

She nods. "I mean, I think. I just came once for the hike, and now I'm wondering if I—"

We don't have time to waste. We're here. Before I let myself hit another dead end, accept that this thing just never yields any answers, I exhale. Fuck it.

I close my eyes, reach out again into that other-space, that place where maybe, sometimes, I get answers. If any of it's real.

Before I know what I'm doing, my hands are on the wheel, and we're going past the sign, onto the private road.

We follow it, windows down so we can hear the tires gripping the asphalt.

After a second, Hannah sits up straighter. "You were right," she says. "This is it."

"What?" I don't see anything yet, no sign or anything, just this windy wooded canyon road.

"We're going the right way," she says.

"How do you know?"

"You don't smell them?"

I shake my head, have no idea what she means.

"Horses," she says. She turns to look at me.

I don't smell anything, but in another minute, it turns out she's right.

To call it a ranch is certainly a stretch, but No Name Equine Therapy definitely has horses. Two large paddocks and a couple smaller ones beyond a small house, a barn at the far end, all in a fairly wide clearing in the canyon. The horses' tails swish, heads turn, eyes catching as we pull to a stop, dust trailing out from behind our car in the early afternoon light. We step out, and I rub my hands together before sticking them in my pockets. Hannah's drawing. My fingers brush against it. I'm starting to see my breath now. The sun shining down into the canyon glints against the horses' coats, against their metal corrals and gates.

"Snow's coming," I say. I reach into the back seat for my hat. "You feel it?"

"No," she says, "but I smell it."

I look at her again. She shrugs, the nose plug still in.

At the far end of the property near the barn, a man whistles in what I guess is a welcome, or a question. I fight the urge to hover my hand over my gun.

It's Ryder Smith, same guy from the video, same guy from the website and our previous interviews. Blue jeans, dirty boots, tan Carhartt, white hat, saddling a palomino. We walk through the paddocks toward him, dirt and gravel crunching and shifting beneath our feet. Horses whinny as we pass.

We stop before the barn. Couple of trucks, equipment, hay. Beyond it, the canyon walls close in, making this place feel like a three-sided shelter of its own.

I watch Ryder Smith as he starts to walk toward us with the horse. Could he be *Wizdumteller*?

"Hi," he says. "C'n I help you?"

The horse huffs, and its eye catches Hannah's. The man turns his attention to her.

"Is Ryder Smith around?" I ask.

The man blinks. "Yeah, maybe." He pauses. "Who's askin'?"

I look him up and down. He has the haunted look of a person who's lived a hard life. Prison will do that, expedite the whole process.

I tap that reservoir again, test my luck a bit. Honesty is what he's gonna respect, that feeling tells me. That other-place that isn't real. I open up my jacket and show him my badge, not long enough for him to see the name on it, just to get a glimpse. "Just have a couple questions," I say.

The horse lifts a hoof, sets it down, swishes its tail. The man pats the horse, whispers, *Shh, easy.*

"Am I in trouble?" he asks.

"We're hoping you can help us with something."

"Is one of my students in trouble?"

"No. Not as far as I know."

He deliberates a long time, looks us both over. Then eventually sighs, hangs his head a little, and takes a step toward me, reaching out his hand. "Sorry," he says. "Old habits. Yeah, this is my place."

"It's beautiful," Hannah says.

Ryder smiles, a little, at that. He keeps his hand on the horse. "I'm proud of it. Been a long time since I've seen one of you," he says to me. "I'm past my probation period."

I glance at Hannah, and I wonder if we take the honesty all the way. I don't know if I'm crazy, but I see her head nod just slightly, as if she knows what I'm thinking.

"Look, Ryder," I say. "We need your help."

"With what?"

"By your students, you mean the people who come here to ride?"

"Yeah," he says after a moment. "We work with rehab facilities, kids with disabilities, kids who've gone down a rough path but want to turn their lives around, all kinds. Anyone who needs a safe judgment-free space to get their lives going in a good direction. We partner with a wolf sanctuary that does the same thing, people who used to own this place. All seems to really help them."

"That's really admirable. Especially doing it all at your age. Impressive."

"Yeah, well . . . I know what it's like. I mean, you know that."

I nod.

"Look, I . . ." He trails off, looks up to the sky. "I can't undo what I did. I was young, and I was angry and lonely, and I was a fuckin' idiot. I didn't want to hurt anyone. I'd never . . ." His head drops again. He looks up with such anguish on his face.

"I wanted to scare them," he says. "I learned a long time later that maybe I just wanted to be noticed. It's just . . . there's no excuse. There will never be. But I'm not that guy, not anymore and not for a really long time. And now, here, every day, I am dedicated to trying to give people the second chance they deserve."

"The horses help with that?"

Even as I ask, I see the horse leaning in now to Ryder, Ryder just slightly leaning back. His eyes are glassy, and he takes a deep breath and lets it go. "Man, it never gets easier, thinkin' about it. We all strive toward peace, but . . . yeah. The horses help. They're . . ." He looks at the creature beside him, standing tall, giving him support.

"They're magic." The words don't come from Ryder. Hannah said them. I turn to her, and she lowers her gaze, doesn't like his attention on her. Maybe doesn't like mine either. She gives a small smile, then steps away from us, slowly walks toward one of the paddocks.

Ryder watches her, taking careful steps through the dirt. She stops beside a paint horse in its own enclosure. The horse steps over to her, and we watch as Hannah reaches up and runs her hand over the horse's muzzle. The horse leans forward into her touch, and after a moment, Hannah drops her forehead to his.

Ryder snorts a laugh. I turn to him, still watching. "That horse," he says to me. "We call her Freebird. She doesn't let anyone touch her. Besides me. And only then maybe half the time."

Freebird swishes her tail, Hannah's hands running up and down either side of her face. Both of them exhaling visible breath into the cold light of day. Ryder snorts again. "Well, I'll be damned. She an agent too?"

"She's . . . No." I don't know why I say it. I'm not really thinking as I watch this woman with the sun in her hair seek such solace in another creature, *give* it. Every time I look at her, really allow myself to look, I think there's something I'm not quite getting. She's . . . That thing she said, feeling like she *knew* me when she first saw me. Was she just saying that she really *does* know me? Is orchestrating all of this? But . . . if I'm being honest . . .

I feel the same, like I know her too.

And yet I think nothing could be further from the truth.

I have to look away. My traitorous body's reaction to her. Just a pretty woman. Beautiful woman. Who is wild and independent and seems to really know herself. Who smiled at me running, and—

And the memory in the park. All of it, I can't quite—

"Horses don't like pressure," Ryder says, eyes on Hannah.

"What's that?" I say.

"Visual, physical, verbal," he says, "they don't like it. That's why they respond to it. They don't like it."

Ryder's eyes flick to mine, imparting some great meaning. "You don't pressure a horse unless you know what you want from it." He jerks his chin toward Hannah again. "She reminds me of my students. You have to be careful."

Again, I think, maybe honesty here. "She's been through some things."

Ryder takes that in, nods once, and softens. "All the horses here are rescues," he says.

"Look," I say. "I'm sorry. I don't have much time. We do need your help."

Again, that nervousness, and the horse beside him shifts a little. Ryder nods.

Is it you? Could it be?

"Did you know anyone by the name of Everett Brown?"

He furrows his brow, thinking. Then he shakes his head.

"What about Kimberly Chen? Ross Thompson?"

Same thing, shakes his head no.

"Ramona Lopez? Pete Noland? Tony Howell?"

Again, a shake of the head. The horse beside him stomps its back foot and swishes its tail.

"I don't know any of these people. Why are you asking me?"

"Can you tell me what a Witchwalker is?"

Ryder goes completely pale. "Did you come here to fuck with me?"

"No," I say.

"Why would you ask me that?"

"It might have something to do with a murder case."

He swears. "Is this that Drifter thing? Again?"

After a moment, I nod.

"I told you all I have nothing to do with that." He shakes his head. "Fuck. Look, I don't want to invite that shit up here. I'm serious."

"Have you by any chance heard of a chat room called DRIFTERS: SEEKING THE TRUTH?" I ask.

"Fuck," he says again, and squeezes his eyes closed. The horse leans into him. "That motherfucker. Did he tell you to come here? Is he fucking with me again?" He's shaken, scared.

"Who?"

He swears again, breathes. He says, "In jail, people talk. They kept me mostly on my own because of what I did. I wasn't a chomo or an animal abuser, but . . . schools have kids in 'em. The guards learned real quick that I needed to be on my own or I wasn't gonna last long. But before they put me in the psych ward, they'd all whisper about it. Not much in prison can scare people, especially the tough guys, but that . . . *thing* . . ."

"The Witchwalker?"

"Jesus, stop. I'm serious."

"What is it? Why did it scare them so much?" *Why does it scare you?*

"I mean, the idea that you might be possessed by something, turned into a killer against your will, what's scarier than—"

"You don't think the killers did it?"

"I mean, I don't know. But in jail, the way people talked, it was like it was real. I had a cellmate for about a month. This motherfucker. He was in for forced labor and SA. Crazy dude. Saw himself as a kind of new Manson. Liked attention, the more eyes on him the better. He would sit there on his bed at night, starin' up at the little window out to the sky, this intense look on his face like he was waiting. Like he was praying with his eyes open. And right as I was closing my eyes to sleep every night, he'd say, like he was talkin' to the fuckin' night, *I feel you watching me. Why don't you take me? Use me too.*"

"They didn't take *him* to the psych ward?"

Ryder looks at me like he doesn't understand. "No, you don't get it. He wasn't crazy. He *acted* crazy, like, we knew that, everyone knew. But even the guards didn't mess with him. He . . . *knew* things. He'd tell us the weatherman was wrong about the next day's report, and he'd be right. He'd tell us what the next ten meals served would be before the distributor had made the drop-off. Sometimes he could even tell you if someone you knew had died and was sayin' hello."

I must make a face because he says, "You don't believe that some people just feel things? That they can access something the rest of us can't?"

I clear my throat, watch Hannah and the horse. "You were afraid of the . . . *thing*? Afraid your cellmate might turn into one?"

Ryder nods. "Afraid any of us might. And it's not *turning* into one, it's like it takes you over. It comes and walks through you. Wears you like a coat. But yeah, he was inviting it in, he wanted it there. And it wasn't always just him. Everybody talked about it. Sometimes we could feel something, comin' in through the window. Passing over our skin. This weird sound. Like it was testing us. Like it was looking for something or someone, and none of us were it. It stayed with my cellmate the longest, would hang around our room, but it always left at the end. And he'd throw these insane fits when it did. Punch concrete walls, bang his head against the bars till he bled, yelling. But that sound when it came. I'll never . . . Sometimes I still dream about it."

"What was the sound like?"

"Um . . . kind of like intense pressure. I don't know how to say it better than that. Like, um, *VOOM*. That's kind of what it was like. Static, and pressure. Like we were sucked into a vacuum. And we were just trapped there, like we couldn't do anything. Just wait."

"How did you know it had to do with the . . . I mean, is it a creature?"

"Yeah. Maybe. No. I don't know. And as far as how we knew . . . we just did. We knew. It was like . . . you know a person when you see him, or feel him." He frowns, shifts. "No, that's not right. I don't know what to say. We just *knew*. But this psycho motherfucker. He won't leave me alone. It's been years, and I can't shake him. He's so—"

"You mean the *Witchwalker*?"

"No, and *please* stop saying it. I'm serious, I'm gonna ask you to leave if you do it again. My cellmate. He's like some kind of freakin' cult priest in Yampa or something. And he's obsessed with the case. The chat room I think is like an extension of his weird congregation, and he sends me stuff, wants me to be a part of his cult. I don't know. I don't want him talking about me, and I don't want anyone here saying that . . . *word* . . . more than they need to. It's serious shit, I don't want to be a part of it. I am not a part of it."

"Do you by any chance remember his name?"

"Yeah. It's Theo. Theo Wharton."

He looks to Hannah and Freebird. A breeze blows through the canyon, rattling a number of trees. Ryder Smith's next words hit me like a drunk truck driver:

"But his congregation calls him Father Sky."

5

Maybe we should say it's important to keep your eyes to the **SKY***.* Mona Brown talking about the vase with clouds on it. "My father gave it to me." The strange emphasis on *father*, the slight pause. The almost reverent, obsessive, possessive way she spoke about him. The way Tillman got her to speak about him. Father Sky.

My father gave it to me.

Where does he live?

Out in Yam . . . Yuma.

Did she mean Yampa? Did she stop herself from saying it?

A quick search, and there he is. Father Sky and his Sacred Life Church in Yampa. Right there in the open. Photos of white-linen-wearing worshippers sitting in the grass around a white dome, faces tilted toward the sky.

I remember suddenly. The flyer I saw in the Mama Tried bathroom on my first night back. FEELING LOST? FIND YOURSELF IN YAMPA. The same slogan running along the bottom of the webpage now for Sacred Life Church. Fuck. It *was* right in front of me. Could he have known that was my bar? Could he have put it there intentionally, to fuck with me?

Father Sky, Theo Wharton. Ryder Smith says he is *Wizdumteller*. The guy in the chat rooms who predicted the killings would start again. Could that mean he's the same one orchestrating them? Seems not too crazy a jump. My pulse races.

I walk toward the car, Hannah following. We may have found him. This might really be it.

And I realize. I don't have backup, I don't have anyone.

We're fucked, have been. Hannah and me. But maybe, maybe if I tell the others, bring them in, maybe there's an out for us.

I get back in the car, agitated, ready. I feel so certain that we have found something huge here, that *feeling* pressing in on me.

This is it. I don't have to be on the run. We don't have to be. This could, and should, clear Hannah and me. Right? Hannah walks toward the car, Ryder Smith watching both of us leave from the barn. My heart pounds, adrenaline coursing through my body. I hesitate, try to decide.

And I do something that either is the best decision I'll ever make or the absolute worst.

I know Jack's number by heart.

I send him a text that might very well save, or end, my life as I know it.

I tuck the phone away just as Hannah gets in.

Theo Wharton. Goes by Father Sky out in Yampa. He's Wizdumteller. Almost 100% sure. We're on our way.

The Sacred Life Church is a round white-stuccoed earthen dome in the middle of a November-brown field with blue water in the lake behind it, pines covering the flattop mountains beyond. Hannah stands on the other side of the car, her eyes intense, darting around the field.

It took us almost two hours to get here, taking the route through Burns, staying off 70 and main roads as much as we could. We hoped for no cameras. The whole time my heart racing. I don't know if I did the right thing texting Jack. I don't know. We could leave, we could just let Jack and the team deal with Theo Wharton. But this place, this property outside the small main town, this sprawling acreage among the rolling hills and mountains. It feels so charged. Feels alive. A thrumming around all of it. I want, *need*, to see.

Hannah seems to respond to it too. Scans the property for the source of the strangeness. For a second, that glitch, and I think I see shadows. Everywhere. Eighty. One hundred. Maybe more. Spaced at intervals across the property.

Then I blink.

And there's nothing.

Just quiet. Wind across the open field.

Hannah's eyes cut to me. I look at her face, every part of me on high alert. And she narrows her gaze for a moment on me, her nostrils flare around the nose plug.

"You're nervous," she says.

I shake my head and lie. "No," I say.

I start the walk across the field to meet Father Sky.

At the edge of the dome, I pause. Wait for Hannah to catch up. She's hanging back, a little. I don't know if it's the strange feeling on the property, or if it's whatever she's seeing in me. Probably the fact that I am feeling now that I might have made an irreversible mistake in texting Jack. I just don't know. Denver is farther than No Name though, I don't know how long it will take for them to get here, if they come. Maybe it'll take care of itself. I can cuff Theo Wharton and leave him for them. But I need to be sure.

We reach the dome. Two large antlers are bolted to the outside of the doors as handles. I pause, try to determine if I hear anything inside. My hand hovers over my gun. I wonder briefly if Hannah still has that pocketknife.

"Ready?" I ask.

She's still watching me, eyes narrowed, searching for something. After a second though, she nods. I open the door.

It takes my eyes a second to adjust to what we find inside. The inside of the dome is painted with rainbow swirling shapes, feels a lot like Denver's International Church of Cannabis. Incense burns at intervals around the space, on either side of the doors we've just stepped through. The ones now falling shut behind us.

The air is thick and choked with the incense, a strange sweet earthy smell to it. Light spills down from stained glass skylights, casting everything in bizarre rainbow color. On both sides of a center aisle sit eight long benches that could probably accommodate ten people each. And at the end of it a multileveled raised dais with a giant sculpture made of what look like antlers and bones. A multiheaded eagle, perched on a tree branch, wings fully outstretched, preparing for flight. Or in a show of intimidation.

In front of the multiheaded eagle, sitting on a floor cushion on the dais in the only stream of light from clear glass above, the only white in the place, like a spotlight, is Father Sky. It must be him. Wearing a white T-shirt and a pair of white linen pants. Barefoot of course. The tanned, muscular physique of a man who spends much of his time outside. Healthy and good-looking in a clothing model all-American way, and with a look in his eye that says he knows he can get away with anything. Has already gotten away with so much. From looks, charm. That violence there. He's dangerous. That edge, that wolfish threat. It's so clear, that I think maybe he wants it to be.

Beads of every color on his wrists, a red bolo tie around his neck.

The same red bolo from my dream, me with Hannah on the mountain.

I blink.

There's no bolo tie.

I take a breath, pull myself together. Nerves, probably. From texting Jack. Meeting *Wizdumteller*, maybe. Finally.

Maybe meeting the person orchestrating all these murders.

Father Sky smiles, watching me.

"You made it," he says, staying seated. "Come on in, don't be shy. All are welcome to the Church of Sacred Life."

I glance to Hannah, who looks around the space, tense, a hand in her pocket. So she does still have the knife after all. Good. We step forward down the aisle, space for both of us side by side to walk through it. We stop at the second-to-last benches, leaving maybe ten feet between us and the dais.

"Wow," he says, leaning back on his hands and shaking his head. "Look at you two. You are"—he glances to Hannah, then to me—"*absolutely sensational.*"

"Theo Wharton?" I say.

"*Really*," he says. "I thought *I* shined bright. I mean, I've made it like . . . my whole thing. It *is* my thing! But . . ." He shakes his head again, leans forward now, rests his elbows on his knees, his eyes raking over us.

"We need to ask you a couple questions," I say.

His attention focuses on me, lit up in wonder. And violence.

Hatred, almost. There, just for a second. My heart picks up its pace.

We might have found him. He might be the one. Someone who would do all this to get to me, to even attempt to frame me.

I try to think if I've seen him before, but I haven't. I don't think I have.

"Ask away," he says, shaking his head again. "To see you both, in person, here . . ."

His eyes cut to Hannah, rainbow light spilling over her. He smiles. She looks away.

"What do you know about a chat room called DRIFTERS: SEEKING THE TRUTH?" I ask.

Father Sky sits very still. Still smiling, still staring at us both like we're a meal he's about to eat. "I'm in it," he says. "My handle is *Wizdumteller.* I run the whole thing."

His words hang in the air. He just . . . said it.

It's not enough to arrest him. There's no crime against posting in a chat room. But if he's the one organizing all the killings, if I can get him to admit it, that'll be it. I can't believe he just said it.

"You're surprised?" he says. "I've been giving you hints, I've been *trying* to tell you."

"Trying to tell me what?"

"Everything," he says. And there's nothing more. He just sits, still, silent. Watching. His eyes never leaving us.

"You seem to have quite a devoted following in there," I say. "The chat room."

"Yeah," he says, tilting his head slightly, his hair falling back from his face. I don't know if I've seen him blink once. "Here too." He nods to the benches. "You should stay for a service."

"You predicted that the killings weren't over," I say. "You said there would be more murders, knew they were about to start up again."

A slow smile spreads on his face. "You get it yet?" he asks me. And I feel something . . . a chill over my skin. I look up to see a shadow moving at the edge of the room. Hannah's watching it too. I tear my eyes from it, focus on Theo Wharton. His words bothering me.

Hannah, in my dream . . .

Do you get it yet?

"Did you go see Ryder Smith?" he asks.

I nod, slowly. The shadow lingers. Another appears, on the other side of the dome. Hannah's eyes flick toward it, and Theo's attention fixes on her. He smiles again. "You're going to ask me about the boogeyman," he says, his gaze cutting to me.

Hannah tenses.

"Do you know who is responsible for these killings?" I ask.

"I know that it knows *you*," he says to me. And the shadows go still. Hannah does too. It feels suddenly very stagnant in here, the air thick, the walls tight. Silence.

"The way you scream," Theo says. "It's so loud. *So bright.*"

"What do you mean," I say slowly. "*It knows me?*"

"I mean you've met it, of course."

"The boogeyman."

He nods that slow strange nod. That predatory smile. "You know the boogeyman."

"I've met the person responsible for all of this?"

He nods again. Glances to Hannah, then back to me, smiles again. "You get it yet?"

"If you have any information that could lead us to someone, even if you're involved in it, we can work out a deal. A pardon, some kind of immunity. We do it all the time. All we need—"

"We're all involved. Don't you see? You, me. Hannah Lawrence." He winks at her. "Even Nat Tillman and Josie Maynor. Even Jack Murphy."

"How do you know my name?" Hannah says. It comes out more like a whisper.

"I'm telling you, I *know. It told me.*"

"Who told you?" I say. "What did?"

Behind Hannah, behind both of us, more shadows gather, drift around the space as though in a procession. More of them pouring in from outside, through the closed doors. We have to be imagining this.

"Hannah Lawrence, afraid of shadows?" Theo says. "You *are* the night. You are the dark and the—"

I glance to the corner. That thick incense swirling from the edges of the room, crawling up and over the low ceiling and coming to fall on us from above.

"What are you burning?" I ask. "What are we breathing in?"

Father Sky smiles. The room starts to sway, a little, and I turn to find every one of the shadows now sitting in rows on the benches. Entirely still. More than a hundred of them packing the space. All the shadows from outside, a congregation in their seats.

"Daniel," Hannah whispers, a look of terror on her face.

I turn back to Father Sky, Theo Wharton, where she's looking. And . . .

He's standing, on the edge of the dais, facing us. His gaze has gone blank. Eyes glassy. I saw Jack's daughter have a seizure once. She looked like this, right before.

I tense, don't know what to do. As Theo Wharton, Father Sky, in the stream of white light shining in from above, starts to convulse on the dais.

His eyes roll back in his head, his face cast up to the sky, arms outstretched, and—

Faster than I can track, his body folds in half.

Backward.

Feet still on the mat, the top of his head hits the floor behind him. Hannah jumps. His stomach up toward the ceiling. Arms outstretched wide above the ground as music starts to play, from somewhere. I don't know where. Hannah is frozen, eyes wide in shock.

Music. Discordant flute or wind instrument plays from nowhere. And Father Sky starts to sway. Slowly. His head making an arc on the floor, face coming around on each side to look up at us, out at the audience of shadows that do not exist. In a daze, I think, this must be what it's like to go to the circus. This is his show, what people come to see. It has to be. Right? The incense some kind of hallucinogenic. Smoke and mirrors. A contortionist. It can't be actually—

He snaps upright.

Hannah and I both take a step back. I reach for my gun.

Father Sky stands before us and looks out at nothing for a moment, above our heads.

Then, as if something huge is shoved to his chest, he is thrown back, trips over his feet. He collapses on the floor behind his mat, in front of the eagle statue. He knocks over one of his singing bowls, the sound of it clanging through the space with the music, reverberating, echoing around us, as it clatters off the dais.

Father Sky blinks, tilts his head one way and then another, cracks his neck, slowly, strangely. His movements different than before. Less fluid, more jerky.

He looks up. And I know even in my head that it sounds insane. I hardly believe it even as instinctually I know it to be true.

He is no longer Theo Wharton. No longer Father Sky.

It's Father Sky's body. But the person before us is now someone—*something*—else.

Hannah gasps. I look to her. Eyes panicked. A whimper in her throat. I think . . .

She's trying to move. But she can't. She's frozen to the spot.

I can't move. I can't—

Father Sky opens his mouth, and when he speaks, it is a new voice, an inhuman one. One that seems to come from all corners of the space, from outside, from the earth itself. So low and rasped and strange that I think it isn't possible. It's ten voices. It's a hundred. It's whatever's in that incense burning in the corner, whatever Theo Wharton has drugged us with. It's the sound of every loss in a life and every moment of pain.

"***DANNY.***" it says.

And I am here, but not here.

Pressure. That strange vibration—

VOOM.

Happy Inn.

Afghanistan.

Every crime scene.

I suck in a breath. I try to take a step, to move away from Theo Wharton, from this room, from whatever any of this is. But I can't. I can't move. I'm—

"***LISTEN.***" it says. "***YOU. WANT. REACH.***"

Outside the window, behind Hannah, there's movement. I can't turn my head, but I can just move my eyes enough to see red and blue flashing lights.

"***TRYING. NEED.***"

Through the drugged haze and the confusion and the music growing in volume and the man before us and the congregation of shadows at our backs, information synthesizes all at once.

They've arrived. Jack's here, probably with backup. I don't know what's happening in front of us, can't begin to understand it.

But I called Jack here, and if there's any chance of Hannah and me getting out of this, of Theo Wharton being apprehended, I need to be able to move somehow. I need control.

I close my eyes, and I remember my body, the way it moves, the way it runs and fights and lives. I know it so well, know sweat and pain and speed and breath more than anyone. It is the place I go when nothing makes sense, when this world feels too painful to spend another second in. I know this. I can do this.

Even as I think it, I move my left foot, slowly, sliding it over the floor, just inches. Psychochemical warfare. They taught us how to do this, how to move through it. How to convince our brains that it isn't happening, that we *do* know ourselves and our bodies and our thoughts, even if it feels the furthest thing from the truth. I can do this. Whatever he drugged me with, however he fucked with the connection between my brain and body, whatever this circus sideshow is, my brain *knows* how to move. My body does. *I* do.

It's all in my mind. I tell myself it's all in my mind. I push harder, feel sweat beading on my forehead. I push. It's all—

I snap back to awareness, and my body is mine once again.

Father Sky opens his mouth to say more. And I turn around to face the doors.

Just in time to see them burst open.

6

Josie, in the doorway. Her gun trained on me. Garcia and two male agents I don't know.

My ex-wife holds up her radio and says, "I have Stansfield, Lawrence, and Wharton. Daniel," she says to me. "You two are coming in, and we're gonna talk. Okay? Don't make this hard."

She doesn't see the congregation of shadows. None of them do. Because the shadows aren't real. Because none of them have been in here long enough to be affected by the drugs. I glance to the incense on either side of the entrance. We only passed through it, got whatever of it fills the room now. But they're standing right next to it.

I can feel Hannah about to run beside me, feel the tension in her. I don't know if she's still frozen.

A voice cuts through my thoughts.

Behind us, Father Sky—not Father Sky—says in that other voice, "***ASK. HER.***"

Josie and the other agents flinch at the voice, the awful sound, the reverberation of it through the chapel, try to find the source of it. Garcia furrows her brow. One of the male agents swears, the other says, *What the—*

Again, that uncanny, terrifying voice behind me says, "***SHE. KNOWS.***"

I turn, just for a moment, to see Father Sky—Theo Wharton, whoever the fuck we're talking to—staring right at Hannah.

Flute music, in the chapel. Tension filling every breath, every bit of air in here choked and thick with it, with the incense. The agents at the front, here to arrest Hannah and me. Theo Wharton on the dais, Hannah Lawrence, terrified beside me.

What does that mean?

She knows.

That other voice, those thousand terrible voices in one, echoes through the chapel, sliding against the walls and falling down back to us from the ceiling.

SHE KNOWS.

SHE KNOWS.

SHE—

We don't have time. I don't have time to parse this out. I look at Josie, think if there's any way out for us from this. I know the look there. I made a mistake, a major one, telling Jack our location. They don't trust me anymore, and maybe I don't trust them now either.

We have to get out of here. I turn back to Josie and open my mouth, start to try and stall them just long enough for the incense to affect them. It shouldn't be long now.

The voice behind me rasps one more time. "***HELP. THEM.***"

A twitch, in the shadow congregation. A ripple, a wave. Heads turning, if the shadows do have heads. This imaginary congregation, starting to move, as a whole.

I hear a clatter and a bang, and I turn back once more to see Father Sky passed out on the ground, fallen back on top of the singing bowls and cushions. The music still plays. The echoes of the crash. I turn back to the agents.

At the front of the chapel, Josie says, "Daniel, you're coming with us, and you're not going to put up any kind of fight. It's good you texted. We're gonna figure this out."

Hannah's eyes shoot to me. Disbelief, confusion.

Betrayal.

Josie jerks her head, and the two male agents start to walk around either side of the dome, around the shadow congregation. All four agents with guns out, trained on us. The shadows . . .

"Josie," I say. And it's a warning, because I don't know what's real.

The shadows have all turned to the agents.

But before I can do or say anything else, the shadows are up and moving.

Two groups of them—four or five each—rush to the male agents on either side of the chapel. They smother them, pile on top of the men, each a writhing, black mass.

One agent chokes, falls to his knees, grabbing his throat. The other is shoved up against the wall, held up above the ground by the shadows.

Josie yells, confused. Eyes frantic. Garcia's head swivels between each of the other agents. No one grasping what is happening.

The shadows are real. They're doing this. Garcia and Josie can't see them, but . . .

They're *real.*

HELP. THEM.

He meant help *us*. He was talking to the shadow congregation.

Garcia rushes to the agent up against the wall, says his name, tries to get to him.

The shadows take her to the ground.

Josie watches all of it, trying to understand. And I can see a glazed look in her eyes, the incense starting to hit. To the side, the shadows swarming Garcia, pushing her down to the floor. Covering her body.

Josie yells, "What is happening? What's happening to them?"

She starts to move, shaking her head and trying to push through the fog of the incense. I don't think she sees the shadows, her attention never moving to the ones still in front of her in the seats. The ones she is inches from. She doesn't see them turning, fixing their attention on her, standing from their chairs, moving.

"Josie, stop!" I yell.

And she does. Just at the edge of the shadow congregation. Maybe some last vestige of marital trust, maybe old habit. But she looks at me with an incredulous expression, and then her eyes go glazed and roll back in her head.

She falls to the floor.

I look to Hannah. She's already moving through the center aisle toward the door. Both of us released. The shadows make no moves toward her. I follow, say, "Wait, just a second."

I bend down beside Josie and feel her pulse, touch her forehead. She's unconscious but alive. The shadows have returned to their seats, the other agents passed out on the floor.

Behind us, Theo Wharton / Father Sky says in his own smooth voice, "Going already?"

I don't turn back. I have more questions. Too many. But . . .

"There are more agents out there," I say to Hannah. "We need to run. Fast."

She nods, and I brace myself for whatever this ends up being. Somehow, the incense isn't affecting me anymore. I don't think Hannah either. We can move normally. We can do this.

I glance back once. One final time to catch Father Sky, watching both of us with that wolfish, furious smile. Dangerous. Every part of him. I know it, feel it. Hatred on his face.

Hatred maybe for me.

"See you soon," he says.

We throw the doors open and run.

I take it all in. The field, the squad lights no longer flashing.

To our right, two agents. To our left, a squad car and of course Nat fuckin' Tillman, looking up at the sky. We've got about a hundred meters between us and the red Wagoneer.

We run.

Shouts, on the right, one of the two male agents. Both of them rush toward us.

One of them is big, not as fast. But strong. The other, smaller than me, is fast.

"Guys, I don't want to fight you!" I yell. "Don't do this." They don't slow down.

The smaller one is almost on us, ten feet away. I swear.

"Don't stop!" I yell to Hannah, and I see her run past me. As I wheel on them.

Small guy is going for the tackle, running at me full force. My mind, body calm. I enter that other-state, the one I've lived in so many times in my life, more than I should have. The fighting quiet. Everything slows down. I don't let myself think about how bad this is, how bad it looks. How royally fucked I will be in every court of law. We just have to get out of this.

I bend my knees, lower my center of gravity, angle my body so he can't make total direct contact. Half a second away. I can see his chest heaving, the breaths he's pushing out. The look of focus on his face. Have to anticipate the moment of contact, when the tackle will come, have to use his momentum, have to—

He jumps, flies through the air. I sidestep, but not fast enough to avoid the hit. His right shoulder collides with mine, knocks me back a step, his arms moving to surround me.

Before they can, I shove my left elbow into his solar plexus and throw my right fist beneath his chin in an uppercut at the same time as my right leg swipes behind his. He's thrown backward, lands on the ground, the hit hard enough that he's still, for the moment.

I look up just as the big man closes in from my side, twenty feet away. He's reaching for his gun, slowing him more. I hold my hands up in surrender. I can't turn to see where Hannah is, or Tillman. The big man takes his time walking toward me. Talks, says that I shouldn't move or he'll shoot, all the normal things. But I'm not listening. I'm watching. I don't hear any of the words he says, but I know he wants me on my knees. I do it, lower myself down. He's going so slow, so fucking slow, as he steps toward me.

I need him faster, need him to move.

Come on, come on, just a little closer.

I put my hands behind my back, and he steps around behind me. He's tall. I sit all the way low so he has to bend down, down, down. My hands almost as low as the ground.

I sense him behind me, bent forward, his head inches from mine. And I throw the back of my skull into his face.

He groans, and I jump up and turn as he steps back, one hand on his bloody nose, the other lifting the gun. I elbow him, knock it from his hand, and it falls to the grass. I step forward, grab the back of his head with both my hands, and long knee him in the throat. I jump back, and he falls to the ground.

I look up, and I can't find Hannah. I don't see her, and a terrible thought crosses my mind. She took the car. She ran, left me here. But no—the car's still here.

Then I see her. Just over by it, past the trees. She's on her knees too. And Nat Tillman stands behind her, tightening her cuffs.

Something shifts in me. More than the fighting calm, more than the adrenaline. Seeing Nat Tillman there, standing over her.

Hannah Lawrence on her knees. There's blood on her chin.

Rage.

I *run*.

I push my legs and move harder and faster than I ever have. Nat Tillman my only focus. Nat Tillman with his hands on her.

I'm there before he finishes, before he has her up and standing. I am there, and I do not think, do not feel, as my arm rears back, and my fist collides with Nat Tillman's face.

I throw a boot into his chest and knock him down to the ground. Blood sprays from his nose, and it is the most beautiful thing I have ever seen.

"Jesus, dude," he says, looking at his hand, covered in it. "What the hell!"

I kick his gun out of his reach and pick up the handcuff key from where he's just dropped it on the ground.

I say, "Josie's inside unconscious. Not from me. Go arrest Theo Wharton, he's the one you want."

I don't wait for a response as I pull Hannah up from the ground and help her get to the car. She slumps into the passenger seat, hands still cuffed behind her back. I close her door and run around to the driver's side, throw myself in, just as the smaller agent gets up off the ground, raising his gun.

He aims it at me and shoots, the crack of the gunshot pulling me back to memories I close my eyes against. I get the car started.

I think he missed, I think I'm okay. I slam the door closed and pull my hand in. I throw the car in drive and peel it out of the lot. His next shot ricochets off the back bumper. We pull away.

And then I feel the pain. I look down.

My left hand is gushing blood. I hold it up higher, swallow, focus.

"Are you okay?" I ask Hannah as we get on the road. She's leaning forward in the passenger seat, blood on her chin, hands still cuffed.

I don't know where we're going. Away from here, as far as we can get. In this unique memorable car that seven agents just saw. I gotta wrap up my hand, get this blood to slow before I pass out. I lift it higher above my heart. Blink myself into focus. Pain. Adrenaline.

Hannah says, "Yeah."

"Here," I say, driving with my left forearm and reaching over with the right to unlock her cuffs. "Lean forward, if you can." She does. It takes a minute, glancing back and forth between the road and her, driving with my hand bleeding and unlocking the cuffs, but I'm able to do it.

She pulls her hands free and throws the cuffs on the floorboard. She reaches into the glove compartment where she finds some napkins and hands them to me, holds herself as far back as she can from the blood, wipes hers off her face.

"You?" she asks.

I nod, hold the napkins to my hand. It's not as bad as I thought, just my pinky's kind of half-on. It fucking hurts. But there's too much going on. Just have to get away, have to think.

We drive, don't speak. I try to take in everything that just happened, try to make sense of it. The sky has darkened. I'm not sure when. Hannah and Father Sky and Josie. I don't know when it happened, but it's dark. Really dark.

Just as I think it, the first snowflake falls to the windshield and melts against it. Then another.

"He hurt you," I say. "How bad?"

She searches through the glove box again, pulls out some wet wipes, slides one over her face. "He didn't," she says.

"But—"

"I ran from him and tripped."

I glance at Hannah. She's holding something in her hand, staring out the window. Her words sound a little different.

"What . . . did you see in there?" I finally ask. "Could you—"

She nods. "I saw them. The shadows."

"It was drugs, right? The incense?" My good hand unsteady on the wheel. I grip it tighter. I don't feel so hot, a little dizzy.

"I don't think so," she says. "It was real. The others, they just . . . couldn't see what was happening to them, they only felt it. I think."

I look at her again. "Why? Why can we see them and no one else? They're not real."

"The shadows are real. And so was that shit with Father Sky." She turns and looks at me. "You texted them. Told them where we were. How could you?"

"The priority is solving this. Apprehending this killer. If we catch the right guy, we're off the hook."

"Are you kidding? That doesn't let us off the hook. We still look pretty fucking suspicious. You haven't given us any kind of chance, and you just totally fucked us. Now they know what car we're driving, now we've fought and actually escaped them. Isn't that another offense? A bad one? I can't believe you—"

Then she goes silent. Tension snakes through the car again. "What is that?" she asks, with a deadly calm.

I look where she does.

At the card that's just slipped out of my leather jacket pocket onto the center console. A six of spades with a fox drawn on it. The one I stole from her cabin.

I clear my throat. "I should have told you," I say.

She stares at me.

"I'm sorry," I say.

"Are you serious? You're—"

Again, her voice a little different. She's holding her mouth in a strange way as she's speaking.

"Are you hurt?" I ask. "Do we need to—"

She's staring at me like I am the worst thing she's ever seen. And my eyes catch . . .

Her hand that's fallen open on her lap.

And—

The ribs. Daphne and me at Linger Eatuary.

The old photographs of the bodies.

A snowflake falls. Then another. As my head spins. As I realize what I'm seeing, what . . .

Wolf depredation.

Veneered or fake canine.

Josie on the ground.

The shadows.

Theo Wharton and—

SHE KNOWS.

Teeth marks.

The snow starts falling in a flurry now, dancing before us.

Do you get it yet? Theo Wharton had said. The same words from my dream.

The words Hannah Lawrence spoke to me, in a dream, on a mountaintop.

The strange way she's holding her mouth.

You've met the boogeyman, Father Sky said.

We drive into the snow, my hand bleeding, the world rapidly turning white.

And I don't know what to do, what to think or feel. Because—

The tooth in Hannah Lawrence's hand, the one she's holding there. The veneer that just came out of her mouth.

It's a canine.

IV

YOUR SWEET LOVE

1

Sometimes snow is a gentle thing that slowly blankets the land, softening the world around you and filling it with wonder.

And sometimes it's an assault. Flurries multiply, thicken, until your vision is white, until the world is muffled then silenced then suffocated then smothered by a force greater than any of us.

Is it the Bad Decision?

Bad Feeling. Bad Decision. Snow coming down hard.

Leaving with Hannah. Fighting the FBI to flee with her.

Hannah's canine veneer in her hand.

It's her. She's the one.

The road stretching in the growing dark. Colorado canyons, mountains, rivers. A hawk soars over us in the snow, and I can almost feel that I see us from its vantage point, red car on long gray road in the white. Soaring higher and higher as we grow smaller below. A finite red point in a sea of blinding white, our headlights barely penetrating.

Time stretching, memories, music playing, almost feeling as though the car is moving of its own volition. As if we are being led forward in some elaborate game. Every player and piece and move leading us toward some great inevitable future.

We are completely blind to it.

By the time we get to Grand Lake, I'm having trouble seeing.

By the time we hit Estes Park, I'm scared we're going to crash. I haven't been going any particular direction, or not meaning to anyway. Just *away* from Yampa. From the others.

Hannah Lawrence did all of this. And Father Sky . . .

The tires slip on the fresh snow, no chains. I need to pull over, need to sort this all out, get somewhere safe.

It's after eight. We need a room somewhere. I squint through the snow and just make out the edges of signs. GAS, FOOD. HOTEL.

I see a sign, take the turn, head up a drive past an unattended guard stand.

We pull up into the parking lot, can barely see. We step out of the car into the whipping cold and snow. I grab the duffel bag, shove the files and knife in it. Grab my cowboy hat. I'd rather have left the knife and the car somewhere else, not where we're staying, but we just have to get inside. We just have to figure this out. The chill bites my skin. Adrenaline. A humming in my ears. It's impossible to see beyond a faint outline of the building.

We walk around to the front of the hotel.

Hannah and me.

She pulls her jacket in tight around herself. She doesn't have enough layers for this weather, even with the puffer. Neither do I. Neither of us prepared because we never thought we'd be here right now.

Hannah Lawrence. Who *ate* those bodies. Who very well might have killed all those people, organized it somehow.

My ears are ringing.

Every body. Every drainage ditch. Years. Years of my life studying this case, working this case, unable to find . . .

Hannah.

Hannah.

Hannah.

Do you get it yet?

Ask her. She knows.

You've met the boogeyman.

A white stately sprawling hotel with a red roof comes into view in the pummeling snow. Light glowing out from the windows. American flags attached to the building above the columns whip wildly in the wind. The snow pelts us as we take the steps up to the front porch and then the two French doors.

The red welcome mat below our feet says THE STANLEY HOTEL.

We open the doors against the wind, and as soon as we step inside, they slam shut behind us, a few small flurries settling down to the red thick patterned carpet below our feet. To our right is a vintage green, yellow, and black Stanley automobile with a fake Colorado vanity license plate that says, in red scratchy letters, REDRUM. In front of us a round entry table like the one at Whileago Manor, holding an elaborate flower arrangement. Behind it is a grand wooden stairway, carpeted in the same red and white as the rest of the lobby, patterned green wallpaper lining the walls, and the thick carved dark-stained wood framing everything, stretching in beams across the ceiling. Sconces glow against the wood, and an old brass elevator reflects the light.

Beyond the flower arrangement is a front check-in desk, the same green wallpaper and dark wood, and to our left a witchy-looking girl manning a séance table. Fireplaces on both sides of the lobby glow, guests and shadows huddled near them in leather chairs.

There are mirrors everywhere. On either side of the lobby, facing in toward each other. Behind and surrounding the stairwell. On every wall. I take a breath, keep my focus.

Hannah Lawrence next to me. Mirrors all around. Every muscle in my body tense.

The guy at the front desk lifts his head as we approach. "Cold out there, huh?" he asks.

Hannah looks around, might be considering running. But where? Where could she possibly run from me now that I know?

Nowhere. Never again. I have no idea what happens next, but I know that whatever it is, this ends here. One way or another.

Hannah Lawrence, who tricked me. Who somehow knew about the Happy Inn, who somehow . . . coerced all the killers? Why not? Didn't she fucking easily manipulate me? Didn't she fool me completely? Still, or because of it . . . I step closer to her. She steps back, and I stay tuned in to her every movement.

"Do you have any rooms available?" I ask the man at the front desk. His eyes trail down to my bloody napkin-covered hand, then back up, flick to Hannah and her nose plug.

"Without a reservation?" he asks.

"Yes."

Hannah shifts, and I tell myself not to look directly at her, even as every part of me is focused on her. And hasn't it been this whole time? Haven't I *known* on some level that I have been obsessed with her, caught in her snare from the moment I first heard her name? Told myself some fantasy that she and I were wrapped up in—

"Ohhhhh, shoot. Well . . . lemme just see here." He winces, makes a big show of widening his eyes and then lowering his brows in concentration, looking at a sheet of paper. "Wi-Fi's down. Been this way for a few hours, gotta consult this sheet. But this is peak season, ya know. Well, one of 'em. I mean, we're really a year-round establishment, but we're really booked up here, I'm just not sure . . ."

"We'll take whatever you have," I say.

I see Hannah flinch at this. Hannah, who has the gall to act like she doesn't trust me. To act like I am the untrustworthy one when she has been—

"Gee, guys, I'm really sorry. It looks like we don't—"

"Excuse me?" A tense voice, behind us. I turn, prepare myself to grab Hannah if I have to, if she bolts anywhere. That feeling when Tillman stood over her, the rage I felt at anyone laying hands on her, touching her, the way I wanted to *protect* her. Tillman, who had her apprehended. I freed a suspect, one who actually deserved to be in custody. Fuck.

But the girl who spoke behind us, one half of a young couple. She looks terrified. "Hi," she says, pushing ahead of us. "We're checking out early."

"Oh, was everything all right with your stay?" the man who's been helping us asks.

"You know, he wanted to do this whole *haunted room* thing," she says, pointing at her boyfriend. "And look, I love Stephen King. I do. I love the book *AND* the movie! *AND* the miniseries! I love 'em! But that *room* . . . that's not . . . and all the people coming up and taking photos with our door while we're just trapped inside with this, like, *ghost*. We just—we have to go."

I glance around, understanding dawning. This is *that* hotel. The one Stephen King stayed in and got the idea for a book. Of course it fucking is. I knew that it was somewhere in Colorado. I tense further, ignore the shadow that brushes by behind us, Hannah stiffening as it passes. Once again, these pieces of my life laid out in front of me. John Denver Sanctuary in Aspen, the motel.

But Hannah couldn't have meant for us to come here, could she? I was the one driving, she hasn't said a word since just outside of Yampa. Father Sky certainly didn't have a hand in us driving here specifically. No, I think this one was all me. And my dumb fucking luck.

The woman drops the key to the counter, and her boyfriend shrugs in an embarrassed apology. But he looks a little shaken up too. Hannah takes half a step away from me, and I move closer to her. She adjusts her nose plug, puts her hand up over her mouth and nose, again that look as if she's in pain.

She doesn't get to do that anymore. I won't feel sorry for her. Not now.

How much of this is an act? Everything, maybe. All of it. And me, so fucking stupid.

"Well," the bellman says, "looks like it's your lucky day! This never happens! Wow, when I tell you this room is booked up months, sometimes *years*, in advance! If I could just write down some of your info—"

"I left my ID at home, could I maybe just pay cash? Sorry, been a rough day."

He watches us a moment, takes us in. "Sometimes these rooms have a way of picking the right guests. Certainly was true one time in 217." He winks. "I think in this instance, we can make it work."

I write down a fake name, address, and email. Hand over the cash.

"What's up with all the mirrors?" I ask.

"Oh. You should really take one of our tours, there's so much to learn! F.O. Stanley's wife, Flora, she was very interested in the paranormal, hosted séances here, collected special items. She believed that by placing mirrors facing each other, she could create portals into other realms. So this whole place very well might be just that! A kind of portal!"

"Great," I say. "Thanks."

"You can go get yourselves a bite at the restaurant or a drink at the bar, I'll send housekeeping up right away and get you in within the hour. I think you two might just be our luckiest guests yet!"

We step into the gift shop and buy another fishing hat for Hannah—hers got lost somewhere in the shuffle in Yampa—and a baseball cap for me, scarves for both of us. There are horror souvenirs everywhere for this haunted hotel. The book it inspired. I don't look at them. I don't look at the shadows milling around the lobby either. The one leaning against the shiny green car. I do not look at the mirrors.

The Cascades restaurant, with its dark carved wooden bar, glowing amber stone bar top, backlit liquor bottles, and copper tin ceiling, gives the sense of stepping into a place out of time. The snow outside the windows is so thick we can't see anything besides white, and the TVs are off. I don't see any cameras in here, but surely they'll have them all throughout the hotel. Still, if the storm can hold and the Wi-Fi can stay out, we might be okay. On the other hand, we might be stuck here until the storm lets up, so there's that too.

Not sure how to deal with my racing heart and the woman in front of me.

Hannah, the center of my thoughts since the moment I saw her. And *still* I couldn't see. Wouldn't see.

We sit behind a long carved piece of glass shaped to look like mountains, at a two-person table. The glass shields us from anyone walking in or at the bar, but not from the two tables beside us, which mercifully are currently empty. Two shadows sit at the bar, and one at a corner table near the window walls. Music plays, low enough I can't quite make it out.

The waitress comes and reads us the daily specials. We don't listen. My eyes don't leave Hannah's face. Those intense green eyes, that wildness I've been so drawn to. The way she's watching me back . . .

"We'll have the ribs," I say. "And a steak."

Hannah's look, accusation, fear, distrust, rage. Hannah with half a canine in her hand.

"That's all we'll have," I say, and the waitress disappears.

After she goes, Hannah says quietly, "I don't eat meat."

I lean back in my chair, lean forward, don't know what to do with myself.

"I don't think that's true," I say.

She goes very still. So still that I think I am looking at a completely different person. Like a mountain lion. Powerful and silent and deadly. For a terrible split second, seeing her across this table, I think that she is the most beautiful thing I've ever seen. How fucking ridiculous that that was all it took to distract me.

"What does that mean?" she says.

I don't say anything, just try to understand. Try to really see.

"How did you know about the motel?" I ask.

She leans forward, lowers her voice, and whispers, "How dare you. *How dare you* accuse me of anything when you broke into my home and stole something, you lied about it, and you completely *fucked* us. You told them where we were. Because of you we almost both—"

"Because of *me*? *I* did this?"

"How am I supposed to believe you didn't do all this? They want to arrest you too, don't they? My life was completely fine and normal before I was taken from—"

"*Who are you?*"

"All righty!" the waitress says, pouring ice water into our glasses. "Did we decide on some drinks to go with the food?"

"I'll take a scotch," I say, never letting my eyes stray from Hannah for a second. Hers that distracted me from everything. "Neat."

"I'm fine," Hannah says.

"She'll have one too," I say.

"I'm fine," Hannah says. "I don't drink."

"Okay," I say. "Then bring me two. Please."

The waitress hovers for a moment, probably checking to make sure Hannah's okay. That I'm not some abusive or controlling husband. Clocking the bruises on Hannah's face, the faint outline of them. If only she knew who the woman before me truly is. What she's capable of.

"I'm fine," Hannah says to her, not taking her eyes off me.

The waitress hesitates, then says, "You just let me know if you need anything."

"Who are you?" I ask again when she's gone. And I feel, looking at Hannah's face in the dim light, the glow of the table candle reflecting against her skin, her eyes, her nose. Her mouth. I feel it is the single most important question of my entire life.

"You know who I am," she says in that lethal quiet calm. And I don't know why, but my chest hurts at that. A feeling pushing up from somewhere.

"No," I say. "I don't."

We sit. The music plays. I can now hear it's "Pancho and Lefty."

Hannah's chest rising and falling. Her focus narrowed in on me.

The waitress brings the food and sets it down between us, along with the glasses of scotch.

The second the food passes in front of Hannah's face, she leans back from the chair, that expression of pain again, rage in her eyes. She locks them on me. The waitress disappears.

Hannah's hands on the table, knuckles white. Her nostrils flare, and she swears, adjusts the nose plug. She reaches across the table and takes one of my drinks, knocks it back with her eyes on me. "Fuck you," she says.

I will not feel sorry for her, I tell myself again. I won't. Not anymore. Not now that I see, finally, what I should have seen from the very beginning.

She stares at me for so long that I think I don't breathe at all.

Finally, softly, just low enough for the two of us to hear and with such a pained expression on her face that I nearly betray myself again, she says, "I didn't kill anyone."

"Now let's see, just to keep track here. You *don't* eat meat, you *don't* drink, and you didn't—"

"Goddamnit," she says, slamming her hand down on mine on the table. "Listen to me." Her skin, my skin, her hand on my hand. She seems to realize, pulls it back, her face flushed. "I didn't"—she lowers her voice—"*kill* them. I just . . ."

"You just what?"

The waitress appears again. "Oh, hi there! I just wanted to let you know that your room is all ready when you're finished here! How's the—"

"We'll take this to go, and the check," I say.

We both reach for the second scotch.

We find our room, have to pass about twenty mirrors to get there. Two young women are taking a selfie in front of it, and they scurry off when they see us approaching. A brass plaque on the wooden door says THE STEPHEN KING SUITE. I open it, wait for Hannah to walk in first. She keeps her distance from me, the take-out container in my hand.

Inside, the red patterned carpet from the hall continues through the room. On our left is a heavy wooden armoire, dresser, and chair. A large dark wood four-poster bed sits in the center of the room with a leather and wooden bench at the foot of it. On the other side of it, a seating area that blocks entry to the balcony. On the wall with the bathroom door is a large desk and chair, and a bookshelf full of books. I don't have to look at them to know what they are.

I stand just beyond the door, my back to it, Hannah hovering between the bathroom and the bed. Her attention moves to the hall door behind me. I'm blocking her exit. A shadow hangs back in the corner by the bookshelf.

"Talk," I say.

Hannah's eyes flick to the take-out container in my hand, then back to me.

"Do you want this?" I say.

"No."

"What's the nose plug for?"

"I can't be close to—"

"You didn't just start wearing it after the motel. What is that tube you keep hiding?"

"Capsaicin," she says quietly. That word sounds familiar. "It's to make it so you can't smell. To deaden the sense."

That spicy smell on her, that's what it is.

"Why did you take the card from my cabin?" she asks. "Why did you lie about being there?"

I tighten my jaw.

She glances at the take-out container again, her nostrils flaring. "Can we get that out of here, I—"

I step forward. "You want it?"

She takes a step back.

I see it there. A flash. Want. Desire.

"No," she says.

"Are you sure?" I take another step forward, reach it out to her. "Here. Take it."

"I—" She shakes her head. Her hand shoots up to her nose. "What do you want from me?!"

"I want the truth," I say. "I want every fucking detail. I want everything."

SHE KNOWS.

My chest is heaving, and I feel like I've just run a marathon, like I want to run another. This woman, right here in front of us, of *me*. Us here in this hotel room together.

"Okay," she says, finally. "Okay. Just. I don't know, put that in the bathroom or something. I can't talk with it in here. *Please.*"

Somehow that *please* sends that protective jolt through me again. I ignore it, even as I put the container in the bathroom without losing sight of Hannah. And when I step back in, she's sitting on the bench at the foot of the bed, looking down at her hands, one of them still holding the tooth. Her feet on the carpet.

"We should bandage your hand," she says, without looking up.

"It's fine," I say. I don't really know if it's fine. I mean it's just a pinky, but I don't know how much a pinky can bleed. It hurts like hell, actually. I hesitate, then call down for a first aid kit. A few minutes later one arrives. Hannah makes no move to leave when I open the door.

"It's a long story," she says, when the porter leaves and I sit against the door on the carpet, open up the kit.

"Great," I say. My heart going crazy in my chest. The snow casting the whole room in that muffled blue-white light. I'm grateful for something to do with my hands.

"Seven years ago, I went to California. I was looking for a change," she says. "In my life. Some kind of, I guess, like, revelation. I was twenty-two, I didn't know anything. And . . . my life before, growing up, it was lonely. In college I studied, mostly, and I had friends but they were superficial relationships. I just never really found anyone who . . ."

She clears her throat. "And then I met Eden."

The pain on her face when she says the name. Anxiety courses through me. Fear, jealousy, maybe. I rip open the alcohol wipes with my teeth and start to clean up some of the blood. I hiss against the pain, do it anyway.

"Lone Pine, California," she says. "I was hoping to hike and just, I guess, get a break from the world. It was meant to be a pass-through. It's where Tumanguya is, Mount Whitney most people call it, even though that's not its name. It's a small town, there's really not much. Manzanar, an old western film museum. Couple bars, hiker resupply, some motels. The Alabama Hills, these rock formations at the base of the mountain.

"My first night there, I stopped in one of those bars, just to get a drink. I'd entered the lottery to see if I could get a permit to summit the mountain from the portal side, and I was waiting to hear. And that's when I met Eden. She was . . . everything I wasn't, I guess. She was there collecting stories, trying to piece together a huge book on this country and the people in it, interviewing locals and getting to know everyone she could. She was . . . *fearless.*"

The look on her face, pain. That type of deep unrelenting grief.

"We hit it off," she says. "And I mean, the kind of hit-it-off that only happens once, maybe twice in a lifetime with someone. Soulmates come in any type of relationship, and you never know when you're gonna meet one, or *if.* If it's even possible. But we knew. It was . . . bliss." She shrugs.

I start to dab the alcohol closer to the part of my pinky that's hanging off. I exhale through my teeth.

"I didn't get the permit, that first night, to summit. We tried a few times, throughout the summer, got matching tattoos of the mountain to sort of will it into existence. And it worked. Finally, we got it. We hiked up, were up at Trail Camp, which is like the last stop just before the top, just us and a couple other hikers and a bunch of marmots. We could've summited in one day, come back down. We were strong. That kind of young and dumb that makes you invincible, almost. But we decided to stretch it out, swim in each lake as we went up, take a couple days. Camp and experience the camaraderie of pre-summit base camp."

She braces herself, takes a deep breath, fidgeting with the tooth. "At the campsite, while we were sleeping, a storm came in. A big one. The kind that gets hikers put on the evening news as the one death for the year. One of the others had told us weather might come, that he was reconsidering his summit and thinking of just hiking back down in the night. We shrugged it off and went to sleep. We were having fun. When we woke up, all the other hikers were gone, and the snow was everywhere.

"We couldn't get down. Could hardly even see. And Eden, it turns out, had a heart condition, and hadn't brought enough medication with her up the mountain since it was just supposed to be one overnight. She hadn't told me about it. I thought we'd told each other everything, but . . ." One tear falls, and she swipes at it with the back of her hand.

"We couldn't get down. The blizzard. We couldn't even find the trails at all at this point, the snow was feet high. So we found this kind of makeshift cave in between some big rocks, and the snow kept coming. We couldn't see, other than just white. Like now," she says, glancing out the window at the flurries that haven't stopped. "We'd only brought food for a day and a half." She swallows. "Eden made it four days before her heart . . . The snow never let up. It got worse. Once-in-a-lifetime record storm."

"I—" She wipes her face again, the tears there, and says, "I was up there for thirty-two more. After she died. Thirty-six days, total."

I've stopped what I'm doing with the bandage. Watching her, listening.

Realization settles over me at her words. Why she is telling me this. What this story has to do with everything.

A young girl trapped and cold and starving, with her best friend's body.

"You survived," I say.

She nods. Takes a long minute, just turns the tooth over and over in her hand, that look of pain on her face. Tears falling. "I had no idea how much a person could hate themselves. I . . . I was really lost, for months. I drifted in and out of towns, but . . . I realized I couldn't be near people, anymore. The *smell* of them. I stopped eating meat, couldn't look at it. And when I met James, the guy who owns the house in Aspen, I needed a place to land, get my life together. He was lonely, just wanted company. He gave me space and never questioned the nose plugs or the capsaicin or any of it. I think he just liked knowing there was someone around. Every day, I'd drive down the mountain and to that trail you and I ran, and I'd run or walk, and I'd think maybe today I just end it all. If I didn't exist, the memories wouldn't either. What I'd done would cease to exist with me. Maybe today I just . . . stop. Have you ever . . . ?"

She raises her eyes to me, vulnerable. Raw. And I know exactly what she's asking. I know the answer I would honestly give, and it's the one she needs. The one she's begging for.

I don't say anything.

Her shoulders slump, and she drops her gaze again. "When it became clear that James wanted more and I couldn't give it . . . I mean, I couldn't even get *near* anyone. There was no way . . . I left. And I walked, mostly. At night. Maybe kind of daring the night to take me, some bad man or big animal. Statistically it'd be the man, I guess. I hiked trails and walked highways. Drove, sometimes. Just . . . drifting. I almost felt like I was between worlds, somewhere not quite here. Nothing between the memories and me. But something about the dark of night, something about no longer existing in the daylight, made me feel as though I . . . No one wants to be the darkest thing in the day. But I was at home at night. I don't know. I was in a hell of my own making, but it was better than trying to live in the daylight world again. Being the darkest thing there and knowing it."

She says, "And there was this other thing . . . Ever since I'd passed into Colorado, I felt this . . . I felt that I wasn't alone. I started hearing things. Static mostly. Sometimes, this sort of . . . pulse, almost. Heartbeat, but strange. *Big.* And I'd wake up sometimes to shadows moving around me. There were—are—shadows, everywhere. So many. I thought that maybe I just had cracked, you know? That my brain . . . after what happened . . .

"One night, I was sleeping in my car, and I just . . . *felt* something. Outside. It wasn't an animal, or a man. Wasn't the shadows. This was bigger . . . I knew it wanted something from me. Somehow, I just knew that. I stepped out of the car and I followed the feeling. It took me down a highway, down the side of the road into a field. An open drainpipe. There was a body in it. It didn't have any skin. I knew it was female, but nothing else."

"When was this?" I ask, my voice barely audible.

She meets my eyes when she says, "Six years ago. November."

And . . .

She's talking about Claire Wright's body. Fourteen-year-old Claire Wright.

My ears ring, the room spins.

"I thought I was dreaming," she says. "It was the worst thing I'd ever seen. Besides Eden. It was Eden all over again. And not. And this *presence*, I felt it push in against my back, all around me, heard—felt, almost—its movement in the night. This out-of-timeness, this feeling that I was insulated from the rest of the world, at least for that moment. Like it had blocked out everything else. And I knew it wanted me to find this. This was my fate, and I deserved to hate myself. I deserved to feel all of it. So I took a step toward it, and then another. And I just . . ."

She stares at the carpet and somewhere else entirely. Then, she lifts her gaze to me and says, "I didn't kill any of them. They just . . . started appearing, where I was. That presence, whatever the *thing* was, pushing me toward them, putting them in my path. I thought it was the universe or God or whatever there is, giving me the punishment I deserved. I thought I was in some kind of hell. And . . ."

She tucks her hair behind her ear, takes a breath. "I got this feeling, that whatever it was that was watching me, that walked with me . . . it liked it. It *liked* me feeling everything I felt—fear, pain, relief in the punishment, almost, and it liked me . . . eating. It happened eight times. The thing leading me there, watching me eat the body. On the sixth body, I broke my tooth on a femur. Had to go get a fake one." She keeps her eyes on the tooth in her hand, turns it over again.

"And then it just stopped after the eighth one. The bodies stopped coming. And I thought, maybe, just maybe, I'd earned my place in the world again. That I was allowed to be here, now that I'd done what it wanted, had owned up to it. Faced what I'd done to Eden eight more times. And then a job came up, away from people, out in the mountains, and I thought it was meant to be. I thought I was being released." She laughs a bitter laugh.

"When it started up again, the killings, I felt the presence again. I felt it wanting me to go with it, and I knew somehow that there was another body. I just . . . I somehow felt it. But I wasn't going to do it anymore. I wasn't going back down there, and I wasn't going to give in. I'd learned to live again, at least in the way that I could. I watched animals, looked after the land, I lived in the quiet. I could exist in the daylight, in nature. But I felt that *tug*, from the night. From whatever the . . . presence, or . . . thing. I could feel that it was upset, didn't like that I wasn't there, wasn't playing my part. It came to me in nightmares, in shadows moving around my cabin, in this dark sort of pulse. But I fought it. Twice. I didn't want to go back, didn't want to feel it ever again. And then . . ."

"Everett Brown came and found you," I say.

She nods.

"And he stuck a tongue in your mouth."

All of it, if I believe her, if this story is true . . .

"I could feel . . . it wanted me to swallow it, to eat it. It was trying to remind me. When we were in Aspen, when you played that video of Ryder Smith talking about the . . ." She swallows. "And that file, everyone saying *it*. I knew that's what it was. That it was the name of this thing that had been visiting me. I don't know how, I just knew."

"But . . . why?" I ask. "Why would it want you? What would it get out of you eating the bodies?"

"I don't know for sure, but I have a theory. Um, do you know about the Egyptian plover?"

"What?" I say.

"It's a bird. Tiny. And it sits inside crocodiles' mouths, cleans the meat from their teeth and eats it. The crocodile lets it sit there without ever closing its jaws because the bird is providing it a service. In turn, the crocodile offers the plover protection. Remoras with sharks, cows and cattle egrets. Symbiosis. I could feel sometimes . . . that's how it viewed me, the thing in the night. The . . . Witchwalker, I guess. In the motel, I could feel it. It wanted me back because it felt we were in some kind of symbiotic relationship. It gave me what it thought I needed, the punishment and giving in to my shame. When you carry that kind of thing for so long, when it sits on your shoulders and your whole being, it feels . . . *good*, almost. To give in to it, sometimes. I . . . when I was eating . . . it was fear and self-hatred and pain and guilt and . . . but it also . . . in an awful unbearable way, felt like *release*. And that thing in the night, I think it liked my company. Like James in Aspen. Protection, in exchange for my being there."

The shadow moves into the bathroom doorway.

"But this isn't my life now," Hannah says. "I don't want to do it anymore. I don't eat any meat, I stay away from people, don't even let myself smell them. I think it wanted me back, and it was angry that I didn't want that too."

"If I . . ." I try to collect my thoughts. "If I were to believe any part of this story, if any of this is remotely true . . ." I run my good hand over my head.

One part of it sticks. One part that makes me think . . .

"You think that's what spoke through Father Sky? The Witchwalker? That it wasn't just some circus act?"

"I know it was. I know its voice, it comes to me in my dreams, whispers along the walls of the cabin. I think . . ." She looks away from me. "I think it wanted us to find each other, for some reason. You and me. It wants something from you too."

"It wants . . ."

"What were you doing when it came back?" she asks. "When the murders started again?"

"I was about to move."

"Somewhere far away?"

"I—"

"And now," she says, thoughts and connections lighting up her eyes. "We left Denver, and there's been another one. It's like the tongue and me. It wants you the same way it wants me. It thinks you're a part of its ecosystem. It doesn't want us to leave. When I ran from my cabin, it pushed me toward you. It wanted this for some reason."

"*This* being . . ."

"You and me. Together. I don't know why."

"But I've never known . . . *it*. Whatever the fuck it is. I've never had some symbiotic relationship of night cannibalism—"

"Well, I don't know!" she says. "I've told you everything. Everything I have, to try and figure this out. Now *you*," she says. "You have to tell me what *your* part is in this."

"I . . ." I watch her. Her story. I don't know if I should believe any of it. I don't know why I should when she's lied this whole time. But that traitorous part of me that is so taken in by her says, *Of course she lied. She was scared. She was alone. And maybe she's a victim in this as much as you are. Maybe more.*

"You don't believe me," she says, her face fallen. "You know what, fine. I don't care. But for some reason they think you're involved in this too, your own coworkers and friends, and if there's one of us who shouldn't trust the other, it's me, with you. You owe me answers."

"I don't have any answers, I told you, I have no idea why this is happening."

"Why did you steal that card from my cabin?" she asks.

"I—"

"Why do they think you're involved?"

"I don't know."

"Yes, you do! Look, I'm trying to help and you're just—"

"Because this sounds insane."

"More insane than killers having no idea why they're doing what they're doing? While they skin an *entire body*?"

More insane than some person somehow stealing my hair and coercing these people into doing these things after tying it around their tongues. I realize now. The simplest answer is that I did it all and left a calling card for everyone to find. And they could say I've muddied and fucked the investigation from the inside, and that's how it's all gone on for so long.

"*I'm* the one who shouldn't trust *you*," Hannah says.

"Why do you then?"

"I don't!"

"Great!" I push myself up to stand, move.

Wouldn't it just make the most sense that I got messed up young by a bad thing that happened to me with my parents, and have somehow been playing it out in these murders, intentionally not solving them, steering investigators off the trail? Isn't that the cleanest possible answer, and won't the judges and the public love it? I'm facing the door, my back to Hannah. Hannah Lawrence who has a knife and could just . . .

Maybe I just let her at this point. Maybe that solves it all.

"I don't think you did it," Hannah says.

Her words sink in, and I turn to look at her.

"How do you know what I'm thinking?" I ask. "How did you know at my house what message I got? That I was implicated by something? How do you always know?"

She stares at me and shrugs, helpless. She says, "You can't pretend you don't feel it."

"What?" I ask. The room very still around us. My heart pounding.

"The connection between us. I've felt it since I first saw you in that motel. I've felt it ever since. It was the same thing I felt when I met Eden. Sometimes, it's just . . ."

The connection between us.

I can't . . . her eyes on me, now. Searching. Is she manipulating me? Of course she is. Right?

I swallow, tell myself to slow down. "So you can read my mind? That's what you're saying?"

"I told you, I get *feelings* sometimes. I don't know. You don't have to believe me about that, I don't care," she says. "But there is *something else* in all this. Something different from us. Something not human. And for whatever reason, it wants you. If the killings stop, it might let me go, might not need me there for the bodies. If we can get to the bottom of what it wants from you, it may be the key to everything. To both of us being freed from it."

I look around the room as if it holds some kind of answer. Standing here by the door, Hannah Lawrence on the bed in front of me. The blizzard outside. "I don't know what to do."

"I think we need to talk to it," she says.

"Talk to it."

"Ask it what it wants. It spoke to us through Father Sky, it's spoken to me before, at night. I bet it can do it again."

"How would we even possibly . . ."

"It comes when I'm at my darkest, my most afraid," she says.

I still don't know what she's getting at.

She takes a long breath through her mouth and exhales. "I think we have to get scared. Really scared. That's when it comes. Before, anyway."

"What are you suggesting?"

"I don't know. I mean, there's no handbook on this."

"Okay. So we get scared." I nod, can't believe I'm going with this.

"Yeah," she says.

"Right. So, um . . . What makes you scared?"

She gives me a look like I am the dumbest man on earth.

"Yeah," I say. "So . . . proximity. Not having the nose plug in, I guess?"

She stares at me and nods, her eyes already filling again.

"And . . . you?" she says after I don't say anything else.

What do I say to this? A million things run through my mind. Everything.

What comes out is,

"Dancing."

". . . Dancing."

I clear my throat. Run my good hand over my head again. "This is a stupid idea. I don't know why I'm listening to any—"

"We can dance."

"I don't want to dance!"

"Well, I don't want to smell you! But if we're going to get anywhere with—"

"*Cowboy* dancing."

"What?"

"Like, um. You know, cowboy waltz. Or square dance, folk dance. Any of it."

"That scares you."

"Didn't used to," I say. But I don't give her more than that. I don't know if I can. "And music. Certain songs. Certain music."

"Okay," she says.

Terror in her eyes.

My heart slamming in my chest.

"Okay," I say. "So . . . we're gonna do this?"

"Yeah," she says. She bites her lip, eyes on me.

The snow outside, the shadow in the bathroom, that book on the bookshelf. That feeling of a great sweeping avalanche, pulling at my feet.

"We call the Witchwalker to us."

2

There's a radio in the room, and as soon as I turn it on, it plays Lee Hazlewood's "Your Sweet Love." I'm turned away, fiddling with it—pretending to, on the bedside table closer to the door. I take a breath to collect myself.

I try another station, and it's the same song. This was the song that played all around us in the mountains in my dream.

I dreamt this, Hannah and me, dancing.

How?

I turn. The shadow in the bathroom disappears, as if it doesn't want to be a part of this.

Hannah is there, her socked feet on the carpet—her boots in the corner behind her—in front of the two chairs. Mine are by the door. I stand again with my back to it.

We watch each other as the song plays. Every nerve in my body at attention.

"So . . ." I say. "We think it'll just . . . come to us? Somehow? If we do this. Do you mean *through* one of us, like with Father Sky?"

"I don't think so," she says. "I mean, it's never done that with me. As far as I know, anyway. But I think . . . it might just *be* in the room, with us. Maybe."

She's maybe five foot five. Standing there in jeans and the green sweater. The shoulder of it has fallen down below her collarbone. My eyes catch on it, move back up to her face. Light green eyes focused on me, she fidgets a little, anxious.

She says, "I think it's like the radio, almost," she says. "My theory, anyway. Like maybe the thing is always *there*, or it's always wherever it is. Um, broadcasting . . . But even if it's trying to reach us, we don't always let it. We don't always turn it on or tune in to the right station."

"You think fear and pain are the right station."

"I don't know if they're the only ones, but they're the ones I've reached it through before. Or the ones that let it through to me, if that makes sense."

She seems self-conscious, nervous both about what we're maybe about to do, but also to propose the ideas. This woman who minutes ago I was certain was the cause of so much pain, so much violence. The one who is so seldom around other people.

I nod.

"Okay," she says again.

She takes a deep breath, her chest rising and falling, the muscles of her neck and collarbone flexing beneath her skin. All of her is tense.

"We don't have to do this," I say. "I don't even know if—"

If I can.

"We have to do something," she says, shrugging that bare shoulder. "They'll come for us as soon as the weather calms." And there is such a look of fear and resignation and sadness on her face that I think maybe she's right.

I nod, again. "Okay," I say.

She takes another breath. Then she steps toward me on the carpet. Body tense, nose plug still in. Then another step. I don't move, not yet.

Up closer, and now that I'm finally allowing myself to look at her, *really* look at her maybe, I can clearly see the bruising on her cheek and brow bones, from the motel. I remind myself that she is the most likely culprit in all this, still. Even if she has the story she has, even if she's here trying to figure things out. Even if seeing the bruises makes me want to hurt the person who did it. All of this could be a distraction. She could have been trying to get me somewhere alone. But to do what? Physically, I could overpower her, even as fast as she is. She might have the knife concealed beneath her sweater, in one of her pockets.

She takes another step toward me. My heart is pounding. She comes within two feet of me and stops. From this close, I have to look down at her. But her gaze has fallen. Her toes scrunch on the floor in her thick socks.

"Sorry," she says, breathy, a little hoarse. "Just need a sec."

I don't move, not even an inch. I can smell her, ponderosa pine and campfire. Capsaicin. I can feel the heat coming off her body, as close as we are. My pulse throbs in my fingertips, on my injured hand. Everywhere.

Then, finally, she looks up and nods. Once, quickly. She swallows.

I don't think, don't let myself. I take the last step and close the distance between us.

Lee Hazlewood's voice fills the room.

My right arm slides behind Hannah's back—warmth, through her sweater, the dip of her lower back beneath my hand. My left hand takes her right, as best it can with the makeshift bandage, hold it out to the side. I pull her in a little closer.

She sucks in a breath at the contact, and I look to make sure it's okay. She jerks her head in a slight nod.

Mom and me, at the Happy Inn. Rose.

The radio playing and Christmas string lights on the headboard and TV, the little dancing Santa in the corner. "Danny, come on, baby. I'm gonna show you how to dance."

I squeeze my eyes tight.

Marianne at Whileago in the living room with the record player. Asking me to show her how to dance like my mom showed me. The two of us, later, in our new formal dancing lessons.

I feel lightheaded. This was the worst idea, and—

I open my eyes. It's cold in here, really cold. Unnaturally. I blink the room into focus and look back down at Hannah. She nods, out of breath, biting her lip. I think I understand.

It's working, is what she means. What we're doing. This might actually work. We might be able to draw the thing out. Ask it what it wants from us, once and for all.

I think . . . we have to keep going. But it's like my legs don't know how to move, like I've forgotten how to be a body. Fear, through my whole body. Adrenaline. Just this dancing, just facing, allowing the memories. I close my eyes, try to breathe through it.

Hannah Lawrence squeezes the palm of my hand in hers. Warm, soft skin against the cold of the room. Her pulse beating through her palm so I can feel it against my own. I open my eyes, watch as her left hand moves slowly, carefully, up my right arm. Comes to rest at my shoulder. It shakes. When was the last time she touched someone? Touched someone by choice? This could be the first time in years. I think of her in the motel, Everett Brown taping her into the bed. Her hands shaking against me, against mine, or . . .

Blood.

I am here and not here, with this woman.

Bathtub.

With Hannah.

I blink at her. Focus in on only her, not the feeling of dancing, not the memories.

That pine and campfire smell. My hand against her sweater, the warmth of her body. The lines of her face, the pain written in all of them. Again, the useless thought.

She is so beautiful, it almost hurts to look at her.

How did this woman and I ever possibly get here?

Still. By focusing in on her, somehow, I start to move. *We* start to move.

Lee Hazlewood sings, the otherworldly strings of the song swelling, filling the room with us, and we turn slowly in a modified waltz. I lead, and she lets me. I don't think it's her first time doing this. The way she moves.

"You can learn a lot about someone from dancing with them," Rose says.

Fuck.

Hannah. Shaking, more now.

It's freezing.

Mom. I—

Shit. I close my eyes, open them again. My fucking heart.

The lights have dimmed, just a little. Flicker in a way that is familiar. It's so cold now.

"It's working," I say. It comes out quiet, half-voiced. I'm not sure I could speak normally right now. Not sure I could do a lot of things.

Hannah nods, licks her lips again. "Yeah," she says.

We waltz. The radio plays the song over from the beginning, a little crackly, staticky. Slightly discordant.

The cold starts to recede. No darkness pooling at the edges of the room.

I look to Hannah. She looks panicked also. It's leaving. Why?

"Shit. Okay," she says. "I can, um . . ." She closes her eyes in what looks like pain, and her hand is off my shoulder. She reaches up to her face and pulls the nose plug free. She gasps in an inhale, nostrils flaring, and she lets out a small whimper. She puts her left hand back on my shoulder, so tense.

"You okay?" I ask. We're close, so close now. Freckles dust her nose. I couldn't see it before, but there's one, very small, at the corner of her mouth.

She raises her eyes slowly, lets them stop and linger on my chest. Her nostrils flare again. Want. Fear. I see it. She inhales long and slow through her nose and closes her eyes again, dropping her head slightly back in what is either pain or desire. Both. Her eyes come all the way up, and I see the tears in them. The want. The room grows cold again.

"Can you keep going?" I ask.

She nods, gives me a look as if to say yes. As if to say please, just do it, so I don't have to. I hope I read her right. God, I hope I do.

I grip her tighter behind her waist and pull her all the way in to me.

She gasps, and I think I misread, start to pull back. But she doesn't let me. Holds me there. Her body, against mine. Her chest and hips and stomach, and her hand holding on to mine so tight I could nearly faint from the pain.

The way she fits against me . . .

Have I ever felt . . . ? Has it ever been—

Movement, at the edge of the room.

Darkness.

My heart pounds.

Hannah's eyes squeezed tight, she swallows. That look of pain.

"Hey," I say. "It's working. Look."

She does. And behind me, she must see the same. Because I feel her press into me just a little bit more, and I swear I feel the world spin.

I hold her tighter.

More black. Moving, swirling in the corner. It's darker than the shadows. Amorphous and thick. Something inky, oily, maybe, sliding along the patterned carpet around us. A split second of telling myself I am imagining it, but at this stage, what's the fucking point? I can see it, and I can feel it. That smell, from the memory at the park with Rose. Chemical, bitter. It's back. The cold so sharp that I think it might burn us.

Pressure. Vibration, static.

VOOM.

Like we've been taken out of time, like the rest of the world is frozen.

Hannah stiffens, and I think she's going to pull away, that it's just too much.

I feel something, coming into the room. Snaking its way toward us from that *someplace else.*

What we're doing is working. But if she pulls back, I'll let go. I'll do it. I let her lead in that, show me what she needs. My heart is . . . I'm . . . We take another three slow steps in our dance, spinning slowly in the room, the black mass starting to lift in tendrils and swirl up and around us, from the floor.

I swallow, my mouth dry. Maybe we shouldn't be doing this. Maybe I'm the one who will . . . We need answers, but just looking at it. Heart racing, blood pumping, body numb. Terror rips through me. Old terror. I close my eyes against it.

And I feel something against my chest. Hannah closes the final gap between us and leans her head on my shoulder.

I almost trip. I can feel her breath on my neck. The tip of her nose against my skin, the way she inhales, taking in the scent of me. And I know what it is, I know what it's from and that it's trauma and that she's stuck in a loop, and that— But . . .

The *feel* of it. Of her.

And this thing in the room with us, this thing that makes me feel—

She squeezes my hand again, and one of her tears drops to my chest. And I am brought back to myself. She's doing it to ramp up the response. Of course. She's doing it to lure this thing all the way in. That's what this is. We need to feel fear to talk to it. That's all this is.

VOOM.

I can't waste it.

"Please," I say to the room. Louder than I spoke to her. I clear my throat and try once more. "Please. We're listening. Tell us what you want." Hannah Lawrence's cheek against my shoulder. The extreme cold, both of us cocooned, almost, in this swirling black mass. Swirling, stretching, almost up to the ceiling around us.

"What do you want?" I say to the room. Holding Hannah steady, holding me steady, still moving, still dancing, the song still playing. Even as both of us are shaking now, as our teeth are chattering in the cold that is unlike any I've ever felt before. That acrid chemical smell on the air. The pressure, like being deep underwater.

VOOM.

The black mass closes in, almost entirely surrounds us. It's dark, and in the few gaps between the inky tendrils, I can see the lights of the room dimming further. I hold Hannah tighter, and say again to whatever's in the room with us, "Please—"

BAM!

Something crashes against the window.

BAM!

Again.

"What was that?" Hannah says.

We can't see through the black now surrounding us. I can't answer her.

"Please, just talk to us," I say, to the room, whatever's in the room. "Just tell us what you want, we're—"

The black presses in on us, and—

Everything goes dark. I lose vision entirely.

Breaths.

Heartbeats.

Hannah's hand in mine. I don't let her go.

I can't see anything. Nothing at all.

Then . . .

VOOM.

I feel it. It's here. Close to us.

Hannah stiffens beneath me, her heart pounding so hard and fast I can feel it.

A sliding, thick, suffocating feeling. The air suddenly clogged with something, though I have no idea what it is. Almost a current, a vibration that is so intense, so overwhelming under and through and around everything, that we are suspended in it.

In a half second of delirium I think of Daphne and her insects, the *Lord of the Rings* movies she used to make me watch. The giant spider that paralyzes the hobbit with her venom. I think that's what this is. But it's not poison. It's energy, sound, vibration. Even now, it mixes with the song, Lee Hazlewood's voice. Contorts and distorts it, makes it discordant and off-kilter and even painful to hear. And still it plays.

Freezing cold. Suffocating. Pressure, on the ears, through the body. Like standing inside a bell tower, inside a wind tunnel. I don't know if Hannah could hear me if I spoke now, don't know if she's trying to speak to me. I don't know if I *can* speak. But I hold her hand and her back, and she holds me, and it's hard to keep dancing, hard to keep moving in this cocoon of black, in this onslaught of strange sound. But we do. Slowly, haltingly.

And I beg it to speak to us, this *thing*. Beg it to tell us anything at all. Hannah's hand is growing colder, her face, her shaking more violent. If it stays cold like this, she could become hypothermic. We both could. Pressure, so much pressure, on the ears, this sound, this feeling so intense.

VOOM.

The thing in the room, moving nearer to us. I can feel it, sense it.

Static. Discordant music, pressure, noise. I squeeze my eyes shut, like it will help somehow. It's loud, so loud, so crushingly—

Every muscle in my body strains against the pressure, my joints on fire, my brain. It's killing me, I think, whatever this is. I don't know if I can take much more. Don't know if—

Hannah cries out.

She pulls away. Breaks contact.

And all the volume stops.

Silence.

Slight ringing in my ears.

The black recedes, pulls back to the corners of the room. It slips away through the walls to somewhere else.

The lights come back on, dim and flickering, but there. The air clears.

There is no one, and nothing, here in this room but us.

I double over and catch my breath as some warmth comes back into my body. Ryder Smith said the thing came to them at night in prison, tested them, as if it was looking for something. Was it like this?

Hannah runs her hands through her hair, holds them there, pulls it back off her face as she tries to come back to herself. "I'm sorry," she says. "I'm sorry, I know we were close, I . . . I just . . ."

"It's okay," I say. "There's probably another way, a safer way."

But when she turns to me, I see it in her eyes. If there is some other way, we have no idea what it is. And time to figure things out is the one thing we know we don't have.

Against the window, red smeared, in front of the swirling snow beyond. I step toward it, see blood in four places, feathers stuck in one of them.

Birds. That was what was hitting the window. Birds . . . at night? In a snowstorm?

I turn back to Hannah, and she's got that look of resolve on her face, of terror. And I think I feel the same way. I think we have this time, this room. For the moment, I don't think anyone will catch up with us. At least until the storm is over. And if there's any way to solve this thing, to even get to the bottom of a part of it, we might need to just do this. Whatever . . . *this* is.

If we're going to communicate with this thing, we need to do it now.

Still, the fear on her face. "We don't have to," I say.

"No. We have to bring it back. We need—"She looks around, frantic. She swears, searching. "I can make it worse," she says. "The fear. Um. Tight space. That's what we need. The bathroom, maybe. The meat, and the tight space, and the dark. It'll be . . ." She chokes, tears streaming, and swallows down the terror. "I think we have to," she says.

I don't move. I don't know what the fuck that thing was or what is right. But her words register. Bathroom.

Hannah and me in the bathroom, together.

Bathroom. Mirror.

"I think it might be now or never," she says.

And the way she looks at me, the resolve with which she holds herself, makes me realize she's right. We have to do this. And if she can do it . . .

Hotel bathroom in the dark. Hotel bathroom with a mirror.

Hotel bathroom with her.

If it feeds off fear and pain and grief and self-hatred, then this is it. This would have to be it. For me. The mirror.

For all the victims, for the killers. And for this person in front of me.

We draw this thing out and find out what it wants.

One more time, I say the word to Hannah Lawrence, and I think it very well might be the last I ever say.

"Okay."

3

We step into the bathroom. A double vanity with granite countertop and two copper sink basins, the mirror behind. I don't look at it. Not yet. On the left is the toilet, and on the right a step-in shower. The take-out container sits on the edge of the counter nearest the shower. Hannah steps in first, and her nostrils flare again. She turns to face me, and I hesitate in the doorway.

"So I'll just . . . come in?" I say. I'm finding it hard to get air in, finding it hard to make my feet carry me forward.

"I guess," she says. "Yeah." Tears fall silently down her face, tension radiating off every part of her. The smell of the meat is strong in here. I can tell already.

I nod, and on the count of three, I pass through the doorway into the bathroom, turn, keep my eyes off the mirror. Hannah steps to the shower side. I'm in front of the vanity, facing her. The closed toilet behind me, the mirror on my left—her right—the door to the bedroom on our other side.

"So we just . . ." She clears her throat. "Close the door."

"Right. And then . . ."

"And then hopefully it comes," she says.

"Have we thought about what it's going to do when it comes?"

"No," she says. "I don't know."

"And if it doesn't come?"

"We *make* it. We'll find a way."

I nod. And she nods back.

Whatever happens, I am certain that once I close that door, there's no going back. I wait until she nods one more time.

I reach out my hand and do it.

The click of the door closing.

We are engulfed, again, in darkness. But the tiniest sliver of light peeks in from beneath the door, just the thinnest line. Just enough for our eyes to adjust and to be able to get a sense of space, a little. After a moment, I can see Hannah's outline. If I turned and looked in the mirror, I'd be able to see myself. I don't. Not yet.

I'm choked, fear flowing through my body like blood. It's not a bathtub in front of me, but it might as well be. I try to regulate my breathing, try to hold myself steady and solid. I can do this. The point is to feel fear. It's worth it, to bring this thing in. To figure out what it wants.

From outside the bathroom, the radio catches on static, Lee Hazlewood no longer playing. Just a droning in-between crackle. Searching for a signal.

I can hear Hannah breathing too, uneven, quick.

Nothing happens.

Hannah takes a small step toward me.

Her breaths. Her body.

Static.

She comes closer.

The radio searching, moving between stations.

When Hannah comes to a stop, she is inches from me. Again, I don't move. I can see her outline, and I can feel her. Smell her, once again. It's stronger now, in this tight space. She leans in toward me. Touches her nose once again to the side of my throat, just almost, just barely grazing my skin. Nowhere else.

She inhales, slow and long and deep.

A disjointed thought comes into my mind. A feeling that everything in my life up to this point was leading to this. As if somehow, on some level, I always knew I would end up here. In this bathroom with her. Her nose against my throat, her body so close. The room spins, and I reach out and hold on to the counter with my left hand, pain as my bandaged finger hits the countertop. I grip tight anyway.

The cold starts to creep in. I can feel the moment Hannah notices too. I don't know if it's the dark or the proximity—any closer, and every part of us would be touching—but . . . something else is happening.

An awareness creeps in at the same time. Like . . . maybe I'm not alone in my thoughts. Maybe a side effect of the fear. Too much adrenaline with not enough movement. Craving fight or flight, not getting it.

Outside the door, the static increases in volume on the radio, tunes into different songs, in and out. Willie's voice. Static. John Prine for a moment. Static. Kris Kristofferson, Emmylou Harris, Jim Croce. Static. A sick feeling enters my stomach, and I know what it's searching for. I tense. Brace myself for the inevitable. Again, this sense that all of this was always coming, a truck barreling toward me in the night. The room spinning. Hannah Lawrence inches from me, breathing me in. Because of what she does to human bodies. What she is probably imagining doing to mine.

The smell of the steak grows stronger in the tight space. I know she wants to reach for it. Again, that awareness, that feeling that in my mind, there is something, *someone* else there besides me.

The cold isn't coming fast enough. The radio still searching. I know what I have to do. It would be so easy. The top of Hannah's head barely comes up to my chin. I can turn, even with her this close to me. Just turn my head. That's it. Just turn my head and look.

My heart is pounding, again, more. Fuck, I could give myself a heart attack.

Dad.

Shit. My palms are sweating now. I might be shaking. Hannah might be shaking.

It's getting colder.

A creak, on the floorboards in the bedroom.

BAM!

Another bird hitting the window. I think.

That creak again. The vibration, whirring.

VOOM.

It's working.

The radio lands on a song. And I knew it was coming, I knew to expect it and that I would have to face it. But still . . .

When the opening notes of "Annie's Song" play, Hannah whimpers. I try to breathe.

The music travels, grows in volume so that it feels as though it plays in the bathroom with us, comes from the floor and walls and ceiling. John Denver's voice begins.

You fill up my senses—

MOM!

I can't get air in. I can't do this.

VOOM.

The vibration, the humming. Getting louder, bigger. Pressing against my ears and my body, and the music growing in volume, and a woman saying something to me, speaking. Hannah saying words. I don't know what she's saying. I just have to—

The song switches. A voice I've heard, once or twice. A newer singer.

Hannah freezes.

Between the static, carried to us on this too-loud, too-heavy, too-strong vibration, he sings, *Queen of the rodeo—*

"No," Hannah says. It's a whimper. A plea. "Not this."

The music gets louder, and she's crying. I don't know what to do.

In my head, the world of my thoughts, that other presence. It's screaming, crying out. I move toward it.

Here between worlds. Standing in this bathroom, and existing in this mind space. Everything, in both, so unbearably loud.

I move toward the other presence in that other-space, and I feel her.

It's Hannah. Hannah, in the bathroom, in front of me. And Hannah there, in the other-world, that in-between. Somehow, both of us, in my mind.

And whatever's in the bedroom, prowling outside the door.

It's here. We've brought it in. I hear the floorboards groan and creak.

The pressure. Static. That crackling strangeness.

Maybe we just open the bathroom door. Maybe we've done what we have to do in here, and the creature, or whatever the thing is, we can talk to it. We've done it. We've brought it here.

I reach out my right hand for the knob, and I turn it, prepare to push it open, for us to be met with whatever this *thing* is.

But the door doesn't move. It won't open.

I step away from Hannah, try the handle again. It's locked.

Hannah realizes, reaches out, tries it. Bangs against it.

"No," she says. "No, no, no."

The song, growing in volume, and the cold, and that static, and—

It switches again. "Annie's Song." John Denver, and

Dad's hands in Mom's hair, slamming her against—

The shower turns on behind Hannah.

The song switches back to the other one.

Hannah crying. Hannah here, and in that other-space. Both of us, in two places at once. All of it confusing, dizzying.

In the bathroom, this body. I stay very still. In the other-space, I move toward her. Am drawn to her. I can't see, don't know if she senses me there, if she's aware of these two worlds, these realities that make no sense but also somehow click every piece of my life into place. In the other-world, I reach out and touch her. And—

I'm on a mountain.

Snow.

Blood. Meat. Body.

Hate. Hate myself.

Teeth, on thigh. Teeth, on stomach. Meat, frozen. Gnawing, tearing, ripping.

Don't look at her face. Can't. look at it.

My friend. My friend.

My friend.

Body in the drainpipe.

Fresh. Blood still warm, still salty.

Blood on my chin, my nose, my cheeks, my hands.

Hands on a shin, hands on a hip, tongue against the muscle of a thigh.

Biting, ripping, tearing, chewing,

Hating

Hating

Hating

Fuck, it's

Good and terrible and I hate myself, I hate—

Mountain

Friend. Eden.

Dancing in the bar. The way she sways, the way she laughs, with me. The way we both laugh. The song playing, Our song.

Queen of the rodeo. Orville Peck's voice.

Eden's laugh.

Eden and me.

Eating

Sucking

Chewing

SCREAMING.

I suck in a breath. Come back to the bathroom. Hannah, before me.

I was in her thoughts.

Those were Hannah's memories. This thing, whatever's in the bedroom, doing this to us. Making us feel this, putting us in each other's heads.

I try the door again. It's so cold in here. Hannah repeating, *No, no, no, please, stop—*

"Let us out," I yell. "Let us out and talk to us! We want to talk to you!"

The door doesn't budge. The song shifts back to John Denver, and the force of it, of *something*, knocks me back into the counter. Hannah stands paralyzed, beside me.

Then I'm—

Mountain.

Motel.

Mom!

Blood, blood in the bathtub. Mom, not moving, Dad standing over her, crying.

Motel

Taped, duct-taped into the bed, a man's body in front of me

No skin. Blood, muscle, bone.

The tongue in my mouth, the feel of it against my own

Hatred and terror and revulsion and—

Something else.

No. No, no—

Please don't do this, I'll do anything. I don't want it, can't—

Blood rushing to my fingers, toes, between my legs. The tongue in my mouth, the feel of it over my own.

Want.

Terrible want.

I want it more than I have ever wanted anything.

Every part of me—

"Please!" Hannah yells, over the unrelenting sound waves, vibrations, static, the songs, now switching back and forth, flipping between the two, all of it so loud.

Static. Music. Noise. Memory—

"Please! Stop! Please, make it stop, make it stop, make it stop!"

Hannah's hands on her face. In both worlds, here, and the other one.

Terror

Hate

Want

I am in the motel as a child, I am in the motel taped into the bed, I am in a bar and on a mountain and in Afghanistan and divorce court and in a car with truck headlights blinding me.

"*Please,*" Hannah says again. Here, or in the other-place. Both. I don't know. I'm dizzy. The meat, and the room, and the smell, and the cold.

Please, make it stop!

She's screaming. Here, in the bathroom, she's screaming, and in that other-place repeating, *Please, please please!*

I don't know what to do. Hannah. Here. Asking me. Begging me.

I see that her eyes are elsewhere. She is elsewhere, stuck there. "Hey," I say. "It's time to come back, okay? We'll get out of here, you just have to come back."

Please, she screams in the other-place, so loud in my head, *PLEASE, MAKE IT STOP, PLEASE!*

"I don't know what to do! I don't know how to make it stop!"

Daniel!

Hannah's voice. In my head. Hannah, frantic, Hannah blind and stuck on the mountain, stuck on the side of the highway, in the drainpipes, stuck in the motel bed.

DANIEL!

Hannah, calling my name.

I don't know, I don't think, just feel so much, fear, want, terror, I don't—

PLEASE!

I don't think. I—

I bend down and press my lips to hers. And . . .

Everything goes silent.

Silence. Stillness.

Dark.

For half a second. For an eternity.

Hannah's lips and mine.

Her skin, and my skin.

Everything suspended. Quiet . . .

Then I pull back.

And it all rushes back in.

Music. Both songs. Static. Vibration. Cold. Loud. So loud. Blood. *Blood—*

The shower, behind Hannah. The smell.

Ears ringing, room turning. This smell, I know. I know it so well, and so does Hannah, and—

Not water. It's not water coming down in the shower.

I don't know how it's possible. Don't know how any of this could be real. But what's pouring down from the showerhead, filling the room with its scent, what's actually physically here.

It's blood.

Hannah. Blood. Meat. Salt. Sound.

Too much, it's too much, it's all—

She grabs me and presses her lips to mine.

Silence, again.

Stillness.

Hannah's lips. Hannah's hands on my shoulder, my side.

Fuck.

Hannah's tears caught on our lips, and—

Relief. So much relief. We hold tight to each other, don't move. A lifeline. A tether, between worlds.

Silence, here. The two of us.

That other-world, the in-between. Memories flashing like a silent movie now, between us. Hers, and mine. All the worst moments, every moment of a life that makes us want to end it all. Every moment that I've carried, that she has. Hannah, who's had to carry all of this alone.

She's seeing it all too, I know she is. My mom, my dad, the motel. The Stansfields. The car crash. Josie and war, watching my friends die. Telling their families. Watching everyone I love die again and again and again.

Me, in Hannah's mind. Her in mine. The things she's feeling, that she's felt. Every part of her laid bare and as clear and visceral as though I am living it now with her, for her. Living it again and again. The mountain, her life before, every moment in the drainpipes and the motel.

She opens her lips, a little. Her tongue finding its way into my mouth, and *fuck*. She groans, presses herself into me. Clings to me.

I don't know if the thing is out there still, but it's locked us here. Her and me together, blocking out the noise. The pain.

A great tidal wave. The avalanche that's always been coming.

What is the point of fighting it at all? When this is what I've wanted from the second I heard her name, saw her drawings in her cabin. Saw her face for the first time. I haven't stopped thinking about her, haven't stopped dreaming and obsessing. Haven't stopped wanting.

Her. Hannah Lawrence.

I want her.

I want her so fucking much.

I move my hand behind her neck, slide it up beneath her hair, and pull her in as close as I can. She groans and meets me, presses her hips against mine. *Fuck*, I breathe again, as she slides her teeth over my tongue, hovers them toward the back of it.

We pause. Her teeth on my tongue. My tongue in her mouth. She could bite down. It would be so easy. She could take it from me. Has me entirely at her mercy.

She hesitates, and I can feel her growing want, her craving. Her *need*. Both our heaving breaths.

I should move. I should do something, protect myself, or . . .

But I won't. I don't want to. I know now, feel with total certainty, that I'd let her do anything. I might as well fall to my knees.

She inhales sharply, and I can feel her need building. She's imagining it, biting down. The spray of hot salt down her throat, teeth sinking into soft flesh. Taking a part of me into her, keeping it for herself. I can feel her, see her, thinking it. Experience it myself, through her. And I think, this is it.

But she pulls back, just slightly. And . . . I can feel what it costs her, how hard it is.

I want to give her what she needs. *Something*. Give her anything.

I reach over to the take-out container, and with us separated slightly, all the sound rushes back. The vibration pushing in, the music, both songs, overlapping, the worst songs from the worst moments of our lives, interchanging, the static, every scream from every terrible moment we've ever lived. The screams of loved ones, our own. Loud. So loud, too loud. This thing outside trapping us here. It's still here. Still so loud.

I take a piece of steak between my fingers and I hold it up before her, fighting through the sound, the pain.

She leans forward, tilts her head back, her mouth open. Hannah with her mouth open before me. Her eyes on mine. She's so fucking beautiful.

I drop the meat to her tongue.

She groans, her eyelids fluttering, as she closes her mouth over the meat in my hand. As I feed it to her bit by bit. Seeing her like this—*fuck*. Juice runs over her bottom lip, drips down from her chin, and as she sucks the end of the meat into her mouth, I run my thumb over that bottom lip, lean forward and kiss the side of her neck, her jaw as she chews. Lick my way up her throat to her chin to get everything that's dripped as she chews and groans and swallows and holds on to me so tight. I'm going to have marks from her nails in me. I can't think of anything I want more. To make this woman forget—everything, all the pain, the suffering.

To make myself forget with her.

I take another piece of the steak, and the vibrations and pressure and cold and sound push in, but I don't care. I don't care at all as she opens her mouth again to receive more. As I give it to her. And as she chews, as I'm hit with another ten memories of hers, of mine, a thousand moments of a life, I do drop down. On my knees, before her, her hands still on my shoulders, more of that juice dripping down her chin. The blood coming down the shower making the room thick, metallic. Warming it up from the cold. I lift the bottom of her sweater and run my lips and my tongue along the skin above her jeans.

A thought presses in, something I feel I should know or see, or—

Animal meat. Human meat. Cows, humans. Animals. Ecosystems. Symbiotic relationships, aspen trees. Wolves. Something I'm supposed to . . .

But Hannah's skin. Her stomach. Here. Right here.

I run my hands up from her hips to her waist. Lick up her stomach to her ribs. Slide my good hand up, and with one thumb, I brush the bottom of her breast. She whimpers, and I do it again. Slowly, I let it glide up to her nipple, just the edge of it. She whimpers again, and I drop my forehead to her stomach, try to collect myself. It's so much. Too much. It's pain and it's fear and it's grief and it's heartbreak, and I have never felt *this*, this much want.

The floor is wet. I blink, my forehead against Hannah's stomach. I look down at it. Try to understand. The floor, wet, beneath my knees. Dark.

I look back up to the shower. I stop, my hands on her waist, my knees in the liquid on the floor.

Blood filling the bottom of the shower, spilling out over onto the floor. Hannah's socks are soaked with it. My knees, my shins. It can't be real. I thought . . .

I reach down with one hand, touch the warm thick liquid. Hold up my hand to inspect it.

It's blood. It's actually—

Mom.

Shit.

Dad, grabbing her by the hair.

MOM!

Dad

"Daniel—"

Slamming her head into the sink.

MOM!

Whirring, vibrating, everything too loud. The music, pressure. Room spinning. Pressure. Blood on my hands.

My mom's blood. It's my mom's blood.

She isn't moving.

MOM! Mom, please!

"Daniel, come back." Hands on my shoulders.

Hands pulling me out of the bathroom, they're taking me away, taking me away from my mom, and she still isn't moving, why won't she answer me?

Mom, please—

"Daniel. Listen to me, you're here, you're not there anymore."

Mom, please wake up! Please!

Hands, shaking my shoulders.

MOM!

Shaking me.

A face in front of me.

Hannah. I suck in a breath, can't quite—

Motel

"Daniel," she says, Hannah says, through the music and the dizzying sound and the cold. "Shit," she says. She turns, tries the door again, but it's still locked. She pounds on it, yells something. I am here and not here.

I am watching them take her away, and she's not moving. Why isn't she moving? Please, Mom—

"Come back to me. Please, Daniel. Come back."

Hands, over my neck, my chest. The sides of my face. Down, back down my chest and my stomach and the top of my jeans. "Come back," she says. That other-Hannah in the other-space calling me too. Two places. I'm in two places. Three.

The motel—

Hannah. Words.

"Shh, Daniel, you're here. It's okay."

Hands on my chest and stomach.

Mom, please.

"Daniel, you're not there. I've got you. I'm with you."

I'm with you.

Those words. The voice . . . saying them.

Hannah.

I'm not there. I'm not at the Happy Inn. I'm at the Stanley Hotel, and Hannah Lawrence is in front of me, and . . .

I'm not there. I'm not back there.

She brought me back. Hannah did. I'm here.

Hannah, kneeling with me in this blood. She shouldn't be here. I don't want her in this. I push through the dizziness and stand, pull her up with me. The blood, hot, an inch thick on the ground now. I grab her waist and lift her up onto the counter.

I go to the shower, try to turn it off. It won't stop. The blood keeps coming. I try the door again, and it's still locked. I don't know what to do. I look around, for a window, for anything to try and stop this. We shouldn't have called this thing here, shouldn't have invited it in.

These songs. This fucking music is going to make me insane, is going to—

"Daniel," Hannah says behind me, through the pressure, the sound. I turn, and she wears that anguished resigned look I've seen before. "I think we have to play it out," she says. "To make it stop."

"What does that mean?"

"Come here," she says. And even as she says it, she steels herself again. To be close to me. To be close to anyone. In that other-space I can feel how excruciating it is for her, how much it ignites that paralyzing want. Every feeling.

"Are you sure?" I ask.

She reaches out, and I take a step forward.

She pulls me in between her knees, my thighs against the counter. Boots on bloody floor.

"I think . . ." she says, touching my chest, "you're gonna have to look."

The music swells and that maddening pressure, vibration, static. Hannah's seen my memories. She's lived them. And . . . I know she's right. Of course I do. Of course that would be the final thing. Maybe what this creature outside the door wants.

But I can't do it. Especially here, especially now. I don't . . . I lean my forehead against hers. "Not yet," I say. It's pitiful, my voice, the words.

"Okay," she says. "Okay." And she reaches up to touch my face as she kisses me.

Again, silence. Just us in the kiss, and that other-world, the one we occupy together. That in-between. I feel it now. Know. Something is in the bedroom still, pressing in on us. And maybe it can access our other-space, certainly some other-space. But this one, the one we inhabit right now, together. It's just us. Just Hannah and me.

And in the bathroom . . . Her tongue against mine, my hands sliding through her hair. Every inch of my body is on fire. No kiss has ever felt like this. I have *never* felt—

It will never be enough. I can't pull her close enough. And the way I feel her, know her, in this moment. That want, that thrumming ache. It's not just mine. Her, tasting me, touching me. Her tongue sliding against mine. I think to grab the take-out container, get the meat, give her more. But the container's fallen to the floor, to the blood. And I know it won't satisfy her anyway.

Hannah, fighting through this hunger, this need, to calm me. To bring me back. Hannah, who is here with me, really here. Sharing this burden, all of it.

I want to do the same. To help her. Give her . . . something.

And then . . . a thought.

I pull back and brace against the sound, all the sounds, flooding back every time we break contact. I lift my bandaged hand. Hannah's eyes land on it. She realizes what I'm doing.

She's about to protest, about to say I don't have to, but I shake my head.

A tear falls down her face, and I lean forward and kiss it. I pull back, her chest rising and falling, and she watches me unwrap the bandage. I swear as it peels the dried blood from my skin, Pain. Want. Certainty.

I let the bandage fall to the floor, and I hold my hand out in front of her.

The wave of desire that hits me is almost unbearable. Her eyes on my hand, the way she's looking at it. I am painfully hard. Have been for I don't know how long. I don't know what's hers or mine anymore.

She reaches up, takes my wrist in both her hands. She locks her eyes on mine.

She opens her mouth and slowly traces her tongue from my wrist, up my palm, to the base of my pinky. My cock twitches against the counter. Everything terrible, incredible.

She licks from the base of my pinky up to the tip of my finger. Over the blood, the exposed muscle, just a light flick. I suck in at the pain. But also the look of her. Her eyes on mine, her tongue on my skin.

She does it again, and I groan, push my hips against her. My cock straining through my jeans. She arches her back, presses herself against me and *Jesus*. I set my good hand down on her thigh. As she leans forward and closes her mouth over my finger. As she sucks slowly from the base to the tip.

The room spins. I don't move. I don't pull it back. It fucking hurts, and I feel sick, but . . . the *look* of her. Feeling, knowing. How much she wants it, loves it. I squeeze her thigh with my other hand, and she moans, staring at my bloody finger, her brow knit in pain and want, and—

She looks up at me, a final ask. I can feel her disbelief, that I would offer this.

Her. Hannah. I'd say yes to anything. I *will* say yes to fucking anything.

I've been a goner from the very beginning.

I nod.

She makes herself pull back, and I can see how hard it is for her. Can feel it. The sound pressing in, all of it. I keep my hand held there, waiting for her, ready when she wants it. Her chest rising and falling beneath the sweater, the outline of her perfect tits I have tried not to notice. She reaches down and fumbles with the button of my jeans. I lean back a little from the sink so she can undo the zipper. I help her with my good hand, slide my jeans down below my hips. I almost tell her she doesn't have to do this, that I'm giving her what she needs, and I don't need anything in return.

But I can feel what she feels, hear what she thinks, not quite in words. But I know. She wants this as much as I do. God, I have never wanted anyone like this. Have never wanted anything as much as I want this, now, with her.

Her, across the table from me at Woody Creek, her with that pen in her mouth at the three-sided shelter, her running on a mountain trail, her in my fucking dreams.

Everything in this whole mess of a life to get us here. She's so unbelievably perfect.

She unbuttons her own jeans. Presses her hands to the countertop to lift herself. I grab hold of her belt loops, work them down over her thighs, her knees, step back and pull them off, let them fall to the bloody floor. She lowers herself to the counter, and I slide my good hand up her thigh, around the back to her ass, squeeze it just a little. She groans, kisses me again. Whimpers. I pull her closer to the edge of the counter.

She touches my chest, trails her hand down until she reaches the top of my boxer briefs. Then she runs her fingers over the length of me, the thin fabric all that's between us.

Jesus, I say. Out loud, in the other-space, I don't know. *You're gonna kill me.*

She reaches for the top of my briefs, slides them down, freeing my cock.

"If I wanted to, I would have already," she says out loud. The half-broken tooth in her mouth. All of her, right here.

I bend forward and kiss her hard. Draw it out, take and give what I can.

She breaks the kiss to spit on her hand, and I think there's a little blood in it. My blood, from my finger. She slides her hand over my cock, with the spit and the blood, and I grip her ass with my good hand and I can feel that she likes it. Loves it. A little hard, a little rough. She leans back up and stares straight into my eyes. I bring my good hand up beside the other one, both hands held before her like an offering, and she knows what I'm asking. She takes my index and middle fingers of my good hand in her mouth, sucks them slowly, covers them in that spit.

I push them into her mouth, watch her, *feel* her lips close around them, her tongue sliding, sucking, tasting. She's imagining it's the other finger. Knowing, anticipating what she'll soon taste. Feel. What I'm giving to her. Again, I push them in and out of her mouth.

Then I pull my hand back. And I reach down, slide those same fingers down between her legs. Fuck, even through the fabric of her underwear, she's so wet. I move it aside, find her entrance, and I slowly push one finger in.

It feels, *she* feels—

She lets out a sound that makes me want to do this a thousand times. A million. That makes me never want to leave this room. She's so fucking wet, it's killing me. Perfect. She is so goddamned perfect. Where has she been all my life, and how is she here now?

Her nails dig into my shoulder, her back arching. I slide the second finger in, and she cries out. I groan. I slide them in and out once more, twice. I pull back just enough to watch them push in and out of her, as she thinks or whispers, *Yes, god yes.* As I rub my thumb over her clit, still pump my fingers in and out, move them so fucking easily. The wet warmth of her.

I see it now too. She's wanted this. Feel the memories, thoughts. Dreams of me in her cabin. Lying on that twin bed beneath the wall of drawings, her hand, traveling down her stomach, into her—

Fuck, Hannah.

She sucks in a breath, and she reaches out, takes my wrist again, the other one. The one I've been holding up for her. It's too much, too hard. Knowing it's there, waiting for her. That it's just there, and it's hers, and—

She can't wait any longer. I don't want her to.

I position my injured pinky in front of her mouth.

She opens wide, her tongue out just a little.

I swear again. The sight of her, the feel of her.

My good hand's fingers still inside her, I push my injured hand forward, place my pinky on her tongue.

Hannah Lawrence. She looks right at me as she closes her mouth around my bloody finger. She starts at the base again, slides her mouth back to the tip. Her spit, the blood.

I suck in a breath, hold the injured hand steady. Pain. Terrible pain. I'm dizzy with it. With more than pain. Everything so intense. The blood on the floor rising, maybe two inches now, beneath us.

I pull my good hand back, slide it out of her. And I move my hips forward, I hover there. The tip of my cock touches her entrance, and I can barely breathe, just feeling that wetness there.

John Denver playing, that other song. Sound and static and pressure and pain.

It's only half a second, this suspension. This pause. But it's a lifetime. It's every moment that makes a person who they are. It's realizing that all of them mattered because they brought you here, and none of them mattered because they weren't this.

Pain. Fear. Blood. Self-hatred, terror, loneliness.

Want.

I thrust my hips forward and slide into her.

She bites down.

I let out a groan. I'm blinded with it. It fucking hurts. It feels better than anything, ever.

I am here, and not here. In this bathroom, in the other-space. I am in a state of pain and ecstasy that I didn't think was possible. I think it might kill me. God, please let it kill me.

If this is death, if this is . . .

I pull my hips back, and I shove into her again as she sucks and she chews on my finger. As she whimpers and moans, her eyes closed, tasting. Spit and blood dripping down her chin. I have never seen anything so fucking beautiful. The room spins, everything pushing in, every terrible memory and moment. The music, the pressure. The thing outside the door that is powerful and wants to maybe hurt or kill us or—

Hannah takes and sucks and chews, and I push into her, again and again.

So fucking terrible and good and—

Hannah's right hand, up my shoulder, my neck. Up to my face. Her thumb under my chin. I know what she's doing. And I know that she has to. That I have to. But I can't do it on my own. I can't. I don't want to, I want to stay here, and fuck this perfect woman, keep fucking her, feeling myself inside her, and—

But I have to. I have to.

So I let her.

She pushes my chin up, and I close my eyes for half a second before I open them.

I open my eyes. I see them in the mirror.

Blood

Bathtub

Fear, Pain

Terror

Mom, Dad

Blood

Blood

My eyes.

My dad's eyes.

Pain in my hand. Absolute fucking bliss of being inside Hannah.

I am staring at myself. Looking at myself in the mirror.

I hate him. I hate him so much.

I am so afraid every goddamned second of everything that's happened before and everything that could still come. Everything that I could be. That he made me.

I fucking *hate* him.

My dad at the center of everything.

"How could you, Rose, how could you?"

Hannah rocks against me, grabs my ass and pulls me in tight to her. I groan again. My eyes on the mirror, on—

She pulls back, releases my finger from her mouth but holds my wrist with one of her hands. She says, "Don't stop."

My eyes on the mirror. I move. Shove myself into her.

"More," she says.

Pull out, push in.

"More, harder. *Please.*"

Hannah. Shove myself in.

"Yes,"

My eyes on the mirror, and the wet slap of—

"Yes, god yes, *fuck* yes."

I drive into her, again and again.

"Don't stop, okay? Don't stop. I'm so close. We're so close. Don't you fucking dare stop."

I groan, growl. My eyes in the mirror, and so much pain, and—

Hannah pulls my wrist to her mouth and closes her lips around my pinky.

Hannah. Sucking, licking.

Taking my finger on her tongue, between her teeth, consuming me, all of me.

Both of us, this pain, this fear.

Sharing it, living it.

Together.

He disappears. My dad disappears from the mirror. That part disappears.

It's just me in the mirror.

It's just her. And me.

Hannah

I push into her again and again, until there is only us in a black universe.

Her body and mine, her heat, her want. Her need.

There is Hannah. Music playing, sound, vibration. Pressure. Static.

A lifetime of events leading to this.

There is us and oblivion.

And when I'm right there, when I can feel that she is too, almost over the edge, almost taking that great leap into the black together,

I push into her one last time.

Just as her teeth rip the last chunk of meat from my finger, taking everything that's left. Sucking, chewing, swallowing. All of it.

There is no life. No death.

There is nothing in the dark.

Just Hannah and me.

Just us.

4

I open my eyes to morning light and snow that only falls softly now.

I sit up. There is no blood on the window glass from birds hitting it. There's no blood on the bathroom floor. I lie back down in the bed and stare up at the ceiling.

Was any of it real? Just as I think it, the pain hits me, and I hold up my hand. There's a bandage on it.

My pinky's gone, the bone too.

I turn my head. She's sleeping, still. Quiet. Her hair fanned out over the pillow, face soft and for once without the look of pain there. For once without the nose plug. I shouldn't disturb her. I should give myself some space, some time to think away from her. Go for a run or go get coffee or something, just to clear my head. But even as I think it, now, knowing what she's been through, having *seen* it myself . . .

And I feel it still. That other-space.

It's still there. A kind of dark open night and Hannah and me standing inside it. I close my eyes and imagine walking toward her in it, imagine reaching out and touching her—

She makes a sound beside me, turns her head, and opens her eyes.

She rolls over to face me and looks at me.

I watch . . . *feel*, maybe . . . her asking the same questions to herself about last night. What was real, what wasn't. I don't remember leaving the bathroom, and I don't know if she does. I don't remember anything after that final moment with her in there. I don't remember re-bandaging my hand. Nothing.

I reach for my phone. Wi-Fi is still out. Cell service too. I put it down, turn back to her.

What happened to the Witchwalker? Why did it trap us in there? Where did it go?

Her eyes search my face, and my questions pause.

Her eyes on me. I feel a deep pulsing ache in my chest.

For once, it's not self-hatred, not fear or guilt or shame or pain. It's something else. So much louder and brighter. But it could still tear me apart, and I'd let it. It happened so fast and feels like it was always here.

"It's different now, isn't it?" she says.

"What is?" I say. I reach out and brush her hair behind her ear with my bandaged hand. But I know what she means. Of course I do.

She's so beautiful in the gray snowy light I can barely breathe.

Still, I want to hear her say it, *need* to hear it maybe.

"Everything."

Outside, something passes by the window, the shadow of a bird. Otherwise, in the quiet falling slow and the mercifully silent radio, it's just us here. Our heartbeats.

She reaches out and takes my hand, lifts it to her face. Her nostrils flare.

She eyes the bandage that will need a change soon, and she lifts my remaining fingers to her lips and kisses them each, looking up at me. Openly, without any kind of guard or filter. And I think, no wonder I've been obsessed with this woman since the day I first saw her. Her, here, taking me in in the same way.

When you've lived in the dark, survived it, it's hard sometimes to explain to others. Really explain how it's with you every second. How it *is* everything. How you're battling all the time, how you don't want to battle it at all. How a part of you grows to know it so completely you don't want it to go.

But Hannah . . .

Daphne, at Linger. What did she say? *When you find her . . . don't fucking let go.*

Hannah and me. Having seen so much of each other, to have lived it, ourselves, in breaths and moments and memories. Having shared all the worst and best moments of a life, lived each other's memories. I don't know that you ever come back from that. I don't know how I could ever want to.

My whole life carrying all of this alone. Up to now.

And she's in danger. Because of me. Because of this Witchwalker.

"We didn't talk to it," I say. "Last night. I couldn't . . . I don't feel any closer to knowing." What's happening, how I'm involved in all this. How I am supposed to solve this case.

She studies my face, but I can feel she's elsewhere too, piecing things together, searching for any clue. "Maybe it did . . . speak to us. In the way it could."

"What do you mean?" I ask.

"I got this sense that it sort of . . . *wanted* us thinking of our pasts, those memories. Maybe it's not just because the dark feelings and memories call to it . . . maybe it wants us to find something there. Maybe not for me, *that* I understand. But for you. It's *your* hair around the killers' tongues, and it's your childhood motel room it brought me to."

She trails her fingers down my wrist, thinking.

She says, "It seemed like there are gaps, though. Somehow. In your memory. Is that right? That memory of your mom in the park. That was in Aspen. But it's incomplete. There are more of those. Did you . . . Could it be something about that room, specifically, or that park, or your life, that it's been trying to get at? Trying to remind you of?"

Flashes. Rose. Other moments.

"Maybe," I say, but I'm caught on what she said. "And for you . . . ?"

"I think for me it's simple," she says, quiet. Her hand on my forearm. Her shin against mine beneath the sheets. "I think I stumbled into something that was always about you. But the Witchwalker, I think it liked me being there. I think it liked being in symbiosis with me. I felt . . . sometimes, when I was eating . . ." She takes a breath, her chest rising. I slide my hand over hers and squeeze. She says, "It felt like it was happy, somehow, that it could feed something. With what it was doing. Like it was satisfied, watching me."

I take this in, try to understand. "But symbiosis, like the bird you told me about. The bird provides a service to the crocodile too."

She bites the inside of her cheek and nods. "Roles in ecosystems change, evolve. We still have wolves, even though . . . well, we'll see if we still do for long. But some wolves found it advantageous to adapt to live with humans. And some humans found that advantageous also. And now we have dogs. The purpose they serve now for us is largely just . . . fulfillment. Some have other jobs, but . . . we care for them, feed them, make sure their needs are met. I think . . . when I'm there, the Witchwalker, it's not alone. And it likes that. I think it recognizes something in me, and maybe something in you."

"You think it wants you to be its pet?"

"I think that it has one main want, and that is whatever it is that has to do with you. And everything else . . . might just be accidents, or . . . maybe it's just stumbling around in the dark like all of us. Existing, trying to understand what the point of any of this is. I don't know, I only feel it sometimes. It's not like you and me in the other-place. I think it thinks differently than us. Like . . . we can and can't speak to dogs. We can and can't understand other species, you know? So I could be wrong about all of it. Also, um." She draws her finger slowly, tentatively, down my chest. "Last night, I . . . did, maybe, get distracted."

I run my eyes over her face. Hannah Lawrence. Here, right beside me. Emotion floods me, one I don't quite know. Overwhelming. Too big.

I lean down and kiss her.

I want—need—to feel her. To slow down this time, to take in every inch of her and make her make those sounds she did last night. This time, without her reliving the pain, without everything else. And the way she reacts to the kiss, the way she presses into me, wearing just her sweater and underwear—I can feel her in both worlds, this one and the other. *Wanting.*

Wanting something I can easily give. At least in this moment. At least one more time.

I roll on top of her. Slip my good hand behind her head, tangle my fingers in her hair as I kiss her harder. She slides her tongue into my mouth, and I press my hips to hers, her back instantly arching to meet me. I can feel how she wants to move, what she wants to give me. I can see it in her mind as she thinks it. Break the kiss, put me on my back, touch and taste every part of me on the way down. But as she tries to lift her arm to touch me, I pin it gently down against the bed. "This time, today," I say, into her mouth, between breaths. "Let me. Let me do this."

"Well," she says, after a moment, a faint smile on her lips. Her lips I kiss again, hovering my body over hers. "If I have to."

I trail my mouth down her throat again, biting, just a little, at her skin there. She sucks in a breath and exhales a small laugh. "There's got to be a cannibalism joke in here somewhere," she says.

I smile, lick her down to her collarbone. Then I feel, in that other-space, just a little, but . . .

Shame. Guilt. Doubt.

Is that from her?

I pull back and look her in the eye, place my hands on her thighs.

It is. She's . . . worried. About my finger, about . . .

She's worried about me.

She feels *shame.*

"To be clear," I say. "I offered that to you. You did nothing wrong. I regret nothing, and I would let you consume every part of me if it's what you wanted."

Doubt, in her eyes. That feeling still there. She doesn't believe me.

"Hannah. Last night was the best of my life."

Her eyes fill looking up at me. Battling that shame, still. How do I tell her? How do I make her understand?

"I took your fox drawing," I say, my hands on this perfect woman, my eyes on her face, "because I thought it was beautiful. And I've touched it and held it and carried it ever since. Since the moment I knew you existed on this planet, I haven't stopped thinking about you. Haven't stopped wanting to see you, wanting you, needing to know anything and everything I could about you. And I didn't want to want you, or think about you. I fought it. Until I couldn't. You, Hannah Lawrence, have consumed my every waking thought since the moment I first saw your face. Since I heard your name. I wanted last night more than I have wanted anything ever. And I loved every fucking second of it."

Her brow furrows again and tears fall, a flood of emotion hitting me from the other side. So much, too huge, for us now. Too big to understand. Painful, and also . . .

Hannah pushes herself up on her elbows and takes my face in her hands, kisses me harder, with more urgency, scrambles to pull her sweater over her head, breaking contact with me just for the moment it comes off.

"Wait," I say, pulling back. I swallow. "Did *I* do anything you didn't want? Last night?"

She stares at me for another minute, and the corner of her mouth cocks in a slight smile. It hits me like a punch to the chest. I'm hard, again, seeing it. Was already, probably. But . . . damn.

She pulls me in again, kisses me harder.

Then I slow the kiss down because whatever's coming next, whatever lies ahead for us, I want—need—her to know what this, what *she*, means to me.

I push Hannah back down to the bed and pin her arms with my hands as I trail my mouth down the most beautiful perfect body I've ever seen.

"What do you call a cannibal who only eats pussy?" I say, between kisses.

"What?" she says on a breath, and I can hear that smile there.

I lick, kiss, bite down her tits, her stomach, her hip bone, across the plane of her abdomen. Her skin, her perfect smooth warm skin. I lift my head just long enough to say,

"A Cativore."

She laughs. It's the first time I've heard her really laugh. It's musical and a little stilted, unused. I want to hear it forever, want to drown in it. "That's not—" she says. "That's the worst—"

And then as I flick my tongue somewhere it hasn't explored yet—somewhere, if I'm being honest, I may have imagined tasting so long before now—she falls back, sucking in a breath.

And in every way I am capable of, with everything I have, in room 217 at the Stanley Hotel with a missing pinky and a feeling of something so right in the middle of all the wrong,

I do everything I can to make Hannah Lawrence feel something other than pain.

5

What happened to John Denver?" Hannah asks. Her head on my chest, my arm around her. We have to go soon. We both know it. I would stay here forever, just like this. "In the end?"

Her hair falls over her face. With my free hand, I tuck it back behind her ear again. I have to focus to hear the words she just spoke. To understand the question.

"He had a kid with a singer in Australia," I say. "He and Annie reconciled . . . kind of. In the movie, he has this camping trip with his kids and they all get on better terms. He hires his dad to pilot his private plane, and his dad seemingly finally accepts his music before he dies. John learns to pilot on his own, and he gets a little restless. The music business landscape changes, and he's no longer the sensation he was before. But he writes songs and he plays and he flies."

"And he dies, flying?"

"I think . . . My feeling is that he wanted to go. That's what it always seemed like to me, in the movie anyway. His dad died. The record deals weren't the same. He'd done all this charity work. Annie and their kids kind of moved on. He started toying around with his prop plane, making adjustments himself, then flying it. He had a malfunction flying near Monterey in California. He crashed into the ocean. But it's just a movie, and just my memory of it. I have no idea what state he was in, in the end."

She stares up at me for a long time, my injured hand in hers, over my chest. She kisses my palm, looks down at it. When she looks back up, she says,

"I don't want to say what I think," she says.

"You can say anything."

"I think . . . I think I know where we have to go. What the

Witchwalker was telling us. I think it knew I would understand. I think it knew I could explain some of this to you, or that we'd get there together."

And because of that thing, linking us in the other-world, because I can almost feel her thought as she's about to say it . . .

Or maybe it's so obvious, and I should have been looking there the whole time.

And . . .

I remember once, Daphne explaining to me. Close family relations can sometimes show up as interchangeable on DNA tests . . . or something like that.

Is it possible . . . how did it not occur to me before? Could *he* be doing this somehow? Would he? How would he not have shown up as a match before?

The only other person who was there that night in the motel who is still living.

Could the hair be his? Could he be a part of this?

"Will you be okay?" Hannah asks. "I'll be with you."

I squeeze her hand, lean into her. I kiss the top of her head and rest my chin there, looking out at the snow.

"Maybe it was always meant to be this," I say. And I know she knows what I mean, I can feel it. Her and me. This. Us, some cosmic fucking wondrous inevitability.

She pulls back and looks up into my eyes. "I'm with you," she says.

A shadow moves in the bathroom, again.

We both stop. Turn to look at it. Because it's . . .

It's not a shadow.

She's not.

She *is*, kind of. But . . . she's *brighter* somehow. More defined.

A *woman* stands in the bathroom. Sort of. A shadow-person. I know somehow that she's the same shadow we saw in here last night, but I can see her much more clearly now. Just almost like a person, glowing, moving in the dark. An X-ray image of someone. Or like a body heat signature in night vision goggles. The woman is cleaning the bathroom. And . . .

The shadows.

The shadows are *people*. Or . . . Memories of people? Echoes?

No. Hannah thinks the word, and I know she's right.

They're ghosts.

And haven't I always known? Hasn't that always been the other piece I wasn't willing to face? That this is real. Ghosts are real, and I can see them. Maybe Rose was right.

The ghost in this room. The haunted room that inspired the book that my mother carried around every day of her life. The book that inspired my name. Over there, on the shelf, with all his others. I finally let my eyes move to it. All the Stephen King titles.

And the one right in the center of them.

The Shining.

Hannah looks at me, and I don't know what to say. Hannah, and me, both of us who see these things. Who both can see, or at least feel, whatever the fuck got in here with us last night.

Both of us, who see each other. Fully. Every dark and terrible thing.

Who joined with each other, in two planes, two worlds. Who now can see things clearly after coming together. After sharing our pain and stopping fighting who we are.

The shadows are real. And I don't know if they're people now, or if they just *were*. But . . . this whole time I fought it. Why have I tried so hard in every part of my life to fight what's inevitable?

The ghost in the bathroom doesn't pay us any mind. We're the visitors here. People come and go, but she stays.

I turn back to Hannah. That connection stretching between us. Radio dials tuning in to the same frequency, Hannah's thoughts and mine. This, here between us, what it could become.

Daphne's words at Linger Eatuary echo through my mind, and I get it now. Lying here with Hannah Lawrence, I get it.

I'm gonna hold on to it, hold on to her, with everything I've got.

And right now, we've got to do the thing I should have done long ago. The thing I've been dreading and fighting my whole life.

Because Hannah's right, and this is what it's been all along. John Denver living so much of his life to gain acceptance or understanding from his father. All these fathers and sons playing out narratives again and again.

Never even looking into my own eyes because I am so terrified of seeing *him*.

Of course the things we don't want are the ones that make us look at ourselves.

I hold Hannah closer, for one more second, the snow falling outside the window. I know, at least, that I won't be going in alone.

Hannah and me, in this together. Going to Sterling.

To the state prison.

We're going to see my dad.

V

AVALANCHE

1

I open the duffel bag Josie packed of my things and pull out my old clothes. The clothes I haven't worn since my parents were still alive. This version of myself too painful to be. The one that, if I'm being honest, I've probably always been.

Black jeans, black pearl snap shirt, black cowboy hat and boots, and leather jacket. A brown and black embossed leather belt with a road runner belt buckle on it that Marianne gave to me.

"You look good," Hannah says in the room, dressed, sitting on the side of the bed.

I clear my throat, feel my face getting hot. She smiles.

The internet is still down, and cell service is spotty. We leave the ghost in the Stephen King Suite. I glance past all the mirrors as we walk down the stairs, pass through the lobby. Until we step back outside into the cold.

We can't find the Wagoneer in the parking lot, every car snowed in, smothered, white surrounding us. No one else will be able to find it either.

We try different hotel staff vehicles until we find one with the keys inside that isn't buried. A gray SUV with STANLEY printed on the side. It's conspicuous, but in the snow maybe it's not easily read. We throw the bag in. The one with the murder weapon, all the files.

We take the long road down from the hotel.

And Hannah was right.

Everything is different.

Not just with her and me. With the entire world.

The shadows, from before, from my whole life . . .

Like the woman in the room. They are no longer shadows at all. And they're everywhere.

Filling the hotel as we leave, the parking lot, the road and the landscape around us. Flickering, in and out. But all around us. Brighter, more defined. Shadowed, and glowing, both at once.

People. Sort of people. In all different clothes. Modern, old, everything in between. Every age. Every type of person.

And other animals. Rodents, birds, wolves, a saber-toothed cat. Dinosaurs. Things I don't even recognize. The snowed-in landscape filled with all of them.

Some of them turn as we pass. Most just go about their business, whatever that is. Most of them there for a moment, and then gone. Just fragments, almost. Echoes. I don't know. But we can see them, all of them. Both of us, Hannah and me. Some of them linger, watch as we pass.

The radio flips back on again. Plays Lee Hazlewood's "Your Sweet Love" on repeat. The song we danced to last night. Hannah reaches over and takes my hand. The world outside is something new. The snow swirling, less violent now, still filling our senses with white. The cold wind pushing against the sides of the car. All these beings, everywhere, drifting in and out of it.

Us, trying to understand. Hannah's hand on mine, holding tight on the center console.

"They don't all seem to be on the same plane," she says. "It's like they're living all on top of each other without even knowing it. They're not looking at the other cars, just ours."

"Maybe because *we* see *them*," I say. Energy, echoes, imprints made by a life, or . . . I think of Daphne, for some reason. Suddenly.

What if . . . what if these things we're seeing, these ghosts, what if they're the equivalent of DNA shed? We leave pieces of ourselves everywhere we go all the time. Could that be it? Could they just somehow be pieces left behind?

But they can see us, feel us, some of them *want* something from us. I feel it. They seem to be consciously here, now, not just an echo of something from before.

"Did we do this?" I ask. "Somehow? Did we—"

"You want to know what I think?" Hannah says, and I wonder how much of my train of thought she can hear. I think what we share, it's more like feelings, wants, images, maybe. She turns in the passenger seat and gives me a look that makes me think the answer is maybe that actually she can hear all of it.

"Yes," I say out loud.

"I think . . ." she says, looking around at this new world in wonder. In fear. "I think they're still here," she says. "But . . . not. Like they've just—" She furrows her brow, turns her head, chasing the thought. Then a new expression crosses her face, a realization.

"Have you ever been locked out of your house at night?" she says.

I nod.

"I think . . . what if it's like that? I don't know why I haven't thought of it before."

"They're locked out? Or we are?"

"No, I mean . . . yes. Them."

I wait, and we pass something on our left that I think is a fucking woolly mammoth. Hannah laughs, a little. Leans further out to see as we drive past it.

"I think," she says, sitting back in her seat, a faint smile on her face, "that maybe death is like getting locked out of your house at night. You get locked out, and your first instinct is to start to try to find a way back in. A weak point, a window you didn't close, a door you might be able to pick the lock for. And the longer you're outside, trying to get in, the more you start to see it all in a new way, the home or life you've built. The lights on inside and the heat or the fire going. All your furniture and art and photographs. It's warm, and it's yours, and you realize, looking at it from outside, finally in a way you only can because you're locked out of it, you realize what you have, what you've built. Maybe even who you are. How beautiful it is, now that you can't access it. And even though you were just in there, you miss it already, maybe desperately, appreciate it in a way you never could without looking in from the cold night.

"Maybe that's what death is," she says. "Maybe it's like . . . you just get locked out one day. And inside, the lights are still on and it's warm and it's everything you know, and the people you love are still there, and you want to go back to them. And maybe sometimes you can just get so focused on wanting to get back in, on wanting to shelter from the night and stay, go back to your home that you know, that you don't realize how actually small a house is. How finite and closed and . . . I mean, you're standing *outside*. *Outside* goes on and on, forever. But it's also dark, especially if you keep staring at the lights of indoors. And it's new, this outside world.

And maybe it seems lonely, even if it's not. I mean, I don't know if it is.

"But what I think is that sometimes maybe someone dies and they can't see that the whole of the world and the universe is at their disposal now, that *all* of it is their *new* home. And it maybe seems dark in relation to the house, dark in some ways and scary, and it's definitely not the warm lit-up house they know and love. But it's so much bigger. Infinite, and full of possibility. If only we're willing to turn around. Let our eyes adjust to the night, to see that it's not dark, not really. If only we're willing to take that step forward, away from the house.

"And maybe after a while we forget the house altogether and realize we were never confined to it totally, we only thought we were. And the people we love exist elsewhere too, not just there, and not just in that way. The house, and the night, matter equally."

Her words settle around us, the snow still falling. Beings, in the white, all around.

"So . . . all these . . . people? Animals? They're just—" I say.

"They're not looking at us, most of them. They're just . . . beyond. They're just right at the edge of our light, and we're not supposed to be able to see them. But you and me, I think it's like we've got special antennas, we pick up radio signals from both sides. Or to go with the house metaphor, it's like we've got night vision goggles. Or something."

"So we see them, but they don't see us. Or they're not really looking. Most of them."

"Yeah, exactly. And maybe . . ." She trails off.

"Maybe?" I say.

"Maybe it's like, you get away from the house. You do, eventually. Turn and embrace the night. But every once in a while, maybe a car drives by. And its headlights are shining through the dark, reminding you of that particular kind of light of your old house, that forgotten kind. And even though the night is far more beautiful, far more luminous and expansive than the man-made three-dimensional home ever was, maybe when we remember it, we get nostalgic, curious because of what it activates in us from memory. We lift our heads, so to speak, and think *what is that*, and think we should walk toward it. Maybe . . . like the radio signals . . ."

“Beings like us,” I say. “We catch their attention by . . .”

My shining boy.

“Shining.”

She nods. “Maybe our headlights just, for some reason, shine a little to the other side. Our signals sometimes just get a little crossed.”

I take this in. And it feels . . . right.

And I’m not alone in it. For the first time.

I squeeze her hand once more, Hannah.

We are speeding through the snow, through an unknown world, to face someone I never thought I would again.

And yet, still, the ache in my chest is something I want, for once.

The radio goes to static, then back to the song. Hannah Lawrence’s hand, warm and solid in mine. Like it was always here, and I just had to reach out and take hold of it.

“And . . .” I say, now picking up her train of thought. The two of us in sync, connected now. Maybe forever. I hope forever. I hear it almost perfectly. “Maybe they’re shining back, in the only way they can.”

2

It should take two and a half hours to get to Sterling Correctional Facility, but with the snow, it's longer. Hannah doesn't roll down the windows. She wears the nose plug again, but she's relaxed. A little more settled in herself. I've never been out here. Have always known it was where Calvin was, so have avoided it. Like so much.

It's a problem, trying to get into a prison. Having to show ID, having to get the prisoner to sign off on visitation, scheduling it ahead of time, being in the logs and on the cameras. Except I have one idea. One card I've known I had for a long time that I haven't ever had a reason to play.

I pick up the phone and call the prison, ask for a guy I haven't seen in years. Tom Banks, one of the security guards. They put me through, and I ask him to call me back on this number from his cell.

"Stansfield. It's so good to hear from you. How are you?"

I hesitate. "I have a major favor to ask," I say.

I test with my sense in the other-space again, decide to tell the truth. We need to get in, and there can't be a record. We need to talk to the prisoner without his approval. But all of this could get Tom into a major shitstorm of trouble.

"I'm so sorry to ask," I say. "I wouldn't if I had any other way."

"Stansfield, I've owed you for so long. If I can help with anything, I've got you."

I tell him what I need. He agrees.

I hang up, grip the wheel tighter.

"What did you do to get that kind of loyalty?" Hannah asks.

I take a breath, put on my blinker to take the exit. "Long time ago, when I was good at my job. His son was kidnapped on a road trip at a rest stop, taken across state lines."

"And you found him."

I swallow, hold myself steady. As we drive toward the prison.

Past all the ghosts, all the echoes of life on earth. Millions of years, the rise and fall of apex predators, of eras and species.

"This is it, I guess," I say. And Hannah grips me tighter.

Out in the snow-covered landscape sits the imposing geometric complex, the large sign in front, American and Colorado flags behind it.

We're here.

I pull into the lot and through the snow, park and open the door before I can convince myself not to. The cold's barely hitting. I'm nervous. I'm so fucking nervous. Thirty-four years old, and the idea of seeing my old man is far more terrifying to me than a world full of ghosts. Hannah walks close to me, presses in against my side. We skirt around a ghost wolf, lingering near the entrance. I don't know the rules, don't know if it matters if we touch them or not. Don't know if they can hurt us. But of course they can. They have, haven't they?

The wolf watches us as we pass.

Inside, Tom's waiting. He takes us to a private room, says the Wi-Fi's been down, meaning we shouldn't have any problems. Lucky. Like the Wi-Fi at the hotel and the car getting buried back there. Like the storm is helping us. Like the world wants all of this to happen, or something does. Just the things a delusional guy thinks before it all comes crumbling down.

Hannah and I sit in two chairs opposite an empty one across a table. I leave my jacket on. Hannah does too. I shuffle my boots on the floor.

My palms are sweating as they go to get him.

Calvin.

We don't talk. It's quiet in here. I try to breathe. I have a Bad Feeling. Of course I do.

The door at the end of the room abruptly opens, and I swallow. Turn.

A guard steps in, an inmate beside him.

Here, in the room with me.

Shit. I—

Bruises on my wrists. On Mom's.

The bottle in his hand, swinging at her.

Both of them yelling, crying, both of them crying. In public. At home. Anywhere.

Dad, and Mom, in the front seats of the car singing along to country music. Smiling at each other.

Dad, showing me how to throw and catch a baseball, in the parking lot of the motel we lived in before the Happy Inn.

Dad, throwing the bottle at the wall behind me, just missing my head.

Dad lifting me up onto his shoulders and making sure I could see the stage at a show at Fiddler's Green.

Mom as he slit her throat.

Dad staring at me through the mirror at the Happy Inn.

Dad. Here. Now.

Bad Feeling.

Dad, here, and me.

It's him.

Hannah squeezes my hand.

Calvin Keller sits across from us.

I blink, try to push past the memories, see him, here, now.

He's shorter than I am, by a few inches. Balding. Heavy wrinkles. He's thin. I remember him with a beer gut, but I guess he can't drink in here. His eyes look the same. They look like mine. All of him, like looking in a fun house mirror, an alternate reality in which I've made his choices instead of my own.

A lifetime of wondering if one day I'd wake up and turn out to be just like him, if it's genetic, if it's a broken thing passed down. Being terrified to get close to people, because what if that same switch flipped in me? A lifetime of hating myself for carrying any part of him forward. Fear, hate. Guilt. The overwhelming, all-consuming guilt for escaping it, for getting a family as loving as the Stansfields, for getting to live in that big house and go to school and have friends and safety and a hot meal in front of me every night. For knowing I didn't deserve any of it.

All of it, from this man in front of me now. All of it, his doing.

Calvin Keller.

It used to be my name too.

He sits down, looks at Hannah with a question in his eyes, and then glances at me, squints at us, trying to figure out who we are.

My heart is pounding, and I feel like I'm four years old. I feel like a little boy who's scared shitless. Maybe that's all I've ever been.

He does a double take at me. Hannah's hand grips mine below the table as my dad sees me for the first time as an adult. As he recognizes me. I want to throw up. I want to run. Hannah's hand on mine, pressing into my thigh.

We stare at each other long enough, Calvin and me, that Hannah nudges me, reminding me we don't have much time. I clear my throat again, open my mouth to speak.

Before I can say anything, he says, "You look so much like her."

His voice, unlocking more memories, more moments. I don't—

Dad, drunk, yelling at Mom to get her nose out of her books and act like a wife.

Mom, gone. Me, hiding behind a dresser. Dad finding me and asking me where she is. I don't know, and he

I try to speak. Try to push this forward and be a man.

"Am I dreaming this?" he asks. My dad asks.

I shake my head, wishing we both were. This man who could be the spitting image of what I would become, if I let myself. This man who is the worst possible version of me.

I clear my throat again, heart racing, palms sweaty. And I take a breath. "No," I say. And I see him flinch at my voice, tears beginning to well up in his eyes.

"You're a man," he says. "Shit. I must be old. You were just . . ."

"I need to ask you some questions," I say.

"Calvin," he says.

"That's not my name."

Confusion flashes in his eyes.

"Picked a new one. With my family," I say.

That hurt him. It's clear in his look. And I know I did it on purpose, but it gives me some resolve. Some momentum. Dear old dad taught me that.

You hurt me, I hurt you. I hurt you, I feel better.

"I . . ." I clear my throat. Again. Shit. "I need to understand. What happened that night. Why it happened. Why you came in yelling at her, what it was about."

A tear runs down his face. He swipes at it with a finger. "I'm so sorry, Calvin. I didn't—"

"That's not my name."

"I'm so sorry."

"Why did you do it?" My voice breaks.

"You know, no one gives you a guidebook on how to be a dad. No one tells you . . ."

"Murder probably wouldn't have been in it."

"Protecting you is all that ever mattered to me. I just knew I had to keep you safe, and she was gonna take you away from me. And I couldn't trust her."

"She was gonna take us away so you couldn't hit us anymore. So you couldn't break bottles over our heads, or throw telephones or books or TV remotes at us. So you couldn't stumble in drunk and beat the shit out of the two most helpless people you could find, the ones who were trapped and waiting for you all day."

"I regret all of that. Every day. And I will for the rest of my life. But you don't know, your mother . . . After she took you to Aspen—"

Aspen.

John Denver Sanctuary. The rock in the middle of the river.

I pause, thrown off.

"What happened in Aspen?" I say.

He stares at me, then says, "You don't remember."

My pulse pounding, in my hands, my throat. I can't talk to him. His voice, so many moments pushing in. Tears burn at the backs of my eyes.

He shakes his head. "She wasn't . . . She didn't mean it. To take you away, to do what she did. She just . . ." He runs his hands over his head. The same way I do.

"I ask myself all the time," he says. "If I regret that night. And . . . I regret that you saw it. I regret the way that must have affected you. I can't imagine. I regret that by doing it I ensured you wouldn't have a dad around anymore. And—" He swipes at tears in his eyes. That nausea threatening again. I want to look away, but I don't let myself.

"I regret all the times I lost my temper and hurt you both leading up to it," he says. "But that night in the Happy Inn was maybe the one time I was a good father. It was maybe the only time I really did right by you. That woman was poison. And if being here is the price for that, I'll take it. I think about it every day, and I welcome it. The pain, the penance."

He stops talking. And . . .

What do I do with that? What the fuck am I supposed to do with any of this?

"If I hadn't gotten to Aspen when I did," he says, "she would have taken you away forever. And that night at the motel, she was going to do it again. I just . . . you're my *boy*. You can't understand, what that's like, what you'd do for your kid."

I see every moment he hit me, feel every ounce of terror hearing the key unlock the door, not knowing if he'd come back and be my dad who loved me, who I could play with, who would hug me before bed, or before leaving. Or if he'd be drunk. And angry. If I was going to have bruises and cuts and the dizzy ear-ringing feeling after my dad's fist colliding with my head.

John Denver Sanctuary. My ears ringing.

Ringing so loud.

Calvin Keller in front of me. John Denver in the movie spending his whole life just trying to win the approval of his dad. All the men on this earth with all the shit fathers.

Except . . . I don't know if I can call myself one. Noel Stansfield was the best dad anyone could have hoped for. The worst thing he ever did was leave this world before I was ready for him to. But I'd never have been ready. And he went with Marianne, didn't make her go alone. Even in the end, he was there for her. He was there for me until then. He was as kind and decent as anyone could be.

Thinking of Noel reminds me of who I am. Even while my heart pounds and the nausea nearly overwhelms me.

I remember. I sit up straight in the chair.

I'm not that little boy in the Happy Inn.

I lean forward, toward him, Hannah's hand still in my own. And this time I hold his eyes. I don't flinch.

Because I'm Daniel fucking Stansfield, and I don't have time for this.

"What do you know about the Drifter murders?" I ask.

Calvin gives me a blank look. "What is that?"

"Surely you get the news in here. Surely people talk." Ryder Smith, Theo Wharton. Different prison, but . . .

"I haven't heard of it. What is it?"

"What about a Witchwalker?"

Again, he stares at me. Those tears still falling. "You really look like her. Miracle, I guess, you lookin' more like her than me. She was so beautiful."

Except I don't think he's right. But it doesn't matter. I swallow, make myself sit up straighter.

"I need some answers," I say, "or we're gonna have to go. We're looking for something, and it's important."

"Well, I don't know what that stuff is. I try to keep my head down in here. Go to services. I've got a lot to atone for, and I'm just . . . tryin'."

I feel the earth moving beneath me and the whole of the sky pressing in. As I once again ask my father the question that's cursed me my whole life. The question that's eclipsed everything. Every accomplishment, every fear and want and hurt. The only question.

"Why did you do it?" I ask again. The words come out softer, more hoarse than I mean for them to.

Pain flickers in his eyes. Instantaneous. He doesn't pretend not to know what I'm asking.

But he shakes his head slowly, the tears falling.

"I need to know why," I say. "Was it just because we were leaving?"

The man in front of me tries to pull himself together, but he can't. "I'm sorry," he says.

"Calvin," I say, his name feeling like poison in my mouth. "Tell me *why*." The last word comes out shaky and desperate, and I don't care.

Why did you take my mom from me? Why did you take my life away? Even if it was to lead to family, even if I'd end up getting everything . . .

Why did you rip her from me?

He sniffs, wipes his face again and presses his fingers to his brow. He is miserable. It's not an act, not for sympathy. He is truly, deeply, profoundly unhappy.

"Why?" I say again.

"That book. The one she always carried around. The Stephen King one. You ever pick that up?"

The hotel room we stayed in last night. That book on the shelf I could have taken, and didn't. I don't say anything.

"She wrote in there, you know. Little notes. All kinds of things, for years. She ripped a page out of the back and wrote me a letter on it. I think she thought it was gonna get to me after."

"After we left."

He looks at me, and I can't read his expression at all. "You should read it, one day. When you're ready. Not the letter, I don't know where that is now. But you should read the book."

"You're saying you read her letter saying we were going to leave, and you came to the hotel, and—"

"I didn't mean to kill her," he says. He sniffs, rubs at his eyes. "Maybe I did. I don't know what I meant to do, I was just so scared, and I couldn't lose you both. I couldn't . . . after she took you to Aspen. . . . You have no idea how much it hurt, the idea of that."

"Yeah," I say. "You're right. I don't know anything about hurt."

After a second, he stops crying, and he takes me in again.

"You turned out strong," he says. "Thank you for coming here. It's a gift. I think . . . seein' you. I think I mighta done something right in this life. I think I mighta done okay."

3

Hannah and I are in the Stanley SUV in the Sterling Correctional Facility parking lot. I don't know where we're going to go, if it's back to Aspen to regroup or somewhere new. I just . . . I need to drive. I need to think.

I talked to my dad. It didn't do anything, didn't give us anything new. Nothing to help us get out of this mess. Of course not. Calvin Keller being useful in any way, the idea of him possibly helping me . . .

I start the car.

WHOOSH!

A hawk shoots out the sky, dive-bombs a smaller bird right in front of our windshield. I see it, as if in slow motion. As the hawk hits the smaller bird with its talons first and then its beak. The hawk breaks the smaller bird's spine in the air.

The small bird drops to the hood of our car with a *thunk*.

The hawk caws loudly, hovers. Then flies away.

Static. On the radio.

"What the fuck was that?" I ask, staring at the dead animal on the hood. I almost can't speak. Calvin Keller. Dad. Dad in front of me. I'm still shaking, probably. I'm—

"He must live here," Hannah says. "The hawk. The magpie probably just moved in. A hawk will do anything to defend its territory."

I look at the small unmoving creature on the other side of the windshield.

"Nature can be brutal," Hannah says quietly, sadness in her voice.

I get out and look in the trunk for some work gloves. There aren't any, but there's an old newspaper. I slide it under the bird as carefully as I can in the snow, telling it I'm sorry. I walk to the trash can and can't bring myself to do it. I take it over to a tree instead, dodging a few ghosts on the way, people, lingering. Watching.

I lay the bird down in the snow beneath the tree. My dad's face in my vision. My dad's voice in my ears. I slide the newspaper out from beneath the little bird. This small body. A life so quickly taken, so carelessly. I leave the bird in the snow and stand to throw away the newspaper, step over to a trash can.

I turn back to the Stanley SUV, but out of the corner of my eye, I see wings flapping. Glowing but shadowed. Rising up to the sky from beneath the tree, soaring up over the car.

Calvin Keller in jail, and me standing out here. The ghost bird flapping its wings.

And if I didn't know any better, I'd say it looked an awful lot like that magpie in the snow. I stand there for a minute, and I watch it fly away.

I step back through the snow to the car, something nagging. A thought, something Hannah said. *A hawk will do anything to defend its territory.*

"Hey," I say. "Hannah, did you—"

I stop in my tracks. Because when I see her, when I come around the side of the car . . .

Hannah is cuffed again. Standing outside the passenger door.

Tillman is beside her.

Tillman, who's pointing a gun straight at me.

"All right, guy," he says. "We do this the easy way or hard way, but you're both comin' with me."

4

Hannah and I are cuffed in the back seat of Tillman's car—her wrists in front of her, mine behind my back—with the child locks on and a paranormal podcast playing. Tillman also cuffed my ankles. *Just in case you decide to try and break anything else on my face*, he said. His nose is bruised and bandaged.

It'll be less than two hours back to Denver.

And then all of this is over. Hannah and me going down for this.

And of course it would be this way. How many nights have I stayed up thinking about the Drifters in their cells, about how they were so certain of their innocence? Of course I would end up here too. Maybe if I go, they'll be let free.

But Hannah.

Silent tears stream down Hannah's face. She's thinking of incarceration, of being indoors. Panicking, being in this car now. I understand, through that other-space we share. It was one thing when she shared the car with me, who she's been close with. Who she . . . Even now my pinky hurts, and I welcome it. But Tillman's a stranger to her. A different scent. And he's now cuffed her twice.

"Can you roll the window down for her?" I ask.

He shakes his head. "No can do, bud. You two are gonna sit quietly and do what you're supposed to for once."

"What's happening with the case?" I ask.

Tillman gives me a look through the rearview.

"It's not us," I say. "I have nothing to do with the murders, and neither does Hannah. What has Father Sk—Theo Wharton said?"

Tillman sighs, flips on a blinker. After a second, he glances back through the rearview, says, "He got away. We have no idea what happened. By the time I got inside the dome, he was already gone."

"Are you serious? Tillman, we need to find him. He's the best lead we've got. He's—"

Maybe the only thing that'll get Hannah and me out of this.

"All right, brother, *we* don't need to do anything. *You* have lied and broken too many laws to count, *you two* are in custody, you put Josie in a bad spot knowing what she did about your past and askin' her not to tell Murphy. And on top of all that . . ." Tillman's voice grows in volume. He says, hands gripping the wheel, "Yeah. You know what? If I'm bein' real honest, and I'm sorry to say it this way, but you're a real shit partner. You keep everything to yourself, you're sneaky, distrustful, and frankly just have a real bad attitude. So how about you just sit quiet for once and let me do my job, since you never intended to help or do it with me as a team."

The car is quiet for a second, aside from his podcast.

I clear my throat.

"You're right," I say. "About all that stuff."

"And furthermore," he says, his voice louder and angrier than I've ever heard it, "you really thought you could just pull up to a jail where they have your dad—who we all *just* found out was your dad—and not think we'd immediately come to get you?"

"We thought the Wi-Fi was out. Thought you wouldn't know."

"Didn't need Wi-Fi. Just regular freakin' logic that you'd come here."

"I just want answers," I say. "And I thought, stupidly I guess, that I'd have more time."

"Well, joke's on you 'cause I was already on my way. And we could have gotten answers together before now if you'd just been any kind of team player."

I shift, try and sit upright with my arms behind me. "You're right, Tillman. You're a good agent—probably better than me. And I'm glad you're here, and that you got us."

Hannah shoots me a look at that. Her face is pale, her cuffed hands held over her nose and mouth.

I take a deep breath and say to Nat Tillman words I never thought I would.

"We need your help."

Tillman shakes his head. "Dude, what are you not getting about this—"

I don't let myself hesitate, don't let myself think. The highway carrying us forward.

For the first time as an adult I say, "I see ghosts."

The words linger in the car, over the voices of the podcast. Tillman is silent.

I clear my throat and say, "I always have, probably always will."

A long pause, again. Then, Tillman looks back at me through the rearview, says, "You . . ."

"I didn't want to admit it to myself, because . . . I mean, I thought I was insane. Or holding on to some childhood fantasy. I don't know. But they are literally everywhere. There's a fucking ghost stegosaurus ahead of us."

"Ghost . . . stegosaurus," Tillman says.

"Let me just tell you. What we've found, where we are with things. You're right that I've been a shit partner, and I've broken laws, and whatever happens at the end of this, I just want to see the right guy go down. We need your help, Tillman. I'm telling you, it's not us."

Tillman deliberates, his podcast playing, driving in the snow. After a long minute, he turns down the volume slightly.

I take that as the best invitation we're going to get.

I tell him everything. Everything except Hannah's part in it. She moves to touch my leg with her own, a movement Tillman clocks in the rearview. Every now and then, Tillman asks a clarifying question. I have no idea if he believes us, if he's really listening to any of this. I wouldn't be, in his position.

At the end of us telling him everything, there's a long pause.

Then Tillman says, "So you two both see ghosts, which you didn't really know were ghosts before, but now you do. There's a thing called a Witchwalker that wants something from you both—unclear what. Daniel's been remembering his mom in a river in Aspen for unknown reasons, Father Sky slash Theo Wharton seems to have, if not orchestrated this all, then at least known about everything. And someone's been trying to frame you both and may have been targeting you two specifically for a long time. Oh and also there's ghost dinosaurs."

"Yeah," I say.

"This radio thing you talk about. How come it's not happening in here, right now?"

"I—"

The radio turns to static, and "Highwayman" comes on. Tillman eyes me in the mirror. I shrug, as much as I can.

"So something's listening in real time," he says.

He thinks. We wait.

"Why the hair around the tongues?" he asks. "Did you ever have long hair?"

"Um, I guess, as a kid. But not since. And for why, we don't know."

"You think . . . you guys think this Witchwalker thing feeds on fear or pain? And that's why it's come to you?"

"That seems to make the most sense," I say. "But I guess we don't know for sure."

"And Father Sky is some kind of like . . . human familiar to this paranormal entity?"

"I mean, that, or he wants to be. But it talked through him, so . . . seems like they've got some kind of thing going on."

It's quiet, aside from the song now playing, a little staticky, a little discordant. Tillman's face looks pained, thoughtful. Sad, maybe.

Sad for us.

After what feels like minutes, Tillman lets out a long sigh and shakes his head. He looks out the windshield, doesn't turn back to me.

"I'm sorry, man," he says.

I exhale, feel Hannah tense up beside me.

A protective surge rushes through me. We're going in, and these murders will all be pinned on us, and we'll spend the rest of our lives in jail. *I'm sorry*, I say to Hannah in that other-place, desperate, frantically searching my mind for any way out. *I'm so sorry*. I can't let this happen to her. I calculate what it will take to get out of this car, whether the three of us can survive what might very well be a crash if I rush Tillman.

I'm not gonna let them take you, I say to her in the other-space. I slow down, try to find the fighting calm, try to prepare myself for whatever's next. Next stoplight I'll need to be ready. I'll just figure it out. But she can't go in, he can't take her. I will not let Hannah be locked up.

Tillman reaches forward and tries to adjust the radio, maybe back to his podcast, maybe to signal that we're done talking.

The radio station won't change. He stares at it for another second.

"I'm so sorry," he says again, and they're the three worst words I've ever heard. We're approaching a stoplight. I brace myself.

Tillman says, "That I didn't make you feel like you could be vulnerable with me."

Music. Snow. Tillman's words.

He's pulling up to the light. And—

"It's important in work and friendships to create an environment of openness and trust," Tillman continues. "Safe spaces. And . . . I'm sorry it wasn't a safe enough space for you to tell me these things."

I . . . what is happening?

"You know, back at the brewery," he says, "I saw your beer go down. It was just upright and almost full, and then it just . . . was on its side."

"You . . ."

"And the way you look at fixed points, the way your eyes track stuff moving through the room, stuff that fully doesn't exist. And cold spots tend to follow you. I don't know if you're even aware of that, actually. Seems like you're not. But I've been walkin' with ya a lot, and they're almost always nearby. And you findin' that motel key . . . I mean, the easy answer is of course that you did it. But . . . why? And I can't think of a good reason."

I'm stunned. I don't even know what to say.

"You . . . believe us?" I ask.

"It didn't sit right, that you guys did this. I mean," he says to Hannah, "I don't know you, miss, but either way it just . . . I didn't think it was you two. And I didn't think it was Oliver Wright either, but he's gonna get tried for it all too probably, since almost every victim or killer is in some way tied to one of his properties as you pointed out. And since he's made himself so involved in the prosecution. And I know, us bros gotta get territorial sometimes, but . . . I'm just relieved you shared this so we can actually get to freakin' work here. Finally!"

The car comes to a stop at the red light. I don't move.

Nat Tillman believes us. He—

"Wait. What did you say?" Hannah, stiff beside me, leaning forward. Her mind whirring, moving too fast for me to follow.

"I'm sayin' we can finally—"

"No, the other . . . Territorial," she says. "Oh my god."

Tillman and I both look to her.

She turns to me. "The hawk. And what he just said, and . . ."

"I don't follow," Tillman says, glancing back.

Hannah's mind, speeding. Mine, fighting to keep up. She says, "The Drifters skin the victims and walk distances with the skins, then drop them. Do you have a map, of all of their routes?"

"We have a map of all the fixed points, but we don't know the exact routes they walked, not most of them," I say. "We've tried to track phone data, but the phones always cut out, and are usually left with the skinned bodies."

"Can we figure out the routes?"

"Um, maybe—"

"Skin has blood," Hannah says. "Smell. Bodies have smell. Do you see? Covering themselves in the blood of the skinned victims, walking . . ."

Tillman says, "Scent-marking."

Hannah nods, excited. "Yes! If . . . if we can get a map, a better one. If we can figure out the routes . . ."

Tillman at the house in Greeley, talking about the path Frank Wheely walked in the grass to us.

The flight path matters.

"Dude," Tillman says. "You're a genius. She's a genius! I can't believe I didn't think of it before."

"What?" I say. "What am I not getting?"

"Ritualized territorial displays," Tillman says.

I look between them.

"A lot of animals use them," Hannah says. "Ways they signal boundaries and needs to other animals. It can be visual, auditory, olfactory. Like wolves—scent-marking and howling, to show what their territory is. We've been thinking like people," Hannah says. "But maybe whoever—whatever—is doing this *doesn't*."

"So," I say, "we redraw the map, see if there's some way to figure out what the territory is. Either Father Sky or this Witchwalker, or . . . if we can see the outer lines—"

"Maybe we can figure out what they're defending," Hannah says. "And from who."

I look from Hannah to Tillman and back again.

Tillman, on board. Listening to us, believing us. And Hannah beside me.

We need space. We need to map this thing. We need somewhere to go.

"Do the others know you have us?" I ask.

He looks at me in the rearview. "Not yet," he says.

"Okay." We can do this. I think this could be something. Maybe. There's a chance.

So I do something else I never thought I'd do. I take a breath, and I say,

"Tillman. You ever been in a haunted house?"

5

The wind howls against Whileago Manor, the world white outside the windows. It's getting dark, the snow still coming.

I light candles around the living room and hand Hannah and Tillman flashlights. Hannah stands far from Tillman. Tillman can't stop looking around the room, his jaw open.

I pull out some of Marianne's big drawing paper and toss it on the coffee table. Hannah and Tillman get started drafting a makeshift map of Denver while I pile some logs on the hearth and get a fire going. For some reason the shadows here haven't changed, haven't become that brighter glowy ghost-version, but have remained shadows, black and lurking in the corners. I don't know what it means, don't understand it.

"You know, it's actually kind of cozy in here," Tillman says.

And as if in response, a door slams, and footsteps run above us.

Tillman looks up, tracks the movement along the ceiling. The floorboards creak.

"Is someone else here?" he asks.

I shake my head.

He watches me. "So this place is really haunted?"

I shrug.

"Can everyone hear it?"

"No."

"So why can I?"

I consider this, watch as the lights glow just a little in the living room above the map. Watch as Tillman's eyes widen when he clocks it too. I shrug, again. "Maybe you've got a little shine too," I say.

I turn away before I can see the grin on his face.

* * *

It takes us the better part of an hour to get it all mapped out. And Pete Noland's path wasn't the only one Tillman suspected was different than we'd originally assumed. Hannah found all the original bodies while they were fresh, and she never encountered one of the Drifters leaving the body. Which means the direction she came from couldn't have been the one they walked. With that information, we're able to redo a few of our original routes.

We rework it again and again, adjust so many lines we would have thought obvious, had thought obvious before. Flight patterns. Pieces aligning to make . . .

We step back, look at it all.

Not a perfect circle. But about as close to one as anyone could get by following roads. One large territory encompassing most of the city and surrounding areas.

And smaller ones within it.

"Shit," Hannah says.

We stand in silence in the candlelight, the fire crackling behind us, the snow flurrying outside the window. The three of us look down at the map of greater Denver, the routes intersecting to make these circles. The lights glow a little brighter.

A long minute passes in which none of us says anything. The house is silent, warm even. Aside from the flicker of flames, everything inside the walls of Whileago Manor is still.

Dizziness, nausea threaten again. As I realize what I'm looking at. As it fully sinks in.

The paths on the map. The circles.

Around Whileago Manor. The Happy/Wander Inn. Josie and Nat's house, and Hannah's cabin. The largest one extending up, below, around the city.

"You said scent-marking is about . . . defending a territory?" I ask Hannah.

"Yeah," she says, thinking.

"So . . . my house. Your cabin. Nat and Josie's. The motel. That's its *territory*?"

"Maybe it views it that way."

"Why?" Tillman asks.

"Well," Hannah says. "If it feeds off fear and pain, and Daniel experienced what he did at the motel . . ."

"Maybe it identified me as a food source," I say. "When I was young. And it's followed me from place to place since. At least as far as it was willing to go."

It never left Colorado when I did. I consider that. "I wonder if it can't go beyond certain places. Maybe there are barriers to its movements? Something it's tethered to, or can't move past."

I bend down and look at the routes on the map, the flight paths, as Tillman called them. I look for the first one. Claire Wright taken from the gas station, her body found by Heather Ridge, her skin ending up near Baker. I put a number one by it. Then I go to the next one, number two. The first three murders, with our new map, the routes the Drifters would have taken.

Creating a perimeter around Whileago Manor.

A phone pings.

I stare at the map and try to think about how any of this makes sense.

Could someone feel they have a claim on my house? My life? It can't be Josie. Or Nat Tillman next to me. It's not Hannah, I know it's not. So . . .

What could this possibly mean? Hannah steps in closer beside me. I reach out and take her hand in my bandaged one.

The phone pings again.

"Whose is that?" Tillman asks.

I realize it's the burner, the same ping from the last time *Wizdumteller*—Father Sky—posted.

I let go of Hannah, grab the phone from its place on the table.

I read it out loud.

Playtime's over. If the gumshoe wants to have some real fun, come join JM and me where it all began.

I look up at Tillman. Panic crosses his face, and I register just as he does.

JM.

Josie Maynor?

Jack Murphy?

Where it all began.

Fuck.

Hannah realizes too. On the map, the circle down below the center.

Because that avalanche, that great tidal wave of snow and cold and dark, has only ever been pushing us toward this all along.

The shadows of Whileago Manor are silent, as the three of us look back to the bottom circle on the map. My vision warps and distorts as I look at it. Almost as though the perimeter is pulsing around it. Beating like a giant heart.

We're going back to the Happy Inn.

6

The snow is thick. Ghost creatures dot the highway, are lit up in our headlights. Denver glitches in and out of reality. White snow, white light, ghost heads turning to watch us pass. Tillman can't see them, but his hands are tight on the wheel, his focus on getting to the motel. Hannah holds one hand over her nose and holds mine with her other.

She's scared. I can feel it in the other-space.

It's gonna be okay, I say. *We're gonna end this. You're going to be free of this thing.*

I'm going to make sure it's true. I have to. However Father Sky is tied in with the Witchwalker, whatever any of this means, we are ending it here. Tonight.

Tillman slows, waits for the exit. And . . .

I see it. The Wander Inn. Glowing white and blue.

Then that glitch. It's orange and yellow in the white night. The Happy Inn.

"Tillman, do you—"

"Yeah. I see it."

I blink. Back to normal, the Wander Inn. Then—

Glitch back, as we drive toward it.

VOOM.

Like we've passed through a section of air charged with something different than the rest. It's not the Wander Inn. The Happy Inn is here. Us, in the glitch world. The memory world.

Off the side of the highway, glowing bright, lit up like a beacon in the swirling snow. In the dark. Just like it was when I was a kid. Brighter even. Wilder. Orange and yellow. Red clown nose and hat. *Free Smile with Every Stay at the Happy Inn!* It's like the Wander Inn never existed, like this was always here and always will be. Maybe it has been.

My John Denver cowboy boots on my feet.

Tillman says, "This is the way it used to look, when you were a kid?"

I nod. I don't know how any of this works, why it's here again. Why we can all see it.

The snow falls slower, over the motel. As if time functions differently in its immediate vicinity. I smell that strange bitter chemical smell, the one from the field, the one from the memory with Rose at John Denver Sanctuary in Aspen. A crackling, static in the air. Hannah shivers.

I turn to look at her in the back seat of the car. Her eyes on mine. The world falling silent for a moment, between us. Hannah who'd had to be in this room for days, even if it looked different.

Adrenaline courses through me already. There's so much I want to say, wish I could give her right now. But I feel her, here, and in the other-space. And maybe that's enough. Hannah and me. Here, and there. Together.

"I'm not letting go," I say. I mean, *of you*. I mean, *of us*.

A tear falls from her eye, and she nods. She squeezes my hand again.

Tillman pulls the car to a stop, the tires crunching over the snow.

And it's time.

Everything seems to go in slow motion. As we jump out, run through the cold. As we see Josie's car is here.

So is the Stanley SUV that we left at the jail.

Can that be right? How?

And Room 6. The door looks exactly as it did when I was a kid, even down to the same indentation at the bottom from when Calvin one time tried to kick it in. Slow motion, as we run to it, as Tillman tries the handle.

It's locked. But we hear voices inside. Tillman swears.

I run to the Innkeepers' Suite. Time, strange. Strained. Everything staticky and crackling. A sign in the window says OFFICE CLOSED. I can just see inside to the drawer where they keep the keys. Or where Sherie used to, when I was a kid. I take my jacket off and then my shirt, wrap the shirt around my good hand, and punch through the window glass. It rains down onto the floor, and I clear enough shards to reach in and open the door. Inside, I pull out the small key drawer.

I run the keys back to Tillman and Hannah, shrug my jacket back on, and close it up against the cold as Tillman digs through the keys until he finds the right one, the orange and yellow plastic key chain dangling.

When he puts it in the lock, his hands are shaking.

The door swings open.

VOOM.

The room looks exactly the way it did when I was a kid. My mom's makeup and jewelry on the bathroom counter. Our cassette tapes and VHS tapes. My cowboy boots. The sunset paintings and scratchy yellow and orange carpet.

The TV's on, playing *Take Me Home* with the volume on. My dad's bottle of whiskey sits beside the TV.

Space feels off. Reality does.

The door slams shut behind us. We all take half a second to understand what we're seeing.

Jack Murphy sits on the edge of the bed, slumped against the headboard, a wound on the side of his head, bleeding. Father Sky stands over him with a familiar crude bone knife, a cold, calculating expression on his face. Intense, wolfish. Blood smeared on his off-white turtleneck and pants, his brown shearling jacket. No wounds on him as far as I can tell. The knife, from Hannah's cabin. From the bag we left in the Stanley SUV with the files. Did Father Sky follow us there and take it?

"Come on in, Danny boy," he says. "Been waiting for you too." He nods to Hannah and Tillman with a smile.

Tillman charges forward, and—

His body flies back through the air, hits the wall beside the front window, plaster powdering. I blink, gun in my hand, try to understand what just happened. Then I see it. I don't know why I didn't at first. This room so strange, making me feel sick, and that chemical smell, but—

Ghosts. It's not just us in here. Ghosts at the edges of the room, three of them. I would guess part of Father Sky's shadow congregation. One of them holds Tillman against the wall by his throat. Tillman chokes, kicks, his eyes wild. I start to move toward him.

I'm thrown back too, into the door, the handle hitting my lower back, hard. I groan. A ghost holding me against the door. It's strong. I try to fight it, but I can't, it's too strong. Tillman chokes, kicks his legs at something he can't see. Hannah stays in the corner to my right, assessing. Jack—

"Stop," I rasp out.

Father Sky waves a hand, and Tillman sucks in a breath, the ghost backing off just enough to let him. Tillman falls to his knees on the carpet, and the ghost lingers beside him, ready to keep him there. The one on me doesn't let go.

"So this is the place where it all began. The origin story of *the* Daniel Stansfield," Father Sky says, looking around the room. "This was where your life changed forever. And mine." He leans back to flip his hair off his face.

"What do you mean yours?" I ask.

"I'm gonna get there. But I just want to say before we begin that I get it. This is actually a pretty great movie." He swings the knife to point at Chad Lowe on the screen singing "This Old Guitar."

"What did you do to Jack?"

"Thanks for leaving this in the car," Father Sky says, tossing the knife from one hand to the other. "Was convenient to find. So you went to visit your old man? How'd that go?"

"How do you know about my life?" I ask. "Do I know you?"

He catches the knife in one hand and then cuts his eyes to me. That strange predatory stillness. "The thing is, you don't. Know me. But I know you. And maybe that right there is the whole crux of this thing." He lifts the bone knife, tilts it back and forth. His eyes never leaving me. I wonder now if he made it, if he is the one who planted it in Hannah's cabin, who gave it to each of the Drifters to skin their victims.

"Are you responsible for the Drifter murders?" I ask.

Father Sky tilts his head. Tilts the knife. Watches. "You know, I couldn't believe it at first. That you people with your jobs and power, that *you* with your *ability*, would have *no* idea. It's just . . ."

He tosses the knife to his other hand, and before I can stop it, before I can even blink, he stabs the knife deep into Jack's thigh.

Jack lets out a groan, head still hanging, slumped against the headboard.

"Stop," I say, and I push against the ghost holding me. It's too strong. I can't move.

Father Sky says, "To answer the first question, I guess you could say I'm a fan. I mean I do *know* who's done all this. And I have been telling you through the chat room the *entire time* that I know. But *who am I*? Just Theo Wharton. Just a no one." He smiles a charming smile. "But there is something I want, and these murders have provided me the opportunity to get it. So no, I'm not responsible for them. You can think of me as a ghost, passing through. Or maybe"—his eyes cut to Hannah, wild—"a carrion bird, coming to pick from what's left."

Hannah stands with her back to the wall beside the TV stand. Watching him.

"Why is Jack Murphy here?" I ask.

It takes Wharton a moment to tear his eyes from Hannah, then he turns and looks at Jack like he has forgotten him. Jack, whose leg is now bleeding. "I called in a hint to the station that maybe you three were here, and then I posted in the chat room saying the agents were here, for you. So . . ." He smiles again. The knife drips blood to the carpet. "Now it's a party."

"Agents?" Tillman says, catching the plural.

"Oh yeah. Maybe you know her. Curly hair, pretty smile, butterfly tattoo right on her—"

"Where is she?" Tillman says.

"Somewhere in the motel. She got a bit . . . cut up. Before." Again, the easy smile, the ever-watchful gaze. "But I think it's been good enough. I just needed extra bodies for pain. And I thought having her here would get you here. You can go find her," he says.

The ghost lets Tillman go, and he pushes up off the carpet to stand.

"Just a word to the wise," Father Sky says. "This place is a bit . . . treacherous. It's a little hard to know which way is up just now. Time, space here is . . ." He shrugs, narrows his eyes, and smiles again. "You can thank your friend for that. Be careful out there," he says.

Tillman glances to me, and I nod. I'm moving, somehow. Sliding to the window wall, next to the door. The ghost holding me is moving us so Tillman can get out. Holding me by the throat, my toes just on the ground.

Tillman opens the door, the cold rushing in, and disappears into the night. The door slams shut behind him.

Father Sky's eyes land back on me.

"Daniel Stansfield," he says. "Calvin Keller. The prodigal son."

"What do you want from me? Who are you?" I ask.

"You have so much power," he says, eyes narrowed on me. "And you don't even realize. You know, *I* can do party tricks. And I'm very good at them. You've seen. I have a devoted congregation, living and dead. But I don't have what you have. No one does, just . . . you two." His gaze cuts to Hannah, that violence simmering behind his eyes. "You two shining *so* bright."

"What do you want?" I say, to get his attention back on me.

"Okay, I'll tell you a little about me. It's privileged information. I make my congregants work for it for a very long time. And . . . they want to." He flashes that smile to us, licks his lips. "But we all know how special you two are, so . . . I'll give you it for free."

He sits down on the bed beside Jack and tilts the knife back and forth slowly. *Take Me Home* plays on the TV. I haven't looked to the bathroom yet. My focus is on Wharton and Hannah. On the ghosts who haven't moved to touch her, but could at any moment.

You okay? I ask her in the other-space.

She nods.

Father Sky whips his head to me and throws the knife across the room. It hits me in the thigh, right where he got Jack. I make a sound, try to move. Pain flashes.

"So rude," he says. "Side conversations, while I'm about to give you such a gift. Every answer. Everything you've been searching for, for so long."

He steps across the room and pulls the knife from my leg. I groan, the ghost still pinning me against the wall, still not letting me move. Hannah watching everything, calculating, trying to see what she can do. That other ghost who held Tillman before hovering, its attention on her.

"I grew up on the other side of the mountains," Father Sky says, backing up again, the bloody knife in his hand. Jack's blood. Mine.

Maybe Josie's. He sits on the bed, flips his hair back. "And I always had a bit of a *gift*, you could say. Saw things, knew things, just . . . enough. Not like you two. But I've always been . . . persuasive." He winks at Hannah, and a dimple shows in his face. "But there was one night that changed everything for me. That broke open my whole world. Can you guess what it was?" The question is directed to me. I don't say anything.

"I'm two years older than you," he says. "I was eight when it happened. When I woke up to the brightest light of my life, shining all through the night. And this . . . *feeling*. I knew. I could tell that something much bigger than any of us had entered the world. I didn't know what it was, where exactly it was, or what it wanted. But I knew, from that moment, that my life was changed forever. Because I had to find out."

He lifts up the knife and slides the blade against Jack's arm, blood spilling onto the bed between them. Jack lets out another half-conscious groan. I try to move, but I can't. My throat held by the ghost, my arms inexplicably somehow glued to my sides. Hannah takes a step forward, and the ghost that held Tillman rushes her. It shoves her down on the floor beside me, all the way down, on her stomach.

"Stop!" I say.

"So I searched," Father Sky says. Hannah, pinned to the floor, her face pressed to the carpet. She whimpers. I fight, and the ghost knocks my head back against the wall.

Father Sky continues.

"I studied religion, physics, science, mythology, because I had to know what it was that I had experienced. I was a man obsessed. A UFO or something like it seemed most obvious, but it just never . . . resonated. Something in me just knew it wasn't it. I went to jail for a bit—unrelated to any of this—and when I saw the first Drifter murders come on the news, I knew, instinctually, that I had found what I was looking for. Finally. I knew that the thing that had entered our world when I was a child was responsible for these murders. And if it sounds outlandish, you'll remember I'm a holy man. I've learned some things, and I've got some"—he waves at the ghosts—"connections.

"So I started following the murders, and I started a chat room because I've found the internet to be a very fruitful place for research, and for finding those who seek to follow. This culture of checking in with the masses to know if an opinion or point of view is okay. Heading to the comments section first thing. It's ideal, really, for cultivating a congregation. I started learning everything I could, about the case, about all of you. I came to Denver, and . . ."

He stands, and I try again to fight against the ghost holding me. Hannah's eyes are squeezed tight on the ground. She's not doing well. I have to do something.

"Hey," Wharton says. "This is where it gets emotional, for me. Pay attention, or I'll have to hurt her."

Hannah breathes, tries to keep herself calm. But I feel her screaming on the other side, the panic at being trapped. I try and calm her there, send a feeling that I'll figure this out, that it will be okay.

"So here's the big part," Wharton says, standing in front of the bed, Murphy behind him. "The big reveal of my life. Can you *imagine* what it felt like to realize? To do a little digging into *your* past, the lead detective on this case, to find simultaneously that the very same night the light appeared to me as a child, a murder took place here at this very motel? So I looked into adoption records and one thing led to another."

He waves the knife around, more blood spattering his turtleneck. "But this is the part you have to understand," he says. "That night changed everything about me, made me who I am, determined every day since. And when I put it all together, when I came here and saw you, how bright you shine. When I truly realized what had happened . . . the light I saw, what I felt that night as a kid, the single most formative moment of my life—spiritually, in every way—what I thought was *God* come to earth, and maybe God calling to me . . .

"It was *you*. It was just another person. A child, a couple years younger than me. Who just shined *brighter.* And pain does shine bright, but this . . . It was *you.* That feeling of a God entering this world . . . that was the Witchwalker coming *to you.*" He laughs, a little. "Me? Well, it turns out I was just . . . inconsequential. I was *nothing.*"

"What do you want from me?" I ask, trying to make sense of anything he's said.

"I told you, I'll get to that." The ghosts dig into us harder. Hannah's breaths come faster.

John Denver sings, and Jack Murphy is slumped on the bed, and Father Sky watches us. He says, "But I will admit to having tampered with just a bit of the case because I just . . . well, I don't know. Maybe I wanted to be a part of it all. Any guesses?"

A memory comes in, from Hannah. A realization. Understanding.

Father Sky in a backpacker's outfit, passing by the cabin while Hannah was sketching something outside. He waved to her, and she waved back.

"There she is!" he says. "You can let her up." The ghost backs off her. She sucks in a breath and pushes up to sit. The ghost hovers nearby, no longer touching her. Father Sky walks over in his moccasins, bends down in front of her on the floor, reaches out, and tucks her hair behind her ear. She flinches back, and he smiles, drops his eyes to her lips, runs his hand down her neck.

"You," he says to her, softly. "You are . . . exquisite. Should you ever want it, there's a place beside me at the church for you. You deserve to be worshipped."

"What evidence did you tamper with?" I ask through my teeth.

"I broke in and took her camera and photographed the person I knew would be the next victim," he says. He sits back on his heels on the floor, looking back and forth between us. The light of the bathroom glowing behind him.

"What do you mean?" I ask. "How did you know who the next victim was going to be?"

"I told you, you are so unbelievably daft. I truly cannot fathom how you didn't feel it."

"Feel it?"

"The Witchwalker. It put a . . . vibration on the two that were going to be next, the next victim and the next Drifter. It did it every time."

"Why? What do you mean a vibration?"

"Not a why, more of a *because*. And maybe vibration isn't the word. Maybe a light. It put a light on them. I don't know how to explain, I just . . . feel it. Know it. *You* have it, the two of you. You vibrate differently, shine so bright. Since it's attached itself to you both."

"What—"

"Danny, with the way you shine, it would be child's play to know. Just by lookin' at them. For the life of me, I have wondered this the entire time, and I can't figure it out. *How* do you *not* know?"

I don't have an answer for that. But if he's right, if any of this isn't an attention-seeking lunatic's fantasies, maybe . . . maybe it's because I've pretended for so many years that none of this was real. Closed myself off from it. And if that's the case . . . if I could have solved all of this so much sooner by just . . .

"Why would you take a photo on my camera?" Hannah asks. "Why would you steal it and put it back?"

Father Sky sets the tip of the knife to the carpet, spins it. He looks up at her with another smile and says, "Because I could, darling."

He tosses his hair back again, turns his eyes on me. "To learn that what I thought was a special calling from Beyond was just . . . some other kid?" He laughs, bitter, angry. "The light that shined that night was *from you*. You screamed, and it was so loud, your grief, your pain, that it shined a light everywhere. And if you scream loud enough, shine bright enough, you're bound to wake something up."

He tosses the knife and catches it.

"You woke up the Witchwalker. And me too."

He tilts his head. "I just . . . wanted to put my mark on the thing. I was looking for Hannah, following her light, and I saw the camera with her and thought, *Why not?* I didn't know if the feds were gonna get her for eating the bodies. But *both* Hannah and the victim being taken to the motel, now that was a twist. I didn't anticipate it, I'll admit. I just thought if the feds did take her, it would just be a fun little trick." He leans back, smiles at her again. "Maybe I have a vindictive streak. I'm not too proud to admit I've been quite jealous of you both."

I strain against the ghost again. Father Sky is only a foot away from me. I can't move. What a fucking joke.

"So, in conclusion, because we don't have all night, I am here because the Witchwalker has attached itself to *you*," he says to me, then points the knife to Hannah. "Both of you. And I want it for *me*."

"To do what?" Hannah asks.

"With the kind of power the Witchwalker could confer on me, the kind Danny here won't just reach out and take for himself, well, I think I'd be pretty unstoppable. Sky's the limit, you might say." His smile grows wider.

"Why Jack and Josie?" I ask. "Why did they need to be a part of this? Why Tillman?"

"You should know better than anyone that the Witchwalker flocks to pain. I needed you to send out your beacon, and . . ." He stands. Takes a few steps back toward the bed, his eyes still on us. "Thank you, for keeping me on track. It's time for the big trick!"

He sits down beside Jack and pins his eyes on me.

"Ta-da!"

He slides the knife across Jack's throat.

Jack—

Blood.

Blood.

Mom—

JACK!

"There it is," Father Sky says, holding the knife to his own chest, Jack's blood spilling down over his hands, into his lap, from the knife. He taps his fingers against the handle.

Tap tap.

"Jack!" I yell. "*JACK!*" I push with every ounce of strength I have, and I can't move, can't get to him. This can't be real. This can't be—

Jack slumps forward, his body tipping over the edge of the bed.

I fight against the ghost hands holding me.

Father Sky's fingers tap against the knife. *Tap tap.*

Jack falls to the floor, and I yell.

Father Sky tilts his head back to the ceiling, eyes closed, and smiles. "Thank you," he says. "So, so bright." *Tap tap.*

"I'll fucking kill you," I say. "I will—"

"Bring him over here," he says. And I am lifted off the ground. Shoved forward. Thrown to the bed where Jack was a moment ago. Father Sky stands, and the ghost, and another, pin me before I can reach for him. They turn me on my back and hold me down. I kick and fight.

Hannah calls my name, screams in the other-place. I see her, out of the corner of my eye. Fighting the one now holding her back again.

Tap tap.

I can't do it. They're too strong, I can't—

"So now the next trick," Father Sky says. "I need to get the Witchwalker to first detach from you and then attach to me. I've done research. A lot. And I found some stories, way way back, of something very like a Witchwalker entering the world. Another time, another place. But they determined that it needed a tether, something physical to tie itself to the person it was attached to. And I was thinking . . . well, there was the tongue in Hannah's mouth. And the hair wrapped around the tongue of every Drifter. Tongues are sacred.

"So my thought is this—maybe this is crazy, but I think maybe I take your tongue. And I put it in *my* mouth. Maybe I have to eat it. I'm not sure. But I'm thinking, if I take it for myself, if I make it *mine*—"

Tap tap.

"The Witchwalker might think I am you. I might be able to trick it."

Tap tap.

"And if I can't trick it, well, you're going to die here tonight either way. If you're dead and it's still stranded here, it will want to attach itself to someone new. And I don't shine like you two, but I shine."

Tap tap.

"And if none of that works, then at least I'll have the satisfaction of knowing a total stranger ruined your life just like you ruined mine."

He flips his hair back. "Want to see another trick?"

He smiles at me. Cocks an eyebrow.

Mountain, snow, trapped.

Hannah cries out.

Jack on the floor, beside me. I can't—

Friend, teeth, meat, hate, hungry, hate—

Scream. In the other-place. *No—*

Hannah. She's sitting in the corner with her head tucked into her knees, rocking back and forth. Whimpering. No ghost holds her down now. She's just . . . sitting.

"What are you doing to her?" I say to Father Sky, who stands at the edge of the bed, watching her.

Snow, wind, blood, meat, ripping, tearing—

"Little supernatural hypnosis trick I learned," he says. "Memory is powerful. And our worst ones can trap us. You know that, Danny. I just led her to it. She's doing the trapping herself. And isn't that always the way."

Ghosts, holding me. I fight against them, try to fight, but I—

I have to do it, I'm so hungry. So hungry, and I can't . . . I have to . . . Oh god, I—

Father Sky steps toward me, holding the knife in one hand and pulling a pair of pliers from his back pocket with the other. "Crude instruments," he says. "But sometimes that's just how you gotta skin the cat. Or whatever they say."

I'm sorry, I'm sorry, hungry, so hungry, I—

Bite. Chew. Rip, tear, squeeze, lick, yes, oh god, I

Hate, hate myself, hate—

Hannah, I send into the other-place. *Hannah, you can get out of this. You're not stuck there, okay? You're not—*

The ghosts push down on me. Sharp pain in my leg. I'm bleeding, a lot, I think. I fight. One of them shoves my shoulder down so hard I think it dislocated it. I struggle against the weight holding me down, the ghosts. I can't move. It's like I have no strength at all in my body.

Hate, hate, hungry, need, hate—

Hannah! I call to her.

Father Sky steps up to me and taps his fingers to my chin, then pulls it down, opening my jaw. I turn my head away, can do that much, but then one of the ghosts holds it in place. I can't move, can't do anything, as he opens my mouth again.

Cold, scared, what did I, oh. My god

Hannah, I call. *Hey, you're not trapped in this. You're not—*

Fuck. How do I stop this? How do I get her out?

Father Sky brings the pliers to my face.

And I think—maybe. Maybe I can't pull her out.

Unless I—

Hannah, help! I call. Like in the bathroom. Like before. *You brought me back before, and I need your help now, okay? You can get out of this. I need you.*

Even as I say it to her though, I can't move. I can't fight it. And he's got my mouth open.

Hannah!

Father Sky pulls my tongue from my mouth with the pliers. I try to fight, I push with everything I have. I can't. I've always been powerless to these ghosts. I've always—

HANNAH!

But she can't hear me. She's too deep in it. Her pain, her shame. I feel it. I feel everything.

Father Sky tightens the pliers on the end of my tongue, stretches it out as far as he can, pain ripping through the back of my throat.

Hannah, I send through to that other-place.

Father Sky lifts the knife.

Hannah, I send. *Whatever happens, I—*

VOOM.

The pressure changes in the room. The air gets cold.

"Yes," Father Sky breathes.

He lifts up the knife with his other hand and angles it down. He presses the tip into the back of my tongue. The knife is dull, but *fuck*, this is—

Pain. Blood fills my mouth.

Black tendrils snake through the room.

The *pressure.*

VOOM.

"Annie's Song." John Denver's singing it on the TV.

Chemical smell. The river in the park in Aspen. My mom. Rose.

Father Sky presses the knife down harder, more blood spilling, hot salt liquid filling my mouth. I let out something between a groan and a yell as he—

The staticky, crackling sound. The oily, inky black crawling over the carpet, up the cabinet to the TV, over John Denver's face. Up the walls of the room and spreading over the ceiling.

Father Sky breathes heavily as he slices down through the left edge of my tongue.

"You know," he says. "I've always thought—"

There's a loud crash. Glass and liquid rain down over me.

Father Sky pauses, lurches forward. Meets my eyes. Confusion crosses his face, then . . .

He stops cutting, releases my tongue. He turns around.

Hannah is there.

Hannah no longer in the corner on the floor. No longer stuck in the memory.

Hannah with her hand on the handle of my dad's liquor bottle. I blink, fight through the haze and pain. The dark. The bottle now sticking out of Father Sky's back. On his right side, just below his ribs. Blood pouring from the bottle like a tap. She lets it go, watches the blood.

I try to stay here. Fight the dark that's pulling me.

Father Sky looks at Hannah and doesn't move for a second. Time stretched and suspended as the black tendrils start their crawl down toward us from the ceiling.

VOOM.

Crackling, pressure, dark, and—

Father Sky swings the knife up toward her.

Toward Hannah.

I snap back to attention. Hannah,

Hannah—

Her eyes on me. The knife, arcing toward her stomach.

I—

I can't speak. Can't move. Blood filling my mouth and my throat, and my vision going dark, and—

The black tendrils descend as the knife makes contact with her.

I scream.

Everything goes black.

7

Hannah. I reach for her, try to feel her in the other-space. But it's thinner, our connection now. It's . . .

Hannah!

I don't hear her. I don't feel her.

I can't find her. I try to feel my body in the motel, but . . .

I'm not there.

I'm only in the other-place. Where is she? I'm only . . .

I'm out in a dark night.

I'm looking at the bright lights of the Happy Inn. Not from the road. Not in our world at all.

In the deep, never-ending night.

Snow falls here, in slow motion. Orange, yellow light from the motel glowing, pulsing.

Cubbyholes of existence, small pockets of warmth behind each window and open door.

I watch Tillman, running, chasing, the rooms stretching in ways they're not meant to. Doors opening to floors. Falling to the ground. Stairs leading back into rooms. Everything stretched and warped and backward and upside down because this is a place out of time. Because the Happy Inn exists between worlds. Because . . .

Because I did it.

What does that mean? I grasp at the thought, know I should know the answer. It's there, just at the edge of my—

Room 6 is dark. It's the only room I can't see.

HANNAH! I scream into the night. I want to run to her, but I can't run. I can't move.

Snow blows. Blood fills my mouth, drips down over my lip and chin. Blood pours down my leg. I can't move my arm. The pain is terrible.

There is silence, on the other end. There is silence here.

I don't hear Hannah. I don't see her.

VOOM.

But I am not alone.

VOOM.

A shape moves in the snow, between the motel and me.

I can't make it out yet. But it's massive.

It comes closer, and I start to see more. Fourteen feet tall. Maybe thirty, it's hard to understand space here, everything stretched, warped in the black. I can't see where the ground begins and the sky ends. A motel, suspended in nothing. A creature floating in the dark.

I crane my neck, look up to try and see its face in the falling snow as it approaches.

VOOM.

I can't see it clearly. It's dark as the night I'm in, black and iridescent, like gasoline on asphalt. Almost camouflaged. Ancient. Long, spindly. As if made of metal or black bones, or . . .

VOOM.

My eyes catch on its spine. Sharp black bones jut out all up and down its back, the longest ones near the back of its shoulders. Forming a brittle spiked wave up and down its body. It stands like a quadruped momentarily on its hind legs. I get the sense that it's fastest on all fours. I can't see its head, too high up in the black above. But I know it watches me.

That black oily ink, swirling around it. Like watching someone through infrared and seeing their heat signature fluctuate, the black tendrils somehow a part of this thing's . . . I don't know what. Energy. Existence.

It's terrifying.

It waits.

Where is she? I ask. *Please, is she okay?*

It stands before me. Close, it could reach out and touch me if it wanted to, could kill me without a thought.

Am I dead already?

HANNAH! I call out again, in the only way I can.

Okay.

It doesn't come as a word, more a feeling. A certainty. A thought in my own head.

It's like the voice that came through Father Sky. This thing, here, communicating. I sway, dizzy, dazed.

You're the Witchwalker, I say, think.

VOOM.

It doesn't say anything.

"Where is she?" I ask out loud. It sounds wrong. My tongue, the blood.

Okay.

VOOM.

"Where?"

Snow flurries down in slow motion around the giant creature, the motel glowing behind it, farther now. Blood in my mouth. Hannah, still alive. The dizziness, nausea, time stretching, warping. Too hard to speak.

I ask, without words, *What are you? What do you want from me?*

It takes a step toward me.

VOOM.

I stumble back, a little. I can do that much. It comes closer.

VOOM.

I—

Stay.

I try to step back again, but I trip over my feet, just barely keep from collapsing. Pain, ripping through all of me.

It approaches, bends down. The movements are slow. It is so big. That crackling, popping static. Like we're underwater. My heart pounds in my chest. Being near it . . .

Life and death and power and fear. I feel sick. I feel like my head is going to explode.

It bends down further, and I think I will see its face soon.

I struggle to breathe. Struggle to hold myself up, as it bends toward me. Arches its spine to bring its head near mine.

And I just see the beginning of its head, I just—

VOOM.

I am ripped from my body.

There sits a black, swirling infinity. An endless night of beauty and rest and creation and destruction and existence. An open plane of possibility. Of matter. Of being.

Of life. And death. And dark.

Burrowed in its depths, suspended among the galaxies, among countless stars and nebulas, a creature sleeps. Curled in on itself. A being of consciousness. As it rests, its physical form shifts, changing all the time. Fluctuating.

It had another home once. On a planet. In a dimension. It does not remember why it is here now, it only rests. Its mind is quiet, at peace. Eternity stretches around it, expanse, sweeping, swirling. Infinite.

It is at home. It is at rest. It is at peace.

It is—

SCREAM.

The sound, so loud. Too loud. The light it emits so bright.

SCREAM.

The creature opens its eyes.

It wakes.

SCREAM, SCREAM. Full of pain.

The creature remembers itself, remembers it is a being, remembers what it is to be, to relate to other beings. To want. To need.

The scream so bright, it calls to the creature. It reminds the creature of what want is. Of need. The light calls it. It needs to go to the light. It wants—

It shakes itself awake.

It follows. Hunts. Searches.

It chases the sound, the bright searing light, across planes, dimensions. Worlds. Universes. Consciousness. It takes a moment, it takes a century.

The scream keeps calling, pulling at the creature.

Want. Need. Light.

And . . .

There.

Somewhere in the great expanse. In a universe in a galaxy on a planet. A pinpoint, nearly invisible to it at first.

SCREAM.

That light shining so bright.

The source of the light is small.

So small. This tiny, terrified thing. Its pain so bright and loud,

That it ripped a hole between dimensions.

A little being in a dwelling of many doors. Orange, yellow, white. Color, and light.

The little boy shine, shines, SHINING his pain.

A scream that crossed existence.

The creature wants. Needs.

The creature pulls itself to the planet, to its plane. Steps through the hole between dimensions, makes itself very small to watch.

Boy. Little boy. That is what they call it in this world. The little one who screamed. Boy. The creature knows this, it remembers or learns.

The boy is gone from the orange glowing dwelling with many rooms and many inhabitants, but his scent is still there. The light from the scream is there. The hole he ripped is there. The blood of the boy's mother is there.

And the creature understands.

Want. Need. Pain.

It takes what it can of the boy, learns what it might. The boy's genetic material on an item it one day learns is called a brush. The boy's shed on the brush called hair. The creature shrinks back through the hole, into the great infinite night. But it watches. Learns. Always notes where the shining boy is, where the light moves.

It watches as the boy goes to a new family. New dwelling, a thin place, a place the creature can watch him through. Not quite the hole the boy ripped in the orange-yellow motel—it learns it is called that—but . . . the creature can watch him there. Feel him. Whileago Manor, they call it.

The creature watches the boy grow. It is very fast, this growing. A blink of an eye. The creature doesn't understand this earth and these beings, but it wants to learn. It wants and needs. Intense want, staggering. It thinks that maybe it has been to this planet and dimension before, long ago. But it was so different. Open land, space. Now it is crowded, too full.

It watches the boy. Doesn't want to leave him. He shines, shines, shines in his pain. The creature can smell it, taste it, feel it in every atom.

The boy grows, leaves. The creature can't find him. It can't move easily in this physical plane. Not with the concrete and buildings and roads and sidewalks. Can't move far beyond the hole. It doesn't understand this, but it tries. It can't find another way in from the other side, there is only the one hole the boy ripped. And it can only move so far.

It waits for the boy to return, and it learns about humans, about all species of this world. It learns it can enter their minds and bodies and experience life, can walk through them. But still, not far from the hole. Not past too much concrete and road and building. It walks as prairie dog and mountain lion and field mouse and dragonfly. It experiences life. As every kind of creature. It watches and walks this earth, steps into it, and it feels . . .

Such want. Staggering, overwhelming need.

This is home now. This is the boy's home, and the creature is tied to him. The light so bright. The need in the creature.

The boy might one day return. Must one day return. The creature searching, always waiting for that shine. Craving it, tasting the air and scenting for it.

And the humans pour more concrete. Dig deeper trenches. Build more dwellings. The animals are restless. The earth is restless. The creature decides.

It calls this place home now and will protect its home however it can.

VOOM.

The boy returns. He is a man now. Grown human. The creature sees in his mind, understands. Violence. War. Blood and Pain and Fear. But the boy has love too now, a mate. He has a new dwelling, with his mate. Near enough to the others that the creature expands its territory, stretches to monitor all their places.

But it feels . . .

The territory is not well.

Crowding. So much crowding, building, pushing in, threatening their range.

Animals, dying. Earth out of balance.

The creature tries to talk to the humans through words, stepping into other humans, trying to speak to them, but their language doesn't make sense to it. It tries to speak with them through feelings, through sleeping thoughts. It tries to walk through other animals and communicate.

The boy is the only one who shines so bright, who might understand the creature. But the boy cannot hear. Does not want to hear. All he sees and hears and feels is pain, violence, fear. He doesn't want to hear anything else, wants only to look at his pain. Again, and again.

So, the creature thinks, the creature wants and needs, and maybe . . .

Pain. Violence. Fear.

Maybe that is how the humans communicate. Maybe that is why they keep pouring concrete and digging out the earth, killing, causing pain violence fear to the other animals here.

The boy thinks only of his pain. Maybe it is what will make them understand.

The creature hatches a plan.

VOOM.

The creature will show the other humans its territory. The boy's territory that the creature shares, that other animals share. It will tell the humans not to concrete and metal and asphalt it. Not to choke the land. More.

It will use pain, violence, fear to ask them. To show the lines of its boundary. It will show the territory belongs to the boy. It will use his genetic material to show it.

Hair. Mark its territory with its genetic material. Show the others. The boy's mother left blood behind in the motel, and her scent has never left it. The creature can use blood. It can use violence, pain, fear. It can enter the bodies of the people, and it can make its need known, in a way they might finally understand.

VOOM.

Then . . .

Another light.

Not so bright, not so loud. But . . . something new in their territory.

A girl. She also shines. She also thinks Pain, Violence, Fear. She also is hungry.

The creature has food. It wants and needs. It can feed her. It gives her what she needs.

And . . .

The land choking stops. The building stops. The animals feel less fear. The girl does not need to feed again. She is happy.

But the boy is not happy.

The creature thinks . . .

He needs to know. Understand. It is the boy's job, his life work, to find answers, to know why. The creature doesn't know why he doesn't understand. It tries to show him.

But the boy won't listen. Does not want to see anything outside this plane, even though things cross over from both sides. Even though he sees these things all the time. He cannot look past Pain, Violence, Fear. Does not want to.

His new parents die, cross the plane. He loses his mate. And the creature feels his Pain, sees the shining light and hears his scream, and it doesn't know what to do. Its need intensifies. Its want nearly blinding.

The light, the light, the light.

The boy leaves again, and the creature waits, despairs. Wants and needs.

But it knows the boy left before, and he came back. It knows that animals migrate.

Then the building, choking starts again. And they have no space here, the animals. The creature. It can't leave this world. It wants to look out for them. The boy, the girl, the animals. It needs to stay.

It feels want, need, for . . .

Its children. The boy. The girl. All the creatures in its territory.

Must protect them. Need, NEED to protect.

It tries to call its children back. Needs their help. Pain Violence Fear. It offers the girl food. She won't take it this time. The boy will not return.

It does it again. Pain, Violence, Fear. Mark territory.

But the girl will not eat. The boy will not return.

The building, choking.

The need that woke it from its slumber, the pain that ripped through worlds.

Protect. Stop light, stop pain. Protect the boy who shines so bright. Who hurts. Who fears. Who is alone.

The creature needs to protect the boy. Needs to make him safe.

It thinks . . . maybe . . .

Maybe if the boy and the girl meet, they will understand. If the boy and the girl meet they will see.

Maybe if they meet, they will help it defend their territory.

Their home. New mate for him.

Mates. The girl and boy. The same. Bright light. Shine. Pain.

She will explain. She knows. She does not fight it like the boy does.

Maybe . . .

VOOM.

I fall to my knees.

In the dark, in the swirling snow.

Static, crackling. Black all around, snow falling in slow motion.

The motel suspended in the dark. The cubbyholes of light.

Room 6 is now illuminated. I can see it. Jack and Father Sky are there.

Josie and Tillman in another one. He found her.

I don't see Hannah.

I call for her. But I—

The creature stands between the motel and me. The creature who I can barely see, camouflaged in the night. The light catching off its iridescent black bones from the motel.

From me.

I look down. Faint light emanates from my body.

I try to understand. Everything I was just shown. Everything . . .

This creature. The Witchwalker.

It heard me screaming that night, *here*. At the Happy Inn. It heard me, and—

I suddenly see the posterboard in Jack's garage. His daughter's project.

Wolves adopt orphaned or abandoned young.

The moment in the bathroom at the Stanley with Hannah when I thought . . . animals. Ecosystems. Something I was supposed to understand.

This thing. This creature in front of me. This . . . Witchwalker, as we've labeled it.

It heard my cry, and it came to answer. It came to . . .

My children.

We thought it *fed* on fear and pain. We thought it wanted the fear, the pain, the light for itself. We thought it liked them, needed them.

We were wrong.

And . . .

After the hotel, Hannah and me. After we were together, after we opened ourselves up to each other. We could *see* the ghosts, not just their shadows. Hear the Witchwalker more clearly. The two of us. We opened ourselves up to it, to the frequency or station.

The Witchwalker was right. Putting Hannah and me together . . .

Mates.

The creature stands upright again, and I can't see its face. This creature who crossed galaxies to come to me. To try to protect me.

Why?

Because pain. Fear. Alone. Because light, pain. Sadness.

The feelings, understanding, flash through me. I blink. Realize I'm still bleeding. Think maybe all of this is me slowly dying. Dizzy.

No reason. No reason other than this creature trying . . . to help?

And . . . the building. What is it talking about with the . . .

You want construction to stop? All construction? I say. Think. *You want people to stop land development?*

Images flash.

Animals. Plains species. Grassland prairie, riparian forests. Denver, its surroundings. This creature, entity. Its home. My . . .

But, I think, *people will never stop building. I can't stop them.*

A feeling comes through. ***Disagree.***

No, I mean it. This violence. And this killing. It . . . You hurt people. You—

Images again. Memories. My own.

Afghanistan.

SWAT kicking in doors of homes.

I shake my head. *It's not the same*, I think.

The feeling again. ***Disagree.***

No, it's not—

Enemy fire. Bullets spraying through the air, shells flying, blood, and—

It's not the same! It has to stop. Please. No more. No more death. No more violence.

The snow falls.

The Happy Inn. This creature, and me.

It's cold, and I sway a bit. I don't think I can stay here long. Stay anywhere long.

Where is Hannah? I reach for her, try to feel her.

The creature watches me. The Witchwalker.

Must protect. Building stop.

No. No more violence. That isn't protecting us. You have to—

It slams me into a memory. The force of it hits me in the chest, and I'm thrown back.

VOOM.

Mom—Rose—in that pink dress at the John Denver Sanctuary. The park Hannah brought me to in Aspen. The one I recognized.

Rose calling me toward the water.

Taking our shoes off, wading through the river, climbing up onto the big rock in the middle of it, looking out at the green grass and trees. At the John Denver lyrics carved in the big stone at the trailhead.

The picnic basket and Mom's crinkled old paperback. The two root beer bottles. The bruises on her face from Dad. The cut on my head from him too.

We've had a perfect day, here. Mom and me. In John Denver's Aspen. I wear a hat just like his. Mom got it for me special.

"You know I love you more than anything, right?" she says.

She hands me my root beer, her book beside her. She holds the other root beer bottle and squeezes my hand. Her hands are both shaking. There's a funny smell.

We had to stop at that old drugstore in town on the way here. Mom let me go upstairs to the kids section and get a toy cowboy there too. I keep it in my lap. She says,

"This is life, Danny. Okay?" she says. "This is the world. It's the sun, and it's green grass, and it's putting our feet in the water together. Nothing scary, nothing bad." She's crying. Why is she crying? Maybe thinking about Dad? I look at the bruises on her face, from him. I don't ever like looking at them. "You know that, right? That this world is a good place? A happy place?"

Tears on my mom's face. The sun shining against the water, against her tears, under the trees. Sun shining against the glass root beer bottles. Mom's eyes on mine. That odd chemical smell, I don't know what it's coming from.

"Mom, what's wrong?" I ask.

"You know that this world is a happy beautiful place, right?" She sniffs, her hands shaking.

I nod. My heart pounding.

Bad Feeling.

"Okay, sweet boy," she says, the tears falling. "Let's drink up, okay?"

I take a sip. It tastes funny. Bitter. Mom is crying. And shaking. I don't know what to do.

Bad Feeling.

I don't know how to help, don't know—

She sings to me, sometimes, when I'm scared and sad. John Denver, my favorite. Her favorite is Blaze Foley. I know how the songs go, we've listened to them so many times.

I turn to Mom, and I hold her hand back. And I sing. "If I Could

Only Fly." I sing the chorus, and the water in the river flows, and I hold my mom's hand, and the sun shines on us, and I hope it works. I hope I can do something to make her not sad. She stops for a second. Listens to me singing.

Her eyes change, they move from the river to me. They go from scared and sad to something else. She watches me, then blinks. Like she just woke up from a dream. Like she can only just now see me.

Then her eyes go wide, and she grabs my root beer bottle and throws it in the water.

And—

After, later.

Sick. Ears ringing. Sweating. Vomiting. Can barely stay awake.

A motel in Leadville. Couldn't make it back to Denver. Sick, both of us, Mom and me. We're throwing up, shaking. Ears ringing so loud.

Dad coming and pounding on the door. Dad taking us to the hospital.

Dad yelling at Mom, in the car. Ears ringing. Dad shaking a box of something at her. Mom crying, her head falling to the side. Like mine.

At the hospital, Dad says, "Kid was playing potions. Put a bunch of BC Powder in his and his mom's root beer. Didn't know what he was doing." I don't know what he's talking about, what BC Powder is.

"Where did the bruises and cuts come from?" the nurse asks.

I don't hear what Dad says to them. Ringing too loud. I feel terrible. Dad runs his hands over his head and watches them wheel me back.

If I didn't know better, I'd think he was crying too.

VOOM.

I gasp, on hands and knees in the snowy dark. Try to clear the ringing from my ears.

That memory, the one that keeps clawing its way out of nowhere. Mom, and me, at the park. *BC Powder.*

Aspirin?

Chemical smell. Bitter.

Root beer. Dad and Mom and—

Jack Murphy in his garage. *It's crazy what you'd do to protect them. Anything. I mean, any—*

Calvin Keller in jail. *That woman was poison.*

My Bad Feeling that night at the Happy Inn. The root beer bottles on the counter.

Mom. *You and me, we're gonna go somewhere he can't find us, okay? Somewhere safe and happy where he'll never get us again.*

Protect.

I look up at the creature, understanding hitting me all at once.

No. It can't be true. It can't . . .

But of course it is. I see it. Remember it now. Maybe I always understood. Maybe some part of me always knew.

My mom tried to kill us both, I think. *Because she was scared. Because she wanted to get away from my dad.*

She—

My singing stopped her the first time. In the river.

My dad stopped her the second, at the Happy Inn.

Dad hit us, and she didn't think we could escape him. Unless we left this world altogether.

My mom tried to kill me.

My mom—

The Witchwalker . . .

It had access to these memories before I did.

Humans. Pain. Fear. Violence.

Violence, in order to protect. Death, in order to defend.

Protect.

Dizzy. Ears ringing. Blood loss. I'm . . . it's hard. To keep thinking.

The creature steps closer.

And a voice calls out, from somewhere far away.

I turn, try to hold on to sight. Light shining, moving away from the motel.

Dizzy.

I blink.

Hannah.

Hannah, coming toward me. Hannah, in the night. Her hair shining, green eyes, her light so bright.

The dark, pulling.

Hannah, I say. Think. Send and feel. *Stay back from the Witchwalker. Stay—*

She doesn't listen. She comes to us, runs through the dark to my side. The creature stays where it is, watches.

She's here. She's okay. I collapse down to my hands and knees, can't hold myself up anymore. She's okay.

Hannah drops down beside me. Both of us here in the falling snow, in the dark.

I couldn't find you, she says, thinks. *I was looking, and I couldn't—*

She reaches for my face, my neck. She pulls me to her, kisses me hard, and I feel her warmth. She's really here. I lean against her.

Did he hurt you? I ask, think. *Did the knife get you?*

She shakes her head against me. *Daniel, hang in there, okay? Your signal is thin. You have to—*

My body feels weak. I lean against her, hold on to her as tight as I can. And I can feel her seeing everything I just saw, being given the same transmission. From me. From the creature. I don't know. She stiffens, pulls back to take in the creature next to us.

Her eyes on the thing that has been stalking her. The thing that has made her face her past again and again.

Somewhere far off, I can hear, feel sirens. Back through the motel, back in our world. I think Josie's hurt. Jack is dead. Father Sky . . . I don't know.

Protect.

It came and took us from the motel when we were in danger. It's been trying to talk to us for so long. Has attached itself to us. That's what Father Sky said.

The Witchwalker isn't leaving. It won't go, and it won't stop killing because humans will never stop building. Humans will never stop working to shape the earth into what they want it to be.

I don't know what to do. The dark, it's . . .

How do we stop this? I ask Hannah.

She looks at me, down to the blood pouring from my leg. The blood in my mouth. Dizziness hits again, and I lean forward, press my forehead to hers.

We have to get you back, Hannah says. *Get to a hospital.*

All of this will continue, I say. *It doesn't want to go. I can't make it stop. Killing, more death. We can't draw it back there.*

Protect.

We can both feel it. It doesn't want to go.

Home.

My vision is getting darker. Harder to see Hannah's face. My ears ringing, like when I was a kid.

Hannah, who understands and knows every part of me, who doesn't turn away.

I say, *Go back.* The dark spreading in my vision, the dizziness. We haven't known each other long, and some part of my brain registers that. But they're the easiest words in the world.

I love you, Hannah.

She pulls back, holds my face in her hands. I blink her back into focus, cling to the image of her against the dark. She kisses me.

There's so much in it, it's everything. I'm dizzy, the ringing so loud. But . . . Hannah. Her lips on mine. Her hands on my face. Tears on her cheeks.

I blink, try to understand. Hannah crying.

Hannah pulling back from me. Hannah standing.

Good, I say. *Go back to the motel. Safe.*

She turns to the creature before us, and her light starts to shine so bright.

Crackling, static. Transmissions coming through. Thoughts from Hannah. Images.

Egyptian plover. Little bird in crocodile teeth.

Time I stop fighting who and what I am.

No, I say. *Wait. Are you—*

Images flash to me.

Us in the Stanley Hotel. In bed. In the bathroom. Her hand in mine in the car. At the jail. At Woody Creek, in the three-sided shelter in Aspen, the first moment she turned and locked eyes on me out the car window at the FBI office, us in Whileago Manor when neither of us trusted each other. Us running together on the trail.

Hannah and me together.

I love you too, she says.

As the dark pulls me, even as I start to understand, start to make sense of what she's doing, saying . . .

No! I call out. Try to—*Hannah, stop!*

But I can't see. I can't see because her light is blinding. Because there is nothing now but Hannah's light, Hannah's pain.

Hannah's pain because she's luring the Witchwalker somewhere else. Because she's hurting enough for it to follow her, protect her. That's her plan.

Symbiotic relationship. Light so bright, so full of pain.

Hannah's pain because she's leaving me.

HANNAH, NO!

The light shines and sears and fills every atom of the universe, and I open my mouth and scream.

HANNAH, PLEASE!

I can feel something new ripping open, a way out, a way somewhere else.

You can't go!

The connection between us, growing tighter, growing dim.

There's another way, there has to be—

Then . . .

Please!

Blinding light, and then suddenly,

I'm alone.

No Witchwalker. No Hannah.

They're gone.

It's dark.

Quiet.

Snow.

A motel, and me. In the endless night.

Hannah—I call out again. But the dark is pulling at me, and . . .

Nat Tillman's voice sounds in my head as the world tilts. As I fall all the way to the ground, lie down in the dizziness, the world spinning. Tillman's voice saying, *Eyes to the skies.*

I look up, delirious, through the swirling snow.

Blink. And I realize.

It's not snow.

It's the sky.

Galaxies, stars, universes. All around, above, below, everywhere around. Suspended, falling, no up and no down. Everywhere in the night.

Stars. Light.

And before me, the glowing orange-yellow motel suspended in all of it. The Happy Inn.

The Happy Inn existing between worlds because of the hole I ripped in it.

Whileago Manor. Nat and Josie's house. Hannah's cabin.

Sitting on a planet in a galaxy in a universe in a dimension.

Denver. Colorado. Earth.

The darkness comes to claim me. And it's the last thing I see.

Our own little cubbyhole of light.

And it all shines so bright.

VI

POEMS, PRAYERS, AND PROMISES

1

I open my eyes to pink-orange light shining through the window, spilling over the bed, pulling me from sleep. I'm in my old room at Whileago Manor, the small one. On the bedside table sit the two copies of *The Shining*. I read half of it last night, my mom's copy, her notes in the margins about me.

Danny saw my mother today, told me that she said she loved us and missed me and that she's happy on the other side. That she'll be looking out for us.

My little boy is astounding.

The memories came again when I woke in the hospital after the motel.

The river, with Rose, at the John Denver Sanctuary in Aspen. Everything Calvin said in the jail. The chemical smell I remembered, the one that kept coming back to me. I blocked it out because that is what a child with trauma will do. The chemical smell of BC Powder, aspirin poisoning.

You know I love you, right?

That night at the Happy Inn, she had written Calvin a suicide note. Explaining why she was doing it. He had hurt us so much, she was taking us somewhere he couldn't touch us. She thought the note would get to him after she'd done it. I know because she wrote practice notes in the back of the book, over the pages of text.

You can't take my boy from me. How could you? Calvin had said.

Calvin saved my life. Calvin killed Rose to protect me from her. Rose wanted to kill us both to protect us from him.

And I had the answer here the whole time. To my life, my past. I just didn't want to look at it. I just couldn't face myself and the truth. And I don't know if she was really going to go through with it. I guess I'll never know.

Halfway through the book is a photograph. Rose, and me, at a western bar. Each wearing matching cowboy boots and hats. She's laughing, her hands in mine, facing the camera. I'm looking up at her like she is the whole light of the world.

I push back the sheets and wince. Stab wounds, dislocated shoulder. A couple fractured bones. One leg, one arm. The ghosts somehow did it. The same leg, higher up, that stab wound from Father Sky. My tongue is healing, should fully heal, they said, but it will take time.

I'm missing one finger.

I can't think about that. I can only think about that.

Please, I say, out into the other-space.

Nothing.

I slowly limp out of bed and down to the basement. I'm in this shoulder sling and these casts for a while. I was in the hospital a week. They wanted me to stay longer, said recovery could still be weeks, months. Said I'm lucky to be alive.

I close my eyes and send out a signal.

Please.

Static, silence.

My phone buzzes. It's been almost three weeks since everything happened. The first week, when I was in the hospital, my phone was blowing up nonstop. Inundated with hundreds of requests for comment. The media frenzy unbelievable. I've made it clear I don't want to talk to any of them. Finally they're starting to slow down. Theo Wharton / Father Sky will be taken into custody once he's out of critical care.

The Witchwalker never stopped searching for me. Sometimes it was drawn by Theo Wharton's light. Not as bright as Hannah's and mine, but still there. Sometimes it went to him at the jail. Sometimes it visited children whose lights shined a little, because kids always shine, a little, I think. But it wasn't satisfied. It wanted Hannah and me. We were the two it had chosen.

The knife has been lab tested, and we can't identify the material it's made of. As far as we can tell, it is made of nothing known to us on earth. I don't know how the Witchwalker moved it, how it took my hair from the motel room, how it moves anything through physical space here. Unless it was by possessing a person and having them carry it. I don't know if it ever possessed Hannah, or me. My best guess is that when Hannah found the knife on her bed, the Witchwalker maybe thought Theo Wharton was a threat to Hannah. That maybe Wharton was back near her cabin, so the Witchwalker gave Hannah the knife for protection. I don't know why it wouldn't just kill Father Sky. I don't know so much.

But then I think of Hannah, what she might say. Interspecies communication can be difficult. It's hard to understand the wants of other animals. Besides survival, we never quite get it. This thing that thinks differently than us, the Witchwalker, that somehow, for some insane reason, decided to spend its life protecting Hannah and me, in the strange ways that it could. I don't get a lot of its motivations. And maybe I won't.

I don't know if it's coming back.

Josie and Jack had enough evidence pulled together to take Oliver Wright down for embezzlement, tax evasion, fraud. And with Wright's involvement with the prosecution of the Drifters over the years as well as his land's ties to the crimes, he might go down with Father Sky for the rest of it all. The timelines match up exactly, between when Wright was building and the Witchwalker was killing. When Wright stopped construction, and when the murders paused. It was right there, in front of us.

I talked to a bookkeeper, figured out my financials. Marianne and Noel left me significantly more than I realized. I put a lot of it into a fund for Jack's family, and for the families of the victims and killers in the case. I should have done it sooner, hate myself for not thinking of it. For not realizing I can use this money for good, just like my parents did.

And with a lot of the rest, I'm buying almost every property Oliver Wright was about to develop. His investors are grateful for the buyout offers, given the crimes he's about to go down for, and I've been put in contact with someone at the city to discuss plans for making the lands public, putting protections in place so there will be no more building, at least where I can help it.

I close my eyes. Reach again.

Where are you? Please.

Silence.

I brace myself, and I limp over to the storage room beside the gym. In the corner, the box of all my parents' papers, photos, sentimental and valuable items. Whatever they deemed appropriate for the Whileago Manor trunk. And for the first time since they died, since their executor handed it over to me, I kneel down—slowly, painfully—and open it.

It takes a long time, carrying the items up the stairs, to the main floor, then the second. To the end of the hall and into the room with the trunk. Piece by piece, book by book. I tried to pick the whole thing up, but with only one arm and a bum leg on that side to support it, I couldn't do it. It hurts, in every way. But it feels fitting that it should take so long. That I should sweat and push and strain to carry these items that were two people's lives. Two of the people who meant the most to me.

Within an hour or so, I've got everything upstairs. I lay it all out on the floor and the bed, where the two copies of *The Shining* used to be. And one by one, I open each item or document or photo album, and I learn even more about my parents. How much they helped the world, how much they traveled. Letters from friends and family revealing how much they impacted other people's lives. Seeing how much they preserved from my childhood, ticket stubs to concerts and games, team photos, yearbook photos, Yule cards from every year. It's December now. Yule will be here soon. The darkest day of the year, a celebration because it means it will get no darker. It means that from that point forward, we are moving toward the light. Or it's returning to us. Marianne loved it.

Death is the worst thing. Taking the people we love and hovering always, waiting to take another. I would do anything to be stringing up garlands with my parents. Jazz on the record player, fire crackling, snow falling outside. The giant tree Noel would let me pick out with him. At the end of the holidays, we'd take the dead tree to the edge of the forest and lay it on its side, thank it for making our home festive. Hang pine cones on it, with peanut butter and seed for the birds. Watch it become home to more creatures. Watch, on our bellies with binoculars in the snow, to see who else might have arrived.

I reach out to the other-place, desperate.

There's no answer.

The house is silent as I hold Marianne's and Noel's lives in my hands, as I prepare to put them in the trunk, in their own box within it. The third owners of Whileago Manor, to rest here with the others, per their wishes. I try to feel it. What it would be like to love a place so much, to want your legacy to continue inside it. To want to rest with those who came before you and didn't know anything about you or your life.

And . . . I do it. What Noel always wanted me to do. I reach in, and I finally do it. I open the other boxes in the trunk. The former owners of Whileago Manor. The history of the house. I learn about them, their lives. Their legacies that live on here, and in families elsewhere.

When I finally close the trunk and look up, I'm not alone in the room.

And they aren't shadows. They aren't Marianne and Noel either.

But two couples. The ones whose lives I just learned about here. A kid, twelve years old, standing with one of them. A young girl with the other couple, and a woman who is her grandmother. The former owners of Whileago Manor. The ones who wanted their memories kept here, whose remaining families I could reach out to, see if they'd want to see any of what's in here.

The shadows that terrified me my entire life. Standing before me now.

Not shadows. Ghosts.

They're just people. Echoes of people.

Denver, Colorado. Whileago Manor.

Noel's voice sounds in my ears as I push myself up to stand and limp through the house, looking for him and Marianne.

Some places just pull harder on you than the rest.

I haven't seen them. They're not here. But maybe, maybe.

I slowly limp back to my room and get back in bed.

I reach out, for Hannah. For my parents.

I reach until I can't anymore.

2

Jack's funeral procession winds through the city ahead of the service. There's snow on the ground, winter in full force, but today the sun is out, reflecting off the white. Josie and Tillman take up the front in Jack's government car, American flags waving from the windows. I drive Emily and the kids in Jack's old Charger from the garage. Brianna holds his Santa hat in her lap in the back seat. We take our motorcade from the FBI office to the church and cemetery across town. It was announced on the news, and some have come out to stand and pay their respects as we pass. After years of these atrocities, the city can rest easy for a bit. And they know they have Jack to thank.

Emily cries when she sees them all.

"He would have loved the attention," she says.

I smile, a little, and watch as a figure fades in and out, among the crowd. Popping up in new places as we go. Just a faint light, just a flicker. Just to watch us roll by.

The light catching on his aviator glasses.

Back at the office after, I take my badge inside to drop it off before I head to the wake.

Inside, it's quiet. I throw a few things together at my desk. A notebook. Some pens. I slide the nameplate into the trash can. I already put in my resignation from the hospital, the second I could. We're hoping there's enough with Father Sky to convince judges that the killers weren't responsible for their actions, and with Oliver Wright unable to still work to keep them in jail, hopefully their convictions will be overturned. It doesn't do anything for Jake Evers and Pete Noland who killed themselves. It does nothing for all the years the others still in jail have lost of their lives. The trauma they'll now always carry. It does nothing for the victims whose lives were lost. For any of their families.

Tillman's the shoo-in now for Jack's position—special agent in charge—and they've already put him temporarily in it. He's the best man for the job, and I gave my endorsement. He found Josie at the Happy Inn, got her to the paramedics. She was cut up all over by Father Sky, but Tillman got to her before there was too much blood loss. Which was good because it turns out she's expecting. She told me in our one brief conversation since.

I'm happy for them.

I pull my badge out of my pocket and inspect it. I was about to hand it in a month ago, back in Salt Lake. Crazy how much can change in a month. In an hour.

Again, I send out the signal.

Hannah.

Static.

Pain, in my chest. Everywhere. Where is she?

I hold out my badge.

Nat Tillman wanders over to my desk.

"Stansfield," he says.

"Tillman," I say, and I hand the badge over to him. He takes it. "I've heard congratulations are in order."

"Josie told you?"

I nod.

He laughs, wrings his hands together. "I'm a little nervous. But I'm excited. It's uh . . . pretty scary. Being someone's dad?"

"Somethin' tells me you're gonna be a good one."

"Dude, stop it, you're gonna make me cry."

"You just gotta teach 'em to keep lookin' up."

He gives me a surprised look, then shoots me with a finger gun. "Finally gettin' something through that hard head of yours."

I smile, run my hand over my face.

"Anything?" Tillman says, his tone serious.

I shake my head. He's asking if I've heard from Hannah. If I've found her. Hannah who disappeared from the Happy Inn that night. When the cops got there, they found Theo Wharton, Jack, Tillman, Josie, and me. Hannah nowhere in sight. The radio frequency just . . . static. I can't find her. I can't reach her or the Witchwalker.

"I'm sorry, man," he says. "But it hasn't been that much time. And you two . . . Look, I mean, some things just make sense in the world. Some things don't . . ." I know he's thinking about Jack. A wave of pain washes over me, settles deep. "But I just think sometimes this world is a kind place. We can't give up hope yet."

I nod.

Tillman studies me a long minute, my badge in his hand. "You don't have to go," he says.

"I'm done," I say. "I'm good."

"Okay," he says. "Well, come on then." He opens his arms and walks toward me.

I groan as he pulls me in for a hug, pats my back.

"'Kay, man, let's keep it PG." I pull away, turn and limp for the door. "See you 'round. Maybe get a beer."

"Maybe two," he says.

I snort a laugh. "Yeah, maybe two."

3

Downstairs, I wave at the security guard. It's my last time walking out of this building.

A relief, such a relief. After all this time.

I take it all in, limp up to the glass doors, ready to walk out into the bright Denver day.

I push the door open to step outside, and it almost hits someone.

"Shit," I say. "I'm so sorry. I didn't see—" I turn and . . .

I stop. Blink.

Here and not here. Glowing. Shadow and light, somehow combined.

His face, calm. Not crying, not miserable. He's—

Pete Noland is standing in front of me, outside the doors of the Denver FBI branch office.

Pete Noland is—

I stare at him, feeling, breathing. I think I'm breathing. I can't . . .

All the guilt. All the shame. The fucking agony of knowing I couldn't fix it.

"I'm sorry," I say. "I'm so sorry." I can feel tears, and I make no move to stop them.

He doesn't say anything, because they never do. The shadows. The ghosts. But he's here.

Pete Noland is . . . okay. Maybe.

We stand that way for a while. Pete Noland and me. In the cold. My breath visible.

And then he slips, fades, and I can only catch a glimmer.

I turn to the parking lot, and . . .

Thirteen more of them. Some just shadows, some clearer, brighter. All standing around the lot, surrounded by snowpacked ground, watching me.

Ramona Lopez, Ross Thompson, Claire Wright, Jake Evers, all the others.

All of them are here. Is this just my brain trying to reconcile with the guilt? With the fact that I couldn't save any of them, that all these murders were because something had attached itself to *me*? Because I couldn't figure it out fast enough?

Tony Howell waves to me. And Pete Noland is again by my side, just for a moment.

He steps up to me and passes through my body, a chill and a tremor running through me. As if to say, *We're real, asshole.*

As if to say, goodbye.

4

The hike up to the cabin is brutal. I don't know how I could be more pathetic. I try three different days, three different times, before I'm able to make it.

I know she's not here. Of course she's not. But I have to try. I'll go to Aspen next. I'll go everywhere she ever lived. I'll climb that fucking mountain in California. If there's any chance of finding her, any chance of seeing her again.

The sun shines in that Colorado way, the snow-covered path crunching beneath my boots. A bird lands on a branch in front of me. A small black bird with white wings and beak, starting to brown for winter. A lark bunting. We learned about them in school when I was a kid, our state bird.

The wind swaying through the pines and leaves. Icicles hanging down.

When I finally get to the top, finally get to the cabin, Hannah isn't there. Just a new ranger.

"Did you know her?" he asks, looking me up and down. "Is she family, or . . . ?"

"Yeah," I say. "I know her."

He hesitates a moment, then says, "Hold on." He comes back with a small box. "These were left here. On the wall. I get a little claustrophobic, so I needed a cleaner surface. But . . . they were so beautiful. I thought it'd be a shame to throw them away."

I know what's in the box before he hands it to me. All of Hannah's sketches, the playing cards. "Thank you," I say. And I'm not sure if I convey how much I mean it.

When I get back down the mountain and to my car, the sun is setting over Colorado. The sky full of thick clouds, orange, pink, and yellow, all of it reflected off the white ground. Geese fly in a V over the snowed-over prairie grass. These plains that butt up against the mountains. That stretch across the belly of a nation. Hannah, waiting somewhere nearby in this grass to photograph that fox. Noel and me lighting up the ecosystems in the museum exhibit. This land nothing but itself, nothing but the life it holds in it.

Which of course is everything.

I blink, as I see a herd of ghost bison walk past in the gold light of the sun, shining.

Denver. The place that built me.

I start the car and head back to the city.

I pass a sign stuck in the ground that says KEEP PREDATORS AWAY FROM OUR HOMES, with an image of a wolf on it.

A hawk will do anything to protect its territory, Hannah had said.

Won't we all?

Protect.

I drive through the night, and I send out that signal. I can't accept that she's not there. That she took the Witchwalker somewhere too far for me to reach them.

Daphne's voice ringing in my ears again. *Don't ever let go.*

I won't. But . . .

Where is she? *Hannah—*

Pressure. A chill.

The radio turns to static. The night feels a little darker, a little . . .

VOOM.

Coyotes yip, as the static gets louder. No music, just sound. Just that crackling in-between.

The coyotes get louder, as I spot them, over on the side of the highway in the field. Not ghosts. Real. Alive. They're in a frenzy, yipping and calling, and . . .

A yelp. A scream. Something calling for help.

I slow, squint, and stop the car. And that terrible sound—

Blood on the snow.

I swear, push myself up out of the car, and shine my light over. To see the coyote pack, blood on two of their faces. And a dog in the middle, trying to fight back. I swear again. Run-limp around to the other side of the car and reach in for my gun.

I lift it, the terrible screams of the dog growing, the static louder and louder from inside the car. I shoot at the ground near the pack. I have to do it twice before they run off, before I can get to the dog and assess the situation.

Maybe forty pounds, some kind of yellow Lab–pit mix, maybe. She's whimpering, whining. Her leg is bloody where they got her. It's freezing, getting colder by the minute. She's not getting up. I hope it's shock. Fuck, it's hard to tell, but—

I don't have time. She's not big. I can do this. I can squat down. I let out a groan as I do, as I feel the wound in my leg reopen, have to stop for a second and try again, the pain making me dizzy.

She's scared of me already. Whimpering and now thrashing against me. In shock from what happened to her.

"I'm sorry," I say. "I'm sorry." I push through the pain that I know is going to fuck me up for so much longer, and I get my arms underneath her. She fights me for a second, and then she lets me pick her up, still crying.

I get her in the back seat of my car, and I get in as fast as I can to drive. She doesn't stop whining, yelping, all the way. The pain is terrible. My pain, hers. The volume of the static. I get the heat on and try to warm her up.

I repeat over and over, *It's okay. Shh, shh, you're gonna be okay. I'm gonna make sure you're—*

There. An emergency vet I've passed a million times. Somehow I get myself and the dog out of the car and into the facility.

I call out, "Help!" when we step into the bright fluorescent light from the night.

Someone comes right away, rushes her to the back, and I collapse into a chair, blood soaking my bandages, my jeans. They rush the dog to emergency surgery. I tell them what happened, how I found her. Someone calls paramedics for me.

The paramedics come. They tell me I'll have to go back to the hospital, and I tell them I'm not leaving her. They field dress my wounds and make me promise to go when I'm done here, and let someone else drive the dog and me home. I nod, agree, don't listen to anything they say. As they're speaking, I feel something in my jacket pocket. I reach in and pull out my badge.

How—?

I sigh, run my hand over my face.

Tillman pulling me into that stupid hug.

Putting my badge back in my pocket.

An hour passes, and I sleep in the waiting room chair. Someone comes out and wakes me.

"She's out of surgery, and I'm so sorry, we had to take the leg."

"Is she—"

"She's gonna be okay. She's just a tripod girl now, but we think her recovery should be pretty smooth."

I exhale, maybe want to cry.

"So you said you found her," the vet says. "She's not microchipped. Are you planning to—"

"Yes," I say. "Yeah."

She smiles a little. "Do you have a name in mind? For our records? We can give her one if you want, just for the system."

Music plays in the waiting room, softly. I didn't notice it before now. Dancing to this song, with Rose. With Marianne. I clear my throat.

"Dolly," I say. "That's her name."

They send us out an hour or so later with medicines and instructions, and she's loopy from the drugs, but she can walk on her own. I lift her into the back seat of the car and get slowly back in.

I talk to her, on the way back. "We're gonna go to the house, and we're gonna pack up some things. And then we're gonna get on the road, and you and I are gonna heal up, and we're gonna find a place of our own, okay? I'm . . . uh, Daniel. And your name is Dolly now, I hope that's okay with you. And . . ." I don't know. Don't know what I'm doing. I look back in the rearview mirror, and she's panting, holding her head up. Seemingly . . . listening. Or watching. So I keep talking. She's not whining at least.

The radio starts to static again. And I feel something in the night. A little pressure. A vibration. My eyes scan the night, everything. Search for the Witchwalker.

For Hannah.

Blaze Foley plays on the radio.

John Denver. Dolly Parton. Static. John Prine. Static.

Dolly whines in the back.

"I'm gonna keep you safe, okay?" I say to her. "You're safe now. Don't you worry."

Hannah? I call.

I near the exit, and . . . I hear something. Something else. Vibrations . . . heartbeats.

Flurries start, snowflakes appearing suddenly, landing on the windshield.

VOOM.

The Witchwalker.

It's back. But—

Next to that pressure, that vibration, beneath or beside it. Smaller, softer.

I hear . . .

Two. Two heartbeats, in the dark.

I reach out, send my signal into that other-space.

Hannah, I say. *Hannah!* I yell.

My heart is racing.

Come on, Hannah. Please.

Time stretching, warping. Static, music, static. Dolly whimpers in the back. I console her, tell her it's okay. Scan everywhere, try to find where they are, how it's—

Movement. Beside my window. I almost swerve to the right, but my eyes catch it, understand just as I do. It's a bat. Just . . .

No. It's a bird, in the snowfall. Flying right next to my window. Like a magpie. Or . . . it's a hawk. No, I—I must . . .

"Hannah!" I yell.

Static.

The music stops. The vibration pulls back. It's gone.

No. No, no, no, please—

I reach, yell, scream into that other-space, send my signal out as hard as I can.

Please, Hannah. If you're there—

Silence.

I start to turn the wheel, start to turn back, but Dolly whimpers in the back, and—

VOOM.

The radio turns back on, switches from station to station. Different voices. Some talking, some singing.

I

Static.

Here

It repeats again, using new voices, new stations, taking time between, but repeating:

Here.

Static.

With

You

Static.

It's her. She's here. My heart. My fucking—

I call into the other-space.

Are you okay? Hannah, talk to me, how do I help you? How do I get you out? How do I bring you back?

The radio shifts again.

Can

Not

"What do you mean?" I say. "Please let me—"

Different

Missing.

But

Miss

You.

But

A hawk sweeps to my left, swerves in front of the windshield, screeching into the night.

I laugh. Cry. I don't know.

That's you? I ask.

The hawk sweeps by again, talons grazing the top of the car.

Lee Hazlewood comes on the radio, the song we danced to at the hotel.

I start to pull over. I can do something. I can find her, and—

The song stops, static, back to switching between stations, voices:

No

Fix

"There has to be—"

Different

"I know. I'm so sorry, Hannah—"

Different

But

Freedom.

And then . . .

No. She can't mean . . .

"You don't want me to help? You won't let me free you from—"

That song again, Lee Hazlewood. "Your Sweet Love."

"You don't want to come back?" It's a plea.

I start to push on the brake, but the pedal won't go down. The car keeps moving forward. The hawk screeches toward the sky, and the radio goes back to static. Static, heartbeats.

Hannah—

Then just static.

Then nothing. The crackling fades. The pressure returns to normal.

Just Dolly and me, the headlights on the road.

As I take the exit for Cherry Hills, Dolly stops whimpering.

Denver night. Hannah gone. I don't know what to do. I stretch through the other-space, but she's not . . .

So I drive. Try not to feel my heart breaking. Try not to feel the worst pain imaginable.

I take the turn, into Whileago Manor.

I can't think about Hannah, about the quiet in that other-space.

She doesn't want to come back. Doesn't want me to try and bring her back. Is she protecting me? We can find another way, I'll go in her place. Or we can find a way to make the Witchwalker happy. I don't—

Dolly lets out a whimper again.

Hannah. I felt her. This can't be the end. I won't let it. I *can't.*

"You know," I say to Dolly, "I was just like you once. Sitting in the back seat of a car that some stranger was driving, taking me to a strange new place. To this place. I was terrified. This exact tree tunnel. It was daytime, but it's always dark in this part. I remember that the social worker's headlights turned on even in the day, just like they are now, that's how dark it was."

Hannah, please—

"It was scary, but . . . it became home. Eventually. It became the best home a kid could ever have. Some quirks, for sure. But . . ."

I pull to the gravel drive, headlights shining toward the house, snowflakes in them. And I catch movement again. By the passenger side window.

The bird scrapes against the window with its wing. Again. My heart races.

Hannah.

I pull the car to a stop. Roll the windows down. And—

I inhale. Fuck.

I smell campfire, ponderosa pine. Capsaicin. The cold wind blows into the car, and the bird is gone, but . . .

A whisper of something. I swear I—

I close my eyes. Send my signal to the other-space. *I can feel you.* I say it out loud, "I can feel you."

Another plea. A desperate prayer.

There's movement, in the headlights, at the far end of the lawn. A rabbit. No . . . a chipmunk. Or . . .

The radio suddenly flips to a talk station. Someone saying:

"You know, it's crazy. Human animals use wide-angle vision only about five percent of the time. For only about five percent of our lives do we take in *all possible information* and then narrow it down to what's needed. Before we even know what it is we should focus on, we've already narrowed in on a finite point. We *live ninety-five percent* of our time on this earth already dialed in, without knowing what we should dial in to. Nonhuman mammals, on the other hand, most of them, live in the opposite visual range from ours. Ninety-five percent wide angle and five percent focal vision."

Hannah—

"And yet, all of us are endangered. Kit foxes from suburban sprawl and habitat loss, the extermination of wolves—for the comfort of human homes, human agriculture—this big fat mess of our local hot-button issue—sending coyotes right up to the dominant mesopredator spot in their shared territories. Which is basically everywhere here. And us, humans, well . . ."

Hannah, are you—

"We're just so dialed in on what we think we should see, what we think matters and what we think life is, that we very often don't see what is right in front of us. We're so tuned in on what we think we want to see that we miss the big picture."

Tillman, talking about UFOs. Keeping your attention open. Eyes to the skies.

And I get it. What Hannah's trying to show me. A tear falls.

Sometimes you really just can't see what's right in front of you, what's been there the whole time.

A light flips on in the upper window of Whileago Manor. The room with the trunk.

In the light of the room, through the window, two figures dancing together. Two figures I've been looking for for years.

Noel and Marianne.

They're here.

This house. The ghosts of my family.

Static, on the radio. A song comes on.

It's John Denver. And I don't fight it. I don't fight anything.

Whileago Manor. The badge in my pocket. The lights on and my parents inside.

John Denver sings,

Today is the first day of the rest of my life.

The rabbit darts across the lawn, but it's larger now. Grows, shifts. A wolf. It looks at me and then howls into the night. Dolly lifts her head in the back, whimpers.

The throbbing, vibrating pressure of the Witchwalker, it's not here. It's somewhere off, distant in the dark, not crossing the perimeter of this property. Or maybe not quite stepping through the hole into this world. Waiting, just outside, for her. The Witchwalker, there. Here. But somehow beyond.

Maybe she's found a way to talk to it, to reason with it. I don't know. There's so much I don't know.

The wolf in front of me in the snow. I blink, and it's not a wolf at all.

It's a fox. The same one from the playing card I've carried since the moment I took it from the cabin wall. A fox, trotting toward the garage. A fox stopping at the door and turning back to face me. Expectant, almost.

And I understand what she meant. Hannah is different now. Different, and not at all.

A future stretches before me, one I am beginning to understand. She'll come and go, when she wants. She'll hunt or exist with the Witchwalker, in another realm, elsewhere, and she'll be with me here. She will go and explore in that vast and limitless night.

Hannah, whose light shines across space and time.

Part of me wishes she would stay forever. Of course I fucking do. In my weaker moments, in a lot of moments, I would do anything for that. But a bigger part of me knows, understands.

You can't tame what's wild.

And there's no reason to want to.

The fox lifts its head to the sky and yips into the night. Dolly looks to me.

The fox waits for us, and I feel her. As if fingers graze my neck. As if a hip leans for one second against mine.

I *feel* Hannah.

The fox turns around and runs straight through the wall, into Whileago Manor.

And when I sigh. It's resignation. But maybe, it's really . . . relief.

It's not fighting anymore. Not fighting who I am or my place in the world. It's facing all of it, the pain, the loss, the fear.

And why would I fight? Why would I keep fighting?

When I have absolutely everything.

Looking in at this house from the night, the lights glowing inside.

The music plays, in the car, all around.

"All right, Dolly," I say.

John Denver sings. *Today is the first day of the rest of my life.*

As I cut the engine, and turn off the headlights.

"Let's go home."

ACKNOWLEDGMENTS

My project of writing about this country and the places within it that particularly inspire me could not be complete without acknowledging our land and nation's history. Colorado has been, is, and will be Apache, Arapaho, Cheyenne, Diné, Lakota, Pueblo, Shoshone, and Ute land. I hope we can continue working toward a future in which we treat this beautiful land, its many varied human inhabitants, its history, and its rich and diverse ecosystems, with the respect they deserve.

This book took a village to write. The idea came to me suddenly and without warning, parts of this story so clear from the get-go, so real to me, that it was almost as though these characters existed already and I'd just somehow stumbled upon them in the dark. And all the rest, I knew almost nothing about. Less than nothing. I really couldn't have done it without my early readers. Please note that anything I got wrong in these pages, it is solely my responsibility and doing, and certainly *in spite of*, not *because of* the contributions of these readers.

First, thank you so much to my family whose Colorado expertise and life experience has been invaluable. Andrew, Andrea, Alex, Brittany, Emily, and everyone who answered my endless questions over years of Thanksgiving meals and weddings and calls, thank you. To Phil, whose legal expertise absolutely saved me, and whose own writing mind helped me work through some of the bigger problems, thank you. I love all of you, and all the rest of our families so much.

Anna Dupre, you absolute goddess and horror queen, none of us deserve you. Thank you so much for your forensic expertise and your friendship. Craig Grossi, I am so inspired by everything you do, write, and put out into the world. Thank you so much for helping me as I try to give veterans the honor and respect they deserve in these pages. And thank you for your service. To every reader here, I cannot recommend Craig's books enough.

To Chad and Adam, the perpetual dream team, I am so lucky

to have you both in my corner. Thank you for everything, always. To the whole of the Nightfire team, who have provided the most incredible home for my books, and specifically Hannah Smoot, Cassidy Sattler, Jordan Hanley, Devi Pillai, Lucille Rettino, Saraciea Fennell, Jessica Katz, Rafal Gibek, Michael Dudding, and Valeria Castorena for their work on this one. To copyeditor extraordinaire Angus Johnston, thank you for your keen eye. To Christine Foltzer and Carly Janine Mazur for the amazing work-of-art covers I couldn't even have dreamt up in my wildest imaginings, and to Ryan Pfluger for the most beautiful, perfect photograph. And to Kelly Lonesome, for your continued belief in and support of my books, and your truly brilliant ideas. I really found the editor of my dreams, and I feel so lucky to get to create with you.

To the whole of the horror writer, reader, librarian, bookseller, bookstagrammer, podcaster community, you have all given me such an amazing home here, and I am forever grateful. Liz Kerin and Chuck Tingle, our writing meetups and friendship have been such an immense joy and touchstone in my life. I got so lucky with you both. To the whole LA horror crew, LA friends, New York friends, friends elsewhere, everywhere, you're all my world, and I love you all more than I can say. And to Rachel Harrison, for your encouraging words and wisdom over drinks one day in New Jersey that got me through this book. I don't think you know what a difference you made, but thank you times a million.

As always, to Kyle, for being the most incredible partner to walk this life with. You are my favorite writer and person, forever and ever. I cannot wait for the world to get to read all your brilliant words this year, and for many years to come. Thank you for believing in this book, and in me.

To my parents, who are the best in the world, and who I am so lucky to have, I love you.

And to everyone I love who's crossed over into that great and beautiful night. I miss you every day. Safe passage in your cosmic travels, and please come back and visit whenever you can.

I'll leave my lights on. And I'll never stop watching for yours.

ABOUT THE AUTHOR

Ryan Pfluger

CJ LEEDE is a horror writer, hiker, and Trekkie. She is the author of *Maeve Fly* and *American Rapture.* Her debut novel, *Maeve Fly*, won the Golden Poppy Octavia E. Butler Award and Splatterpunk Award, and earned a Bram Stoker Award nomination. When she is not driving around the country, she can be found in LA with her boyfriend and rescue dogs.